DOMINIQUE DAVIS

The Price of Revenge

First edition

This book was professionally typeset on Reedsy.
Find out more at reedsy.com

Dedicated to survivors shattering the 'perfect victim' trope, one story at a time.

Contents

Preface

Readers, before you begin to move on through the pages of this story, I want to ensure you are fully informed about the content that lies ahead. This book delves into various themes and experiences, some of which may be sensitive or triggering for certain individuals. If certain topics are off limits for you, please assess the QR code provided to see a comprehensive list of trigger warnings before reading The Price of Revenge. The same information can be found here: https://ww w.dominique-davis.com/trigger-warnings-in-the-price-of-revenge. If you prefer to avoid spoilers altogether, you can skip it and begin reading.

iv

Get the free eBook Version

As a special thank you for purchasing this physical copy of The Price of Revenge, readers receive its digital version for free. Simply scan the QR code below or visit my website to access the proof-of-purchase form and upload your receipt or the book's cover to claim your complimentary eBook.

1

A Nightmare At Alpha Phi

It all started innocently enough, as these types of stories always do. It was the last day of the spring semester and our campus was electrified with anticipation for the impending summer break. Like the A+ student I was, I completed my assignments early, leaving me with an empty schedule. My morning was devoted to some much-needed rest, but that afternoon I embarked on a shopping spree alongside my best friend and roommate, Sabrina Price. Brace yourself, you'll be hearing her name a lot.

How does one begin to describe Sabrina Price? She's almost indescribable, but I'll give it a shot. If you can visualize a young Alicia Silverstone with a hint of a Boston accent, then you're on the right track. Within our circle of friends, Sabrina assumes the role of the no-nonsense one. She likes to have fun, but also possesses an uncanny ability to detect bullshit from a mile away.

If she thinks you're trying to play her, you'll be cut out of her life faster than you can say "go". However, if you can do the impossible and coax out her rare, radiant smile she usually likes to keep to herself, congratulations. It's a sign she deems you worthy of keeping around. I should know.

With a smile that could light up a room, an audacious personality, and the privilege of being white, blonde, and able-bodied, Sabrina possessed all the attributes to become an "It Girl" in the glitzy world of Hollywood. That is, of course, if she had been born into the right family. Unfortunately for her, fate had other plans.

Sabrina was born to a lawyer mother and a pilot father, which meant her rise to stardom was confined to being the "It Girl" of our humble, small rural hometown. She and I had been inseparable since the day we met on the playground at the tender age of five. Fourteen years later, we found ourselves attending the same college and sharing a rented apartment as roommates.

It's safe to say we did a lot of things together. That day was no exception. We went to the mall, eager to find ourselves new dresses for the dinner we had planned that evening with our significant others. It was a routine for us to go out as a foursome, but this night held a deeper significance. It marked a bittersweet occasion because the approaching summer was destined to keep us apart.

My boyfriend, Luke, had secured an internship at a prestigious law firm in New York, which meant he would be immersed in the hustle and bustle of the city for months. Sabrina's beau and my longtime friend, Mike, was dedicated to helping renovate his family's vacation cabin in Maine. Sabrina intended to divide her summer between assisting him and renting a van and going on a road trip of her own.

My plans were decidedly less interesting. I was returning to my quaint and overwhelming white hometown of Wayland, Massachusetts, where I'd grown up with Mike and Sabrina. While part of me yearned for an exciting summer like my friends, my obligations beckoned me back home. My grandmother, Winnie, was scheduled for hip surgery and with my parents tending to their own patients in another country, it fell upon me to care for her. However, it wasn't a complete disappointment.

I cherished my time with Winnie, and being able to spend as much time as possible with her while she's still here is something I'm always grateful for. The only downside was the separation of our group for the next three months. We would resort to FaceTime and texts to stay connected, but it wouldn't be the same as seeing each other in the flesh. We were determined to make our final night together an unforgettable one.

"Shall we raise a toast? It feels like the fitting thing to do," Luke suggested as the dinner wound down.

Mike, already clutching a beer, readily agreed, though he had one condition. "Let's skip the sappy shit. There's no need for it."

"By 'sappy,' do you mean I shouldn't say how much I'll miss you all? That my world will feel a little dimmer without you guys in it for the next three months?" I paused, teasingly grinning, before continuing. "Is that what you're getting at?"

Mike shook his head like he was annoyed, but he never was. At least not with me. I was something of a sister to him since he never had one, which worked out great for me because I was an only child too.

"Okay, but in all seriousness, I am going to miss you guys. Especially you two," I said toward Sabrina and Mike. "No offense, babe."

"Some taken," Luke replied.

"It's just that Sab, Mike, and I have been three peas in a pot for as long as I can remember. We have never been apart for longer than a few weeks. Three months seems almost unimaginable to me."

"And since I only joined at the start of last semester, making this trio a quartet, it's easier for you to be away from me? Do I have that right?"

"Ooh, tread carefully, Whit," Sabrina chimed in, playfully wagging her finger.

I chuckled nervously, trying to find the words without saying the wrong thing. Before I could reply, Mike interjected with, "I think what

Whitney is trying to say is that the bonds we've forged are so strong that even a temporary separation feels like a monumental change. We've become an integral part of each other's lives. The bond we have with you is different, but it's still there and just as important to us."

"What he said," I quickly added, resulting in a choir of chuckles.

"Nice save." Luke leaned over and left a barely there kiss on my cheek.

"You should thank Mike for the assist there. One second longer and you would've had to pay for your own dinner," my best friend joked.

"Oh, the horror," I feigned, mocking her by placing a hand over my heart. Still, I took Sabrina's advice and mouthed "thank you" to Mike. He nodded and then signaled to the server it was time for the check.

On our way back to campus, Sabrina made a proposal that would have lasting effects on everyone in the car. "A end-of-the-year party is happening over at Alpha Phi. We should hang out for a little while."

"I don't know," Luke said apprehensively. "I haven't finished packing yet and I leave in the morning."

"How is that our problem? You should've packed ahead of time like us." Sabrina leaned forward and looked at both me and Luke. "Come on, let's stop by. We don't have to stay for long."

"You just don't want the night to end," I guessed. Though she hid her emotions most of the time, Sabrina was going to miss Luke and me a lot. She'll have Mike for some of the summer, but our group being apart was as difficult on her as it was on me.

"Will you hold it against me if I admit it?"

"They won't, but I will," Mike replied, while trying to coax her back into her seat. She wasn't budging.

"Come on, please. We'll stay for an hour or two. That's it." She put the puppy dog eyes on Luke, then me.

I moved my head to look past Sabrina to see Luke. I lightly tapped on his chest with my knuckles to get his attention. "Babe, I think we can spare an hour."

"Alright, fine. But if I don't make it to my flight on time tomorrow, I'm blaming you."

"No, you won't. You'll blame yourself, not my girl." Sabrina punctuated it with a hug, her arms wrapped around my shoulders. The unexpected closeness sent a shiver down my spine. Her lips, stained with a vibrant red hue, pressed against my left cheek, leaving a lasting mark behind on my burning face.

"Oops. It looks like Winnie kissed you," she exclaimed, her laughter ringing out in its full glory. Her laugh was so infectious that I chuckled too. She withdrew from me, her eyes as mischievous as a Cheshire Cat. With the finesse of an artist, she licked her thumb, then gently erased the lipstick smudge from my cheek.

Catching her eye, I asked, "Did you get it off? Or did you make it worse and make me look like a clown?"

"I honestly can't tell if I got it all or not. It's a coin toss, whether that shade of red on your cheeks is from my lipstick or from you blushing like a schoolgirl."

Her rib drew laughter from Luke and Mike. I joined in briefly, hoping my car's air conditioning would kick in and cool my fiery face before we made it to Alpha Phi.

By the time we arrived, the party was in full swing, and it quickly became apparent this was unlike any party we had been to before. Frat parties had become somewhat routine over the course of our freshman year, but this one surpassed all our expectations. The house swelled with a crowd that pushed its capacity to the limit. The loud music reverberated through the neighborhood. And the drinks and drugs were flowing freely.

Ordinarily, I would've suggested we retreat to another party or head home. But this was the grand finale of our freshman year, our last chance to break away from our usual rhythm and embrace the whirlwind of the party that was unfolding before us.

Sabrina and Mike, without a second thought, dove headfirst into the festivities. They laughed, danced, and engaged in PDA that bordered on reckless abandon. Their unbridled behavior was both infectious and irresistible, and against my better judgment, I joined in the intoxicating revelry, indulging in a few drinks of my own.

The trouble didn't start there. That came an hour later when Sabrina began feeling ill. "Make sure you get it all out of your system," I advised her as she retched into one of the frat house toilets. Sabrina had dragged me into the bathroom, kicking the previous occupants out so she could be sick in private.

"Thanks for the helpful advice," she said, before flushing the toilet.

"Anytime," I replied with a smirk. "Are you feeling any better?"

"Not at all. This doesn't feel like drunk vomiting. It feels like food poisoning."

"Well, you ordered the lobster."

"I know. Why did you let me do that?"

"Me?" I balked. "Mike's the one who recommended that place. Remember?"

She sat on the toilet seat after shutting the lid. "Believe me, when I find that boyfriend of mine, I'm going to give him a piece of my mind. Until then, I'm blaming you."

I gave her a sympathetic smile. "What do you need from me?"

"I want to go home and lay in my bed. Preferably with a wastebasket."

I took my phone out of my jacket pocket and sent a message to Luke, telling him to meet us in the bathroom. A minute later, there was a knock at the door.

"Open up. It's me."

"Mike?" Sabrina asked, lifting her head up to look at the door."

"That's Luke. I texted him to come."

I opened the door slowly and watched Luke's eyes widen as they adjusted to the scene of Sabrina, looking as un-Sabrina as she had ever. Her complexion, normally kissed by a healthy glow, resembled that of a ghost. While she was sick, I made her wavy hair disheveled by clutching it. Her eye-catching tan cocktail dress now clung damply to her body. Even her red lipstick had lost all its luster, as if to reflect her own dwindling energy.

"When you texted come to the bathroom, I was expecting a quickie. Not this."

"Did you mistake me for a character in Euphoria?" I joked.

He laughed. "No, but Sabrina could pass for Cassie right now."

Sabrina would have made him choke on those words if she was feeling well. The fact she didn't told me how awful she must've felt. "No more joking. I need you to take Sab to the apartment. She got food poisoning."

"I knew getting the lobster wasn't her best idea."

"Now is not the time. You see her. She isn't feeling well and wants to go home. She needs someone to take her."

Luke had been named our designated driver. I'd expected him to complete my request, no questions asked, but he was annoyed. "Why can't Mike take her?"

Mike disappeared after he and Sabrina danced. He went outside for a smoke, but neither of us had seen him come back inside. "I don't know where he is. What matters is Sabrina needs to go home. Can you take her or not?"

"Of course I can take her. I drunk nothing, just like I said I wouldn't.."

"Good," I replied, holding up my cup. "Because I'm halfway through my third cup of rum, so clearly I can't do it."

Luke nodded. "I'll need your keys."

I pulled them out of my pocket and gave them to him. We helped Sabrina stand, but not before she asked me, "Aren't you coming with us?"

"I think I'll stay for another hour. Try to enjoy the last night before I become Winnie's live in nurse for the next three months. Unless you want me to come with you?"

"No. It's fine. You should have fun, enjoy your last night. Don't let me ruin it."

I gave her a quick hug, then opened the door for them. Luke glanced my way then said, "I'll drop her off, help her settle in, then I'll come back to get you."

I smiled at him, appreciating his thoughtfulness. Since we met at orientation the previous summer, moments like that constantly happened, reminding me of how in sync our connection was. I watched as he walked Sabrina out. There were few people I would entrust with the care of my best friend. Luke was one. Sabrina would be in safe hands with him.

After they left, I made a conscious effort to do what she had advised of me: have fun. Over the next couple of hours, I surrendered to the classic pop hits that had been missing from my life and my playlists for far too long. I chugged down enough drinks to make even the lamest of jokes seem hilarious. I put on my best social butterfly impression and flitted from classmate to classmate—some familiar faces, others I hadn't met before.

It was liberating. For a brief moment, I was back in high school, relishing the company of my peers without a care in the world or with my unfounded worries tagging along. I felt invincible, like nothing or no one could hurt me. I let that feeling override my best sense of judgment. It didn't occur to me that what I was feeling wasn't real. That I wasn't invincible, that I could be hurt. It didn't occur to me at all until it happened.

Exhausted from dancing, I plopped onto a nearby couch, only to feel my vision blur and distort. As I rose shakily to my feet, the room became a swirling vortex of lights and sounds. I sought support against the nearest wall, attempting to steady myself. The dull throbbing of an impending headache thumped along with the song that was playing, an unwelcome reminder of just how much I had drunk - and how much I was regretting it.

Taking my phone from my pocket, I saw it was past 1 a.m.. Two hours since Luke left. I sent him a text asking if he was on his way back, but sighed in response to the lack of a reply. Still, I reassured myself. There was no need to panic — he would come back.

I tapped the shoulder of a girl and inquired, "Do you know if there's somewhere I can lie down?"

"The guest rooms are upstairs. You can see if there's a free room."

I thanked her and made my way slowly up the stairs. Two doors were open and clearly occupied from the glimpses I had. It took me passing four more rooms until I came across one that was free. I winced, closing the door shut behind me.

The harsh, bright light coming from the fluorescent bulb above me was making my already throbbing headache worse. It was a beacon of misery, making me wish there was some Advil for me to take. I turned the light off and blundered through the blackness until I felt the soft embrace of the bedspread. Plopping onto the cozy mattress, I noted I was in a stranger's bed. Not ideal, but I had to quiet the pounding in my skull. I chucked my jacket under my head like a pillow and gave in to the sleep that was calling me.

The sound of the door opening and closing woke me about an hour later. The room was so dark, as if someone had taken a permanent marker and colored the windows until they were pitch black. I didn't know, but I guessed it was after midnight from the darkness outside matching the darkness inside.

I sat up, the pounding in my head returning with a vengeance. As my eyes adjusted to the darkness, the silhouette of a man standing by the door came into view. "Who's there?" I asked aloud, fear gripping me as I wondered who it could be.

"Who do you think?" The man's voice whispered, audible enough for me to hear.

I breathed a sigh of relief when I heard that familiar voice. "Luke, you came back. I was worried you wouldn't."

I held my hand out to him and felt his hand engulf mine. I guided him to me until his body crashed on top of mine. "God, you're heavy. You need to be in the gym over the summer when you're not busy interning."

I felt a rumble of laughter against my chin, like a distant thunderstorm that made me giggle too. "I missed you," I whispered close to his ear. The night had been perfect, but there had been one thing missing: him. I wanted Luke there, singing and laughing with me. He was doing something far more important in taking care of Sabrina, but that didn't stop me from missing him. But he was there then and everything was okay.

He showered my neck with kisses in response. He always did this, whether in public or in private, like then. It was his understated way of telling me how much he wanted me.

"I want you too," I replied, my voice husky.

Luke's mouth, hot and insistent against my skin, moved from my neck to my face. His tongue traced the seam of my lips as his hands found their way to every part of my body. It was a more passionate kiss than I had ever had before. I chalked it up to him wanting to make our last night together before the break memorable for us both. His muscles tensed as he pulled me closer, and I knew he was feeling the same way that I was. We didn't want the moment to end.

Amid his desperate kisses, I felt around until I found the button on his jeans. I undid it and slid down his fly. Luke broke the kiss to pull his pants off. Then he helped me remove my black tights off before he tugged my black dress up high enough to expose my underwear. His lips made me shiver as he grazed the lace of my undergarment and planted a trail of kisses over my abdomen.

Luke's fingertips traced patterns on my skin, creating a soft tingle wherever he touched me. A warm breeze feathered across my cheek and stirred the strands of my hair. It felt as good as water in a desert because every nerve ending in my body felt on fire. As my panties were tossed somewhere on the floor, I felt all the emotions at once. Exposed, but loved, self-conscious, but desired, reckless but safe; all at once.

I didn't bother to ask if he had a condom before he positioned himself in between my legs. We used them, but I was on the pill so I was okay with us foregoing condoms this once. As for sexual health, I was safe on my end and I trusted Luke. We hadn't been dating for that long, but we were committed to each other and were monogamous. He would never cheat on me, and vice versa.

I sucked in a breath when he entered me. That was the first time I had ever let a man enter me without a condom. People told me it was a unique sensation. "It was so hot," Chloe, a friend from high school, told me one day after she had done it. "I loved how big he felt inside of me and how I could feel him moving. It felt so good how we could feel each other's heat."

I took her word for it then, but I didn't feel that way with Luke. Him moving inside of me was intimate, but I didn't feel how hot it was. I felt how much it hurt. Every thrust was jarring and painful, that I gripped the sheets on the bed. Not from the pleasure I was expecting, but to keep from yelping. He moved through my body like he owned it, and for a moment, I felt like he did. And for that moment, I hated him. For taking my body away from me and making it his.

The pain was unbearable, but I refused to open my mouth in fear of unleashing a scream. Tears pricked at my eyes. He didn't notice that or when I winced. I was glad he didn't. I didn't want to be the one to make him stop. I didn't want to disappoint him. He pushed himself further inside me until the pain subsided and turned into numbness.

"Are you close?" I breathed out.

A grunt was the only response I got back.

With one last thrust, he came inside of me. The warmth of him trickled down my thighs and slipped out from under him. His orgasm was my personal victory, as well as my failure. In one act, I'd gotten physical evidence of how much my boyfriend wanted and desired me. But I felt dirty, unsatisfied, and disposable. Not the feelings you want to feel in the aftermath of being with the man you love.

He stayed inside of me after he was done and laid down on my chest. I felt him nestle his head into between my shoulder and heard him sigh. "You don't know how long I've wanted to do that."

"Yeah, you and every other heterosexual man on the planet." I snorted. "Don't expect that to become a habit. From now on, we're only ever using condoms."

He kissed me underneath my earlobe. "No. That's not what I meant."

"What did you mean?"

"You don't know how much I've wanted to do that with you, Whitney," he whispered.

A lump formed in my throat. Luke never called me Whitney. He had a cousin named Whitney that he was close to and didn't like the idea of referring to the both of us by it. So he started calling me Whit. A nickname Sabrina gifted me with years ago. Everyone else called me Whitney, but Whit exclusively belonged to Sabrina and Luke.

"Since when did you start calling me Whitney?"

"I always call you that."

"No, you don't. What are you talking about?"

A thick eerie silence fell over the room. The only sounds were the muffled music coming from downstairs and a dog barking in the distance. I waited for Luke to answer me, but the seconds ticked on and he never did. I couldn't even look him in the eye to see what he was thinking, because his face was still buried between my shoulder and chest. If it weren't for how tense his body felt pressed against mine, I would've thought he had fallen asleep. His breath blew hot air into my dress as he exhaled.

I pushed his shoulders up so I could look at him. It was so dark, but even then, I didn't recognize the eyes looking down at me. "Luke?" I squinted, begging for a yes.

"I'm sorry."

No. No. No.

"Get out of me," I hissed through clenched teeth.

My chest rose with each breath I took. Whoever this was, was still inside of me as if we were wrestling for control over my body. Even though it was mine. Forever belonging to me, never to him. "Get off of me!" I shouted, pounding my fists on his chest.

"I'm sorry," he repeated, his voice breaking.

With one quick movement, he was out of me. My body convulsed in pain as waves of sensation overwhelmed me, causing me to clutch my stomach. I fought to stand and felt my feet land on top of my underwear. I put them on in such a rush; they were backwards. I didn't care. I rather they be on backwards than give his eyes another glimpse of me in my most vulnerable state.

Reality sunk in as I pulled my dress down to my knees. I cheated on Luke with a stranger, unprotected. My body felt like it had been torn apart and half haphazardly been reassembled. Guilt and shame bubbled up in my head and my stomach. I would've done anything right then for the ground to swallow me and make me feel nothing.

"Oh, my God. How could I do this?" It didn't occur to me that what happened wasn't my fault. I wasn't thinking clearly enough to grasp this wasn't something I chose. Someone had done this to me. That realization would come later.

I hurried to the door, but stopped when I was in front of it. Whoever did this would not get off easy. I wouldn't let him. I lifted my hand toward the light switch and turned it on. A heavy sigh came from behind me when the lights flicked on. I tried to prepare myself as I twisted back around, but nothing could've prepared me for this.

"Mike?"

2

The Last Girl Scout

One second I was looking him in his vacant blue eyes, and in the next I was on top of the stairs overlooking the guests partying below. I don't recall how I got my feet to move or how they found their way back near the entrance of the house. My body was on autopilot, and I had to trust it knew what was best for me because at that moment I couldn't do that for myself.

Downstairs, the remaining partygoers were laughing, dancing, and drinking, blissfully unaware of the events that occurred in one of their bedrooms. I wanted to be mad, but I couldn't. If I had been in their shoes, I would've basked in the bliss of ignorance too. It would've been better than startling at the sound of floorboards, creaking under the weight of his footsteps.

I didn't turn to look. I couldn't do it. My stomach tightened with a dread just at the thought of seeing him. I descended the stairs and pushed through the crowd, ignoring their groans and complaints. As I stepped onto the porch, the late night air sent shivers down my spine.

I instinctively reached for my jacket, forgetting I left it upstairs. There was no way I was going back to get it. The place my feet wanted to go was in the opposite direction, not back into the frat house. They took me across campus in my black open-toed heels, making me regret ever having chosen to wear them. But it wasn't anything compared to the rest of the regrets piling up on my list.

When my feet stopped in front of the administration building, I was relieved to see it was open. A guard was posted at the entrance and he noticed me immediately. Other than him, I was the only one around and my body was visibly shaking from the memories of what transpired inside that bedroom. It was safe to say I stood out.

He sensed the gravity of the situation and ushered me inside. Clayton arrived not too long later, looking like she had been woken up by the call, but her well-known prowess broke through her tired appearance. I stood as she approached me. "Would you like to join me in my office?"

I nodded, my voice caught in my throat, rendering me unable to respond verbally. I trailed behind Clayton to her office. Although I had never been there, the students who had, shared their horror stories. Dean Clayton's reputation was one of strictness and a no-nonsense attitude, but also one of fairness and understanding. I hoped the fair and understanding side would be the one I got tonight.

I took a deep breath and sat across from her. She looked in no rush to begin what would be a draining conversation. "How about you tell me what happened tonight?"

"Shouldn't we wait for a counselor or something? Isn't one required to be here?" I didn't know who our counselors were, but I would've felt better with one present.

"Unfortunately, all our counselors have already left for the break. I can try to contact one if you need one to be present."

"It's fine." I was being a nuisance for coming here and demanding a meeting before we were all supposed to be on break. I didn't want to become a bigger one by requesting more than what I needed.

Clayton nodded. "Then why don't you tell me what happened?"

A shaky breath preluded my explanation. "I was at the party at Alpha Phi. I was there with my friends Sabrina, Mike, and my boyfriend, Luke. After we arrived, Sabrina came down with food poisoning and had to leave. Luke took her back to our apartment."

"You didn't go with them?" Clayton interrupted to ask.

"I was having fun and wanted to prolong it for as long as I could. I didn't think it would be a big deal."

"What happened after they left?"

"I was drinking before they left and I drank after. I was having a good time, and I didn't want to let up, so I kept drinking."

"What happened next?"

"I got a headache and went upstairs to lie down." I gulped, knowing what I would have to admit to next. "I fell asleep, but woke up an hour later to who I thought was Luke coming to pick me up."

"It wasn't Luke?"

I looked at my hands while I shook my head. "No, but I didn't know that until it was too late. I was intimate with them."

"Did you find out who this person was?"

"Yeah... it was Mike." The words rushed out like peddles down a hill, but their impact was like a brick. Saying the words out loud made it real. Before, I could've dismissed what happened as a bad dream I fabricated in my head. Except I don't remember my dreams. Fragments of my dreams linger in my head when I awake, only to be replaced by another soon-to-be-forgotten dream. This wasn't that.

I remembered more than just fragments. The memory survived in its vivid, haunting, clarity, replaying in my head so many times until I could recall the nuances of every detail. Like how the hue of his shirt harmonized with the blue of his eyes after I turned the lights on. Or how his sweat coated his brow and neck once the realization he'd been caught set in. However, it was the scent of his cologne that remained etched in my mind.

When he laid on top of me, the scent of Nautica Voyage lingered on him. I could smell it then, not from the memory, but from how it hung off of me now. The facts of what he did remained, and unlike my dreams, I wanted them to vanish. I wanted to forget the cornflower blue of his shirt, forget how scared he looked, forget our bodies now shared the same scent. But I couldn't wield any of it to leave me. That's how I knew it was real.

"What am I supposed to do?" I finally brought myself to ask the only person I figured would have the answer.

Dean Clayton cleared her throat, then started. "I'm sorry. No one deserves to experience something like that. If you want to bring charges against Mike, you should know it will be extremely difficult to prove what you're saying happened. It's going to come down to your word against Mike's. The unfortunate truth of the matter is the accused is usually favored."

"You're not telling me anything I don't already know."

"Okay, good. That might make this next part easier for you to hear."

I stared blankly at her. "What are you trying to say to me? Please, just spit it out."

She leaned back in her chair and sighed. When she was ready, she sat back up and faced me head on. "It might be easier for you if you were to let this go."

"Are you joking?" I knew she wasn't, but an inappropriate timed joke would've gone over on me better than her suggestion. "Let this go? Mike took advantage of me. He violated me and you want me to let what he did go? What kind of advice is that?"

"Whitney, it's important to be realistic here." She took a breather before opening her mouth to say the words I'll never forget. "There is little justice in the world for rape victims. That's the brutal truth, and what's worse is that there is even less justice for victims that look like you."

I didn't need Dean Clayton, a white woman in her 50s, to tell me the system doesn't do right by rape victims, especially when they're a woman of color or Black like me. I found this out early in life. Growing up with two doctor parents who have experience treating rape victims means you get lectures on how to keep yourself safe, so you never become the patient they have to treat.

They told me because I was a woman; I had a target on my back. Because I was a woman of color, the target was bigger and I needed to do everything in my power to not increase the chances of it happening to me. To not only save myself from the trauma, but because the likelihood of the person responsible for it being held accountable would be slim to none, even if I knew who they were. The only thing I stood to gain from Dean Clayton reiterating what my parents always told me was proof they were right.

When I said nothing, Clayton continued. "I was a dean at two universities before coming here. In that time, I've dealt with rape cases where the victims went forward and pressed charges against their attacker. What always happened was they ended up becoming re-traumatized by the case and the scrutiny they faced by the defendants trying to get their client off. Cases like yours where the victim initially consents to the encounter are even more traumatizing."

"I only consented because I thought Mike was Luke. If I had known it was Mike with me in that room, I never would've allowed that to happen."

"Why couldn't you tell the difference?"

"What?"

"You said you only consented because you thought Mike was Luke. I assume you've been intimate with Luke before. Correct?" I hesitantly nodded. "Then why couldn't you tell the difference between the two men?"

"I don't know. The room was dark. They're both white, medium build, their voices aren't noticeably different. It was an honest mistake. One I wouldn't have made if I was sober."

"But you must have noticed something was off," she countered. "The kiss, the act itself, even their cologne. There were signs it wasn't Luke, and you ignored them. Was it because you were inebriated or because you secretly wanted to be with Mike and you saw this as the perfect opportunity to do it without the backlash from Luke and Sabrina?"

"I did not want to be with Mike."

"How else do you explain why you were willing to ignore so many signs it wasn't your boyfriend who you were with?"

"No," I protested. "I have never once thought of Mike in any way other than as a friend. Even if I did, I would never hurt Sabrina or Luke by ever pursuing anything with him. I didn't want what happened between us. I didn't want him or what he did to me."

"Did you tell him you didn't want it?"

"No."

"Why didn't you?" she pressed.

"You know why." I was becoming more and more frustrated with Clayton's line of questioning. "I thought he was Luke."

"In other words, you liked it."

"Are you trying to blame this on me?" I balked, not understanding how we got here. "I was drunk and confused. Most people aren't aware of their surroundings in that state. To insinuate I wanted this to happen, that I wanted to be with him, is ridiculous. He tricked me into sleeping with him. He knew what he was doing all the while I didn't. This was on him. Not me."

"Don't you understand? This is exactly the treatment you will receive if you get up on a stand. Mike's lawyers will tear you apart. They will set out to make you question your memory, make you doubt yourself. They will use everything they can against you, your alcohol consumption, your sexual history, everything. They will paint you out as someone who wanted this to happen and they will make it look like you are lying. And with the lack of evidence, it will be your word against his.

Clayton rubbed her eyes, trying to temper her frustration. "I understand you want justice. You want Mike to be held accountable. You need to know, though, the legal system is not a fair one. It's difficult to prove cases like yours. There's too much doubt. Too many holes that could be poked in your story. I'm not saying this to hurt you, but to protect you."

My veins burned with seething heat as the seconds ticked by. Clayton never struck me as manipulative and self-serving until now. She was supposed to be different. I assumed because she was a woman, she would be a champion for women, but I couldn't have been more wrong. She was just as malicious, if not worse, than any male dean. "You're not protecting me. The only person you're protecting is yourself."

Now I was the one to catch her by surprise. "What?"

"You want me to drop this because you don't want this to ruin your reputation. Your credibility. You don't care about me or the other victims on campus like me. You care about protecting yourself and the school."

"Okay. Let's say I am telling you to drop this to protect myself and the university. Can you say anything I have told you is a lie? The legal system never does right for rape victims. Why would it be any different for you?"

She didn't wait for me to answer before she continued. "If you try to make this a case and testify, you will be eaten alive and all Mike will get is a slap on the wrist."

"What am I supposed to do?"

"You should get tested and get the morning-after pill." Clayton rattled this off like she'd said these exact words a hundred times before. "The counseling center can provide you with information on medical care, counseling, and support services."

This was the expert advice she had for me? Turn to the university for support? The same university whose dean was telling me to let what happened go? I would have laughed in her face if I wasn't stuck in a state of disbelief.

I picked my mouth off the floor to ask, "Will Mike be suspended? Kicked out?"

"If you would like an investigation, but it will be the same thing I told you before. He'll say it was consensual. You'll say it was under false pretenses. We could always do a rape kit, but I doubt it will show anything except you two were intimate. Unless you have a witness that can back up your story, it's your word against his. Do you have a witness to the assault?"

"Do you seriously think he would've done what he did if someone else was around?"

"So that's a no and we are right back to where we started. It's your choice if you want us to continue forward with an investigation, but the chances of this ending in your favor are low. But you already knew that."

"I just want him gone. Seeing him again… I can't stomach it."

"I doubt he will want an investigation to happen unless he truly thinks he did nothing wrong. I can bring up transferring to him. That way, you get what you want and his reputation remains intact. Everyone wins."

Including Clayton and Lakeview. They wouldn't have to deal with the publicity a rape investigation launched against one of their students would bring. Before I could bring this up to Clayton, she was already moving on.

She stood from her desk and held her hand out toward me. "Remember, the university is here to support you. We are committed to providing a supportive and safe environment for students like you and we will do whatever we can to ensure that."

The scoff I let out was involuntary, but I couldn't be upset at myself for not holding it in. After all we talked about, Clayton had reduced our conversation down to the same corporate jargon she spews to the school's board of trustees. If I hadn't already been convinced what a good minion she was for them, this would've made me see the light.

I rose from my chair, realizing I no longer had a reason for being there. She looked me straight in the eye and said, "Whitney, I'm sorry for what you've been through. I wish we could do more for you."

I left her office, imagining her smiling when I closed the door, proud she saved the school from a scandal. The thought of her being proud of what she did to me, what she likely done to other victims who came to her for help, made me more physically ill than I already was.

The saddest thing of all the sad things was that even though the things she told me were said out of her own self-interests, there was a kernel of truth to her words. I knew myself well enough to know I wasn't strong enough to withstand the scrutiny a trial would bring. Even in the most clear-cut cases, accusers are questioned as if they are the accused, and have their pasts pried through by lawyers looking to smear their names.

They're harassed by news outlets and trolls who examine their body language to prove they're lying. Strangers chastise them, accusing them of trying to bring a good man down. If I went after Mike, the same allegations would be leveled at me. He was the son of a rich white Boston family with their own connections. I stood no chance.

Clayton was right. I would be eaten alive trying to prove what happened to me. I would be torn apart by his lawyers, news sites, social media trolls, and the people in my life who took his side. Add in the misogynoir I would receive, my heavy drinking, and me initially consenting to the encounter, a jury would never consider me deserving of justice. I would never meet their standards for a "perfect victim".

Clayton hadn't told me anything I didn't already know, but she confirmed the doubts in the back of my head and pushed me to make a decision I will always wonder was the right one. I never went to the police. I never reported Mike. With that one conversation with the dean, my fate had been sealed. What neither of us knew was how it would seal hers too.

3

The Object of My Hostility

By the time I made the walk home from the 24-hour pharmacy I stopped at, it was 3 a.m.. I avoided feeling sick when I brought the morning-after pill, but on the walk home, nausea bubbled up in my gut. It wasn't from the pill though, but from the thought of facing Sabrina again. I didn't know what I would tell her. How do you tell someone their boyfriend assaulted you? It would be hard to tell a stranger that, but how do you tell your best friend that? These were the thoughts I was pondering as I walked home.

As I reached the street of our apartment, I noticed some clothing in the bushes and paper in the air. I picked one off the ground and recognized it as a paper I wrote earlier in the semester for an anthropology class. Panic swept over me as I realized what was happening. I entered our lobby and raced up the stairs, not bothering to wait for the elevator.

In front of our door, I reached for my keys, only to remember I loaned them to Luke. Realizing my mistake, I banged on the door. "Sab, let me in."

My pleas were answered by the sound of the door unlocking. Sabrina appeared in the doorway, her eyes puffy and red. Her face twisted in rage when she laid eyes on me. "The nerve of you to come back here."

"I don't know what you've been told, but it's probably not the truth." It was late. I was exhausted. I badly wanted to wash the smell of Mike off of me, but more than anything, I was scared about what Sabrina knew.

"Mike came here and told me and Luke what happened. I know you slept with him."

I shook my head before she could get all the words out. "No. That's not true."

"Don't deny it. I can smell him on you."

"Please let me explain. I didn't sleep with Mike. That's not what happened."

"Why would Mike lie? For the life of me, I can't see why he would make this up."

I let out a deep breath. This was my chance to make everything right. Except things wouldn't be right. In a world that was right, everything would be how it was a few hours ago. Mike would be Sabrina's boyfriend and Luke's friend. He would be the guy I thought of as a brother. Not what he was to me now.

"Mike raped me." I had avoided using that word the entire night, because I didn't think what happened to me constituted the use of it. But standing in front of my best friend and having one chance to redeem myself in her eyes meant I had to be honest. Honest with her, and honest with myself. I was raped by Mike, and there was no way I could sugarcoat it for her benefit or my own.

"Don't do this," she forewarned.

"Don't do what?"

"Don't be the girl who cried rape because she regretted who she slept with."

That was the end. I didn't realize it, but that was it. The end of our

15-year friendship. I thought it ended when the conversation was over, but it ended at the very beginning. Everything that followed was just further proof we were done.

"I am not making this up. Please give me the chance to tell you what happened. Please."

Sabrina reluctantly stepped out of the doorway to let me in. I closed the door on my way in and followed her into our living area. She sat on a loveseat, while I sat in an armchair facing her. Her eyes were fixed on mine. It was a hard stare. I'd seen her give it to people who annoyed her, but never to this extent. And certainly not to me.

"After you left, I kept drinking. Eventually, I got an awful headache. I wanted to come home, but Luke hadn't come back. I went upstairs to sleep until he came back. When I woke up, the lights were off and someone was in the room. I thought it was Luke, and he didn't deny it. One thing led to another, and we slept together. It was only afterwards he revealed he wasn't Luke. I ran to turn the lights on. That's when I saw it was Mike."

While I was talking, I kept looking at Sabrina, waiting for the moment where her icy demeanor thawed. The moment where she was horrified to hear how alone I felt when she and Luke left. A sign she believed what I was telling her. Anything to show she cared. It never came.

"Do you want to know what Mike told me? He said he went upstairs to check on you and when he got there, you came on to him. You practically jumped his bones, telling him how much you wanted him."

"That's not true. He's trying to make this look like my fault. It wasn't. I called him Luke. He knew I thought he was Luke, and he still did what he did."

I was begging her to believe me. In a span of two hours, I lost my dignity, my pride, and the love I carried for a friend. I couldn't afford to lose my best friend too. "Sab," I whispered, the nickname I gave her when we were kids. "We've been best friends for most of my life. I don't have any memories of my life without you being somewhere in them. You could say the same thing about me."

"What's your point?"

"My point is in the almost two decades you've known me, have I ever once given you a reason to believe I could do something so malicious to you?"

The answer was no; I hadn't. For as long as I could recall, we had been attached to the hip. Not to sound like Dom Toretto, but we were more than friends. We were family. Our bond transcended beyond casual acquaintanceship or close friendships. Sabrina was the sister I never had, and I was the sister she wished she had. Our bond was unbreakable, or at least that's what I had thought.

"You know who else I've known for almost my entire life? Mike. Do you expect me to believe that secretly, all along, he's been this monster waiting for the perfect moment to pounce on you? It's easier for me to believe you both betrayed me than for me to believe he did what you're saying."

"Are you fucking kidding me?" I blurted as I stood. "How can you sit there and accuse me of making this up? You know me better than that. I would never lie about something like this. I know this is hard for you to accept, but you have to believe me when I say I'm telling you the truth."

"Do you love him?"

"What?" I looked at her like she'd spoken in a foreign language. Sabrina stood to meet my eyes. "Do you love Mike?"

"No. I don't. I never have, not in the way you're imagining."

"Are you sure about that?"

"Yes. I am. Where is this coming from?"

"When Mike came here and told me what happened, I was angry. I was sad. I felt betrayed. What I wasn't was surprised. He may have been my boyfriend, but he looked at you sometimes like you were the one he loved."

I had no idea what she was talking about. Never once before tonight did I ever think Mike felt something for me other than friendship. "Sabrina, come on. Are you being serious right now?"

"I am. Mike never said anything, but I noticed how he looked at you. I said nothing because I loved him and I didn't want to push him away. Especially not into my best friend's arms. Looks like it didn't matter. You got him anyway."

"How many times do I have to tell you? I'm not in love with Mike. What happened was not consensual. He misled me into believing he was Luke. He took advantage of me. How can you not see that?"

"What I see is my best friend telling me she slept with my boyfriend. I see she's afraid of losing me and our friendship so badly she's willing to say my boyfriend raped her, so I don't have to hold her responsible for screwing me over. That's what I see."

She wasn't on my side. She didn't believe me. Every word that came out of her mouth felt more painful than the vile act committed against me. "How are you going to believe him over me? I'm your best friend, not him. There's no one else in the world you trust more than me."

"Whit-"

"What? Are you going to deny it? You can't. It's the truth. Memory lane is on my side. In the 7th grade, who was the person who bought you tampons because you were too embarrassed to ask Bryan and your mom was too busy playing mom to someone else?"

"Whit, stop."

"Was it Mike?"

"Whit-"

"Was it?" I raised my voice.

"No," she begrudgingly answered.

"Was Mike the one who sat with you in that horrible waiting room all day when your grandfather was on his deathbed? No, it couldn't have been him because he couldn't be bothered to pick up his phone. You know who was there? Me!"

"You've made your point."

"No, I haven't, but I'm about to. Since Mike is such an amazing boyfriend, he must've been the one holding you when you cried on your 18th birthday because your mom had to take care of a sick Jordyn and couldn't fly out for it. Do you remember that night? Because I do. I remember wiping your tears away, listening to your grievances against your mom. I remember I held you until you cried yourself to sleep. Again and again, it has been me who has been there for you. Not Mike. So how can you choose him over me when it's my turn to need you?"

Maybe I imagined it, but I could've sworn there was a glimmer of guilt in Sabrina's eyes after I was done. As quickly as it was there, it was gone by the time she spoke. "If you had told me the truth instead of continuing with this lie, I could've chalked this up as a drunken mistake and forgot it happened, but you can't take any responsibility."

My fingernails dug into my palms, preventing me from lunging at her. I squeezed them in so hard I thought they would come away bloody. "I won't take responsibility for something that happened to me. Something out of my control. Something I didn't want."

"Mike told me a different story."

"He's lying! Why can't you see that? He knows the truth makes him look worse, so he made up this lie to make me look like I was the instigator. He's the liar here."

"I think the only one lying is you."

"If you truly believe that, then we were never friends, never sisters."

Sabrina nodded to herself. "First thing we've agreed on this entire conversation."

"So what? In a blink of an eye, our friendship is over? Just like that?"

30

"Our friendship died when you fucked my boyfriend. It was put into the ground and buried the second you lied about it."

Sabrina turned to walk away, but I wasn't having that. I grabbed her arm and forced her to look at me. "15 years of friendship gone because you can't trust my word?"

"No. 15 years of friendship gone because you couldn't keep your hands to yourself. Was Luke not enough for you? That you had to go after my boyfriend too?"

"I'm sorry that I didn't realize it was Mike until it was too late, but don't do this. I need my best friend now more than ever. Please don't throw our friendship away because of an honest mistake."

"It wasn't a mistake. It was a choice you made to sleep with my boyfriend. Owe it."

"No, I won't ever do that because that's a lie. Worse, it's his lie. I won't back it up."

The tears fell then, and I hated myself for them. I hated myself for letting this happen, for wasting the little dignity I had left to apologize to Sabrina for her boyfriend raping me. Despite hating everything that was happening, I loved her more. I needed her on my side. If that meant eating a bullet to get her support, then so be it.

"Say something."

She pulled away from me for the last time. "I didn't throw our friendship away. You did. Remember that when you're the only one who shows up to your pity party."

"Why are you being like this? Even if you don't believe me, I made one mistake. Do I have to pay for it with our friendship?"

"You didn't make one mistake. You fucked my boyfriend, lied about it, accused him of being a rapist, and now you're guilt tripping me. That's what I can't forgive."

I wanted to yell, scream, and cry, but I didn't do any of that. Instead, I stood there and watched as Sabrina walked across the room and grabbed a trash-bag full of stuff and the jacket I was wearing earlier. She threw both at me. "What is this?"

"Mike dropped your jacket off before he left. As for the bag, it's your stuff. I don't want you here anymore."

I looked around our apartment. We had decided to lease it together when we moved to Chicago to attend Lakeview together. It was filled with memories of our freshman year and the enduring strength of our friendship. Memories that would now be tainted by the events of the night.

"This is my home. You can't kick me out."

"I'll find some way to buy out your half of the lease." She went up to the coffee table and picked up my keys that Luke must have left behind. She tossed them at me. "I threw the rest of your clothes and belongings out. If you go now, you can catch some of them."

I couldn't believe what I was hearing. Sabrina always had a mean streak to her. I saw it be brought out several times during our friendship, but I had never been on the receiving end of it until then. "I shouldn't be surprised you're getting some sort of twisted pleasure from this. You've always been this kind of person."

"And what person is that?"

"A cold-hearted bitch who only cares about herself."

"I'll take that over being the girl who rather cry rape than take accountability for her actions." She walked away, slamming shut the door of her bedroom and the coffin on our friendship. I gathered my bag, jacket, and keys and left. I walked out of the building, knowing I had lost my best friend for good.

Outside, I found some of my clothes on the ground. They were caked with mud, but I picked them up anyway. I paused in my search of my things when I felt my phone buzzed against my hip. I took it out of my jacket pocket and saw there was a text from Luke.

Luke: In case you didn't know, we're done. Don't even try to convince me to forgive you. You made your bed the moment you slept with Mike. Goodbye Whit.

I felt like my world had come crashing down. Luke's text was a culmination of everything that had gone wrong that night. Luke, my once reasonable and level-headed boyfriend, suddenly became irrational in a matter of hours. Dean Clayton, who I thought I could count on, turned a blind eye and dismissed my concerns. Sabrina, my supposed best friend, betrayed me in the worst possible way.

Then there was Mike, the person at the center of it all. His actions caused everything that had led to this moment. I couldn't comprehend how one person could have such a negative impact on so many lives. As I sat there on the grass, clutching the remnants of my shattered night, tears streamed down my face. The finality of it all weighed heavily on me. I reached a point of no return, where things would never be the same again.

4

Crazy, Stupid, Revenge

If you think you want to hear how my summer went, trust me, you don't. For three excruciating long months, I helped Winnie get around and refrained from using social media while crying myself to sleep. Fun times I would rather not relive. The actual story you're here for began on the last Friday in August, the day I returned to campus.

As part of the university's "effort to support me," or what I like to call, paying for my silence, I was given a private dorm to stay in. The one caveat being I had to attend mandatory therapy with one of their counselors. Dean Clayton let me pick from the lot and I chose Dr. Johnson.

She was a Black woman in her late 30s that I hoped would make for a better time than the old and stuffy white therapists the university had employed. "Why are you here?" She asked in our first session.

"Don't you already know? I'm sure Dean Clayton briefed you about me."

"You're right. She did, but you didn't have to show up. You could've blown this off and finished settling into your dorm, but you're here. Why?"

I shrugged. "I didn't want to give them a reason to take away my dorm."

"And why is that?"

"Why don't I want my private dorm to be taken away?" I cocked an eyebrow at her. "Because I don't want to live in a dorm with another person. I don't want my personal space to be invaded."

"Why?"

"Do you only ever reply in a form of a question?" I was agitated. I already didn't want to be there, discussing problems I wish I could forget.

"I'm sorry. I'm trying to get a sense of what's going on with you, a sense if you're going to take this seriously or not."

"I'm here, aren't I?"

"Physically, yes. Mentally, though, I feel you're checked out."

"Of course I'm checked out. I don't want to be here rehashing the last few months of my life with you. I relive it over in my head every day. It doesn't help when I do it alone and it won't help to do it with you." After a deep breath, I released it slowly. "But even though I feel that way, I am here. Maybe I won't always be here mentally, but I'll be here physically and I'll do what you ask me to do, no matter how pointless this seems to me."

Dr. Johnson nodded, content with my answer. "Alright, then let's start with creating some goals for our time together."

After a half an hour of Dr. Johnson and I conversing about goals I should try to achieve during the semester, I was free. It was 3 p.m. when I started to walk across the campus to my dorm. I lived in Chicago for a year, but I hadn't gotten used to its weather being nipper in the fall. Still, I came prepared, dressed in a sleek black hoodie, matching cargos, a snug black beanie, and pristine white sneakers. If I was honest with myself, I was wearing the outfit not just for warmth, but for comfort too.

The previous year, all I wore was form fitting clothes. I was confident with myself, unbothered by the idea of showcasing my body for others to see. Ever since that night with Mike, the thought of strangers eyeing my body became unbearable. I covered it up as much as I could, trading my blouses that highlighted my cleavage for oversized hoodies. The skirts and denim jeans that hugged my curves were replaced with baggy sweatpants and cargos. All my makeup products were discarded, along with any concern I had for my appearance.

I was initially worried the change in my appearance would make me stick out, but it had the opposite effect. I blended in with the other students on campus much easier than before. Which can explain why the Price family didn't recognize me when I stopped right in front of their car.

I stood rooted in place, watching as Sabrina's mom, Eliza, and stepdad, Bryan, unloaded boxes from their shiny new-looking Range Rover. I hadn't seen them since the after party they held for Sabrina after our graduation ceremony. That was two years ago, but from where I was, they more or less looked the same.

Eliza wasn't in her usual attire of an elegant dress or pantsuit. Instead, wearing a long-sleeved white cardigan and jeans. Her honey blonde hair was pulled back into a messy bun, some strands of it sticking to her fair forehead. Bryan, who was holding a stack of moving boxes, was in a plaid shirt and khaki pants. He had grown out a beard that covered his chin and his cheeks, giving him a distinguished look that complemented his bronze skin tone.

As if I were a stalker, I crept closer to a nearby tree, using it as a shield, while I watched them unload boxes from their car and enter Porter Hall. I knew they would be on campus to help a certain somebody move in, but I hadn't expected to run into them. Now that I had, my mind was running wild with possibilities.

I waited for another person to go inside and then rushed to catch the closing door. Inside, the pounding of my heart echoed in my ears. Over the summer, I fantasized about what it would be like to get back at Sabrina for ending our friendship the way she did. It was like an intrusive thought that kept popping up in my head, no matter how wrong I knew it was. Despite its wrongness, it also felt like a comforting dream, one I now could make come true.

Porter Hall was arranged like the hall I was now living in. There were three floors. I was on the first, where a large receptionist's desk was in the center of the space. The woman manning it looked to be in her mid 30s and was intently focused on whatever was on her computer. I tapped on the desk lightly to get her attention. She looked at me, a question written on her face. "What can I do for you?"

"Oh, it's so silly. I just moved into my dorm today with my parents' help. I received my key card earlier, but I didn't have the chance to look at it before my mom took it. Now they're somewhere around here with my key, and I have no clue where they are."

"You didn't get your room assignment? It should've been sent to your email address we have on file weeks ago?"

"Um, no. I looked out for it, but it never showed up in my inbox."

"It must have gone to your spam folder. In any event, I can tell you where you need to be. What's your last name?"

"Price," I answered with as much confidence as I could muster.

The woman typed the name away on her computer. "Jordyn?"

"Correct." I smiled.

The person Eliza and Bryan were moving into Porter Hall was not Sabrina, but their other daughter, Jordyn. For months Sabrina bitched and moaned about how Jordyn got accepted into Lakeview and would attend in the fall. She hated they would be co-existing in the same place again, even if they never saw each other.

I thought nothing of this information at the time. The little tidbit was tucked away in my brain, likely never to be thought of again unless

Sabrina complained about it. Never in my wildest dreams did I think I would use it to my advantage, but here we were.

"Jordyn, it looks like you're in room 204."

"Ah! Thank you so much. I thought my days of getting lost at school ended with high school," I joked.

"Don't worry about it. No one likes to admit it, but everyone is always a little lost at college at first. It takes some time to get adjusted, but you'll get there."

I thanked her for the information and her kind words, then took the elevator up to the second floor. I could see from down the hall that the door to room 204 was slightly ajar, giving me a chance to look inside. It would've been perfect if I was looking to spy or eavesdrop. Except I wanted to do much more than that.

I stood outside the door, far enough not to be seen from the crack, but close enough to hear what they were saying. "Alright, you two, the open road is calling your names. And let's be honest, it would be rude to keep it waiting any longer. Am I right?"

"Subtle," Eliza mocked her daughter.

"Don't get me wrong, I love you both for helping me unpack, but I got it from here. There's nothing else you guys need to do here."

I fully pushed the door in and witnessed their bodies shift towards me in surprise. "For my sake, I hope that's not true. I would like to think you guys would want to see your third favorite daughter before leaving."

Stunned silence was the response I got as they took in my appearance. I didn't look like the same girl the Prices had known for 15 years, but I could say the same about them. A closer inspection of Mrs. Price revealed new wrinkles under her eyes. Then not only did Mr. Price grow a full beard, but specks of gray appeared in it. Yet it was Jordyn, whose appearance had changed the most.

Jordyn embraced the tomboy look when she was a kid, but her

new appearance was on the next level. Her once brunette hair had been shaved into a buzz cut. She now had nose piercings, including a diamond stud on one nostril and a silver ring on the other. Her wardrobe now featured dark green cargo pants and tight black tank tops that showed off her freshly tatted full sleeve. A pang of envy hit me from how comfortable she looked in her own skin. All the while, I was trying to sink deeper into my own.

"Whitney!" Mrs. Price exclaimed, rushing over to give me a hug. "What a surprise. We didn't know we would see you today."

"Neither did I, but I saw your car out front and thought I should stop by and say hello."

"I'm glad you did." Mrs. Price lowered her arm to the small of my back and guided me into the room.

It reminded me of the first time I'd visited their home. I felt so out of place and nervous, having been invited to my first sleepover. I stood outside their front door for half an hour until Mrs. Price peeked out the window and saw me. She opened the door like she hadn't seen me standing there with no intention of coming inside.

I immediately respected she didn't make me feel embarrassed by asking me why I hadn't rung their doorbell. In fact, she didn't ask me anything at all. She greeted me with a warm smile and offered me her hand. She guided me inside and up the stairs where Sabrina and her friends were.

There were plenty of friendly gestures sent my way that weekend, but that one by Mrs. Price was the nicest of them all. Because of that and many more gestures like it in the years to come, Eliza Price became more to me than just my best friend's mom. She became like a second mother to me too.

"It's so good to see you."

"You too," I replied, feeling myself blush. I hadn't seen or spoken to Eliza in two years. I didn't know what to say or how to act.

39

"What about me? Am I chopped liver?" Bryan asked, his arms wide stretched.

"I see you haven't lost your sense of humor." I laughed as he enclosed me into a bear hug, then looked me up and down.

"You're right. I haven't lost my sense of humor. You know what else I haven't lost? My phone number. I thought I told you before you left for college, you could call me or Eliza for anything."

"I know, I'm sorry, I just…"

"Whitney, it's okay. We're all just glad to see you," Mrs. Price said, giving me an out.

"It's actually Whit now. Like officially."

"You legally changed your name?" Shock colored Bryan's tone and expression.

"I did. It's a long story, but it was something I needed to do."

"Oh, how Cher of you."

It wasn't hard to find where that snarky comment came from. The smirk on Jordyn's face gave her away. Though her appearance had changed, her brand of humor was as unfunny as ever. She thought spitting out sarcastic one liners would make her the Seth Cohen of the Prices, but really she slot more into the Ryan Atwood role of being the dull, brooding hermit of the family.

That's not to say Jordyn didn't have friends. She had two close friends back home and even a girlfriend. Her inner circle was small, but that was a deliberate choice on her part. She once mentioned she surrounded herself with individuals she believed would push her to be her best self. That didn't include her sister. Or me.

"I thought you would appreciate my name change, since you know so much about reinventing oneself," I fired back.

"You're right. I know a lot about that, but when I reinvented myself, it feels like a natural progression of my growth. Not a desperate try-hard attempt for attention."

"Jordyn, stop it," Eliza begged, trying to break up our spat early.

"It's okay, Mrs. Price. Jordyn's opinions have never carried any weight for me. Why would they start to now? It's not like she has ever exemplified great decision making skills of her own. Case in point," I replied, striding up close enough to poke at the fresh ink on her tawny skin. "You realize this stuff is forever, right?"

"Says the girl who shortened her name to a word that literally means a tiny amount. A synonym for speck, iota, scrap. Are you trying to tell us something?"

"I don't know what you're implying."

"Like you need so many things to be, let me spell it out for you. Your life is so inconsequential. You accidentally internalized it and changed your name to reflect that you're just a speck of a human. Not a whole one."

"Jordyn!" her parents cried in unison. They were used to refereeing fights between her and Sabrina, but seeing her be outwardly hostile to someone else caught them off guard. Not me, though. Jordyn never tried to hide her sharp tongue around her sister or me. So while her comments were not surprising and may have once been hurtful, after the hell I've been through, some rude words from a girl who has never liked me weren't going to phase me.

I leaned into Jordyn, so her parents wouldn't hear what I said next. "Nice Sabrina impression, little Price. Although I have to say if you're going to emulate your sister's mean girl act, you're going to have to do much better than that."

"Alright, that's enough. As much as I'm going to miss having a full house, I can honestly say I won't miss this," Bryan added bluntly. "Also, we felt the same way about that tattoo. She asked for it for months and we tried convincing her it wouldn't be a good idea. But once she asked for it as a graduation gift. We figured better a tattoo than a car."

"Why not both?" Jordyn shrugged slyly.

Eliza let out a hearty chuckle. "Nice try, but you already made your bed with the tattoo. No car."

I stood there watching them like I was an intruder as they continued to talk. They weren't my family, but I observed them affectionately as though they were. I couldn't help but be envious of the dynamic they'd developed and made work for their family, a dynamic I lacked with my own.

"Whitney- sorry. Whit, how have you been? I've asked Sabrina about you, but she barely likes to talk to me about her own life, so that conversation didn't get far."

"I'm doing okay. I made the adjustment to college as well as to be expected. My 3.7 GPA serves as proof."

"That's fantastic, honey. I'm proud of you and I'm sure Sabrina is too." I nodded, not wanting to tell her otherwise. "How is she?"

"Eliza," Bryan drew out like he was warning her not to go down that rabbit hole.

"What? I'm not asking her to invade her privacy. I just want to know how Sabrina is doing from her best friend's perspective."

This was it. My chance to indulge in my worst impulses and spill something about Sabrina that would wreck her parents' image of her. This was my golden opportunity and... I couldn't go through with it. Looking into Eliza's eyes, I saw the pain it would cause, and I couldn't hurt a woman who had always been nice to me. The want to hurt Sabrina was still there, but I couldn't do it by going through her mom. "Um... Sabrina is good," I answered finally. "She enjoyed doing the van life thing over the summer."

"We saw that on her Instagram. Hopefully she'll talk about it with us once we stop by the apartment. Do you need a ride there? We can take you. It's our next stop."

"Thanks, but that won't be necessary. I don't live there anymore. Sabrina rents that apartment with someone else now."

42

Eliza's face fell. "I'm sorry. I didn't know. What happened?"

Quick on my feet, I said, "I couldn't keep up with my half of the rent. Sabrina tried to cover for me, but I didn't want to take advantage, so I told her to get a new roommate."

"We would've paid for you like we do for Sabrina. It wouldn't have been any trouble," Bryan chimed in.

"I would've felt like I was taking advantage of you."

"Take advantage. These two do it all the time."

"The difference is I'm not your kid and I don't need you guys to pretending like I am."

Eliza and Bryan's eyes went wide. They were not used to people rejecting their offers like that. Even Jordyn watched me intensely, maybe thinking if she did it for long enough, she could figure out the source of my frustration. "I'm sorry. I didn't mean for that to come out so harsh. I'm just not interested in being anyone's charity case."

After a long pause, Eliza nodded, signaling she understood my feelings.

"Aside from tattoos being tatted and beards being grown. What did I miss in the last two years of the Prices' lives?" I asked, trying to steer the conversation off of me.

"Nothing major. We three took a vacation over the summer to celebrate Jordyn heading off to college. Again, another gift she got."

"Still doesn't make up for a car," Jordyn whispered loud enough for me to hear, but not for her parents.

"Bryan and I are doing great work at the firm. It'll keep us busy with both of our baby birds now leaving the nest."

"Mom, please, don't start with the empty nest stuff again."

"I can't help it. I'm going to miss my babies." Bryan brought his wife closer to his chest and kissed the side of her head.

"You guys don't have to worry. I'll keep an eye out for Jordyn, keep her out of trouble."

She scoffed, but Eliza was too preoccupied with what I can only describe as staring at me with heart eyes to notice her child's snark. "Knowing you girls are going to watch out for each other puts my mind at ease."

"Dad, can you please take mom and leave before she cries again?"

Eliza looked like she might protest when Bryan nodded. "That I can do. Just right after we get one more hug."

Jordyn rolled her eyes like she was annoyed, but her body language gave her away. She went up and wrapped her arms around her parents, who looked a little surprised by the sudden show of affection, but were so grateful for it.

They stood there for a minute, clutching each other tightly. Eliza drew back first. She took her purse off the twin sized bed and started walking out, but stopped when she was in front of me. "No more of this being a stranger stuff, okay? You said it earlier as a joke, but you are considered a part of this family, Whit. That won't ever change."

I nodded at her heartfelt words, emotional at hearing them because it confirmed my biggest fear hadn't come true. Sabrina hadn't told her mom our friendship was over. If she had, Eliza surely wouldn't be saying I was a part of her family. If she knew her daughter cut me out of her life, she would've done the same. It hurt knowing that, but I put it aside and allowed myself to enjoy the moment for what it was.

She hugged me again before turning and following her husband out of the dorm. I watched them go, feeling conflicted until the sound of a cough rattled me. I turned and saw Jordyn eyeing me closely. "Why are you staring at me like that?"

"What's the real reason you aren't living with Sabrina anymore?"

"How did you know?"

"I've seen Sabrina and you lie to my parents enough times over the years to tell when it's happening," she chirped, so cheerful at catching me in a lie. "So what happened? What caused the one thousandth

44

fight between Blair and Serena?"

"You're exaggerating. We never fought that much." Though our biggest blowups were reminiscent of those between the iconic Upper East Side pair. "Wait, am I the Blair in that scenario?"

"Of course, you're Blair. You don't have the legs to pull off being Serena." I didn't have time to react to her dissing my legs, as she was already talking again. "Now that we got that out of the way, care to tell why you moved out? Did you realize she's as bad of a roommate as I always claimed she was?"

"Sorry to disappoint, but it wasn't that. Me and your sister decided we were better off not being friends anymore."

"Are you being deadass right now?"

"You tell me since you claim to know when I'm lying."

Jordyn's piercing stare scanned my face in search of clues that I was lying. But the longer she stared, the less intense her gaze became. "I don't understand."

"What's there not to understand? Friendships end. It's normal. Not anything out of the ordinary. A tale as old as time."

"Your guys' friendship was anything but normal. It crossed that line a long time ago."

"What are you talking about?"

"You guys made plans to buy a house and live together in your eighties if you were both widows. And now? You're just done? How is it possible that you went so far from one extreme to the other?"

"It just is."

"It just is," she repeated mockingly under her breath. "That's all you have to say to your lifelong friendship ending?"

"Despite years of saying otherwise, we weren't meant to be friends forever. We were what each other needed for a time, but that time has passed. It's time for us to move on from each other."

"What triggered that realization?"

I shook my head before she finished asking the question. I wasn't going there. "The specifics don't matter. Don't bother trying to get it out of me."

"Ah, so it was Sabrina's fault."

"I never said that."

"You didn't have to. Look, I more than anyone know how difficult Sabrina can be. You know that's true."

"I do."

"Then help me understand why you're still protecting her when you're not friends anymore?"

"I'm not protecting her."

"Yes, you are. Why?"

"Why do you care?" I was not expecting Jordyn to care at all that my friendship with her sister was over. She was never interested in it. Why the sudden investment in it now?

"I don't care," she said, not so convincingly. "I just like gossip."

"Get it from a magazine. I'm not going into what happened between Sabrina and I."

"I'm not asking for a play-by-play. I'll be content with a one-sentence summary."

"Not happening."

"Alright, fine. I'll get it out of Sabrina. She was always the easiest to break between the two of you."

"Thanks... I think."

"Don't forget to lock the door on your way out. Oh, and if I don't see you for the rest of the fall, have a good semester."

Putting aside how she casually dismissed me, I was confused where she got the idea this would be the last time we ran into each other. "What makes you think we won't see each other again?"

"What makes you think we will? Did I miss you switching from communications to economics?"

"Did you miss me making your mom a promise to look out for you?"

"You were being nice when you said that. No one took what you said seriously."

I wanted to shut Jordyn up by telling her I meant my promise. That she shouldn't have presumed the worst about me. I didn't tell her that though, based on her being right. I was just being nice when I told Eliza I would look out for her younger, reclusive daughter.

She looked concerned about Jordyn being on her own. It was like Jordyn's first year of high school all over again, only this time, she'd be in a different state. I wanted Eliza to be less worried, so I made the promise out of the goodness of my heart, even though I had no intention of following through on it.

"Would us becoming friends really be all that bad? You would have someone to show you around on campus, tell you what classes to avoid, make sure you don't get lost."

"And what benefit would I offer you? Make sure you aren't lonely to the point of wanting to kill yourself?"

This was a perfect microcosm of my relationship with Jordyn. Me offering to do a nice thing for her and her blowing me off. The reason she was always hostile toward me wasn't unknown. My relationship with her sister was the culprit. Neither of them ever admitted it, but I knew Jordyn was reluctant to get close to me because I'd been claimed by Sabrina.

I'd accepted this absurd reason for why she was so distant towards me, but it sucked since we could've had our own friendship if Jordyn had ever wanted it. The issue was she never did and still didn't. What had changed was I was going to make it my mission to befriend her.

The worst part about your best friend becoming your enemy is that you entrusted them with all your secrets. The best part? They entrusted theirs with you. The biggest secret I was ever entrusted with by Sabrina was how she really felt toward her baby sister. To put it plainly, Jordyn may have been the only person to rival me on Sabrina's shit list.

For reasons I could never get out of her, Jordyn's very presence annoyed Sabrina. Every chance she got, she opted to avoid being around her. She kept her distance from her sister like she was the embodiment of the plague. I remember her being over the moon when she got accepted into schools out of state. She was getting what she always wanted, a plane ride between her and Jordyn.

When she received word Jordyn would join us at Lakeview, it was the angriest I ever saw her prior to our last conversation. "Yet again, Jordyn swoops in and takes something that's mine," she complained to me while we were hanging out in her bedroom.

"What do you mean by again? What else has she taken from you?"

"Don't act like you don't know. She always gets what she wants. It's always been like this."

At the time, I didn't put too much thought into that conversation. I chalked it up as Sabrina venting, but the more I thought about it, the more I knew how to get back at her. If Jordyn getting into the same school as Sabrina got her so riled up, how would she react to her little sister cozying up with her ex-best friend? I didn't know, but I was looking forward to finding out.

"I'm not trying to be rude," Jordyn prefaced. "But I can't picture a world where you and I could ever get along for longer than a minute. Let alone see a world where you and I become close friends. Can you?"

Without missing a beat. "I can."

"You're full of shit."

I laughed bitterly. She was not going to make becoming her friend easy. "I'm not the same person I was a few years ago. I like to think you might like the person I am today."

She looked skeptical, but I kept talking before she could voice her doubt. "There are some parties happening tomorrow night to ring in the new semester. I'll be at the Alpha Phi one if you're interested in stopping by and seeing what the party scene looks like."

"Yeah, you've really changed. Still inviting me to parties when you know I hate them."

"Trust me, you'll want to come to this one. There's going to be fireworks."

"Metaphorically or actual?"

I smirked at her, my eyes glinting with mischief. "You'll have to come to find out."

5

I Could Never Be Your Friend

Although by my sophomore year, I had attended hundreds of frat parties; I arrived at the welcome back to campus party with butterflies in my stomach. This could've been because it was my first party post rape. In actuality, it was because the party was taking place where my rape occurred. I was returning to the scene of the crime when I should have been as far away from it as possible, but there was something more I wanted, and I could only get it by going back to where everything went wrong.

Stepping inside the Alpha Phi house, the thumping music mirrored the rapid beat of my heart. Everywhere I looked, there was movement, laughter, and people having a good time. All of whom were drinking from what I could tell. I would've never noticed it before, but I was hyper-aware of things like that now.

I moved past the guests in the living room and entered the house's den. It was spacious and allowed me to breathe without bumping into another person. I searched around for Jordyn, but couldn't find anyone who fit her description. I kicked myself for not getting her number. Normally, I would have, but I didn't want to come on too strong. I needed to befriend her, but it had to happen on her terms.

Or at least let her think that was the case.

"Hey, excuse me?"

I tapped a girl nearby on the shoulder. She turned back, a sour frown on her face from me interrupting her conversation with a guy. "What?" she barked.

"No need for the attitude," I said, trying hard not to sound frustrated. "I was just seeing if you'd seen a girl-"

"I've seen plenty of girls."

"Yes, and you'll let me finish I'll give you a description of the one I'm looking for. Jordyn is her name. She's about two inches taller than me. She has a cool full sleeve tattoo on her left arm, a blonde buzz cut, and nose piercings."

The girl looked around, evidently unfamiliar with Jordyn's name or the image I'd drawn of her. She shrugged her shoulders and turned back around to the guy.

"She's probably in her dorm reading a book instead of socializing with us civilized folk," a voice calmly yelled over the music blaring from the room over.

I turned around slowly because despite the loud muffled music, I would recognize that voice anywhere over anything. Sabrina's hazel eyes bore into my soul as she sat alone on a couch in the corner, a red solo cup in hand. She looked the same apart from a tan.

She donned a cropped pink tank top and tight blue jeans. Her blonde hair was pulled back into a high ponytail. She didn't make a move to get up. Expecting me to approach her, fulfilling the role of the peasant to her queen. And like the docile friend I once was to her, I did what was expected of me.

"What are you doing asking about my sister? According to my parents, you two have already seen plenty of each other."

"I see that got back to you."

"Did you think it wouldn't?" She tilted her head, her gaze never leaving me. "I didn't think I needed to say this because I thought it was self-explanatory, but stay away from my family. We aren't friends anymore. You no longer have access to my mom, Bryan, or my sister."

I scoffed and closed my eyes, which enraged her even more. "Do you think that's funny?"

"No. What I find funny is you staking a claim over Jordyn like you suddenly give a fuck about her. You don't."

"And you do?" she asked, looking eager to find out my answer. I wouldn't give it to her.

"I didn't come here to fight with you."

"Then what are you doing here? Looking to screw someone upstairs again?"

"Go ahead, hurl your petty insults. They lost their effect on me. And I don't owe you an explanation for why I'm here. Like you said, we aren't friends anymore."

"Fair enough. I only asked because if you were raped like you said you were, I figured you would be too traumatized to come back to the place where it happened."

She thought me coming here was proof I lied. She'd finally be vindicated for not believing me. But her victory was short-lived, as I immediately busted her bubble. "I'm not traumatized by being here. The only thing traumatizing is the sight of seeing you again after what you did to me."

"I didn't do anything. Everything that has happened has been your fault. Luke breaking up with you, Mike and I splitting up, him leaving to go to a new college, our friendship ending. All of it comes back to you not being able to own up to your mistakes. That's not my problem."

She stood, making us to face-to-face. Or, as close to face-to-face as you can get when one of you is four inches taller and towers over the other. "I don't understand why you've taken an interest in Jordyn.

Maybe you think you can get access to me through her. If that's the case, you're more delusional than I thought. She will never be friends with you, and I will never let you get close to me again."

I mumbled, "Wanna bet?" under my breath as Sabrina turned and walked off. If my plan worked as envisioned, not only would I become Jordyn's closest confidante, but I would find any way to get under Sabrina's skin and make her life the living hell she had made mine. Because no matter how badly I hurt her, it would never be enough.

* * *

I spent an hour searching the house for Jordyn, only to keep coming up short. By the time hour two rolled around, I concluded she hadn't come. Sabrina was right. Jordyn was likely reading in her dorm like she did every Saturday night. During high school, she developed this habit of declining invitations offered to her by Sabrina or me. It got to where we stopped asking her to join us. I broke my bad habit by inviting her out tonight, but it looked like Jordyn was refusing to break hers.

"Looking for someone?"

I turned around and sighed a breath of relief. It wasn't Sabrina again. Then again, the person I was facing wasn't that much better. "Tyler, I was hoping I would run into you, but I doubt that feeling is mutual."

"Don't be like that."

"Like what? Bitchy?" I asked, daring him to agree. "That's what we're both thinking. You won't admit it though, because that would make you look like a hypocrite since you're the one who has been dodging me."

Tyler Morris was the average white frat boy with a scruffy head of hair. The only thing that made him special was the title of Chapter President of the Greek being bestowed upon him. We met last year when we had a conversation where I complained about how all their parties blended together. He gave me his number, so I could offer suggestions for how they could improve them.

I saw through the gesture for what it really was, a way for him to express his interest in me. I didn't want to take his number because I was with Luke, but I did it anyway because I didn't want to see the person Tyler might've turned into if I had said no.

It turned out to be a good thing though because I spent the summer texting Tyler, offering suggestions to him. They weren't about how to help make their parties better, but how to prevent sexual assaults from happening at their events. After two weeks of this, Tyler stopped returning my texts and calls. Never one to be deterred, I didn't stop leaving them.

Tyler, at least, had the sense to look remorseful as I confronted him. "I'm sorry, but you were leaving me 10 messages a day. For my sanity, I had to mute you."

"I admit I was being excessive."

"You think?"

"You need to look at the bigger picture and at the content of my texts. Sexual assaults are frequently happening at your events every semester. Doesn't that scare you?"

"Of course it does."

"Then we can both agree something needs to be done about it. I was hoping we could get something agreed upon before the summer was over, but you ignored me."

"Because you weren't telling me anything I didn't already know."

"I'm glad to hear you're aware of this. Now, what are you doing to prevent this from continuing to happen?"

He was not as quick to reply like before. Silence stretched between us because I would not bail him out. He was going to offer me an answer, whether or not I liked it.

"You seem to think there's some sort of quick and easy solution to fixing this and there's not. If there were, every campus in the world would have implanted it by now. We all want to stop sexual assaults from happening on campus, but there's only so much we can do about it."

"Yet you can't name me one thing you're doing to fix this." He sighed like I was the one who was getting on his nerves, when I was the one who should be irritated at how this conversation was going. "I'm not asking you to solve a problem that's been happening before we even existed. I'm asking you what you are doing to prevent these assaults from happening on your watch."

"I'm doing what I can," he replied matter-of-factly. He acted like I was the one who was being unreasonable by asking for something tangible. He went to take a sip of whatever was in his red solo cup, but before he could bring it up to his mouth, I snatched it from his hand. "Hey! What are you doing?"

I downed what turned out to be beer before responding to him again. "If you're going to stand there and continue sprouting bullshit, I'm going to need a drink to withstand listening to it."

"I'm not—"

"Yes, you are!" My voice raised another level, and people turned their heads to see what was happening. If I kept going, I would've caused a scene. It was the last thing I wanted, but I was fighting for something important. Embarrassing myself in front of a hundred people was worth it if I made my point heard.

Tyler noticed people staring. His expression changed from mild annoyance to full-blown nervousness at lightning speed. "You need to calm down. This is not the place for us to be having this talk."

"Where would you like to have it? It's not like I can arrange a meeting with you. You muted my number."

"If you leave right now, I promise I will un-mute you and set something up where we can talk about this in a more appropriate setting."

"Do you think I don't know what you're doing? You want me to leave because you don't want your party to be ruined by me, the Debbie-downer. You don't actually care about this."

Tyler's jaw clinched, containing his anger like a snapped trap catching its prey. "I don't care? As I seemed to recall, you weren't trying to get involved in this until you were affected by it. Why did it take you getting assaulted for you to care?"

"Fuck you," I whispered as I poked my finger into his chest. The little composure I had was slipping away from my grasp.

"Did I lie? You only care about this because it happened to you. If you hadn't been raped, you wouldn't have batted an eye at this, just like everyone else. So don't act like you're better than me. Unlike you, I've been doing the dirty work for a while. Not just when it's convenient to me."

My lips tightened as I tried to think of a comeback, but there was none. Tyler wasn't wrong. It pained me to admit that, but it was the truth. I hadn't been carrying a picket fence demanding for change until I was affected by the problem. Tyler's words hurt, but not because they were a lie. They hurt because of what it said about me.

His watchful eyes stayed on me until I pushed his cup into his chest. I pushed past him and the rest of the guests in my way. He called my name as I approached the front door. I didn't turn around. He could have the satisfaction of knowing he was right about me, but he would not have the satisfaction of seeing me on the verge of tears.

The cool breeze of the night air was a relief to my burning face. I was relieved again to find there were only three people hanging around. I went outside to escape an audience not to entertain another one.

I descended the porch steps and started toward the vacant patio bench on the side of the house. It was separated from the rest of the home by a tree that hung above it. The privacy it provided was exactly what I needed to pull myself together before I made the trek back to my dorm.

After I sat down, I closed my eyes and took a series of deep breaths. Slowly, I inhaled through my nose and exhaled through my mouth. I repeated this ten times until I felt in control of myself. With so much time on my hands during the summer, I looked into ways I could help myself when I felt like I was on the verge of losing it. Deep breaths did the trick. It didn't work all the time, but it worked enough times for me to keep doing it, even though I was sure I resembled a monk.

"I can't tell if you're channeling your inner Zen master or audition-ing for the role of a yoga instructor. But hey, if it's the latter, the role is yours to lose."

"I thought you weren't coming," I said as I reopened my eyes. Jordyn was standing on the other end of the bench. She was wearing faded blue jeans with rips in the knees and a loose graphic tee that clearly had been run through the washer one too many times.

"You intrigued me with your promise of a fireworks show. I like metaphorical and actual ones." She pointed at the empty seat next to me. "Want some company?"

"No, but I'll make an exception. Sit." And she did.

Now that Jordyn was here, I didn't know what I should say or do to build a bridge between us. It used to be so easy for me to make friends, but so much had changed. I no longer made connections so easily. Plus, Jordyn was always a tough nut to crack. Building a friendship with her wouldn't be anything less than difficult.

"What was up with the deep breathing exercises? Did I stumble upon you having a panic attack or something?"

"No, but if you did, maybe don't joke about me looking like a yoga instructor?"

"My fault. In my defense, you really looked like one." She chuckled lightly. I side-eyed her until she reined it in. "Seriously, though, when did that start? I don't remember you doing them in Wayland."

"I don't remember wanting to punch so many people in Wayland. Here, I do."

As I stared at the night sky, I wondered what Jordyn was thinking as she looked at me. Was it the same thing I'd thought when I put on another black sweatshirt, sweats, and sneakers? That the version of me she knew wouldn't have been caught dead wearing this ensemble to a party? However, the new and not so improved Whit Robinson would? I'm sure she had questions, but I wasn't ready to answer them.

"You said before you had changed," she spoke again, interrupting the not so awkward silence. "Other than you shortening your name and dressing like you raided through Aaliyah's closet, I saw nothing different about you."

"And now?"

"The jury is still out, but you're meaner than I remember."

"I don't know if you meant that as a compliment, but I will take it as one."

"You didn't let me finish. You're meaner than I remember to everyone except me. Why is that?"

Because I want something from you. "I was never that kind to you before in Wayland. It was everyone else I sucked up to."

"Are you saying this new version of you is just the inverse of your old self?"

"When you put it like that, yeah. Out with the dresses and heels. In with the hoodies and sweatpants. I'm also done trying to please everyone. Telling people to fuck off is a lot more fun."

"And now that Sabrina is out as your best friend, there's room for me to fill the role."

"I'm not trying to replace Sabrina with you, if that's what you're implying."

"Aren't you though? I mean, why else would you invite me out tonight? If you and Sabrina were on good terms, you would've gone with her to this party and not given me a second thought."

"Is that how low you think of me?"

"In the past, whenever you two got into a fight, Sabrina would hang out with another one of her friends until you guys made up, and then she promptly forgot about them. Tell me how that's any different from what you're doing."

"For one, I'm not using you." Not yet, I thought. "Second, Sabrina and I didn't get into an argument. She said things to me no one should ever say to a friend, let alone their best friend. We can't come back from what was said. We're done. Consider our friendship deader than MySpace."

Jordyn let out a half snort, but she wasn't laughing at me like she so often did. I coaxed a laugh out of her. I wanted to give myself a pat on the back for the minor achievement, but I stopped short of doing so. I still had work to do to earn her friendship and trust.

Once her laughter died down, her line of questioning continued. "If what you're saying is true, why haven't you cut me off? It's not like we have ever had a relationship separate from Sabrina. Cutting ties with her should realistically mean you're cutting ties with me. Yet here we are."

"The only reason you and I were never friends was because of my friendship with Sabrina. With her out of the picture on my side, there's no reason we couldn't be friends now."

"I wouldn't say that was the only reason we weren't friends."

"Really?" I asked, genuinely surprised. "Why else weren't we friends?"

"My sister is a bougie narcissist who mostly only thinks about herself. In my book, any person who willing chooses to spend time with her has to have something wrong with them. And other than Mike, you were her longest running companion."

"Sabrina is all of those things, but I was witness to the times when she cared about someone other than herself." I bit back a smile at a memory. "In the 6th grade, this white girl in our class touched my hair without asking and called it nappy. Before I could say anything, Sabrina had taken her hand off my hair and threatened to shove the girl's fist down her throat if she did or said anything like that to me again."

"She never told me that," Jordyn replied.

"I'm not surprised. She liked to keep quiet about things she did that were good. She had a reputation to maintain. No one could know she had a soft spot."

"A soft spot reserved for you and you alone."

There was an implication in Jordyn's words, but I didn't know what it was. I tucked the question away for a later date and continued. "I excused her undesirable traits because she let me see the good in her. It didn't hurt that I also knew where those traits came from. That was enough for me to ignore the bad. That's why I excused her behavior for as long as I did. I shouldn't have, but I did."

Jordyn nodded, not wanting to talk about it anymore.

"Was that it? Were those the only reasons that stopped us from connecting?"

Jordyn laughed quietly to herself. "You're the reason we never connected."

"What? Me? What did I do?"

"Don't be obtuse."

"I'm not," I insisted, my voice high. "What did I do that was so wrong to you? I reached out. I invited you to hang out with me and Sabrina when we went to Natick or to a party. You always declined."

"Do you not notice your invitations always had a caveat to them?

Let's go over to Natick, but only if Sabrina joins us. Let's go to a party, but I'll spend most of the night talking to everyone but you. You never attempted to connect with me one on one."

"I didn't know you wanted that."

"We lived in a town whose percentage of Black residents was an abysmal 1%. At four years old, you were the first Black girl I saw who wasn't on TV or reflected back at me in the mirror. Of course, I wanted to connect with you. I wanted to learn things from you. Like who you went to get your braids done. Or how to decline someone's request to touch your hair politely. Or how to respond when your teacher confuses you for the only other Black girl in class. I wanted to ask you so many things because you were the only person in my orbit who I could've asked who would understand, but you never made yourself available to me. Then, as time went on, I no longer wanted anything from you."

Jordyn shifted her body and stared everywhere but at me. I didn't know she felt this way, or had been carrying this around. Why our interactions over the years were the way they were suddenly made sense. It explained why Jordyn was so dismissive, snarky, or even hostile towards me. I closed myself off from her when she needed advice about growing up as a Black girl in a predominantly white town.

She couldn't get that advice from her family, who mostly resembled the very town she was seeking help in navigating. Sure, she had her dad, but his experiences as a Black man differed from hers as a Black girl. There was no one in her family who she could fully see herself in or relate to. The closest person she had to that was me, who was oblivious to how much she needed my guidance.

It was no wonder Jordyn was against us becoming friends. I wasn't around in the way she needed me to be when she was younger, and she was now closing herself off to me. And she saw through my

61

justification why I wanted to hang out with her. She knew it was only because my friendship with Sabrina was over. If I wanted any chance of becoming her friend, I needed to make things right.

"Do you know Mrs. Sandra on Third Street?"

"Yeah. Why?"

"She's friends with my grandma and did my braids as a favor to her."

"Where was that answer when I had hair?"

I chuckled. "As for your second question, I would've responded with something like, 'No, I don't want your grubby hands in my hair. Now fuck off.'"

Jordyn looked at me then. A faint outline of a smile assembled on her face as she said, "Grubby? How is that polite?"

"That was your first mistake. You can't be polite with these white people when they ask to touch your hair or they'll think they can ask again later. Be rude to ensure they never ask you again."

"See, this is the wisdom you could've passed down to me." Her faint smile became a real one. "What about my last question? What would you have done if you were me?"

"That one is easy. I would've said, 'Excuse me, Mr. Smith, my name is not Sasha. It's Jordyn and you'll be wise to remember that because both my parents are lawyers and neither of them are afraid to sue you for discrimination.'"

"My English teacher was Mr. Wheeler."

"Even better."

Jordyn threw her head back, her perfect teeth shining like pearls. I couldn't stop staring at her as she laughed. Aside from her laugh being the prettiest I've ever heard, she looked so happy and content. Emotions she never showed when she was around me. I didn't know if I would ever have the pleasure of seeing her in that state again, so I took in every detail of the moment, committing it to memory.

"I'm sorry," I said after she quieted, hoping she could see I was being genuine. "It probably doesn't mean much now, but I wish I'd done things differently."

"It's okay. Looking out for me wasn't your responsibility."

"I should've made it mine. I knew how living in Wayland wasn't always easy. With my parents away, I only had my grandma to hold up as an example of how I should act while living there. You needed a similar Black female presence in your life, and I should've been that for you. I feel like I failed you by not being conscious of that."

A tear ran from my eye to my cheek in record time, opening the doors for a colony of them to fall. I wasn't always this sensitive, but tears seemed to have a way of pouring out of me nowadays. I cried every night for the first two weeks of summer. The irony of my depression raging on during the bright sunny days of summer was not lost on me.

Gradually, my tears lessen over the break. I hadn't cried in weeks. I figured coming back to campus would trigger their return. What I didn't expect it was for it to happen so soon or with an audience watching. I hated being vulnerable in front of people. I was making things awkward, and worse yet, I was probably scaring Jordyn off.

"I would offer you a tissue, but I never anticipate pretty girls breaking out in tears at the sight of me."

My ears perked up like a dog who heard the word treat. "Did you just call me pretty?"

"Note to self, ways to get Whit to stop crying, call her pretty. I think I'll need to use that trick again."

Hearing her use my preferred name made me grin from ear to ear. It was a small thing, but it made my heart flutter. The same feeling repeated itself when Jordyn pulled her shirt away from her chest and leaned closer to me. With a gentle touch, she used its collar to wipe away my tears.

"Whit, you don't have to beat yourself up over this. It's okay. You were only a year older than me. You didn't know what you were doing. We were kids, too self-involved to notice what was going on with other people. I'm sure we would've done things differently if we knew then what we know now."

I swallowed the bundle of nerves lodged in my throat. They formed at the realization if I'd leaned any further into Jordyn, I would've head-butted her. That's how close we were. Her brown eyes were kind as she damped at my cheeks. Her usually reticent brown eyes were magnetic right then. Jealousy overwhelmed me when I realized I was the last person in her inner circle to see them like this.

I found my voice again after she finished and fell back into her spot. "You didn't have to do that. I've made your shirt gross with my tears."

"This shirt has seen plenty of tears over the years. It's nothing a run through the washer won't fix."

"I know you aren't a kid anymore, but I still have wisdom I could pass down to you if you ever wanted to talk."

"I don't know."

Just when I thought we were getting somewhere, Jordyn pulled back. It wasn't like I thought we would become BFFs overnight, but I needed us to end things on a good note to make this night worth the tears and humiliation. "Tell me this, since you were making mental notes to save about me, you do plan on seeing me again, right?"

"What answer can I give you that won't reduce you to a puddle of tears?"

"Yes. This won't be the last time we see each other."

Jordyn inhaled deeply, as if this might be the hardest thing she ever had to repeat. "Yes, Whit. This won't be the last time we see each other. Happy now?"

"Nope."

"What else do you want me to-"

A sharp cracking sound that boomed nearby made Jordyn jump out of her skin. "Nice. I see I get to play my favorite game of fireworks or gunshots here too," she laughed off.

"You can breathe easy." I pointed up to the sky, where a fury of colorful fireworks spread across the glowing stars. Jordyn took it all in with a wide grin. I experienced it last year and had a similar awe at the beautiful display. It was just as good, if not better, watching it from Jordyn's perspective. "Now, I'm happy."

6

Adventures In Blackmailing

When Tyler promised me a meeting, sitting across from Dean Clayton again was not what I had in mind. Yet that's where I found myself two days after the party. Like three months earlier, I sat across from her, a desk separating us, as she lent me advice I wasn't going to take.

"I will not tell you what you can and can't do with your life, Whitney. What I will say is attending a party at the same place you were assaulted will not help you move forward."

She sounded so condescending. It made me want to put my fingers in my ears to drown her out. "That place is going to be triggering for you for a long time. Maybe one day you'll get to a place where you can step inside of the house and feel normal, but that day isn't today."

I nodded along. It was the quickest way I could leave if she thought I was taking her advice. "You're right, Dean Clayton. I thought I was ready to face it, but I'm not. I know better now."

"Good. I'm glad to hear it. It makes this next part easy. You're not allowed to step a foot inside Alpha Phi house or any other frat or sorority house for the rest of the semester. I'll talk to Dr. Johnson about her stance on this issue next semester to see if the ban can be lifted."

"Um... what?" She wasn't happy when she heard about my outburst, but to go as far as banning me? "Where is this ban coming from? Did Tyler suggest this? Dr. Johnson?"

"Neither. I decided it myself. I think it is in everyone's best interest you avoid the frats and sororities out of an abundance of caution. Those places could stunt your recovery."

"Is this being done to help me or to help the frats?"

"I don't know what you're suggesting."

"Are you afraid I'll out the frat system for being complicit in the sexual assaults having on campus? If I had raised my voice any higher at that party, everyone would have heard my complaints."

Dean Clayton kept her expression unreadable as she pulled closer to her desk. She wanted me to hear her next words carefully. "I'm not afraid you'll out the frat system because there's nothing for you to out."

Even though I shouldn't have, I scoffed. Right in her face. I wasn't prepared to hear that, and I let my real emotions go unchecked. "I'm sorry, but I wasn't aware we were going to pretend our last conversation never happened."

"No one is pretending we didn't talk about your allegations before the summer, but I fail to see how that correlates to what we are discussing regarding the fraternities."

"Fail to see?" Was she being intentionally obtuse, or was she really not seeing how her fraternities were complicit in what happened to me? "Your frats are supplying guests who are under the legal drinking age with alcohol, then do nothing to ensure they're safe when their parties are over. How is that not being complicit?"

"You're right. Our Greek system needs to be doing a better job of confirming what guests are 21 or older. I will talk to Tyler about checking guests' IDs before letting them drink."

"Okay, and what else? What happens after their guests get drunk?

They leave them to fend for themselves?"

"We have a campus ride sharing service where students can call and get a ride to their dorm safely. Inebriated students should have the forethought to call or text the service before they take part in drinking."

"Some of them do, but let's not act like that's the majority. More safety precautions need to be put in place to prevent any type of assault happening during Greek events or after."

"I agree, and I love how passionate you are about this. Remember, you can always leave suggestions on how to improve safety on campus with our campus hotline."

A hotline? The one no one has used in the last century? She was directing me to that? "What exactly happens to the suggestions people leave on the hotline?"

"They all get streamlined and the best ones get sent to me. I review them and if they satisfy all our criteria, we add them to a list for eventual implementation."

Eventual? More like never.

"That sounds great. I will check it out," I deadpanned, while playing with the straps of my hoodie. "Was there anything else, or can I leave?"

"One more thing and you can be on your way. I spoke to Tyler and without violating your trust, he admitted some concerns to me about you."

"Oh, did he now?"

"He did and through this meeting with you, I have to say I agree with his assessments."

"Assessments?" I repeated. "I must have missed Tyler becoming a psychologist. Or that I appointed him to be mine."

"I'm sorry. I realize how that sounds. This is a chat where I offer you advice. It's not supposed to be a lecture because you have done nothing wrong."

Yet. I hadn't done anything wrong yet. I suppose it's possible she didn't mean it that way, but that's how I took it. "What are your concerns? Maybe I could alleviate them."

"It's just that you seem to be angrier than normal."

"You know why."

"I do, and that's why I insisted you attend therapy with one of our counselors to help you process the trauma you've undergone."

"And I'm attending," I drawled. I was doing what she asked me to do, and it still didn't seem like enough. "What else do you want from me?"

"Nothing. Only for you to give therapy a real chance, not just with the trauma you've experienced, but with your anger as well."

"I don't have anger issues." I was, in fact, angry, but it wasn't an issue. My anger was the reason I was standing up for myself and for others on campus who didn't have a voice. Labeling my anger as an issue—as if it was something I needed to rid myself of was an insult. One I would not feed into, to make Dean Clayton, Tyler, and anyone else who was uncomfortable with it happy. "I've had a rough summer. It has followed me into the fall. I have been angrier as a result, but that's all it is. It's not a problem."

"I'm not so sure about that. You haven't been acting like yourself recently from what I've been told. It seems to me you're angry at everything and everyone, including me."

"Dean Clayton, I'm not angry with anyone. Especially not you, not when you've been my biggest champion after my rape." I fought the urge to laugh at the lies I was spewing. What I was saying felt so fake to me, but Clayton seemed to buy it based on how she was hanging on to my every word. "I promise I'm okay and I'll keep doing the work to better myself."

"I hope so. You're too bright of a star, Whitney, to let your light be diminished by your emotions getting the better of you."

I wanted to tell Clayton my emotions weren't holding me back. Being in touch with them was an advantage to me, not the disadvantage Clayton made it out to be. I didn't tell her that, though. Instead, I mustered an ecstatic smile and replied, "Thank you, Dean Clayton. I'll make sure to keep in mind everything you've told me."

* * *

After I left Clayton's office, I made a pit stop at the reason for my latest troubles. Once at Alpha Phi, I pounded my fists on the front door and waited 20 seconds before a white guy with dirty blonde hair opened the door. He was shirtless and shielding his eyes from the harsh sunlight on his undoubtedly hungover eyes. "From your knock, I thought you were the police."

"How lucky for you it's not." I rolled my eyes before bypassing him inside. The place was a wreck. Evidence of a party they had last night was everywhere. Red solo cups and paper plates littered every surface in the living room. The smell of beer and vomit hung in the air. Plus, three guys were passed out, two on the floor and one on the couch.

I stepped over the two losers on the floor to get a good look at the one on the couch. I peered down and recognized the guy as Tyler. "Do you, um… need something?" The guy who let me in asked, looking very confused.

"Yes. Make yourself useful and get me a cup of water. Please," I added there at the end. I was in a foul mood, but this rando was not responsible for it. I didn't need to take it out on him. With his head down, he grunted an okay and went into the kitchen. I listened to the water run from the tap and his footsteps until he was beside me.

"Thank you." I grabbed the cup from him and, with a quick flick of my wrist, dumped its contents onto Tyler's slumbering face.

His upper body popped up, resembling a vampire emerging from its coffin. The water soaked his brunette hair and, as he sat up, it dripped down into his gray t-shirt. Realizing what happened, he looked up at me, shivering. "What the hell?!"

"Dude, I didn't know she was going to do that."

"You can go now." I shooed the rando away. I wanted this to be a private chat.

Begrudgingly, he headed upstairs. I turned my focus back to Tyler, who was shivering like a dog on its way to the vet, but this dog was giving me the death stare.

"Instead of looking at me like that, you should thank me. I gave you the shower you desperately needed."

"Dean Clayton told me you were supposed to be banned from here."

"I am, which is why you're not going to tell her about this chat of ours."

"Why the hell would I protect you after you just dosed me with water?"

I glanced around the room until I saw what I was looking for. There on the display stand that held the TV was a half-empty can of beer. On the other side was a translucent baggie of what appeared to be marijuana. I left Tyler's side to pick up both items.

"What the hell are you doing?" Tyler asked as I took two photos with my phone. One of me drinking out of the beer can and the other of me holding up the bag of weed.

Putting the items back where I found them and sliding my phone back into my pocket, I smirked. "Consider this blackmail. Because although Dean Clayton will be upset at me for breaking her ban, who do you think she'll be more upset at? Me, the traumatized 19-year-old rape victim? Or you, the senior supplying me with drugs and alcohol despite me being underage? I'm going to guess it'll be you."

Tyler ran his hands through his wet hair while shaking his head. "Blackmail? This is a new low for you."

"I plan on going even lower."

"What is it you're after? You want the frats to get suspended? Is that it? If that's the case, you need to realize that even if you get us suspended, assault and harassment will still happen on campus. There's nothing anyone can do to stop it completely. Not even you, no matter how much you try."

"You're right. It wouldn't stop, but it would be lessened. That's enough for me."

Tyler stood and approached me slowly, like he was afraid I might strike him. "You're playing a dangerous game trying to start a war with the frats."

"I didn't start this. You did the second you threw me under the bus to Clayton. Before I was content with leaving you alone, but no. You had to screw with me. Did you think I was going to take that lying down?"

"I didn't get you banned. You did that on your own. Take some responsibility for that."

"Why? You guys never do. People get assaulted at your parties, and somehow it's everyone else's fault but yours."

"I've been patient with you ever since you told me you were raped at one of our parties. I felt guilty it happened under our watch. So I let you yell at me and berate me because I felt sorry for you. Well, I don't feel sorry for you anymore. You have used what little sympathy I had left for you up. If you want to go after the frats, go ahead. Be my guest, but prepare yourself because you've just made every one of us your enemy. Is that what you want?"

He was trying to intimidate me, get me to back off. I wouldn't. Nothing I did would save myself from what happened with Mike, but if I could stop this pain from burdening someone else, then nothing or no one was going to stop me.

I laid my hands on Tyler's shoulders, leaning in close to his right ear. From an outsider's perspective, it appeared as though we were engaged in a private and intimate moment, and in a way, we were. "I may not have started this war between us, but I'm sure as hell going to enjoy finishing it," I whispered, my breath tickling his skin.

I let go of his shoulders and pulled back. The smirk on my face was priceless, almost as good as the steam coming out of Tyler's ears.

"I'll be seeing you," I said in an upbeat tone I didn't have to fake. On my way out, I left behind a parting gift of two bruises onto the backs of the passed out boys on the floor. The groans they elicited as I left were music to my ears. My size six Nikes caused minimal damage, but it was a preview of the real damage I was going to inflict onto them. I smiled at the thought, the biggest I'd had in months.

7

Chasing Jordyn

Tuning out Dr. Johnson's words, my focus zeroed in on the clock positioned directly behind her head. The session would be over in ten minutes. Not long, but not short enough. These sessions were more tortuous than my classes this semester. Having to discuss that night and my feelings stemming from it over with a dean appointed counselor was insufferable.

I shifted in my seat, trying to keep myself from rolling my eyes at my therapist's endless pep talks. Dr. Johnson, noticing my discomfort, changed subjects. "How are the goals we created last week coming along?"

I glanced down, my hands fiddling with my nails. "They are going fine."

"Do you mind telling me what steps you've taken to complete them? Starting with your goal of creating a safe environment for yourself."

"I've finished moving into a private dorm on campus. No room-mates, just me. Living by myself makes me feel safe."

Dr. Johnson nodded in approval. "That's great. What about the other two?"

The second goal was to build a support system. "My parents have been supportive. I talk to them almost every day." Of all the lies I've told recently, that one was the easiest to get through. My parents would've been supportive during my time in need if I had told them what had happened to me.

"I know it's only week two, but have you made any friends?" she inquired further. "It would be helpful to you to have a support system outside of your family."

I looked at the clock. Seven minutes to go. Ugh. Maybe Dr. Johnson would end the session early if I told her what she wanted to hear. "I have made a friend. It's early days, but it could be the real thing."

"That's amazing, Whit. I'm so proud of you. What's your friend's name?"

"Jordyn," I said because in due time that wouldn't be a lie.

"What class did you meet her in?"

"I didn't meet her in class. We're from the same hometown. Jordyn is actually the younger half-sister of my ex-best friend, Sabrina."

"Oh." Dr. Johnson's smile fell. "Do you think it's wise to be making friends with someone who is closely related to someone who has hurt you?"

I went into what happened that fateful night, including Sabrina's role in it with Dr. Johnson during our first session. She knew the truth because no way was I going to be keeping track of every lie I told her. It was better I kept being truthful with her about the big stuff.

"Jordyn isn't like Sabrina. She doesn't have the worst qualities of her sister and she isn't going to hurt me like Sabrina did. We aren't that close for her to."

"Alright. You know what's best for you and if you think this Jordyn person is good enough to be called a friend of yours, I will respect that. I want to ask you a question, though, and it's not to piss you off."

"Oh, this should be fun."

She ignored my wise crack and continued. "Is this friendship with Jordyn genuine? Or is it your way of getting back at Sabrina off?"

"Ever consider that it could be both?"

"No such thing. Either you're enjoying this girl's company for the right reasons or using her for the wrong ones."

I couldn't feasibly tell her what I was planning. I trusted Dr. Johnson would not tell my business to anyone, but I didn't want her to think of me as a psychopath who cared more about getting even with their enemies than being concerned about the people I was hurting.

"Doc, my reasons for becoming friends with Jordyn are perfectly innocent. I enjoy being around her. There aren't many people nowadays who get that distinction, but she does. I wouldn't try to ruin that."

She nodded along, like she really wanted to believe what I was saying. "Good. I hope you remember that. It may tempt you at times to rub in Sabrina's face your newfound friendship with her sister, but don't. Don't snoop to her level and hurt an innocent bystander in your feud."

Dr. Johnson gave me a knowing look that I was growing familiar with. Clayton gave it to me at our meeting and Tyler had given it to me at his party. It seemed like they were all trying to tell me, don't mess this up. They each meant something different. Don't expose the university's wrongdoings, don't ruin the frats' reputation, and don't fuck up one of the few good things that has happened to you in months.

Only one of them I took to heart.

"I'm not going to hurt Jordyn. That's not who I am. I'm not Sabrina."

* * *

"Come on," I said to myself as I slapped the back of the printer. I was in an empty library, printing off an essay for class. At least, that's what I was trying to do. "Why isn't this thing working?" I asked, not expecting anyone to respond. The only other person there was the librarian, who was enthralled in a conversation over the phone.

"The printer's been jammed all month," a voice replied. Distinctly not the librarian's, who was still rambling on the phone.

As I straightened my body from bending over the printer, I noticed Jordyn at the far end of the row of computers. She must have come in while I was fighting with the printer.

"That explains why no one is here." I moved back to the computer I was on, closed out the tab, and logged out. "I guess I'll have to find another place to this print off."

"Maybe not." Jordyn swung her bag over her shoulder and met me in the middle of the row. "Follow me."

Any other person I would've said no and left without another word, but Jordyn was actually talking to me of her own volition. It was either a miracle or she was warming up to me. I followed her to the librarian's desk, stealing her attention away from the phone.

"Mrs. Campbell, how are you today?"

"I'm doing great, Jordyn, but I'm busy at the moment. Is there something you needed me for?"

"I was wondering if me and a friend could use your personal printer in your office? We'll only be a moment."

"I don't know. If word gets out that I let you both use it, then I'll have to let everyone do it."

"Who would find out? I won't tell. You won't tell. Whit won't tell. Right?"

"Um... yeah." I nodded, still adjusting to Jordyn calling me a friend.

Mrs. Campbell hesitated for a moment longer before relenting. "Fine, but just this once, and only for a few minutes. Leave my office exactly as you found it."

"Thanks Mrs. Campbell!" Jordyn grabbed my hand and pulled me towards her office.

I looked down and watched our entangled hands as we made the short walk. Jordyn's soft hands were a hard contrast to the large, bold tattoo covering her left arm. Yet another example of her contradicting herself. Similar to her soft-spoken tone of voice, being a rival to her sharp as a razor blade tongue.

Jordyn was an assortment of contradictions. I liked every single one of them because they made up who she was. The traits that made her up were like puzzle pieces, and if you could put them all together and make them fit, you were rewarded with this beautiful portrait of Jordyn. I felt like I was on the verge of unlocking it.

When we entered the office, Jordyn released my hand and located the computer. "You can print your stuff off first. I'm not in a rush."

"Thanks… friend," I said with a wink before jumping to log onto the computer.

"You're a real comedian."

"Hey, it was your words. Not mine."

"I said you were a friend. I never said you were mine."

"Is that because you're too busy making friends with librarians to add me into your exclusive group?"

"Friends with librarians? Where are you getting that from?"

"Um, hello?" I looked at her as if she had the intelligence of a newborn. "We're only here because of you being in Mrs. Campbell's good graces. So, tell me, how did you get so chummy with her?"

"I don't think we're especially chummy."

"You've been here for two weeks and already know her name. I've been here for two years and didn't know it until you said it."

"That's more of an indictment on you than me, don't you think?" she asked while canvassing her way around the office.

"Yeah, yeah. I'm a selfish asshole. That's what everyone keeps telling me."

"You mean someone was brave enough to say that to your face? Was it Sabrina? Because if it was anyone else, I'll be truly shocked."

"It wasn't your sister. It was this guy."

"Was he upset that you guys only did what you wanted on your date?"

"Now, you're the one who's a comedian," I mocked. "I'm not dating. And if I did, it wouldn't be with him. He's an asshole."

"Sounds like he got under your skin. The prime makings of an enemies to lovers story."

"Did you not hear that last part? I would never date him."

"All heroines in enemies to lovers stories say that. And yet..." she trailed off.

"It's more likely we end up staring in a love story than me and him."

"Wow, I'm truly honored to know I'm a step above rock bottom for you. Thank you."

I side-eyed her while half smirking. She knew how to twist everything I said to make me look bad. Not that impressive of a feat because I kept putting my foot in my mouth, but it was annoying. "Other than making friends with Mrs. Campbell, what you've been up to? How are your classes?"

"You don't have to do this."

"Do what?"

"Pretend like you care. I know, I guilt-tripped you before for not taking an interest in me, but seriously, you don't have to start now."

I paused typing into the search bar to face her. "If I didn't care, I wouldn't have asked. Do I look like the kind of person who asks about people's classes out of the goodness of my heart? I'm selfish, remember?"

"While you can be selfish. Your class superlative was 'most generous'. So that does sounds like something you would do."

"What was your class superlative? 'Most likely to be pessimistic

79

about everything for the rest of her life'?"

"Close, but not quite. It was actually 'Most likely to overthink everything.' So, you were in the ballpark with the pessimism angle."

"I can see that. Case in point, you thinking me asking about your classes is out of guilt when I just want to know how they're going for you."

Jordyn leaned back into the beige wall behind her and crossed her arms. "If you really want to know, my classes are fine. They're all general requirements, so I'm not interested in them, but they aren't hard."

"I hated those classes. I thought they were an enormous waste of time. The only one I liked was oral communication because it was actually a part of my major."

"Oral communication is the one class I detest so far and the reason I'm here. I have to print off this speech I'm giving next week. I'm not looking forward to it."

"No surprise there." I clicked the print button on the computer and waited to hear the printer whirl to life. "You've always hated having to talk."

"Not true. I like talking just fine."

"Yeah, with your friends. What were their names?" I pondered for a second. "Melissa... and Carrie?"

"Alyssa and Sherry."

"Right!" I said enthusiastically before standing and grabbing my essay. "You enjoyed talking to them and that girlfriend you had. You hated having to talk in any other scenario."

"I may not be like you and Sabrina and enjoy talking people's ears off, but I can hold my own." She pulled herself away from the wall and replaced me at the spot on the computer. "It was public speaking I always hated and still do."

"I get that."

"No, you don't. You've always excelled at public speaking. It's thrilling for you and it should be. You're good at it."

"How would you know? I was a grade ahead of you. We never took a class together for you to have seen that."

"You hosted the school assemblies, remember?"

"Yeah," I smiled at the memories. "I thought you skipped out on them and hid in the library until they were over."

"Yes, but sometimes when I got caught and was forced to attend, I caught your performances. I saw how good you were firsthand. It didn't matter if you were reciting a speech or introducing the acts, you did every task with confidence. Those assemblies were unbearable, but you made them somewhat watchable."

Her words sent a pleasant warmth through me. I couldn't explain it if I tried, but beneath Jordyn's reluctance to befriend me, there was something warm, a friendliness there. It was what I was determined to latch onto to make a connection between us real. "You thought I was good?"

Jordyn blew a raspberry, sabotaging the vibe we had going. "Please don't get a big head. I already watched it grow three sizes when I said you were pretty. If it grows any larger, I'm afraid it'll explode."

Just as I was about to respond, the printer whirred again. Seizing the opportunity that presented itself, I grabbed Jordyn's paper while she was busy logging off.

When she got up from her seat and noticed nothing was in the printer, she glanced at me. "Whit, cut it out. Give me back my speech."

I held the paper behind her back, a mischievous smile tugging at my mouth. "No. Not happening."

In a few quick steps, Jordyn closed the distance between us and reached behind my back to retrieve the paper. I was nimble and kept it just out of her reach, maintaining my teasing smile.

"Is an apology what you want? If so, I'm sorry for saying you have a big head. Happy? Can I have my paper back now?" I shook my head back and forth. Her frustration grew and her eyes narrowed on me. "What's it going to take for you to give me my paper back?"

"It's simple. Have coffee with me. My treat, then I'll give you your speech back."

"What is this? The Notebook?" she asked, not even a little tickled by the turns of events. "Whit, I don't know if you know this, but I'm not Rachel McAdams and you're not Ryan Gosling. He could get away with blackmailing her into a date. You can't. You're not as cute or as charming as him. So stop this."

"Good thing I'm not looking to go on a date with you. I'm looking for a casual outing between us as budding friends."

"Budding friends? Is that what we are?"

"Do you have a better name for it?"

"Yeah, how about 'stubborn intruder and helpless victim who can't get away'?"

"You don't look so helpless to me. In fact, I think you enjoy our repertoire. Otherwise, you wouldn't encourage it like you do."

"You're ridiculous," she replied, noticeably not denying my accusation.

"Ridiculously entertaining?"

"More like annoying," she shot back.

I leaned closer, my voice taking on a more sincere tone. "If I am that annoying, you can put an end to it by taking me up on my offer for coffee. I'll give you your paper back and leave you alone."

"Can I get that in writing?"

"Sorry, lawyer's kid. You're going to have to take me at my word for this one."

There was a pause as Jordyn considered my proposition. After a moment, she sighed, her walls crumbling. "Alright, fine. I'll have coffee with you, but I make no promises that I'll be a pleasant guest."

The grin on my face went from ear to ear. This was it. My best and last chance to make Jordyn want to be my friend. There was a lot riding on this one cup of coffee, and I needed to make sure I didn't let it go to waste. However, I also needed a fresh approach, because kissing Jordyn's ass was not working.

"Little Price, if I wanted to hang out with somebody pleasant, I wouldn't be asking to hang out with you."

Her eyes widened in disbelief as a burst of genuine laughter escaped her lips. The sound caught me off guard, my eyebrows shooting up in surprise. Any tension lingering between us seemed to dissolve in that moment as her laughter echoed in the air.

I blinked, momentarily taken aback, before breaking into a smile myself. Jordyn wiped a tear of mirth from her eye, her face still adorned with an amused grin. "Is there anything I need to bring to our coffee date besides my unpleasant self?"

"No, not even your wallet. I'm paying for everything."

"Great. In that case, I'll order the most expensive thing on the menu."

"I wouldn't have it any other way."

8

Walking The Line

As I sat in the campus' cafe two days after my last interaction with Jordyn, fifteen minutes after our agreed upon time, I wondered the impossible. Was I being stood up?

That sounds self-absorbed, but it was a genuine question. I never been stood up before. I didn't have practice in this scenario to know the difference between someone being late and someone not planning on showing up at all. Before I could have a full on meltdown, Jordyn put me out of my misery and walked in through the door.

She was wearing a black henley shirt, a black leather jacket with spikes coming out of its shoulders, dark wash slim-fit jeans, topped off with a pair of sturdy black boots. She looked like she had just met up with a biker gang. That wasn't necessarily a bad thing. If she sweet-talked me over coffee, I might have been inclined to join her.

"Did your motorcycle gang keep you?" I inquired as she sat in the booth across from me.

"What?"

"I knew you were going to be unpleasant. I mean, when aren't you? But I thought that would start after you arrived, not before."

"Are you seriously upset I was fifteen minutes late? Do I need to remind you that you blackmailed me into coming?"

"At least I wasn't rude about it."

"You are impossible." She slid out of the booth in record timing. "I don't know why I thought this would be fine. You're as big of a headache as my sister, but lucky for me, I don't have to deal with you."

"Wait! Please?"

She was looking down at me, waiting for a reason she should stay. I reached down and unzipped my backpack, that was under my feet. I went through it until I found what I was looking for. Holding her paper out to her, I said, "Here. I'm sorry for taking it."

She didn't hesitate to take it. "You're just giving it to me? Wasn't the whole point for us to have coffee, then you give it to me?"

"Yeah, but you don't want to be here, and I will not force you to stay. You're off the hook. I hope you do well on your speech," I said genuinely.

While I knew Jordyn leaving meant my plan to get back at Sabrina was over, I was at peace with it. I could always find something else that didn't involve putting someone in the middle of our feud. What I wasn't okay with was making both her and me miserable. If she didn't have the tiniest bit of interest in staying, I didn't want her time or mine to be wasted.

While looking down at my water, I absentmindedly stirred the ice cubes with my straw, then noticed Jordyn's shadow lingering. She was flipping through the papers with a confused expression. "What is this notebook paper you attached? It's riddled with notes."

"I read your speech. I know, I'm sorry. It was an invasion of privacy, but I knew you were nervous and I wanted to proofread it for you. I made a separate sheet of notes for you. I thought we could go over it together while over we drank our coffees, but you can read it in your dorm and still get what I was trying to say."

I prepared myself for Jordyn to blow up at me, but it never came.

She sat back down, still rifling through the pages. "You put in this much effort to help improve my speech? Why?"

"I told you. You were nervous, and I wanted to help."

"No, seriously, what's the catch? You must want something. If you were queer, I would think you wanted to get into my pants, but you're not, so what is it? Do you want me to put in a good word for you to Sabrina?"

"I wanted nothing except to share a coffee with you."

"Why is this so important to you? You and Sabrina aren't on speaking terms, but surely you can make other friends. Why are you so obsessed with me being your friend?"

"No one is obsessed with you. You're not Mariah Carey. Also, I've never been stellar at making friends. I caught a break getting close to Sabrina. Her friends became mine. Unfortunately, when her friendship went away, so did theirs."

"You don't speak to anyone from your high school group? Not even Mike?"

My eye twitched a little at the mention of his name. "No, especially not him. He was never my friend. None of them were. They were Sabrina's. Now that it's just me, I don't know how to do this. I don't know how to make friends."

"I don't believe that. I mean, someone has to want to be your friend," she softened her voice, trying to make me feel better.

"Little Price, if I had a line of people knocking at my door trying to befriend me, why would I need to blackmail you into having coffee with me? Face it, we're not that different from each other."

"Meaning?"

"I'm not interested in scouring high and low for friends. If I can connect with one or two people, then I'll be happy. I just want one real friend to call my own."

"You think that could be me? Your ex-best friend's sister?"

"It's not ideal, but yeah. I think it could be you. That is, if we could get over this minor hurdle."

"By hurdle, you mean me not liking you?"

"Yes, that hurdle. If you could get over that, then I think our friendship could have the potential to be great."

A chuckle left her lips as she shrugged her jacket off and let it settle around her hips. It was subtle, but it told me she was growing more comfortable. "How do you propose I get over that?"

"You could stay and we could talk, for however long you want. The moment you get too annoyed with me, we can stop and you can leave. No hard feelings."

"What would we talk about exactly?"

"Anything you want. The purpose is for you not to hate me."

"You think one conversation is all it'll take for my opinion of you to take an 180?"

"A 180? I was hoping the dial was already being turned in my favor."

The corners of her mouth upturned, suggesting she was cautiously curious. "45 minutes. Don't make me regret staying."

"In that case, how about a round of rapid-fire questions? Answers have to be limited to 10 words or fewer. That way, neither of us can overthink them. By us, I mean you."

She rolled her eyes, but continued. "Okay, but only if we answer the questions honestly. There's no point in doing this if we're less than a 100% honest."

I knew what Jordyn was doing. She was planning on asking me about Sabrina and she wanted me to be truthful. The thought made me nervous because I had no clue what she wanted to know about us besides why our relationship ended, but I wasn't in a position to deny her request. "Deal."

"Why Lakeview University?" she asked, kicking things off.

"Sabrina wanted to come. I didn't want to leave her. Same question."

"Their economics program is the best. What's with the new wardrobe?"

"Not interested in anyone seeing my body. Still with your girlfriend from Wayland?"

"No. What's with the attitude transplant?"

"I stopped trying to please everyone. Why did you break up?"

"We never dated anyone else. Time for a change. Why did you change your name?"

"Same answer." My smile widened as I embraced the chance for an authentic conversation with her. "Why did you shave your hair?"

"I got tired of maintaining it. How did your parents react to you changing your name?"

"Don't know. Never told them. Why a full sleeve tattoo?"

"I needed it to complete my stud initiation," she replied with no trace of seriousness in her tone. "What's the deal with your parents?"

"They love their job more than me." Jordyn's face fell like I guessed it would, but I didn't miss a beat to ask my next question. "What made you realize you were a lesbian?"

"Um… Hayley Kiyoko in Lemonade Mouth. She was a revelation. What made you realize you were definitely straight?"

"I don't know. I guess I always knew. Were you afraid to come out?"

"Not to my parents or Sabrina. Have you ever been in love?"

I thought back to my relationship with Luke. It wasn't that long ago, but so much had changed. It felt like a different version of myself was the one who was in love with him. "Yes, but I was wrong. Same question."

"Yes, but it might've been just puppy love. Do you miss Wayland?"

"Not even a little. You?"

"I miss my parents. Not much else. Do you miss Sabrina?"

"I miss having a friend. Not particularly her. Do you miss your ex?"

"Not lately. Who was your first time with?"

"Alex Gregory. His bedroom during a free period. Yours?"

She gave me a 'who do you think' kind of look. "Jenny Liao. My bedroom while my parents were away. Was it everything you were hoping it would be?"

"No. It never is. You?"

"Yes. It was perfect." Her answer was said with such genuineness, I had no choice but to believe her. "Are you really not dating?"

"I'm not. I hope to keep it that way. You?"

"No, but I'm open to it. Are things really over between you and Sabrina?"

"Yes. It is. Why did you care so much when I first told you that?"

"I couldn't believe you finally got tired of her. What irked you about her the most?"

"How she lashed out at people when she was hurt. Were you happy to hear our friendship was over?"

"Yes, but I wasn't proud of it." She leaned forward over the table. Her smirk was as playful as ever. "Who do you like better right now, me or her? Remember, be honest."

I leaned against the back of the booth and saw a subtle shift in Jordyn's expression. Her narrowed eyes seemed to be focused intently on me. Like she was studying my features, trying to decipher what my answer would be. It's possible I imagined it, but there was an apprehension in her gaze, as if she were bracing herself for the answer she feared.

"You," I said after a moment. Suddenly, that apprehension wasn't there anymore, a sparkle was. "And frankly, it's not even close. Does that feel good to hear?"

"Yes, but don't read too much into that," she said with a laugh. "Do you regret missing out on a friendship with me in favor of her?"

"Yes, but I'm trying to fix that. Why can't you accept that I've changed?"

"A leopard doesn't change its spots. Why do you really want to be my friend?"

"I'm lonely. You're good company. Do you believe me?"

"Not a chance. Why won't you tell me the real reason?"

"Believe me or not, I'm telling the truth. Is there another reason you hated me that you haven't told me about?"

"Maybe. Is Sabrina the reason your guys' friendship ended?"

"Yes. Did you ever have a crush on me?"

For a second, Jordyn's focused expression faltered, revealing a flicker of vulnerability. Her nose crinkled and a brief pause hung in the air as she considered her answer. It was the first time during our game she seemed genuinely taken aback. In an instant, her answer slipped out of her lips like lightning. "Yes. Did you ever hook up with my sister?"

I had no time to make sense of Jordyn's answer because of her ludicrous question. I wondered where it came from. Was it from actual curiosity or deflection? "What do you think?" I finally replied. "Do you still have a crush on me?"

"No, and not for a long time. Again, did you ever hook up with my sister?"

"She's straight. I'm straight. Do the math. Why does Sabrina hate you?"

"Our mom prefers me to her. Have you ever been with a girl?"

"No. Did Sabrina know about your crush?"

"She might've had an inkling. Have you ever thought about being with a girl?"

"Not explicitly. Why are you so curious about my sexuality?"

"You know what they say about inquiring minds. If Sabrina told you she wanted to be friends again, what would you say to her?"

"Go to hell. Why did you meet with me when you could've just printed your paper off again?"

"I was suffering from boredom. You're a cure for it. Why did your friendship with Sabrina end?"

"She thinks I'm a liar. I can't change her mind. Do you really hate me?"

"No. It's closer to dislike. What does she think you lied about?"

I swallowed at how intense this had quickly become. I should've ended things here, but we both had been so honest with each other. It didn't feel right to say my trauma was the line that couldn't be crossed when Jordyn surely shared things she didn't want to share. "It was over something that happened before the summer. Could we ever become friends, or am I wasting my time?"

"Nothing about this is a waste. Would it kill you to be a little more specific?"

"Yes, it would. When did you have a crush on me, and why?"

"When I was thirteen to fifteen. You were mildly attractive. Why are you still protecting Sabrina? You're not friends anymore. You don't have to keep protecting her."

"I'm not. I'm protecting myself. Why did your crush on me end?"

"I don't like to fantasize about things I can't have. Are you trying to fill the gap Sabrina left in your life with me?"

"My therapist would probably say so. Does that upset you?"

"No, it doesn't. Did I make you feel uncomfortable saying I had a crush on you when I was a kid?"

"No. I consider it an honor. Did this exercise make you dislike me less?"

"A little," she replied bluntly. "Do you want to stop and order something?"

"Yes, please."

The air felt charged around us, but despite the lingering tension, there was an undeniable sense of progress. I could've been projecting, but it truly felt like something had changed between us. Silently, we went up and ordered our coffees. Then, with our freshly brewed coffees, we settled back into our booth.

Sipping on my latte, I contemplated what to say to Jordyn. We had emotionally opened ourselves up to each other. Where did we go from here?

"Are you this awkward on dates?" Jordyn threw the question at me so unexpectedly, I almost choked.

"Oh. I didn't realize I was being awkward. I'm sorry. In my defense, it's been a while since I've been on a date."

I didn't realize what I said until I saw the biggest smirk on her face. She looked like a kid who had just found out a secret about their sibling that they would hang over their head forever.

"You heteros may think getting coffee is enough to be called a date, but I expect a lot more. Don't expect to get me into bed if you aren't buying me dinner or taking me to a movie, at least."

I wanted to shrink myself into a ball under the table and die. She just told me she used to have a crush on me and what do I do? I slipped up and say we're on a date. Did she think I was making fun of her? "I made everything more awkward, didn't I? Wait, don't answer that. I don't want to know."

"It's cute how nervous you are about this. It's a real role reversal since I was the one always awkward and nervous around you when we were younger."

"When you had the crush or before?"

"It was the whole time. You were like a towering skyscraper in my life, embodying everything I aspired to be. You were beautiful, smart, nice, and unapologetically outspoken. Before I had a crush on you, I kinda wanted to be you. I held you up as the standard, thinking I needed to be feminine, social, and giving like you were in order to be loved and accepted in Wayland. As time went on, that feeling shifted. With the crush came the realization I needed to find my own identity. I couldn't continue trying to mold myself after you."

Taking a moment to sip her coffee, a sense of self-assuredness took hold as she spoke again. "After I realized that, it wasn't long before I discovered what made me happy. I found joy in embracing traditionally masculine clothing and sketching tattoos. I paid more attention to myself and recognized I was my happiest when I kept to myself and was selective with my generosity. I understand the person I am isn't everyone's cup of tea. Some people learn to appreciate and acquire a taste for it, while others never do. But it doesn't matter, because this way of being works for me. As long as it continues to work for me, I'm going to continue being this way."

"You're pretty fucking incredible, you know that?" I asked, but it wasn't a question. It was a factual statement because she was undoubtedly amazing. I couldn't believe how privileged I was to sit there and listen to her as she talked about the journey she went on to become who she was.

"I don't think I'm special, but I will gladly take the compliment."

"You are though. Not everyone is strong enough to give an entire town a giant 'fuck you' and not conform to their ways of life."

"It's not about being strong enough. It's about realizing what's more important to you. Conforming to the rules and doing what you think makes everyone else happy. Or doing what you know will make you happy. It wasn't an easy choice, but I landed on the second option. I was fortunate to have a support system in my family, as well as Jenny, Alyssa, and Sherry. Without them, I might have succumbed to fear and chosen the first option for the sake of safety."

"Looking back on when you came out, I wished I had been there for you more."

"Don't do that. We weren't friends. You owed me nothing. You were accepting and never treated me any differently, and that's all I wanted. If you would've tried to become my friend then, I would've thought you were taking pity on me."

"Still, I wished I could've been a part of the support system you had."

"You seemed pretty supportive right now." Jordyn smiled as she took another sip of her drink. I didn't want to get my hopes up, but it seemed like she was extending me an invitation of sorts.

"Tell me this, is this the most vulnerable you've been on a date?" I asked, keeping up with the lightness of the mood.

"Yes, yet another reason this is a lousy date. You feed me coffee and get me to be all honest and revealing. Yuck. Where's the fun? Where's the dinner and a movie?"

I drank the last bit of my latte in a rush, then slid out from the booth. "Come on. Let's go. If we leave now, we can get something to eat and have time to catch a movie."

She stared back at me, wide-eyed. "Whit, I was joking. You know I don't actually consider this a date, right?"

"Will you consider it one if I buy you a hot dog and take you to watch something?"

"Are you deadass?"

"I am." I enjoyed taking Jordyn by surprise, but I would've liked it more if she hadn't been surprised at me wanting to do a nice thing for her.

Jordyn stood and met me where I was. "Can I get relish on my hot dog?"

"You can get anything you want."

She smirked ever so slightly. "Then what are we still doing here? Let's go."

* * *

After leaving campus, we walked a few blocks over to a hot dog vendor. As promised, I brought Jordyn one with relish while I treated myself to one with ketchup.

94

"Is this everything you thought it would be?" I asked as we started gingerly walking to our next destination. "A date with your childhood crush. This must be a dream come true for you."

"I should've lied. Your head is definitely too big for your body now."

"You're the one who demanded we be truthful."

"I know. I'm kicking myself for it now," she snickered. "By the way, you're not special. Lesbians have new crushes every week. I know I did and still do."

"You said you crushed on me from when you were thirteen to fifteen."

"Yeah, off and on. It would've ended sooner and for good if you had stopped coming by the house so much, but you treated that place like a second home."

"My parents were never home, so my house was empty a lot. Winnie was around, but she would go to Bible Study and bingo with her friends. I hated being there when it was just me, so I went to your guys' place. Your mom and dad never made me feel like I was intruding."

"Since you've been so nice to keep bringing up my old crush on you, it's only fair I ask you about your parents."

"What do you want to know?"

"What you said back at the cafe, do you really feel that way about them? I've only met your parents twice, but they've seemed like nice people."

"They are. That's the problem. I used to joke with Sabrina that I wasn't my parents' firstborn. Their firstborn was their job, and I was the accidental pregnancy that disrupted everything. Is it any wonder why she never laughed? It was never a joke."

I avoided eye contact with Jordyn. I needed to get this out before facing her again. "They love me. I'm not in denial about that. Nor am I trying to throw a woe is me party, but my parents love their jobs to where they put it before me."

"They work with Doctors Without Borders, right?"

"Yeah. And I know it's not easy for them to miss out on time with me. They are the personification of selflessness for making that kind of sacrifice for their job. The problem is that I didn't. I didn't get to choose to miss out on time with my parents. It was decided for me. They've missed out on so much of my life that when they come home, they feel like they're a step above strangers. I try not to complain about this because I don't want to sound selfish or ungrateful."

"You don't. You sound like someone who misses their parents," she reassured me, her voice gentle.

I closed my eyes, determined to express myself without breaking down. "I do, but I'm angry at them, too. But how can I be? They're away because they're off saving lives. It's not like they're abandoning me. They're helping people who wouldn't be helped if it weren't for them. It's not right for me to be upset at them for what I'm feeling."

When I opened my eyes again, Jordyn was reaching out to place a hand on my shoulder. "It's okay to feel angry and hurt. Your emotions are valid, and they don't diminish the love and respect you have for your parents. You're allowed to express what you're feeling, even if it seems conflicting."

"Now look who's the one vulnerable," I tried to laugh to lighten up the mood, but it came off as forced. "I'm sorry. You probably weren't expecting to listen to my sob story when I asked you to join me for hot dogs."

"I don't mind. I always envisioned what our conversations would be like if we ever got past formalities. I never imagined we would get to a place where we could talk about stuff like this, but I'm glad we are."

"Careful now. I might get the idea that we're friends."

We continued our walk in comfortable silence, the gentle autumn breeze rustling around us, providing us with a soundtrack. As I took another bite of my hot dog, the wind swept through my hair, causing strands to fly across my face. I struggled to keep them in place, and a laugh came from Jordyn's direction.

"I don't miss having to deal with that. Shaved head perks."

"It suits you. You could give Kristen Stewart a run for her money." That got another laugh out of her, but it wasn't a joke. "It wouldn't work on me, though. It takes an extraordinary beauty to pull off a shaved head. I'm not that."

"I'm not trying to make your head any bigger than I already have, but you're beautiful, Whit. How else do you explain the grip you had on me when I was a preteen?"

"You were dazzled by my kindness and intellect?" I suggested half-heartedly.

"Did those things help? Yes, but the main reason was you were obnoxiously pretty."

"Were? What, do my baggy sweats not do it for you anymore?"

"The rapid-fire questions ended an hour ago. I'm not obliged to answer that."

"I'll add it to the list for next time."

"Jumping the gun, aren't you? This date hasn't even ended yet."

"Let's just say I'm hopeful."

I got my hair to stay put long enough to finish my hot dog and throw it into a trash can. We were a block away from the movie theater when I got the urge to ask something that might ruin our evening. "I want to ask you something, but I don't want it to ruin the rest of our time together," I cautioned as we got closer.

"Should I be nervous?"

"No, but I think I should. Earlier you asked about me and Sabrina, hinting at our relationship being more than just friendship. Where did that come from? Did Sabrina say something to make you think we were ever more than friends?"

"No. She didn't have to say anything."

"What do you mean?" I stopped walking to digest whatever I was about to be told.

Jordyn sighed, unsure if she wanted to go there. "There's no easy way of saying this, so I'm just going to come out with it. Whit, you and my sister had what we lesbians call an intense homoerotic friendship."

I blinked at her like she was speaking in morse code. "I don't know what that is."

"It means the line between platonic and romantic can be a little fuzzy. Trust me, I've been there. Jenny and I were friends for a long time before we became a couple. She was out before I was and helped me on my journey. After I came out, I realized that for our entire friendship, we had been acting like a couple. My relationship with her differed from my ones with Alyssa and Sherry. I talked to her about it and we ended up kissing. Everything clicked then why I felt closer to her."

"Sabrina and I were nothing like you and Jenny."

"No, I guess not. Since you two never realized what your friendship actually was."

I laughed bitterly. There was no way she actually believed my friendship with Sabrina was comparable to the one she had with her girlfriend. "You're being for real right now? You aren't playing with me?"

"I'm not. I'm being completely serious."

"Okay, enlighten me. What did Sabrina and I do that put out the vibe that we were more than friends?"

I thought Jordyn would need a second to come up with examples, but she rattled things off like she'd been waiting for this day. "You two were always touching each other. You guys would find any excuse to hold each other's hand or fix the other's hair or makeup. That's not even getting into how you slept over at our house more than Mike ever did. In the same bed as Sabrina, no less. Then there were the couple nicknames you had for each other."

"Whit and Sab? Those were not couple nicknames."

"Maybe they weren't explicitly coupley, but you both uttered them with the same affection one would say 'babe' or 'honey' to their significant other. Don't even get me started on the way you looked at each other. You guys exchanged glances at each other like you were the only people in the room. Everyone noticed it."

"Everyone? Who is everyone?"

"My mom and my dad. For a while, my mom definitely thought she had given birth to two lesbians."

"Two people is not everyone."

"I wasn't finished," she warned. "When I came out, I vividly remember kids at our high school being confused because they thought if one of the Price sisters was going to come out of the closet, it would've been Sabrina."

I rubbed the back of her neck and chuckled, albeit nervously. "I didn't know we gave off that vibe. Me and Sabrina were close, but deep down you had to have known we never crossed into that territory."

Jordyn looked me up and down, skeptical. "Not even a kiss as practice before doing 'the real thing' with boys?"

"No!" I yelped. "We never did anything like that. Sabrina was my best friend. I felt comfortable around her in a way I wasn't with anyone else. Maybe because of that, I did things with her I didn't do with other people in our group, but I never saw Sabrina as a romantic interest."

"Okay, calm down. I'm not accusing you of anything. I just always thought there was more to your guys' relationship. It's possible I was projecting, since that's what happened with me and Jenny."

"Yeah, that has to be it," I replied, hoping to put the topic to rest. We resumed walking, shifting our conversation to other subjects until we arrived at the movie theater.

As we settled into our seats and the movie began, I tried to focus on the storyline, but Jordyn's words stuck around in my mind. She was wrong. Nothing about my friendship with Sabrina was homoerotic. She wasn't carrying a torch for me, nor I for her.

Nothing about our relationship was unusual. Was it toxic? Yes, but what friendship wasn't? There was no hidden meaning to the bond Sabrina and I shared, like people wanted there to be. We had a completely normal platonic friendship. Why couldn't anyone but me and Sabrina see that?

9

Friends with Ulterior Motives

I felt positive about the state of my relationship with Jordyn. After the movie ended and we made the walk back to campus, she wasn't ready to declare me her new best friend, but I got the consolation prize of exchanging numbers with her. A major step forward for us.

Over the last week, we hadn't seen each other because we'd both been busy with classes, but we did text. Okay, fine. I texted. Jordyn sent back variations of emojis and gifs. Case in point, I asked how her day was going and she replied with a thumbs up emoji. I sent her a video of those cakes that are made to look like something else. She responded with 'Nope. Don't like that.' gif from The Office.

She read no more of my messages after that.

I wouldn't let that deter me. It was Friday night, but in the morning, I would ask her if she wanted to hang out tomorrow. I hadn't yet because I was busy with my classes and she was busy with hers. Also, I didn't want to come off looking clingy, asking her to hang out when she wasn't even responding to my texts. She was close to accepting me as her friend. I didn't want to scare her off, but I wasn't sure how much more I needed to do to get her to where I already was.

Distracting myself, I turned the volume up to my TV and flipped through what was new on my streaming apps. This was how I was spending my Friday night. If you would've told me from last semester that, I would've guessed I was sick. In a way, I was, but it was a sickness that wasn't going away. I would have to accept and get used to it. What other choice did I have?

I pulled my comforter up to my chest and settled on a rom-com. After about 30 minutes of watching, the screen lost its sharpness, and my eyelids drooped. Sleep was beckoning to me, and I didn't resist from following it into the darkness.

My sleep was disrupted by the blaring of my cellphone. As my eyes re-adjusted to the brightness of my television and my lamp, I reached over my bed until I found my phone. I saw it was after midnight, two hours after I fallen asleep. Not only that, but the call wasn't spam, like I was expecting. It was coming from the only person I would want it to be from.

"Is your building on fire, Little Price?"

"Fire?" she questioned. "Is this your take on is my refrigerator running joke?"

"No, it's a legit question. Since I can't imagine any other reason, you would call me after midnight. Unless my building is the one on fire and you wanted to warn me so I don't burn alive?"

"How do you know I wouldn't let you burn?"

"You like me too much to do that." That was wishful thinking, speaking, but I was hoping she would agree. Instead, I heard nothing and then her taking a swipe of something. "Jor, are you still there?"

"Physically? Yes, but mentally? Let's just say I'm currently exploring uncharted territories in the realm of questionable decision-making."

"Meaning?"

"I'm wasted. I've had three tequila shots, a glass of vodka, and I'm currently finishing my first beer. Proud of me?"

My body flew up from my pillow. I bent over my bed and canvassed my floor for the sneakers I was wearing earlier. Jordyn being drunk was as worrying as Rory Gilmore getting arrested. Something was wrong for this to have happened. I held my phone up to my ear with my shoulder as I reached to pick up my shoes. "How did you get alcohol? You're barely eighteen."

"They didn't card me."

So much for Dean Clayton saying she would make the frats and sororities do better at checking who among their guests were under the drinking age. My expectations for her promises being made were low, but I wasn't expecting to be proven right this fast. Hell, I never expected to be proven right at Jordyn's expense.

"Where are you?" I asked, trying to gather as much information as I could.

"Delta Zeta."

"I'm confused about how you're even there. You hate parties."

"Yeah, but my roommate is rushing, and she wanted me to tag along. I didn't want her to go alone, so I said yes."

"Where is your roommate now?"

"She met someone."

"And let me guess, she left you for them. Not much of a friend, is she?"

"That's not fair. I told her to go and said I would take the campus ride service thingy back to our dorm."

"What's the name of it?" I asked, trying to prove a point.

"I don't know. I was calling to ask you."

Point made. Dean Clayton stressed to me students who get drunk should have the foresight to order a car, but how were they supposed to do that when they didn't know the name of it? They rarely touted the app. Mentioning it in a student pamphlet and promoting it with one or two signs on campus wasn't enough. More needed to be done, but Clayton was content with doing the bare minimum.

"Don't worry about finding out the app's name. I'm coming to get you."

"Whit, that's not necessary."

"I already have my shoes on. There's no stopping me." I hung up before she could challenge me again. I had a ten-minute walk ahead of me and didn't have time to waste.

Standing tall among the trees, the Delta Zeta home exuded a timeless grandeur. The white façade stood out against the thick greenery, producing a picture-perfect image. The design was a mix of old and modern, with a porch embellished with elaborate woodwork elements. A flag planted by the front door with the sorority logo waving in the night's breeze, welcoming those who passed by or planned on stepping inside. I never thought I would be a part of the latter group, but this year kept on surprising me.

You would think Sabrina and I would have been all for being Delta Zetas or a part of any sororities, but that wasn't the case. I hated the clique nature that so often found their way inside the fabric of a sorority's being. And for Sabrina, well, she thought she was above them. Being on the lower end of a sorority totem pole would not have been in line with the reputation Sabrina gathered for herself, so neither of us ever tried joining. To think Jordyn would be the one out of the three of us willing to enter Delta Zeta's house was surreal.

The front door was unlocked, so I entered with no carding. I was immediately welcomed by the hugest living room I had ever seen, even bigger than The Prices'. A marble table separated the two whirling white staircases that lead up to the bedrooms. On the right was a grand piano, headshots of past leaders followed you everywhere you moved, and paintings of horses filled in the rest of the walls.

The left side of the living room had a grand fireplace with an ornate mantel, a coffee table with years old magazines, and two plush white sofas with pink, neon, and purple pillows. The walls were decorated with antique items, including a portrait of a woman and an enormous grandfather clock. I was in a trance with the beauty of the house. I almost didn't hear the screeching woman behind me.

"Oh, my god!" the woman screamed. "Another pledge!"

"Oh, no. I'm not-"

Before I could finish, she was interlocking her arm into mines and dragging me toward their back door that led to their courtyard. "We have to hurry! They're almost done with the pledging process."

"But I'm not-"

"Prepared? It's okay. We're laid back compared to most. So much so, I think Emily may overlook your tardiness and give you a chance. What's your name?"

I didn't know how to tell her I wasn't interested in rushing. She may kick me out before I could get to Jordyn, so I played along. "I'm W-," I stopped myself, remembering Dean Clayton had banned me from the frats and sororities. I wasn't sure if she had given my name out to every Greek organization, but I wasn't taking the chance. "I'm Willow."

"Oh, my god! I love that name. It's the name of my favorite character on Buffy."

Her infectious energy made me smile. "I was always a Cordelia girl."

"I loved her too! Oh, I have a good feeling about you. I'm Leah, by the way. I'm a sophomore member here."

"I take it you like Delta Zeta then?"

"I love it. I didn't have many friends back in high school. Having over fifty now is weird, but also nice to have," Leah answered with a laugh.

I nodded my head, understanding. I followed her out into the courtyard. It was huge, with large palm trees, white marble fountains, and a Jacuzzi. There were several lounge chairs and umbrellas set up, providing guests with shade as they mingled. By my estimate, there were fifty girls lounging around and talking to each other. I kept my eyes focused on finding one, Jordyn.

"Come on, you have to meet Emily," Leah said while pulling me toward a corner where a group of three girls were talking. "Emily! I found another pledge."

The three girls turned in our direction, and my face almost cracked when I saw one was Jordyn. She was wearing a sage green button-up shirt with the sleeves rolled up, black slacks, and black combat boots. She looked like the Jordyn I had become accustomed to, but seeing her in this kind of environment puzzled me. And that was before I saw the red solo cup in her hand.

"Emily, this is Willow. Willow, meet Emily."

"Hi," I directed to the brunette standing in front of me. Behind her was Jordyn mouthing "Willow" with an incredulous look on her face. And that stole my attention.

"Nice to meet you, Willow. But if you want to be a pledge at Delta Zeta, the least you can do is show up on time."

"Understood."

"So you understand why we won't be offering a spot in?"

"I do."

"Oh, come on, Emily. So she was two hours late. She still showed up. You got to appreciate the boldness. I know I do," Leah interjected on my behalf.

"I see your point, Leah. But I don't think we'll offering her spot in. She can try again next year. We'll give her a fresh start then."

I smiled weakly, pretending to be sad over the rejection. "Can I ask you a question before I leave?"

"Sure, why not?"

"You know you're supplying those under the drinking age with alcohol, right?"

"Oh, yeah," Emily nodded. "They're allowed to have a drink or two while they're here, so long as they're not getting drunk."

"Who is monitoring that? Do you have a spreadsheet of how many drinks each pledge has?" I said, pointing out how ludicrous her justification was. "Also, how many of your pledges are rushing? I'm gonna guess more than half, which means they're having drinks at each sorority they visit. So saying, they aren't getting drunk here doesn't mean much if you're helping them get drunk somewhere else."

Emily's expression of shock froze in place as she processed what she just heard. She wasn't expecting that kind of push back. She shook it off as best she could and replied, "You make a good point. We should keep tabs on our pledges and how much they drink. I'm just not sure how we're supposed to do that when, like you said, they attend other sorority parties and drink there."

"Maybe stop serving them alcohol until you figure it out. Just a thought." I look over to Jordyn, who, similar to Emily, sported a surprised expression. "Jordyn, let's go."

"Right. Thanks for a surprisingly enjoyable night, Emily. And it was nice meeting you, Sarah and Leah."

"You too," they echoed her.

Jordyn followed a few steps behind me as we made it in front of the Delta Zeta House again. She was quiet until we were out of earshot of the remaining guests. "Just when I think I have a handle on you, you confuse me all over again."

I looked back at her, but didn't stop walking. "What are you talking about?"

"I don't remember you being preachy about underage drinking when you and Sabrina were doing it in high school. Suddenly it's a problem when I do it?"

"Do you seriously have a problem with me for looking out for you?"

"I never asked you to do that. I can handle taking care of myself fine."

"Everyone always thinks that, but we all need someone to watch out for us sometimes. You might not like me for it now, but you'll thank me later for it."

The sound of her boots on the pavement stopped. "Why are you behaving like you're my mom or my sister? You're not anything to me."

That made me stop walking and turn around. "Excuse me for thinking we were becoming friends."

"Why do you want to be friends with someone who only tolerates you?"

"Because I think you more than just tolerate me. You want us to be friends, but you're holding back for whatever reason."

"What reason would that be, since you have everything figured out?"

Her arms were folded across her chest and she looked at me, waiting for me to say something. "I hurt you back in Wayland. I wasn't there for you in the way you needed to me to be. You're afraid of giving me a chance to get close to you now because you think I'll hurt you again and this time it'll hurt worse."

She took a step back; her face paling. "That's not—"

"Yeah, that's exactly it. You're afraid I'll hurt you if we become friends. It's nonsense though, because I wouldn't."

I took a step closer to her, but she took a step back, her face panicked. "I don't know what to think about you. You're confusing me. You have since you walked into my dorm. You're different from how I remember you. At first it was the clothes, then it was everything else. I assumed you wanting to be friends was because of you needing a friend after losing Sabrina."

"You don't think that anymore?"

"I don't know what to think. I'm waiting for the other shoe to drop. Something to prove to me I was right to be skeptical about you. That you're still the same self-involved person I remember you being in

Wayland."

Anger was boiling inside me. I had done everything in my power to be there for her, to prove to her I was worthy of her friendship. And yet, she continued to push me away. "Jordyn, you don't have to be so damn defensive all the time," I spat out. "I'm not the same person I used to be. I've changed, grown up. You should try it sometime."

Jordyn let out a small laugh, but there was no humor in it. "Is that right? You've changed? From where I'm standing, you're still the same person you've always been. You still think you know better than everyone else, better than me. You still think you know everything there is to know about me when you don't know a damn thing."

This was not what I had expected when I came here. I came to show Jordyn what a true friend I could be, but things were just getting worse. I took a deep breath. I couldn't let my anger get the best of me, not when there was still a chance for us.

"Okay, you're right," I said, taking a step back and lowering my voice. "I don't know everything there is to know about you. No one ever does, but I do want to get to know you better. I want to get to a place where we can genuinely become friends. It doesn't matter if we take things slow or dive in headfirst. We can do whatever you want. I just think we could miss out on something special if we don't see where this could go."

"This is why I'm reluctant," she mumbled, her expression impossible to read. "It's never been this hard with anyone else before. You seem perfect one minute, knowing just the right thing to say to me or how to behave around me. Then in the next, I'm wondering what you're really up to. I want to believe we can make this- whatever this is- work because deep down I know it could be good... but I've had good friendships before. They were never this complicated. Isn't that a sign?"

"I don't know. All my friendships have been this complicated and full of drama."

She chuckled and some of the tension eased out of her posture. "You mean you were handing out intense speeches like this to other friends of yours?"

With a wry smile, I shook my head. "No, because I never wanted their friendships as much as I want yours."

Her expression softened at this admission, and I knew I had finally made some progress in getting through to her. I took a step closer. This time, she didn't back away. "Okay," she whispered. "Let's give this a try. Let's try being friends, but it has to be slow. No more intense speeches or dramatic confrontations."

"I'm willing to take it slow if that's what you need," I replied, trying to temper the chirpiness in my voice.

"Then it's decided. We'll give this a try to see if we can build something good out of this mess. I have one condition in order for this to work. You got one thing right earlier, which is I am worried about getting hurt. Not exclusively by you, but by everyone. It's why I enjoy keeping to myself. So if we're going to become friends, I need you to promise me you won't intentionally hurt me or break my trust."

I wanted nothing more than to give her that promise, but I was hiding the real reason I sought a friendship from her. And it had nothing to do with her but my own selfish interests. If Jordyn ever found out how I was intending on using her to get back at her sister, it would certainly end things between us forever. So instead I told her, "That's not something you have to worry about. Not from me."

I said my empty promise with conviction, which gave Jordyn the reassurance she was looking for. Deep down, I knew if she ever found out the truth about me, she would be proven right. But despite the potential pain this secret could bring her in the future, at least now we had a chance to become friends. Maybe we'll reach a place where nothing could drive us apart, not even my hidden motives.

10

We Need To Talk About Sabrina

The perks of becoming Jordyn's friend were long and benefited me greatly. For one, she didn't keep me at arm's length nearly as much. She listened and talked to me. There was no more leaving my texts on read for days or waiting for me to be the one who initiated things. She responded to me as quickly as she could. More importantly, she reached out to me whenever she had something to share.

If she was reading one of the many horror books she collected, she would text me a summary of what chapter she finished and make me as equally freaked out about the murders and plot twists as she was. Even when it left me with some colorful dreams, I embraced being that friend for her. She still kept in touch with her friends from back home, but I felt like I was becoming a part of her life in a way that was uniquely mine.

It didn't appear to be any downsides of being Jordyn's friend. Well, that was until one afternoon where I was hit with the realization that every rose has its thorns. For Jordyn, hers was her sister.

It was a Tuesday, and I sat back against the door of Jordyn's dorm. We planned to link up after her class ended at 2:45 p.m. to go eat and then catch a movie. She was running late, so I occupied myself with a crossword puzzle on my phone. I finished solving it when I heard footsteps approaching. I looked up, expecting to see Jordyn, only to find Sabrina striding towards me with a displeased expression.

"Do you have amnesia or something? I told you to stay away from my sister and now you're seeking her out at her dorms?" she said, lowering her voice just enough so she wasn't being disruptive.

I remained sitting on the blue spruce colored carpeted floor because if we were going to have this conversation, I was going to at least be comfortable. "It's none of your business, but Jordyn invited me."

"Yeah? That why you're sitting out here by yourself looking like a lost puppy?"

"She's running late, genius. And her roommate, Amelia, isn't here because she writes for the school's newspaper and they're having a meeting. Not that you would know any of that, since you never talk to Jordyn about anything besides yourself."

She brushed off the insult with a roll of her eyes. "I've tried to be nice about this."

"Nice? Nice where?"

"Nice by not telling my family about what you and Mike did before the summer. My parents loved you guys. It didn't feel right telling them how you both screwed me over by screwing each other, so I never told them. But I can. I can also tell Jordyn how you lied on Mike's name. I don't think she'll want to be your friend after that. Do you?"

"So what? You're going to tell your version of the truth to your family if I don't stop being friends with Jordyn?"

"Something like that."

"Do it," I said confidently, no trace of fear in my voice. "Because I don't think you kept our friendship ending from your family because 'it didn't feel right'. I think you kept it from them because you knew they wouldn't believe you. Eliza and Bryan would never believe I had knowingly slept with Mike."

"But you expect them to believe Mike raped you? You're delusional."

After scanning the area to make sure no one else was within earshot, she looked at me again and said, "Being the daughter of two absentee parents must be hard. I wouldn't know, but I assume it is. With that said, I suggest you find another set of parents to leech off of. Mine are off limits, and so is my sister."

It shouldn't have, but her comment stung. I told her in confidence how I felt about parents and how I took comfort in thinking of Eliza and Bryan as a second mother and father. Every secret I told her, every detail of my private life that I'd foolishly thought was safe with Sabrina could now be out in the open for anyone to know if she so desired.

That's the worst part about losing a best friend. Finding someone you thought you could trust with your most intimate thoughts, hidden insecurities, and paralyzing fears is hard enough as it is. To think you found that person only to have them betray you is a blow you never fully recover from. I certainly wouldn't.

While Sabrina spoke, I realized that as her adversary, she had the capability of hurting me however she wanted to. The only course of action I could take was to respond in kind, even if it meant hurting the one person I didn't want to. Finally, I stood and met her eyes. I wanted her to hear this next part loud and clear. "You want me to stay away from your parents? Fine, but not Jordyn. I'm not you. I don't abandon my friends."

"Friends? You can't actually believe what the two of you have is a friendship. Either she's using you because she's lonely or you're using her thinking it's going to make me mad. It doesn't matter which because it won't last. One of you will get sick of the other and end this sham."

"Are you describing me and Jordyn, or me and you?"

Sabrina looked stunned at my line of questioning. She recovered quickly though and replied, "Do you notice the common denominator in both is you? That would give most people the foresight to see the problem is them."

"I see the problem, but it's not me. It's you. You're the one who's always looking out for number one. You're the one who gets joy from making the people around you feel like crap. It was the story of our friendship, but I won't let it define us now as strangers. You don't get to put me down anymore or make me feel lesser than you. And I'll be damned if I let you control my life when you're not even a part of it."

Her gaze shifted away from me and settled on something behind me, her expression completely emotionless. Once I heard the voice, I knew why. "What's going on? Why are you two bickering out in the hallway for everyone to hear?" Jordyn inquired as she approached us in bewilderment.

"Me and Whit are just having a chat while waiting for you."

"A chat? It sounded like a screaming match from what I heard."

I exhaled heavily, aware this was throwing a wrench into our plans. Jordyn didn't tolerate bullshit or petty drama. She enjoyed watching it from afar, but she never wanted to be roped into it. "Your sister is concerned about us being friends. In fact, she wants me to ditch you."

"I didn't say she should ditch you," Sabrina clarified. "Just that it would be in everyone's benefit if this new friendship of yours ended before one of you got hurt."

Jordyn rolled her eyes to show her disdain. "Sabrina, is your life in any way, shape, form affected by me and Whit hanging out?"

"I mean, it's only a matter of time before she asks for an invitation to cousin Sean's wedding or to Thanksgiving. Eventually she's going to want to be part of our lives again and I didn't sign up for that when I cut her out of my life."

"That's why you're against us being friends? This has nothing to do with you feeling concerned for me or worried I might get hurt? All you care about is how my friendship with Whit affects you? What a world-class sister I have."

"Jordo," Sabrina pleaded affectionately. "I am worried about you. I was friends with Whit for years and she stabbed me in the back. Of course, I'm concerned she'll do the same thing to my little sister."

"I didn't stab you in the back, but if you want to believe that, fine. But don't repeat those lies as facts to her."

"Will the both of you just stop?" Jordyn demanded, her voice raising on each syllable. "Your issues are with each other. Not me. I'm not a part of this, so don't put me in the middle. Sabrina, you're my sister. I love you, but I won't let you decide who I'm friends with. It's none of your fucking business, so stay out of it."

"And Whit, I've enjoyed hanging out with you these last few weeks, but I hope you don't expect me to feel the same way you do about Sabrina. No matter how many times we fight or are at odds, she is still my sister. That will never change, so don't push your luck."

Sabrina beat me to the punch by nodding her head first. "Jordo, you're right. I'm sorry. I fell into the overprotective big sister trap. It won't happen again."

"Good." Jordyn accepted her apology so easily. It annoyed me. "How about you, Whit?"

I squared my shoulders and met her gaze. "I'm sorry, too." Not that sorry, but she didn't need to know that. "Jor, I won't try to push my feelings about Sabrina onto you. I respect the relationship you have with your sister, and I'm not trying to mess with that."

Her tight-lipped glare transformed into a satisfied grin as she nodded. But as quickly as she was standing there, she was quicker to open the door to her dorm and closed it behind her. Effectively killing the plans we'd made in a matter of seconds. I spun around to look at Sabrina and saw she was heading toward the stairs that exited the building.

I lingered alone there in the hall for a moment, feeling relieved and disappointed. Relief that the tension between Jordyn and me was gone as quickly as it appeared. Disappointed the opportunity to get closer to her had been blown. All because of Sabrina.

11

To Flirt with Danger

Jordyn whispered, "I'm sorry," in my ear as she approached me from behind. As her words sank in, I felt a chilling sensation crawl down my back. He spoke those exact words to me on that terrible night—the two simple words that confirmed my gut feeling that something was wrong. I was seated in the campus coffee shop, engrossed in my phone, when her voice intruded upon my thoughts. I hadn't noticed her enter.

Had I seen her coming, my body's reaction would have been different. The fine hairs on my arms and the nape of my neck would have remained undisturbed. My hands wouldn't have quivered, forcing me to conceal them beneath my thighs, away from prying eyes. My eyes wouldn't have involuntarily closed, as if trying to remind me I was in the here and now, not five months ago, in an unfamiliar room with unwanted hands touching me in places they were unwelcome.

The air was filled with the intoxicating scent of freshly brewed coffee and warm pastries, but it couldn't erase the dreadful memories weighing on me. Jordyn's hushed voice filtered through the thick fog in my mind, and I forced my eyes open to see her speaking. "This is partially your fault too, you know? You need to stop arriving at our hangouts so early. That way, I'll stop feeling like a bad person when I'm a little late to them."

"What?" I asked, trying to get my bearings.

"Are you okay? You seemed out of it," she frowned, taking her leather jacket off.

"I'm fine. I was lost in thought."

"You know, I was just kidding, right?"

"Kidding about what?"

"About you needing to stop showing up to stuff early. I like when you do that. It makes me feel you value my time and are putting forth a genuine effort in being my friend. I just feel bad keeping you waiting. I want you to never get the impression that I don't care as much about this friendship as you do. I want to make this work."

"I know. I don't mind waiting, honestly. It's just a habit of mine to be early." A habit I had specifically made during the early stages of my friendship with Sabrina. We were kids when we became friends, but she already accumulated a certain social status at our school. It was known her parents worked and lived in the richest neighborhood in Wayland, and everyone wanted to befriend because of it.

Knowing this, she became selective with whom she let into her inner circle. No one who was too eager. That was a sign of them having ulterior motives. No one who was too enamored by her. She wanted friends, not minions. People who would challenge her, but remained loyal to her, too. She didn't want to be surrounded by a bunch of people pleasers, but she didn't want friends who would go against her either.

Somehow, I ticked all her boxes. I learned what lines I could cross with Sabrina and which to steer clear of. Toying that line was a specialty, and I mastered it long before anyone else did. I like to think it was because I treated Sabrina like she was a sort of test. If I was going to live in a predominately white small town until I was eighteen and could leave, I needed to learn how to read people, how to fit in, and how to survive. Tools I would need living as a Black woman in America, anyway.

The way I saw it was if I could earn Sabrina's acceptance and friendship, I could earn anyone's. And that's what I did. I became her sounding board, her confidant, her loyal friend. In return, she shielded me from criticisms from our peers, opened up her home and family to me, and made sure I was never left out of anything. It was a perfect trade-off, a seamless friendship. Until it wasn't.

"I didn't know if you wanted the same thing you got the last time, so I ordered you a water," I told Jordyn when she glanced at it. This was our first hangout since she canceled our plans. Whatever hostility she was holding onto toward me about my spat with Sabrina seemed to have lifted when she asked me out for coffee.

"Thanks, because if I have any more coffee, I will get the jitters. I had two while I was out helping Sabrina."

"Helping her with what?"

"You don't want to know. It's boring."

Not being forthcoming with details was unusual for Jordyn, which made me all the more intrigued by what Sabrina was up to. "Were you helping her with a project or something? God knows she can't get a passing grade without help."

"Have you not heard she's running for Social Chair?"

"I'm not up to date on that stuff, in case you haven't noticed. I don't pay attention to those stunts anymore."

"Well, Sabrina does, and she's running. That's where I was before coming here. She roped me and her new boyfriend into passing out flyers with her face on it."

I couldn't help but cackle at the image of Jordyn carrying around flyers of Sabrina, with her toothy smile and flowing blonde hair.

"I'm glad you find that so amusing."

119

"Sorry, but it's funny. If she and I were still friends, she would've definitely made me do that. Now you know what it feels like to be the best friend of Sabrina Price."

"Mind taking the duties back?"

"Nuh-uh. She's your problem now. I'm free of her."

"Good for you, because I never will be." She took a sip of her water as a reprieve from talking about Sabrina, but I wasn't done on the subject yet.

"Didn't you say she had a new boyfriend? Let him handle her high maintenance ass."

"He seems like he is. I've only met him twice, but he seems to know how to handle her and her Sabrina-ness. Still, I'm not sure if he'll be around for long."

"Why not? What's wrong with him?"

"Nothing from what I could tell, but everyone thought her and Mike would last forever and out of nowhere, she broke things off with him. What's stopping her from doing the same to this new guy?"

There was so much I wanted to say, but I swallowed my comments and settled for, "You're right. This guy could be yesterday's news by tomorrow."

"Yeah. What's that saying, 'boys come and go, but sisters last forever'? That applies here, except the sisters' part is quite literal for me and Sabrina."

"Correct me if I'm wrong, but your relationship with her is almost as tedious as mine with her. Why are you so inclined to always being there for her?"

"Your question is giving only child energy."

"I wonder why," I mocked. My tone was jovial, but the question I posed was serious. Jordyn knew it was too, hence why she was avoiding answering it. "Come on, humor me. Every time Sabrina needs your help, you're there. Can you say the same thing about her?"

"I thought you weren't going to do this."

"Do what?"

"You said you wouldn't try to force your opinion of Sabrina onto me."

"Is that what I'm doing?"

"Yes, it is. And I would prefer if you would just own it instead of acting cute about it."

I raised my hands, genuinely apologetic for venturing into territory Jordyn wished we didn't explore. "My fault. I just wanted to be sure she wasn't taking advantage of you."

"Is that what you think she did to you? Took advantage of your friendship?"

I hesitated for a moment before answering. "Sabrina had a way of making me feel lucky to be her friend. Like she was doing me a favor. For a long time, I believed her."

"Until?" Jordyn asked, her eyes searching my face.

"I wish I could tell you one day I woke up and realized Sabrina wasn't half the friend to me that I was to her, but she called it quits on us. She believed I wronged her, and she stopped doing me the favor of being my friend."

"She can be a real bitch sometimes. Or, like all the time."

"Don't I know it?" I replied with a wry smile. "Still, I'm glad things turned out this way. It made me realize I don't need her toxicity in my life and it allowed me to make new friends, real ones like you."

Jordyn's face briefly contorted into a sly smirk, but she suppressed it. "Happy to be included in that group."

"Included? You're the only person in it."

"You seriously don't have one friend beyond me? Chloe? Owen? Brooklyn? Hell, Mike?"

I stiffened at the mention of him, but I tried to hide it. "I'm not friends with them anymore. Like I said, the high school crew were always closer to Sabrina than me."

"What about Mike? You guys were like the three musketeers."

I sighed, knowing I couldn't give her a halfhearted excuse. She wouldn't buy it. She would need more, but I didn't know how much I was comfortable offering to her. "Before he transferred, I found out Mike wasn't who I thought he was."

"What do you mean? Who was he?"

"A person I don't want to be friends with."

Her curiosity was piqued, and she leaned in closer. "What did that floppy haired golden retriever do?"

"It doesn't matter. He's just not someone I want in my life."

"Why do you have to be so cryptic about everything? First, Sabrina, now Mike? My imagination is going to run wild with possibilities of what he could've done."

"I can't tell you. Please, can we just leave it at that?"

She leaned back in a huff. "You and your secrets. Will I ever be privy to them?"

"They're not secrets you would want to know."

She recognized I was being serious and stopped pushing the topic. "I want to ask you something, but I feel like I already know your answer."

"Try me."

"Sabrina is formally announcing her bid for Social Chair on Saturday. She's reserved one of the ballrooms at the Campus Center. I am going and I'm sure I am going to be bored out of my mind."

"I'm sure you'll have a great time," I lied, trying to sound optimistic.

"Well, I'm sure I won't. Unless... you come with me."

"You want me to be your date?"

A noticeable blush spread across her cheeks, betraying her embarrassment. It was cute as hell, but I wouldn't embarrass her further by pointing it out. She crossed her arms on the table and looked at me. "Yeah, but not in the romantic sense. More in the 'it would be nice to have someone to talk to' sense."

"Spending a night dedicated to boasting about your sister sounds like hell."

"I know it does, but I could use a friend for this."

The last party I attended, I wound up in a screaming match with Jordyn. The one before I ended up in tears. Before that one, I was assaulted. I came to the conclusion parties were not my thing. Then again, spending an evening with Jordyn wouldn't be so bad. Plus, seeing Sabrina's face when she found out I was there would be priceless. She might get so mad, it may end up ruining her night. The thought of that made me happy.

"I'll go, but you better thank me by going all out. I mean, picking me up from my dorm, paying for my drinks, dancing-"

"Dancing?" she scoffed. "Haha, no. I don't dance."

"Okay, Chad. I'll settle for you picking me up and buying me drinks."

"I can do that, but don't expect me to seal the night with a kiss."

"That's too bad. I was hoping you would." She nudged my knee hard with her own underneath the table. Her knee collided with mine underneath the table, catching me off guard. "Ouch."

"That's what you get for being such a shameless flirt."

I didn't know how to tell Jordyn I had never flirted with my friends before, that it was something I never did. Hell, flirting in general wasn't something I did at all anymore. The thought of entertaining a connection, let alone a romantic one, filled me with an overwhelming repulsion.

Yet, inexplicably, entertaining it with Jordyn felt different. It felt good. Safe. Right. With her, the prospect of a connection didn't seem repulsive. It felt like something akin to hope, a thing I wondered for months if I would ever feel again. I didn't know how to explain that to her without scaring her, so I stayed quiet and let my smile speak for my heart that couldn't.

12

In the Heat of the Moment

Gathering what little courage I had, I lifted the drape that hung over my floor-length mirror to reveal the body I hadn't seen in five months. How did I avoid looking at myself for that long? It was pretty easy, actually. I spent the summer at Winnie's house and rarely left. Food was delivered, clothes were shipped, no friends called to hang out. Every single thing that would have pointed to the way things had changed about me were the things I avoided.

By staying at Winnie's, I was safe. I knew where the mirrors were and I evaded them every time. The mirrors in my bedroom and bathroom were hidden by drapes I threw over them. By bypassing them, I could act like nothing was different about me.

I couldn't avoid them forever, but the longer I stayed away from them, the more I could believe everything was normal on the outside — even though I was crumbling within. Seeing my reflection would have forced me to have to confront what had happened; at a time when it felt safer to ignore it.

Had I not been invited to Sabrina's party, I would've tried to avoid my reflection for the rest of the semester, delaying the inevitable. Having been invited, I knew it was time to face the music and take a look at myself. Upon first glance, nothing appeared drastically different about my appearance, giving me some relief. Upon closer inspection, things weren't as they had initially seemed.

My face looked fuller than before, especially around my cheeks, where excess puffiness made me resemble a child. The bags under my eyes were more pronounced than ever and took up most of my eyelids. Months had passed since my last hair appointment and it showed. My curls were a frizzly mess. My added weight gain in my stomach and waist area was the least surprising change.

I started gaining weight prior to the rape. As a freshman on campus, I fell prey to the infamous 'Freshman 15.' Eating at local restaurants and fast-food joints because it was convenient and easy added up after a while. I at least had a campus gym at my disposal to help me lose it. I didn't have that over the break. Depression hit me hard over the summer to where making any walk that wasn't to the bathroom or to the porch felt impossible, so exercising wasn't an option.

For three months, the extra pounds kept piling on. I didn't know exactly how much weight I gained, but it felt closer to 25 pounds than just 15. I tossed my old clothing to accommodate this change, a closet full of oversized tees and hoodies that helped conceal my new figure. With my new wardrobe, I was allowed to accept my new body and let it grow in all the ways it wanted to. I liked my body and a new number on a scale would not change that.

I glanced at my phone and saw I had two hours before Jordyn was supposed to come pick me up. In a rush, I went over to my closet and looked to see what I had. My eyes fell on a black long sleeve shoulder cut top in one box labeled 'shirts'. Navy denim jeans in a box labeled 'jeans'. Black combat boots in one box I simply titled 'shoes'. Wordsmith, I was not. The boxes had been in my closet stuffed haphazardly into the corner like they were exiled from my life in favor of my hoodies, sweatpants, and sneakers. But today called for their return.

My torso looked perfectly hugged by the flattering fit of the shoulder cut top. The pair of navy denim jeans were worn at the knees, but would make do for tonight. The hem of the jeans brushed against my boots as I walked up to my mirror for one last look. For some reason, putting on the outfit and seeing how it looked on me made me feel closer to myself than I had in months, though I wasn't sure which version of myself that was anymore.

Just as I finished styling my hair into a high, curly ponytail with bangs, Jordyn came to the door. When I opened it, her eyes and mine did a double take on each other. Trading out her ripped jeans and graphic tees for a white button-down shirt and khaki pants. I wasn't sure if she got dolled up for the party or for me. We stood there for a second, looking at each other like two deer in headlights, and then laughed nervously.

Jordyn smiled warmly and said, "Well, hello gorgeous."

I giggled before saying, "Hi, nice-so bad yourself."

A blush crept up my cheeks as I realized I flirted with Jordyn. The second time in the same week I had done it. I didn't know what was coming over me. I wasn't a flirt. Of all the guys I'd dated, they'd been the ones to initiate things. Not the other way around. I was never the one to start the flirting with a man, let alone with a woman. Yet here I was doing exactly that with Jordyn, and I couldn't explain why.

Jordyn must have noticed my confusion because she switched subjects. "Did you like my shoes so much, you had to go out and buy your own?" She pointed down at them. "Your boots. They suspiciously look like a pair I own. Is it possible I'm rubbing off on you?"

I shook my head. "Nah. Combat boots simply fit the style I'm going for now."

"Which is my style."

"I don't remember you trademarking hoodies and combat boots."

"Didn't you know they practically belong to us, lesbians?"

I was still getting used to bantering in jest like this with Jordyn, but I enjoyed it. A lot. "Oh really?" I raised my eyebrows, challenging her back.

"Absolutely. No one pulls this look off better than us."

"But you can make a little room for me, can't you?"

She smirked, her eyes crinkling at the corners. "I suppose we can make an exception for you, just this once."

I couldn't wipe the stupid grin off my face even if I tried. I took a step closer, close enough to smell the exquisite sandalwood fragrance Jordyn was wearing. "We should probably go. Doing this whole 'standing in front of the door talking' won't get us anywhere."

"Right." She looked as disappointed as I felt. "Let's go."

Once we were outside, we hurried us across campus to the campus center. The lights were on and music was flooding out of the building. My heart hammered in my chest, nervous about walking in, not knowing what to expect. The party was going to consist of people Sabrina invited. I was the odd one out.

As much as I loved the idea of seeing Sabrina's face when she saw I was there, having it turn into a reality scared me more than I cared to admit. My anxiousness wasn't helped by her voice being the first thing I heard as we stepped inside. She was making a quick plea for the guests to not bring their drinks with them to the dance floor to avoid spilling it. Sound advice, but hearing her authoritative voice boom from the speakers as I walked in did not ease my nerves.

I distracted myself by checking out how decked out the hall was. The walls, ceiling, and floor were made of amethyst mosaics, as if they had been grown from it. There was an area to the left that was allocated for the DJ, including a stereo system and other equipment he needed to make the music blare. In the far back was the stage

Sabrina was speaking on earlier. A bird eyed side view of the room would make you think it was ready for a wedding reception, complete with the table cloths draped over the tables and floral centerpieces decorating them.

Surveying the room, I tried to see if I recognized any familiar faces. I didn't. Either Sabrina hadn't invited her inner circle, or I couldn't recognize the new people in her life now that I was cut out of it.

"Are you okay?"

I tore my gaze away from the other people in the room and placed it on Jordyn, the one who mattered. "I will be once we get this over with."

"We won't be here long. Do you want a drink in the meantime?"

"Yeah, but nothing alcoholic."

"Non-alcoholic, bet. Stay here. I'll be back."

"Where would I go?" I replied as Jordyn started walking away. She halted her walk and cast a knowing smirk over her shoulder. Her confident smile was enough to glimmer even in the midst of the party for her sister. It made such an impression on me I thought I could still see it as she resumed walking again.

Inwardly I smiled because Jordyn, the quiet as a mouse, snarky wallflower, baby of the family, had blossomed into a scene-stealer. She wasn't the blonde bombshell like her sister, but she was something better. The party itself may have been for Sabrina, but Jordyn was the brightest star in the room. If only she and everyone else there knew it.

I was so lost in thought about Jordyn that I was surprised when someone bumped into me from behind. "I'm so sorry," the man said as he bent down to pick up the phone he dropped.

"It's fine-" I cut myself off when I realized who I was staring at.

It seemed like years had passed since I'd seen him last. Though it had only been months. His hair was cut shorter now, but the same shade of chestnut brown still hung over his eyes. There was a hardness to his eyes that wasn't there before, and I knew I was responsible for it.

"Whit... it's been a minute," Luke, pointing out the obvious, said.

"A minute? More like four months, Luke. How have you been?"

"I'm fine. Thanks for asking." I could have believed him if his eyes hadn't betrayed him. Before, Luke looked at me as if I was something to be studied and deciphered. Now he looked at me as if I was a task he needed to avoid.

"You don't look fine. You seemed tense. Is that because of me?"

He let out a deep sigh. "I don't want to do this tonight."

"Do what?"

"Talk about us. It won't end well, and I don't want to ruin Sabrina's big night."

I almost laughed. The only reason I was there was to ruin Sabrina's night. If I could do that by having a much needed talk with Luke, I'd be killing two birds with one stone. "Don't you think we should talk? I don't know about you, but a two sentence break up text provided little closure to me."

"Maybe you need closure, but I don't. I was done with you the moment I found out what you did."

"I did not cheat on you. You would know that if you bothered to talk to me. Instead of getting my side, you believed what Mike told you. We were together for almost a year. You knew me—knew the kind of person I was. You could've given me the benefit of the doubt, but you didn't."

"Are you telling me Mike lied about what happened between you two? That he destroyed his relationship with me and Sabrina over a lie? I find that hard to believe."

"If you would let me explain-"

"You don't have to. I know what story you're going with. Sabrina told me you said that Mike took advantage of you."

"He did. This shouldn't be up for debate," I snapped. By insinuating my version of the truth was a lie, Luke was feeding into the false narrative Mike had created. What pissed me off more than him questioning me was how my integrity was in question too. "I was drunk, and he knew that. He knew I wasn't in the right state of mind and he made me think it was you with me in that bedroom. He tricked me into having sex with him."

"I can't understand how you could've confused us with each other. Mike and I aren't twins. We don't have the same voice. He is taller and heavier than I am. There were signs and you ignored them."

I expected this victim-blaming from people who knew my side of the story, but it still hurt to hear. I averted my gaze and looked at the floor, too embarrassed to look him in the eye. "The room," I stammered. "It was dark."

"That's your excuse?!" Luke said in the loudest tone I had ever heard him use. "That's how you defend the fact that you cheated on me? You might as well have said he slipped and fell into you. That might've been more plausible."

"Why can't you see it from what it was?" I pleaded, desperate for him to understand. "It wasn't sex. Him manipulating me wasn't foreplay. If you would get past your anger toward me, you would see what happened wasn't consensual. It was rape."

"Just stop!" he shouted at me, his eyes filling with anger. "Whit, I wish you would just own up to your mistake instead of just blaming Mike for what happened. You were both complicit. Stop trying to blame this entire thing on him and paint him out as a rapist."

"I'm not painting him out as that. It's what he is."

A thick, syrupy quiet settled between us like the air after a thunderstorm. I could feel him trying to put his finger on what was bothering him about my story, but he gave up, knowing it would only result in more fighting. "Why didn't you come back for me?" I asked, my mind not letting good enough be enough. The question had burned a hole in my chest for months and I needed an answer.

"Come back? What are you talking about?"

"That night, before you left to take Sabrina home, you said you would come back to get me. For hours, I waited for you, but you never came back. Why?"

"I-," he stammered. Before he could decide on the right words, a voice pulled his attention away from them.

"Babe, I've been looking for you. Did you see me out there?" She stepped forward, closing the space between her and Luke. She leaned in, their eyes still locked together like magnets. Their lips met and like a gunshot to the heart, I knew why he never came back.

He had chosen her over me.

When they broke apart, Luke's eyes flew over to mine. He had the decency to look guilty, but it didn't lessen the betrayal I felt right then by them both. I didn't think it was possible to feel betrayed by two people you'd already given up on, but apparently it was.

"I guess I have my answer."

I tried to turn to leave, but Luke grabbed my wrist and spun me around to face him. "It's not what it looks like."

"You aren't fucking Sabrina?" I spat, already knowing the answer.

"It's not like that. We didn't start anything that night. We got together a month after we broke up."

"Oh, you waited a month? That changes everything. I feel so much better."

He shook his head, exasperated with me. "At least, we waited. You and Mike didn't respect us enough to even do that."

"Have you not listened to one word I've said, have you? I don't even know why I keep bother trying to explain. I should just save my breath. It's clear neither one of you is ever going to believe me about what happened that night."

"Hey. They had nothing non-alcoholic, so I got you water. I hope that's fine." I cast a quick look to my left and saw Jordyn standing there with a water bottle in her hand, offering it to me. When I didn't take it, she looked between me, Sabrina, and Luke, then asked, "Everything okay?"

"Everything's perfect," I said, finally taking the water bottle from her. "Thank you for this. It's exactly what I needed."

Without hesitation, I twisted the lid off the bottle and poured water over Luke's shaggy brown hair. Some droplets ran down onto his face, slowly dripping off of his chin while others made their way down into his eyes and soaked through to the ends of his thick locks. I watched as it slid down his skin and pooled in small puddles on the floor. His forehead was still dripping with water as he frantically tried to shake it off.

He glared at me, his face bright red with rage. "What's wrong with you?"

"You, and her!" I couldn't fully voice my anger without sounding like the mad woman I looked like. I shoved the bottle into Luke's chest and stormed out of the building without looking back. I was so mad that I didn't realize I'd backed out of the promise I made to Jordyn until I was already out of the door. I wanted to be the supportive friend she needed, but I couldn't bring myself to go back inside and watch Sabrina and Luke do the same thing they crucified me for.

"Whit, wait!" I stopped walking and faced the entrance, and lo-and-behold, there was Jordyn, jogging towards me. "What happened back there? Why did you throw water in Luke's face?"

"Do you know who that guy is?"

"Yeah… Sabrina's boyfriend. Do you know him?"

"Do I know him?" I stared at her, agape. "Yeah, intimately."

Her face soured, like she had just taken a bite of a lemon. "You mean-"

132

"That I fucked him first? Yeah, I did. We dated for a year and your sister had a front-row seat to the show. I guess she liked it so much, she wanted to experience it for herself. Fucking bitch!"

I wanted to hit something. Something that would knock some sense into my reeling brain. I tried to make myself sit down at the bench less than a foot away, but my feet wouldn't cooperate. All I could do was stand there and watch as Jordyn's face fell.

"Whit," she murmured, inching closer to me, "I'm so sorry. I had no idea."

"No idea?" I echoed, incredulous. "You're Sabrina's sister, and you didn't know she was screwing my ex-boyfriend?"

"I know you're angry, but don't lash out at me."

"Angry? No, I'm not angry. I'm upset. Sabrina was my best friend and the second things went south between us, she goes out of her way to hurt me in the worst way imaginable. And the person who I thought was becoming my friend decided not to tell me? Why? Because her loyalties lie with her sister, even when she's in the wrong."

"I swear I didn't know," Jordyn reiterated. "Sabrina just introduced me to the guy last week. Neither one of them mentioned his past with you to me. They knew if they did, I would, of course, side with you."

"Really?" My tone softened. "You're on my side?"

"Of course. You don't go after your friends' exes. That's like girl code 101. Unless you're gay. Then dating each other's exes is a time-honored tradition."

Despite the sadness and anger I was feeling, Jordyn made me crack a smile. When she saw her move to lighten up the mood had worked, she tried it again. "But even though I'm on your side, I have to admit, I'm not totally on board with the whole 'punishment by water boarding' thing. That was a little too extreme."

A small chuckle escaped from my lips to fill the air between us. "What punishment do you think would be a better fit for Luke?"

"Being with Sabrina should be punishment enough. I mean, he went from dating you to dating my sister. I can't think of a bigger downgrade than that."

I looked at her, a genuine smile on my face. "You think so?"

She stepped closer, evading every bit of my comfort space, but I didn't mind it. Her chest nearly pressed against mine as she slid a loose lock of my hair back behind my ear and said, "You were the girl everyone back home wanted. Not her."

"Now I know you're just trying to make me feel better."

I started to pull away, but she pulled me back inside of her embrace. "Does it feel like I'm trying to make you feel better?" she asked in a low tone that I felt in my knees.

My cheeks flushed under Jordyn's gaze. I felt overwhelmed by the intensity of the moment and all the unexplainable emotions that were coursing through me. So much so, the only word I could get out was, "Jor..."

"Because there are a lot of different ways I can make you feel better. None of them has to include words. Do you want to hear them?"

My heart was beating fast, my mouth was dry, and I had no idea what we were doing or how we had ended up this close. I was afraid of ruining this, whatever this was, so I stayed planted where I was, merely nodding until my voice reached our ears. "Yeah," I croaked out. "I want to hear them."

Jordyn's smirk widened, but she took a few steps away from me. Disappointment hit me when she did. Her choice to put distance between us made my heart feel like it was in a free fall, while my heart rate returned to its usual boring pace. I wanted to dismiss the effect she'd had on my body, but the loss of her closeness made it undeniable.

"Well," she started. "I could give you a hug, and you can cry on my shoulder if you need to. Oh, uh, I could buy you some of your favorite food—pizza always helps those in a crisis. Unless they're lactose intolerant, then pizza would cause another crisis. Or, you know what, I could go back to your dorm and listen to whoever you have on your playlist these days. What do you think?"

I looked down at my hands, worried she would see the smile on my face wasn't real. "Pizza sounds great."

"Why do you sound like you're disappointed?"

I shrugged. "It's nothing. I guess I thought you were going to suggest something else."

"What would you have wanted me to propose?"

"Nothing. Forget it." I shook my head, trying to shake off the awkwardness I created. "Pizza is perfect."

13

Wicked Intentions

In the wake of Sabrina's party, there were many thoughts accompanying space in my mind. One person took up an entire estate, but I was desperate to evict them. The best way I figured out how to do this was to put all my attention on my enemies and how to destroy them. Forgive me for the melodramatics, but this was where my head was at.

I devoted a lot of thought to the two people that at one time mattered the most to me and how they had found another way to betray me. The only silver lining I could find about it was they didn't rub it in my face until later. I don't know how I would've reacted to the news of them becoming a couple during the summer, but I know it would've not have been well.

Sabrina and Luke caused me a lot of pain by not believing me when I told them what had happened with Mike. On the days I wanted to give them the benefit of the doubt, I told myself they were acting from a place of hurt. That once their anger subsided, they would realize they were in the wrong and beg for my forgiveness. However, with this latest betrayal, there was no more benefit of the doubt to give.

There were either two reasons they became a couple, and both reasons did them no favors in my eyes. Either they saw the two of them dating as the perfect way to get back at me for "sleeping" with Mike. Or they'd been harboring feelings for each other while Sabrina and I were friends and Luke and I were still together. It didn't matter which reason it was. Both made me to see red.

I didn't have to convince myself I wanted revenge against my former friend. My mind had already been made up on that. That was the whole point of me becoming friends with Jordyn. And though Sabrina hadn't hidden her frustration at our newfound friendship, I didn't consider just being friends with Jordyn to be enough anymore. If I wanted to get back at her, targeting her relationship with Luke was the obvious path forward.

But don't be mistaken. The plan formulating in my head to screw with Sabrina's relationship wasn't solely about her. I wanted to screw Luke over just as much, if not more. Although Sabrina had violated girl code by going after my ex, it didn't surprise me in the slightest. That was her wheelhouse. All bets were off when she told me our friendship was over. She has a vindictive side to her. I would've been foolish to think she wouldn't go after me in the same way I've seen her go after others who'd hurt her.

What I couldn't have predicted was Luke being a willing participant in her revenge plot against me. Luke wasn't like her. He wasn't a vindictive person. Over the year we were together, I never even saw him kill a fly. That wasn't who he was; it wasn't in his character. His willingness to sink so low startled me and only fueled my desire for retribution. I wanted them to pay for how much pride they took in hurting me.

The only question that remained was how. How could I get back at them without either of them figuring it out? The most glaringly obvious idea looked to be the one that might actually work, if it was executed right. I was going to have to break them up, and I would have to do it without them knowing it.

I wanted revenge, but I needed plausible deniability. If they knew what I was up to, my plan would fail before it came to fruition. Having this in mind narrowed down how I could go about it. Nothing could lead back to me. This meant I couldn't spread gossip about Sabrina to Luke or vice versa. They would figure out what I was up to fast. And they probably wouldn't have believed what I told them, anyway.

For this to work, the discontent in their relationship would have to come from one or both of them, not me. I thought about how to build doubt in their relationship without putting myself into the middle of it. From what I saw of them at Sabrina's party, they were in the honeymoon stage of their relationship. Breaking them up would be harder than just spreading unfounded gossip or rumors about them. I needed actual evidence of something tangible that would spell the end for them.

Cheating was the clear route to go. I knew firsthand how both of them not only detested it, but weren't forgiving when it came to it. But how? How would I get one of them to cheat on the other? Between my parents and Winnie sending me money and me selling my car over the summer for some extra cash, I had some money to burn. Did I have enough to hire someone to seduce Sabrina or Luke? It was a long shot, but desperate times called for desperate measures.

Grabbing my laptop off my desk, I sat down on my bed and opened it. I clicked on the incognito tab and began my search. I typed in phrases I never even in my wildest dreams imagined typing. Phrases like 'professional seduction services' and 'hire a seduction expert', anything that could lead me to someone who could help me out.

For what seemed like hours of searching through websites and forums, I had found four services that were advertising what I was looking for. The problem was that the two couldn't look more like a scam, and the two that looked legit would cost me close to my tuition.

I closed my laptop, my frustration mounting. If I couldn't trick one of them into cheating, this plan would fall to the waste-side.

I sat against my headboard, deflated. Every idea I had was riddled with holes. Hiring someone to seduce one of them was too pricey of a road to go down. Seducing Luke myself was out of the question. He was so angry with me, I couldn't see him wanting to be with me in that way again. Not even in a weak moment, and honestly? The thought of sleeping with Luke to get back at him and Sabrina made my stomach turn. I was willing to do a lot to get what I wanted, but that was a bridge I couldn't bring myself to cross.

So what was I left with? Hiring someone on campus to do my dirty work for me? The idea intrigued me, but it was too risky. Too *10 Things I Hate About You*. Besides, things ended well for Kat and Patrick. I would be the Joey of this scenario and things didn't end quite as well for him. Plus, I couldn't trust anyone to keep this secret to themselves. I would be setting myself up to be found out if I included someone else. I needed to do this alone.

As I laid back onto my bed, watching the shadows play on my ceiling, a thought stirred in the back of my head. An idea that made its way slowly but surely until it sprang full-fledged into consciousness. It was so obvious. I didn't have to trick Luke into cheating on Sabrina. I just needed to make Sabrina think he had.

I sat up and grabbed my laptop again. I typed in yet another address I never thought I would, but it was thankfully less outrageous than 'professional seductress'. Behind me, my wall was drowned in the white and red of Windy City Mingle's webpage popping up on the screen. I clicked on the create account button and when it asked for my name, I typed Luke's. Question after question, I answered as if I was Luke.

Name: Luke Burton

Gender: Male

Orientation: Heterosexual
Age: 20
Location: Chicago, Illinois
Bio: ...

Biography was the trickiest part. I needed to nail Luke's voice, so there was no doubt it wasn't him. It had to be perfect. I stared at the blank space for a few seconds before typing again.

Bio: I'm a college student studying law in Chicago, and while my mom is supportive of my work ethic, she's also encouraging me to get out more and have some fun - aka why I'm giving this a shot. If you're looking for someone to share some laughs and create memories with, let's start by grabbing that beer and seeing where it takes us.

That should do it, I thought to myself as I finished inputting the details. All that was left was one more thing. I crossed my fingers as I logged into Instagram for the first time in months. I checked in once to spy on Sabrina's page and found I was blocked. I was hoping for a different outcome with Luke. I went down my following list and found Luke. I clicked it and waited for it to load.

When it did, I let go of the breath I'd been holding. Luke hadn't blocked me. I was about to cheer when rows of pictures of Luke and Sabrina appeared. The most recent photo was a photo dump from her party. The caption read: "My girl. This is just the beginning. Can't wait to make more memories with you. #blessed."

To stop myself from gagging, I focused on the photos. There were five. One of the venue, another of the food. However, it was the three photos of the happy couple I was most interested in. In one, Luke's arm was wrapped around Sabrina's waist like they were posing for a prom pic. In another, they wore big smiles while conversing with guests.

It was the last photo that felt like a knife in the gut. It was of Luke and Sabrina sharing a passionate kiss in the middle of the party. I could tell the photo was taken after I'd dumped water onto him because he was now wearing a zip up jacket over his shirt. Even through the photo, you could tell his hair was damp. And yet, it didn't matter. My antics hadn't ruined Sabrina's big night. She looked happy, and so did he. Happier than I had ever seen them before.

I couldn't wait to ruin it.

Scrolling past, I found a solo photo of Luke. In it, he was wearing a sleeveless gray tank top, running shorts, and a pair of tinted sunglasses. The sun was blaring down on him and it looked like whoever had taken it called his name just before snapping it, because he was barely looking up at them. He was sporting a casual smile that always caught my eye. Now I hoped it would catch another woman's eye too.

I downloaded the photo and uploaded it as his profile photo. I plucked out a few more photos to make the profile look real. And then, just like that, Luke was on one of the most popular Chicago local dating apps. In less than a minute, the profiles of potential matches rolled in. Beautiful women around his age that lived close by accumulated on screen.

Each woman's profile presented something different; hobbies, job titles, music preferences. They were all fascinating in their own unique ways. If I was queer and was doing this for myself, I would've swiped right on all of them. But alas, I was acting as though I was Luke and I needed to think like him too.

Who of these women would Luke be interested in? I knew little about his dating history except that he had one serious girlfriend before me. My best guess about who he may like was to consider myself... and Sabrina. I thought about what we had in common and what may have attracted Luke to us. We were both outspoken, independent, strong-willed, stubborn, and prone to lashing out. Oh, and conventionally attractive.

Keeping that in mind, I narrowed down the women. After scrolling through profiles and swiping right on the ones I believed matched that criteria, I heard a knock at my door. "Whit, it's me." I jumped out of my skin, hearing Jordyn's voice.

I closed the laptop, and I got up. Before I opened, I checked out my appearance in the mirror. It was 6 p.m. on a weeknight. Jordyn and I hadn't talked about meeting tonight, but maybe she wanted to go hang out? I reevaluated my appearance just in case she did.

I was in a pair of burgundy leggings and a matching Nike hoodie. The knocking started again, but I didn't go to it, instead I pulled my hoodie over my head. I was wearing a gray tank top underneath. In the mirror, I saw how much side boob I was giving, but I didn't move to fix it. When I went to grab my brush, I realized what I was doing. I was making myself look presentable, like I was about to face a crush.

I chuckled at myself. What was I doing? Jordyn was my friend. Not some crush I needed to impress. I stopped what I was doing and went to open the door. "Hey," I said in a cheery voice.

"Hey," Jordyn said back. She was carrying a drink and a plate with a burger and fries on it. "I hope I'm not interrupting something."

"No, not at all," I assured as I took the food from her. "You got this for me?"

"The cafeteria was about to close and I saw they still had some burgers left. I assumed you hadn't eaten yet. Was I right?"

"Yes, thank you. That was nice of you." I might have mentioned to Jordyn one of the good things the cafeteria served was burgers. I took a bite of it, savoring the flavor. It'd been a while since I ate a burger this good.

"No problem." She looked around, taking my dorm in. "This is my first time getting a real good look at the place. It's huge."

"Yeah, it is. So if you ever get sick of Amelia, you can always crash here."

"I told you, I like Amelia. She's the best roommate someone could ask for."

"I don't doubt it, but even the best roommates can be exhausting. The offer stands."

I was lost in thought, realizing I just casually offered my place to another person and felt no regrets about it when Jordyn stepped closer to me and reached out for my hand. Not the free hand, the one holding the burger. She brought it up to her lips and took a small bite, her eyes never leaving mine. I watched, transfixed, as she swallowed. I should have pulled away, but I didn't. Caught in her gaze, I was spellbound. When she dropped her hand from mine and laughed, my trance was broken. "Did I not mention that was the last burger? You didn't mind that I took a bite, did you?"

"No, of course not." I sounded meek, even to my own ears. I cleared my throat and took a step back. "Sit. I'll find a knife and we can split it."

I went into my kitchen area and pulled open the drawer and picked out a butter knife. I washed it off in the sink and returned to my bed to see Jordyn sitting and glancing over at my phone. "What are you doing?"

"Sorry." She sat upright. "Your phone lit up, and I caught the beginning of the notification and I couldn't believe it. Are you on Windy City Mingle?"

I sighed. When I made Luke's account, I used one of my backup emails. They must have sent a notification saying I had a match. "Um... yeah," I said, embarrassed.

I thought Jordyn was going to laugh at me, but she gave me a reassuring smile. "Did seeing Sabrina and Luke together push you to do this?"

"Sort of." I sat down across from her and grabbed my phone from her reach. "I'm just ready to move on."

"And you think a dating app is the way to go?"

"What other way could I go?"

"Uh… I don't know. How about meeting someone on campus or close by?"

"I'm not looking for a boyfriend. I just want to get my mind off of Luke."

"You can meet someone to take your mind off of Luke in the real world. You don't have to go virtual to find what you're describing."

"And I should take relationship advice from the woman who has only ever been in one because…?"

Her mouth dropped, and she slapped my knee with the back of her hand. "Hey, my one relationship lasted longer than any relationship you have ever been in."

I couldn't even say she was wrong, because she wasn't. It dawned on me then that even though I had more experience than Jordyn; she was the only one between us that actually ever experienced true love.

"What do you recommend I do, then?"

"Go out and meet people. There has to be somebody out there that wants your annoying ass."

I bit back a laugh and gave her the knife I had been holding. I watched as she cut the burger in half and gave me the bigger piece. "Speaking of going out, do you want to do something on Saturday?" I asked after taking a bite.

"I can't. Amelia and her friends are taking me out to this all ages club Saturday."

"A club?" I yelped. "That's a perfect place for me to meet people."

"Are you inviting yourself to my hangout?"

"Yeah. I mean, if you think Amelia would be cool with it. I wouldn't want to intrude."

"You wouldn't. Amelia would love to meet you."

"As do I her."

"It's just that… I'm not sure you'll like the club."

I tilted my head to the side. "Are you going to be there?"

"Yeah-"

"Are you going to ditch me?"

"Not unless you ask me to."

"Then I'll like the club just fine. As long as I get to spend time with you, I'll be happy."

Jordyn's eyes lit up and a broad smile slowly spread across her face. She smiled for what seemed like an eternity, and yet I still couldn't look away. "Okay. I'll pick you up at eight."

14

Whit in Wonderland

"Don't say I didn't warn you," Jordyn said, as she watched me stand agape, realizing just what kind of club we were in.

"You didn't tell me it was a gay bar. Am I even allowed in here?"

Overhearing us, Amelia appeared from behind me. The three of us drove in an Uber and I got the chance to get familiarized with Jordyn's roommate and friend. "Of course you're welcomed here! This club is for everyone. The staff is welcoming, just like the club itself. I guarantee you won't be sorry you came."

"What she said," Jordyn echoed.

"I thought you hadn't been here before."

"I hadn't, but if you've been to one. You've been to them all. And the one I've gone to was amazing, so this one should be too."

My eyebrow raised after hearing that. "You've been to a gay club before? I don't remember there being one in Wayland?"

She bristled, like I had told her the funniest joke ever. "Oh, there is still so much you don't know about me."

"Levi and the rest of the gang got here before us and got hold of a table if you ladies want to sit with us?" Amelia offered.

"Lead the way." I started to follow her, but Jordyn held my arm back.

"Are you sure you want to hang with them? They're not like your usual group. Between me not being completely honest about the nature of the club and this not being your scene, I would understand if you want to stay by the bar and just hang out with me."

"It sounds like you want to spend some alone time with me, Little Price."

"Whit, I'm being serious."

"I am too." I sighed, trying not to grow defensive. "Jor, I'm not a child. I'm not scared off by different environments or new people. These people are your friends, right?"

"It's fairly new, but yes. I like them enough to say they're my friends."

"Then, of course, I want to meet them. I want to learn more about you by seeing how you're reflected through each one of your friends. As for this scene, no, it's not my usual thing. But it's yours and I want to learn it. Now, will you come on before we lose our seats and have to stand?"

Jordyn stared at me with a look of unbridled admiration, as if she was seeing me for the first time. "You keep on surprising me."

"That could only be a good thing because you had a low opinion of me before."

"Not anymore," she whispered over my shoulder. "Come on. You have some names you need to memorize."

With that, she took my hand, and we made our way towards where Amelia was waiting for us with a group of people sitting on a long, black leather couch. As we approached them, they all stood and put on smiles for us. I could feel the warmth in Jordyn's grip as she held my hand tighter, giving me reassurance I was making a good move by sticking around.

The group introduced themselves one by one. There was Levi, one of the nameless white swimmers on the university's swim team I could finally put a name to. His stature was large, which made his friendly, gentle demeanor even more ironic. To Levi's left was his boyfriend, Wes. His major was in education and he minored in ASL. He was a CODA and wanted to help educate deaf students, particularly those who were POC or Black like him. He had a kind and caring look that I could immediately clock would make students gravitate to him as a teacher.

Then there was Mahina. They were the brainiac, majoring in computer sciences. They seemed to have a shier personality than the rest. The only outwardly bold thing about them was the tatu they had on their arm, highlighting their Polynesian heritage. Finally, there was the aforementioned Amelia. She specialized in journalism and ran the school's newspaper. I knew this about her already, but it was better hearing it from her. The pride she took in her work was clear by how she talked about it. When she said her name, Amelia Castro was going to be famous one day, you believed her.

I settled in between Levi and Wes while Jordyn went to the bar to pick us up some drinks. "So now that we've spilled stuff about ourselves, are you ready to share something about yourself with the class?" Levi volunteered, opening the floor for me.

"What do you want to know?"

"Everything, but I'll settle for a basic introduction for now."

"Um... I'm Whit. Well, technically, I'm Whitney, but I changed it legally to Whit recently."

"I thought about changing my name when I came out as nonbinary, but I'm too attached to Mahina. It would feel weird being referred to as anything else but it."

"I didn't have that problem because Whit had been my nickname as a kid, so it wasn't a learning curve."

"How did your parents react? Mine would've thrown signs at me I would've never seen before. Mind you, I know most of the bad words in ASL." Wes laughed, and we joined in with him.

After things died down, I answered. "I haven't told my parents."

I heard a unified "What?" from them.

"How is that possible?" Wes asked.

"My parents are a part of Doctors Without Borders, so they're gone a lot and I'm here. It hasn't come up during our weekly phone calls."

Amelia and Levi nodded their heads, understanding. But Wes and Mahina looked like they wanted to say something. "I know you two have something to say. Please do. Don't feel you have to bite your tongues around me. I like honesty."

Mahina cleared her throat. "It kinda sounds like you're using your parents being away as an excuse to not tell them about this big life change of yours. Maybe... that's a symptom of a larger of problem between you and them."

A quietness fell onto the area we were in until Levi had the guts to break it. "Good going, Mahina. You're scaring Whit off before she even has a chance to decide whether or not she likes us."

"You're not scaring me off. You'll have to say a lot worse to scare me off." Mahina looked relieved to hear that. "And honestly, they're right. My parents and I don't have the greatest relationship. I wish it was something we could fix, but they're never around for us to fix it."

"Sorry to hear that. If it is any constellation, you can join Levi and I's group."

"What group is that?"

"The 'our family sucks' group. We don't have meetings, but we cry and complain on the phone a lot," Amelia laughed.

I exchanged a quick glance at them both and then nodded. "I'm in."

"You're in what?" Jordyn questioned as she returned from getting our drinks. She handed me my Sprite, but the question still hung in the air as she sat down.

"We were just accepting Whit to our group. You know, the one where our family sucks," Amelia explained with a giggle.

"I leave for two seconds and you guys are already digging into her childhood trauma? It took me 15 years to go there with her."

"So what you're saying is we're more efficient than you," Wes deadpanned. Our laughs blended together, and I knew I had made the right decision by staying.

"How about this? Instead of talking about our families like a bunch of killjoys, we actually make good use of being at a club and have fun? I know that's a foreign concept for some of you," I joked while looking in Jordyn's direction. She didn't hesitate to show me the finger. I laughed and continued. "But why are we here if not to have a good time?"

"Jordyn told us you were here to meet guys. That is, before you realized this was a gay bar," Amelia teased.

"Laugh now, but when I leave here with a bisexual or a pansexual man, I'll be the one laughing."

Wes shook his head but couldn't hold back the smile that was on his face. "I thought Jordyn was exaggerating when she said you were full of yourself, but no. She got you down to a tee."

"You say full of it. I say appropriately confident."

"How confident are we talking?" Jordyn inquired.

"Why? What did you have in mind?"

"You said I didn't know how to have fun."

"Jor, it was a joke."

"One you meant," she countered. "And that's okay. I just would like the chance to prove you wrong."

With my curiosity admittedly piqued, I yearned to learn more. "How do you want to go about that?"

"A bet," she suggested with a smirk. "I bet I can leave the bar first with a girl before you can with a guy."

"Interesting proposal, but there's one problem. There's at least 50 girls here, all who are queer. I'm betting there are a lot less bisexual or pansexual men here who would be interested in me."

Levi sat up from the couch and pointed at me. "Hey, what happened to you being confident that you could pick up any interested guy here?"

"I'm not going back on what I said. I'm merely pointing out she has more options than I do."

"Either you think you can do it or not."

I fought hard to keep the smile from spreading on my face. "Fine," I relented. "You're on. What do I get when I win?"

"You mean when I win," she corrected me.

"Okay, wait, you two. If you're serious about doing this, then let set some ground rules and decide collaboratively on what the winner gets." Leave it to Amelia to take control and settle things down.

"What rules do you think we should set?"

"For starters, there has to be some sort of physical contact that proves you left as a couple with the person you picked up—no handshakes or high fives allowed."

"That's fair. What else?"

"No embarrassing each other while trying to make a move. Keep it classy."

"Anything else?"

"Um…" She thought it over. "You can't tell the person you're interested in picking up about the bet. I don't think either of you wants to win this because you got pitied."

She was right. A pity victory would be worse than losing. I nodded, then cracked a smile, excited to win this. "This should be fun. So what does the winner get?"

We all exchanged glances, each of us thinking what would be the most fitting for the challenge, then Jordyn spoke up. "The loser has to do one thing the winner wants."

"Like wash their clothes or something?"

"If that's what you want."

It wasn't the most creative option, but it allowed room for interpretation and that I liked. I agreed with her idea and we shook hands to finalize it.

"Wait! One more thing," Amelia interrupted.

"Oh, come on. Amelia, let them start." Mahina was getting impatient. I couldn't blame them. I was eager for things to get underway too.

Amelia went to her purse and pulled out a notepad. "What is that?" I asked, laughing.

"Write what you want if you win and keep it in your pocket. That way, you can't change it a million times later."

She tore off two pieces of paper from her notepad and handed us each one, along with a pen. On opposite ends of the table, we both bent down and silently jotted down our secret desires. Little did we know this game would turn out dramatically different from what we expected.

* * *

Standing amid the crowd of the club, I realized how out of my depth I was in. I had little to no experience picking up men. I would've been out of element at a regular nightclub. This being a gay club made it even worse.

With my head down, I made my way towards the bar. It was cramped, but I squeezed through. "Hey," I yelled to the bartender, who was tending to another customer.

"I'll get to you in a second."

"Oh, I don't want a drink. I want to know if you're by any chance bi or pan," I uttered as casually as one could.

The bartender stopped what he was doing and chuckled until he realized I was being serious. "Are you doing some type of LGBTQ+

scavenger hunt where you have to find someone of each orientation?"

"No," I shouted over the music. "My friend and I made a bet. Whichever one of us takes someone home first wins. I'm straight so..."

"You realize this is a gay bar, right?"

"Hence why I'm looking for a bisexual or pan man who can help me win."

The bartender snickered and pointed to a corner of the bar. "There's your best bet—the group over there." I followed his gaze and sure enough, there was a small clique of men sharing stories with one another.

"How do you know they're-"

"Trust me, they're bisexual. Just go talk to them." He said with a shrug before turning away to help another customer.

I took a deep breath and stepped towards the group of men, feeling more than a little nervous about what I was about to do. Still, my competitive nature wouldn't let me back down from the challenge.

As soon as I was close enough, one man turned to me and offered a smile. "Can I help you?" he asked, his voice warm and inviting.

I gulped hard before finally finding my voice. "Do you any of you find me to be attractive?"

Laughter rang out from the group, and I scolded myself for being so brazen with my wording. "I'll take your laughter as a no. Thanks."

I turned around to leave when another one of the men's voice called after me. "Love, come back. We meant nothing by the laughter. You caught us off guard."

I hesitated, not sure what to do. He continued, "We all think you're attractive, and we'd love for you to stay and chat with us."

His words sparked something inside of me, making my heart leap in my chest as I realized they were being genuine. I turned around and approached the group again. "Sorry for being so straightforward before. I don't normally do these things."

"Things?"

"Pick up men."

"That's what you were trying to do?" one of them asked.

"Yes, I was being bold. I see now I was making a fool of myself."

"Why don't you start again? We'll pretend to forget what happened."

"Okay, cool," I replied. "Hi, I'm Whit. What are your names?"

The group exchanged glances before the one at the front spoke up. "My name is Matt," he said. The one next to him introduced himself as Brian. The others stepped forward and shared their names as well, introducing themselves as Wyatt and Drew.

"Take my seat," Drew offered, standing up.

"Thank you. That's sweet of you."

"So, what brought you out tonight?"

"Trying to distract myself from my ex boyfriend who I found out is now dating my former best friend."

The group grew silent as they exchanged glances. Matt was the first to respond. "That... sucks." He said, his voice soft and sympathetic.

Brian spoke up next, putting a hand on my shoulder in a gesture of comfort. "It sounds like you need some serious cheering up right now. Why don't we make it our mission to do just that?"

"I would like that very much."

I leaned back away from the bar to look at Wes, Levi, Amelia, and Mahina in the corner. They were watching me closely, their eyes bugging out, seeing I made a few friends. Mahina winked at me, giving me an encouraging smile. I returned it and gave them a thumbs up.

"Mind if we order you a drink or two? However many you want?" Wyatt inquired.

I hadn't planned on drinking alcohol tonight, but if I was going to be flirting with men, I needed the liquid courage. "Sure, why not?"

Over the next hour, our conversations become more natural. Each of the four men bought me a drink, and I grew more relaxed as the night went on. With each sip of my fourth vodka cranberry, I became less worried or nervous about being rejected. I decided no matter what happened after I left the bar, as long as I could say I had fun, tonight was a win.

"I'm cutting myself off. After my four drinks, I get reckless."

"How reckless are we talking?" Matt questioned, his eyebrow raised.

I laughed and shrugged. "Nothing too ridiculous. Just a few embarrassing stories that I don't want to explain later."

"Fair enough. Let's get you some water to sober you up." Brian waved to the bartender and signaled for a water bottle.

I threw my arm over his shoulder and leaned on him. "You're taking such good care of me," I said, hoping it sounded as flirty as I had meant for it to sound.

"No problem. My sister is about your age and I would hope someone would look out for her like I am for you."

"Aww." Fuck. Brian was equating me to his sister? Not good. I removed my arm from his shoulder and his name from the list of prospects I could take home.

I took the water bottle from the bartender and swallowed a big gulp. When I put it down, I felt a hand touched my elbow. Before I jerked it away, I saw the hand belonged to Mahina. "Excuse me, guys. But can I borrow my friend for a second?"

Nobody protested, and I got up to follow them. "Hey, watch my water. Make sure no one does anything to it."

"We got you," Wyatt reassured.

Trusting them, I followed Mahina to the gender neutral bathroom and saw Levi was already there waiting. "What's going on?"

"We don't have a lot of time, so we'll get straight to the point," Levi prefaced. "Jordyn is hitting it off with a girl whose foot she stepped on."

"Stepped on?"

"Long story. On a time crunch, remember? Anyway, we think she's getting close to leaving the bar with her."

"Meaning, you need to speed up the pace with the guys at the bar. Have you found out if any of them are into girls?" Mahina chimed in.

"Wait, why do you two care?" I thought about it for a second. Then it hit me. "Oh my god, did you all place wavers on who would win the bet?"

"Yes, we did," they admitted sheepishly.

"I can't believe this."

"What, you two are the only ones allowed to have some fun off of this? Also, you should be happy. Mahina and I bet on you. That's why we're telling you to pick up the pace."

"Hell, more than pick up the pace. You need to pick one of them."

"I know, but I don't know which one of them is interested in me other than Brian who is definitely not interested."

"Which one is that?" Levi asked.

"The older one who is wearing the denim jacket. He told me he's 27. Drew is 23, Wyatt is 21, and Matt is 24."

"Which one is the Hanson brother reject lookalike?"

I hated I knew which one he meant. "That's Wyatt."

"Go with him. I've seen him checking you out. He's just doesn't want to make it obvious."

Mahina shook their head. "No, no. I like the one who looks like Mason Gooding."

"That's Drew."

"Go with him. He has the flirty eyes whether he looks in your direction."

"You two are not making this easy for me."

Mahina's phone dinged. They pulled it out and gasped. "Jordyn and that girl are going on to the dancefloor. I guess that's the physical contact proof we were asking for."

Jordyn dancing? This I had to see. "That girl has never danced a day in her life. This is going to be hilarious."

"You know what won't be funny? You costing us each $50," Levi complained.

"Okay, fine. I'll ask if any of the boys want to dance with me. Whoever says yes is the one I'll ask if they want to leave."

"Have you decided where you would go? His place or yours?"

I snorted. "The bet was which one of us could leave here first with someone. We never said we had to take it back to either of our homes."

"You know what, let's not worry about where you go for now and just focus on getting someone to leave with you."

Listening to Mahina's advice, I went back to the bar and to the guys. I thanked them for keeping my water safe, then with as much confidence as I could muster, I asked, "Would any of you boys care to dance with me?"

Drew glanced at Wyatt and then at me. "Actually Wyatt and I were just about to go out the dancefloor ourselves, if you don't mind tagging along with us?"

I smiled in relief. "That would be great!"

We all made our way to the dancefloor. Although I rarely ever danced, I got into the rhythm almost immediately and soon was dancing with as much enthusiasm as any of the others. I was graceful and loose-limbed, my body moving like it had a mind of its own. I flowed from one movement to the next, my arms languidly encircling Drew and Wyatt as they stood mesmerized by me.

"You can touch me, you know. Don't be shy."

Drew and Wyatt looked at each other like they were wondering which I was talking to. I put them out of their misery by answering, "I was talking to you both. Let's dance."

My hips swayed as I moved between the two, Wyatt in front of me and Drew behind me. Drew's hand rested on my waist and my arms went around Wyatt's neck as I nestled myself in between Drew's crotch and Wyatt's. My hands reached up above my head enticingly before sliding down Wyatt's chest.

I was in my own world, being pulled further and further into the music. I leaned my head back on Drew's shoulder and watched the different lights mingle together on the ceiling. For the first time since that night, I felt free. Most importantly, I felt safe. And unlike that night, I knew this was real.

I moved my hands further down Wyatt's chest and hip, feeling the tension in his body as he became lost in the moment. Drew's hips moved to meet mine and between us generated an energy that coursed through our veins like electricity. The music took over every sense of me and all I wanted to do was stay right there, forever suspended in it.

When I lifted my head from Drew's shoulder, I caught Jordyn's eye from across the dancefloor. She was the Drew of her routine, with a girl swaying back and forth against her. And yet, Jordyn's eyes were nowhere on her. They were on me.

As good as things felt between me, Wyatt, and Drew, I couldn't stop myself from wondering how much better it would've felt if Jordyn was the one I'd been dancing with. It was a dangerous thought. Jordyn was my friend. Not a romantic prospect. I couldn't explain why my mind was insisting on treating her as one. At the same time, I couldn't deny that while I was sandwiched between two gorgeous men who wanted me, my mind keep going back to her.

The song came to a close, and I watched Jordyn lead her date off the dancefloor and head toward the exits. Once they left through the doors, the bet would be over and I would lose. I knew this, and I did nothing to stop it. Instead, I peeled myself off of Drew and Wyatt and left the dancefloor by myself.

"Is everything okay?" Drew asked, him and Wyatt following closely behind me.

"Yeah. I'm okay. I needed a breather, that's all."

"Are you sure?"

"Yeah. You guys can go back. I'm done for the night."

"We actually had something we wanted to ask you," Wyatt segued. "We hope we aren't coming off too strong by asking you this, but Drew and I are a couple and we actually came out tonight looking for a third."

"Oh." I had gotten what I wanted. Not only did I find one bisexual man who wanted to go home with me, I found two! And yet, I couldn't bring myself to care. "That's nice of you guys and I'm flattered, but-"

"We understand," Drew said. "We figured it may go this route, but we had to try."

"It's really not you guys. It's me."

Wyatt shook his head. "You don't owe us an explanation. Plus, I think we already know. You're hung up on that ex of yours, right?"

"I'm certainly hung up on someone." The words flew out of my mouth before I could think twice. Although I didn't say it. I knew who I meant.

"Well, we hope that person comes to their senses and realizes what a gem you are," Wyatt said.

"Thanks guys. I appreciate it. You're both amazing." We shared a quick hug and said our goodbyes before I watched as they headed back over to the bar, hand-in-hand as always, looking for their third wheel for the night—a role that would never be mine to fill.

I walked back over to Amelia, Wes, Mahina, and Levi, who were back sitting on the same couch we sat on earlier. They had emphatic expressions on their faces. "You don't have to tell me. I saw Jordyn leave with the girl."

"You put up a worthy fight," Wes said, trying to soften the blow of the loss.

"Any idea what she wanted me to do?"

Amelia shook her head. "No, she didn't say. I guess she'll let you know tomorrow."

"Well, regardless, tonight was a blast."

"Speak for yourself. Mahina and I both lost $50 dollars." Mahina lightly slapped Levi across his chest. "I mean, yeah. We had fun too."

I smiled weakly. "I'm glad, but this is where my night ends. It was great meeting you all. I'm happy to have confirmed Jordyn has great friends looking out for her."

"We feel the same way about you," Amelia said in a manner that told me she meant it and wasn't just being nice. "You know, we just ordered an Uber. We're having a last round of drinks while we wait for it to come. You can stay and join us."

I appreciated the offer and spending more time with Jordyn's friends didn't sound like a bad way to end the night, but my head was still spinning from the thoughts I shouldn't have been having about Jordyn. I wanted to go back to my dorm, shower, and sleep these feelings away. "Thanks, but I'm tired. I'm going to wait for my Uber outside. You guys enjoy the rest of your night. I'll get your numbers from Jordyn."

I waved goodbye to them and walked to the exits. Outside, I checked my phone and saw it was a little after 10 p.m.. There were some people standing around. I couldn't tell if they were going in or leaving like me. Walking up to the curb, I pulled out my phone and looked for the nearest Uber around.

"Did those guys decide they wanted each other and ditch you?"

I turned around and didn't hide the grin I was sporting. "For your information, they were already a couple, and they liked me a lot. They wanted me to be their third for the night. I turned them down."

Confusion colored Jordyn's face. "Why?"

"You had already won. There was no point."

"So that's the only reason you turned them down?"

"Honestly? I never planned on going that far with whoever I picked up. I never would've taken them home or gone home with them."

"I thought you wanted to have fun. Distract yourself from Luke?"

"What about you? I thought you and Jenny broke up because you two had never been with anyone else and you wanted to explore being with other people? You had the prime opportunity tonight, and you did what?"

Jordyn shrugged. "Like you said, I was never planning on going that far with her."

"Why not? Scared to take the plunge?"

"No, but because I would've been wishing she was someone else and that wouldn't be fair to her."

I couldn't process her words because a group of friends walked through us to get into the club. Annoyed, I took Jordyn's hand and walked into the alleyway. It provided enough privacy and darkness for me to understand what she was trying to say.

"You... you like someone else?" I stammered, barely registering the surprise in my voice. "Is it Amelia? Or no, it's Jenny, isn't it? You still aren't over her. Which makes sense. She's your first love. You were with her since the ninth grade. That's hard to beat."

I was rambling, and I didn't know why. If Jordyn liked someone, this was a good thing. She deserved to like a girl and have them like her back. Why then, was I so scared by the idea of that?

"It's not Jenny or Amelia."

"Oh." I was relieved and confused at the same time. Who could it be then? Jordyn had been single for months, so I forgot she could have feelings for someone else. "You don't have to tell me. It's not my place to know. What I do want to know is what I have to do for you. You know, since you won our bet."

161

I thought changing the subjects would make both of us less nervous, but I seemed to have added to Jordyn's. "We don't have to talk about it now. I'll tell you tomorrow when we're both sober."

"Way to make me more curious. Come on, tell me."

"No, I think I should wait."

She looked so unlike herself then, nervous and unsure. "What is it? You can tell me."

"What I wrote…" She looked down, not meeting my eye. "It's so embarrassing. I think I drank too much before I wrote it."

"Jor, what is it?"

She sighed before looking up at me. "I wrote that if I won our bet, I wanted you to kiss me."

My brain went haywire. There was no way. No way that was what she wrote. She had to have been messing with me. "If this is a joke—"

"It's not. I told you I had a crush on you years ago and I always wondered what it would be like. As we became friends, I started wondering about it again. Then there were a couple of times where I thought I caught you wondering what it would be like too."

"It's stupid," she continued. "I know you're straight. I'm just projecting my old school-girl crush onto you and that's not fair. I'm sorry. Please forget I ever asked you to do that."

"Jor." I touched her arm to stop her from walking away. "What if it's not stupid? What if you were right, and I have wondered what kissing you would feel like? What if I were wondering that right now?"

She shook her head, looking down at where my hand was on her arm. "You're just saying that because you're drunk. Don't deny it. You had four vodka cranberries."

"Tell me this, when you're drunk, do you ever get the urge to kiss a guy?"

"No, but that's not the same thing."

"It is. Me being having four drinks isn't making me want to kiss,

162

the want has been there for weeks. The alcohol is simply giving me the courage to admit it."

She pulled her arm away and started pacing up and down the alley. She was scared. Scared to believe me, scared to trust, I wouldn't regret this when I was sober. There was only one thing I had that I knew would make that fear go away.

Digging into my pocket, I took out the piece of paper I had written my wish on. The wish I wrote before I had a single drink. The wish I wrote before knowing how Jordyn felt. The wish I wrote that would prove I felt the same.

I handed it to her. She looked at me, then it with confusion before unfolding the paper and reading what I wrote. I watched her eyes as she read the words: If I win, I want Jordyn to kiss me.

Before I knew it, she'd dropped the paper and grabbed my waist, pushing us back into the brick wall. Our mouths met instantaneously. It felt both familiar yet different from anything I had experienced before. Her lips were so soft, the softest I've had the pleasure of tasting. She was gentle too, giving me control of how deep or far I wanted this to go.

I pulled back ever so slightly, my mouth hovering just above her lips. "Don't hold back. You don't have to be gentle. I want to feel everything."

She didn't hesitate to capture my lips again. This time, her kiss was more insistent, demanding my full attention. I complied eagerly, deepening the kiss as we explored each other's mouths. Our tongues battled for dominance, hers winning. She coaxed mine into submission, and before I could stop myself, I was moaning into her mouth.

I should've been embarrassed, but I wasn't. This kind of desire had laid dormant within me for months. I hadn't imagined it would awaken like this or by her, but I welcomed it. I wasn't going to let it go, let her go.

I ran my hand down her back, over her jeans, caressing her ass. She whimpered into my mouth, pressing harder against me. I pouted when I felt her pull away, only to realize where her lips were going. Using her hand, she angled my chin up, exposing my neck.

She kept her hand there and teased me mercilessly, alternating between light bites and small kisses. Rubbing the inner skin of her hand, I planted kisses along the column of her wrist. I could feel her pulse thumping hard against my lips, matching the rhythm my heart was beating at.

She finally broke away, chuckling softly. "I think we might have gotten a little carried away there."

The moment her lips left me for good, I felt the loss like a physical pain. It was intense, aching. I wanted her back. I needed her back. I ran my hands over my face and took a long, shuddering breath before meeting her gaze. "I'm sorry."

Her smile was gentle as she tenderly cupped my cheek. "Don't be. I know I'm not, but we are going to have to talk about this and what it means."

"Not tonight," I begged. I wanted to live in the fantasy of that perfect kiss. Not in the one of our crushing reality.

She nodded, then extended her hand out to me. "Can I take you home?"

I took her hand and intertwined our fingers. "You're the only one I would want to."

15

Dial M for Mistake

I woke the next morning with a headache, dry mouth, and a sensitivity to the sunlight streaming into my room. As I laid in bed, contemplating whether or not to sleep in, a knock at my door interrupted my thought process. I wiped the sleep out of my eyes before I opened the door so I saw the image of Jordyn standing at there clearly.

She was wearing her usual a band tee, jeans, boots and her leather jacket. What was new was the tinted sunglasses she wore. I couldn't tell for sure, but I thought I could see she was feeling what I felt, the consequences of last night.

"Good morning. I thought if you felt at all like me, you would need this." She took a coffee from the cup holder she in her hands and gave it to me.

"Thank you." I took a sip, savoring both the flavor of the caramel Frappuccino and the fact she knew it was my favorite. "So, did you stop by just to give me this?"

"No. I was also hoping we could talk. You know, about last night..."

I'd been dreading this conversation the moment she broke off our kiss last night. Things were awkward enough between us on the Uber drive back to the dorms. I couldn't imagine how much more uncomfortable us talking about what transpired could be.

Jordyn walked fully into the room and I sat down on my bed, not having enough energy to have this conversation standing up. "Can we not talk around this? This is me and you. We've never held our tongue around each other. Let's not start now," she asked of me.

"Okay. Let's talk bluntly then. We kissed, and it was the best I've felt in months," I admitted with no shame. "I liked it and I don't regret it. I hope you don't either."

She sat down across from me and put her hand on my knee. She was searching for the right words to say. "I've thought about what it would feel like kissing you since I was thirteen when you were just my big sister's oblivious best friend. Last night in so many ways, felt like a dream come true. Then morning came and reality hit me."

"What do you mean?" I asked, though I was nervous to hear her answer.

"Before we kissed, we both admitted to wanting to kiss each other out of curiosity. Now that we have and that curiosity isn't there anymore, that want won't be, either."

Before I could get a word in, she kept going. "You were curious about what it would feel like to kiss a girl, just like how I was curious to kiss my longtime crush. We got our answers, and that can be all it was."

I listened to her closely, not sure how to respond. This felt like her rejecting me. At the same time, she was right. There was no other explanation for why I suddenly had the want to kiss a girl when I had never felt that way before. With her, no less.

"I think you're right," I said after pausing to think. "Us kissing doesn't have to mean more than what it was. It was a kiss, a fantastic one." That got a smirk out of her. "But that's all it can be."

Relief looked to have washed over her. "I was worried this would be the thing we couldn't come back from and that's scared me. I've enjoyed our time being friends, and I don't want this kiss to have ruined it."

"You don't have to be worried or scared about that. Our friendship might be a little different now that I know how good of a kisser you are," I joked, trying to lighten up the mood. She shook her head, somewhat amused. "But it isn't going anywhere."

"I'm happy to hear you say that because I got a favor to ask of you."

"Seriously? I'm still paying for the last favor I did you." It was a joke, but there was a kernel of truth to it. If I never did her the favor of being her date to Sabrina's party, I might've still been in the dark regarding her relationship with Luke. Then I wouldn't be impersonating Luke on Windy City Mingle with two of the women I—or more accurately, he matched with.

"Yeah… I wish I could promise you this favor won't be as bad as that one, but that would be a lie. Especially since it involves Sabrina and Luke."

I closed my eyes as I took a deep breath. "What is it?"

"Sabrina said that since you're going to be in my life and Luke is going to be in hers, she wants there to be peace between the four of us. To prove that, she inviting us to have dinner with her and Luke next Friday night."

"She wants peace, but I can't picture anything more torturous than that dinner."

"I know, but she has a point. Whether or not Luke is temporary in her life, you aren't in mine. So I would prefer if you could coexist with Sabrina, even if it's just fake niceties."

A sigh escaped me as my shoulders slouched. I hated to admit it, but Jordyn and by extension, Sabrina had a point. I needed to get along with Sabrina to save face with Jordyn. She needed not to get any whiff of my plans for revenge against her sister. Though the two had their differences, Jordyn would've thought I was mad if she knew what I was up to and that I couldn't have.

"Alright," I agreed reluctantly. "I'll go, but I can't promise I'll be pleasant."

"If I wanted someone pleasant as a friend, I wouldn't have befriended you." I laughed at her calling back at what I said to her back in the library a month ago. It was amazing how far we had come in just that span of time.

"She set the reservation at O'Donnell's at 7 p.m.. I'll pick you up and we'll go together."

"Sounds good to me."

She stood and eyed the door. "I'm going to go now, but I'm glad we're okay."

"Me too."

I walked her out of my dorm and when I returned; I saw my phone lit up with a message from Alexis, one of the girls I was as Luke. We'd been messaging back and forth on the app for almost a week. Some texts were flirtier than others, but nothing explicit. If I wanted Sabrina to think Luke was cheating on her, I needed to create more than some suggestive texts.

That's when the idea came to me. I grabbed my phone and texted her back.

Alexis: Good morning. Any special plans for today?

Luke: No, but I have some in mind for me and you next Saturday.

Alexis: What did you have in mind?

Luke: O'Donnell's at 7 p.m. We can meet each other there. Does that sound good?

Alexis: It sounds perfect. I can't wait to meet you.

Luke: I can't wait either.

16

Karmic Justice

Walking into O'Donnell's, I understood why Sabrina picked it for our peaceful dinner. The restaurant held an air of elegance that created a mythical ambience. Marble and velvet covered everything, with walls adorned in opulent tapestries. The ceilings' chandeliers provided a cozy ambiance, casting a warm glow over the tables and their plush chairs. The servers, dressed in crisp white outfits, hurriedly carried trays of exquisite dishes, while soft music played from hidden speakers.

It was the definition of high dining. Any chaos happening behind the scenes was tucked away from patrons' view. Someone would have to be foolish to cause a scene in such a place like this. I smiled at the thought, knowing what was to come.

"Should we have a code word or a signal? In case things go to shit or you get the urge to throw water onto either of them?" Jordyn asked while the host went to grab our menus.

"Can't we just text?"

"Then we get up to leave? Yeah, that won't be suspicious at all."

I placed my hand on the small of her back to steady her. "Jor, it'll be okay. There's no need to worry about anything."

She moved away until my hand was no longer touching her. "Let's keep our hands to ourselves this Saturday, okay?"

I chuckled. She was acting all jumpy with me since that kiss. While I found it adorable, I kinda wanted things to get back to the way they were before. "Okay. No touching."

"Thanks."

The host told us to follow her, and she led us to where Sabrina and Luke were. Luke was wearing a business casual shirt and khakis. His just as evil half wore a dusty blue floral pleated midi dress. She brought that dress during one of our mall outings. I didn't know what to make of that. Was it supposed to be her way of showing there were no hard feelings? Or did she not even realize the significance of wearing it?

I tried not to give it anymore thought as Jordyn and I approached them. Sabrina stood and tapped Luke's shoulder until he did too. "Jordo! Whit! You both look great!"

Sabrina's observation wasn't far off, at least not regarding Jordyn. She dressed up a bit by wearing a gray striped button up v-neck vest and matching trousers with a black belt. She looked phenomenal, me not so much. I found a ruched collar blouse and black slacks to wear. My favorite thing I was wearing wasn't even mine.

I was searching for a jacket when Jordyn arrived. She told me she had one in her dorm and we went back and she lent it to me. It was a brown faux leather jacket, and it hugged me perfectly. I wasn't planning on taking it off. I was going to guard it with my life and keep it close to my heart.

"Thanks. You guys look great too," Jordyn spoke for us.

We sat down, Jordyn across from her sister and me from my ex. Somehow, that was the best option. Only second to not doing this dinner at all. I took a swallow of the water that either Sabrina or Luke ordered for me to hide my displeasure at being here. It would be worth it, though, to please Jordyn and for what I had planned to happen in less than thirty minutes.

"Whit, thanks for agreeing to this dinner. I think it's important we moved forward, for Jordyn's sake."

Jordyn's eyes landed on me, making sure I behaved. "I'll do anything for her, even agreeing to awkward dinners like this one."

Luke and Sabrina chuckled. I couldn't tell if it was to appease me or if they were relieved to have the quiet part said out loud. The server came to take our orders, making the conversation lull for a few brief moments. When he left again, Luke took a deep breath and cleared his throat. "Anything interesting going on with you lately, Whit?"

"I was invited into a threesome."

Sabrina coughed into her napkin while Luke's face twisted into one of horror and confusion. Jordyn seemed more entertained than anything. "You did what now?"

"I met these two guys at a nightclub last week. They were bisexual and wanted to spend the night with me, but I turned them down. I was much too tired."

"You're serious?" Sabrina asked.

"I am. Jordyn can back me up. She was there."

"Yeah, it's true. There were four guys into her that night. She could've had her pick of the litter, but she went home instead."

Went home after making out with you, I thought. Sabrina and Luke didn't need to know that part, so I stayed quiet. It brought me joy to think about implanting the image of me making out with Jordyn in her big sister's head, but I didn't want to hurt Jordyn by doing that. That moment was just for us. No one else.

Sabrina snickered. "I'm sorry. This just reminded me of jokes about us in high school."

"What jokes?" Luke asked for clarification.

"People used to say me, Whit, and you know who, made the perfect threesome. If only they knew."

Jordyn leaned over my chair. "Mike?"

I nodded. She looked like she was going to ask another question, but my phone dinged. There was a message from Alexis telling me she parked her car.

Alexis: I hope it's okay I'm early, but I was excited to meet you. Are you here?

I didn't respond. It wouldn't make much sense to since she was about to walk in on her forgetful date who forgot he scheduled a double date with his girlfriend with his first date with Alexis. Luke was in for the shock of his life and I was going to revel in it.

Sure enough, I spotted Alexis near the entrance. She was on her phone, no doubt looking for Luke to message her back. She was in a red halter dress and black pumps. Her black curls framed her face, and she wore a light smokey eye.

My eyes stayed on her even as the conversation at the table continued. I only looked away when my name was called. "I'm sorry. What did you say?"

"Are you coming to the election results party this Wednesday? Hopefully to see me win social chair."

"The votes have already been cast?"

Luke nodded, like no shit. "Yeah, where have you been?" Planning on sabotaging your relationship, I thought, but obviously didn't communicate.

"What do you think? Are you coming?" Sabrina asked, looking for hopeful for a yes.

So I gave it to her. "Sure, I'll come to support you. Even though I didn't vote for you. Or anyone, for that matter."

The entire table lightly laughed again, but it was short-lived because of who was approaching our table. "Luke?" Alexis squinted at the back of Luke's head until he turned around to face her.

"Yes? Do I know you?"

Alexis's face was a cross from laughing and a "are you serious?" expression. "Stop messing around. I didn't realize our date was going to include three other people."

Now Luke carried the look of confusion. "I'm sorry. I don't know what you're talking about."

"Are you being serious?"

Jordyn and I exchanged a look. Something was about to go down.

"Yes, I'm serious," Luke said slowly, as if he wasn't sure what he was getting himself into. "I don't know who you are or what date you're referring to. You got the wrong guy."

"Your name is Luke, right? And you don't have an identical twin by that name, do you?"

"No! What is going on? Did *Punked* get revived, and I missed it?"

"If anyone gets to ask that question, it should be me," Alexis declared, her voice rising. "You invited me here and now you're pretending you don't know me?"

"I don't know you!"

Sabrina leaned over Luke's chair and whispered into his ear. "Should we call the police? What department handles mental health emergencies?"

"I'm not having a breakdown, but thanks for the concern," Alexis said sarcastically.

"Okay. Listen lady, if my boyfriend says he doesn't know who you are. I'm inclined to believe him. Not some stranger dressed like a hooker."

I covered my mouth to keep from gasping. Jordyn leaned over again, whispering, "What is happening?"

"I don't know, but I'm enjoying it."

Alexis unlocked her phone and opened the Windy City Mingle app. "Does this ring a bell?" She shoved the phone into Luke's hand.

Sabrina read the messages over his shoulder as he scrolled. Her mouth dropped after a minute.

"You're on a dating app?!"

"What? No!"

"But that's your name, your photos, info about you only someone who knew you would know. This sounds exactly like you."

"And he invited me here for a date. He must have forgotten he already had a date with his girlfriend when he scheduled one with me," Alexis guessed.

"I'm telling you. This isn't me. Someone must be catfishing as me." Luke seemed desperate to prove his innocence, but neither Alexis nor Sabrina seemed to buy it.

"Yeah, right." Alexis folded her arms, pissed at being yanked around. "A catfish would know you would be at O'Donnell's at the same time you asked me to be here? Yeah, that makes a ton of sense."

"I- I-," Luke stammered.

"Don't bother. I'm not even that hurt. We talked for a like week. Believe me, there are other, better fishes in the sea. I'm just pissed at you for wasting my time and for not owning up to your actions."

"Owning up? I have done nothing wrong. I'm the victim here."

"Really, dude? Your girlfriend is right there." She shifted her eyes to Sabrina to address her. "You should know he told me he never met a girl who he connected to so quickly before. He clearly doesn't think highly of you."

Sabrina's eyes widened in disbelief. Luke shook his head and turned toward her. "That's not true. This is one big misunderstanding. Think about it. Why would I cheat on you? With her, no less? She's not even my type."

Alexis took my glass of water and looked at me. "Can I borrow this?"

"Be my guest."

She took the glass and poured it on Luke's head until he was soaked. "Asshole," she taunted before turning around and going out the entrance.

The other patrons were watching in disbelief. Luke was too busy wiping the water out of his eyes to notice. Sabrina was staring at her hands in her lap, too angry to look up.

"Am I magnet for water?" Luke joked while wiping his face with a napkin.

Without warning, Sabrina grabbed her strawberry lemonade and tossed it in Luke's face, undoing the progress he made in drying it.

"Fuck you," she said, nearly in tears. "You knew about my trust issues, and you still did this? I thought you were better than Mike, but I was so wrong. You're just like him." She stood up from table and covered her face as she hurried into the parking lot.

"Sabrina, wait!" Luke got up and chased after her, hoping to fix the damage he had done. Aka the damage I'd done.

I was so giddy on the inside, I barely registered that Jordyn talking. "Whit?"

"I'm sorry, what?"

"Tell me, should I check on Sabrina and see she's okay?"

I shook my head. "Those two kids need to talk things out. Don't get involved. Not now."

"Do you think Luke was telling the truth? Maybe he is being catfished?"

"If you had asked me before last month, I would've said no. Luke didn't seem like the guy who cheats, but he also didn't seem like the guy to date his ex girlfriend's best friend. So, I don't know."

Jordyn followed my advice, then retorted, "Aren't you glad I dragged you along to this dinner now?"

"I always enjoy a dinner and a show."

We laughed softly, then we noticed our server approach our table but without our food in hand. I knew what was coming. "I'm sorry, but we're going to have to ask your party to leave."

"We understand." Jordyn and I stood and paid for our drinks. Plus Sabrina and Luke's drinks. I was definitely going to hold that one over their heads.

Afterwards, we walked out to the entrance and witnessed the end of the conversation between Luke and Sabrina. I expected to hear curses and shouting, but it looked peaceful. The opposite of what I wanted. Except that wasn't even the worst of it. After their last words, Sabrina hugged him! Hugged him. Like, what the fuck?

I wasn't the only one confused. Jordyn looked stunned. We both knew when Sabrina felt betrayed by someone, she would light them up a new one. What was this non-aggressive bullshit?

Luke got into his car and waited, presumably for Sabrina to get in since they arrived together. "Hey, Sab!" Jordyn called out for her. "You can get a ride with us if you want."

She looked between Jordyn and Luke. Her face was pensive as she walked up toward us. I didn't have a good feeling about this. "What's happening?" Jordyn asked.

"I'm going to go back with Luke. We had a conversation about and I think I overreacted. He showed me his phone, and I saw he never downloaded that app before."

"He could've used its website," I interjected. Neither sister looked at me liked I was helping the situation. "Sorry."

"Anyway, we're going to talk things out, but I think we'll be okay."

Jordyn went quiet and then turned to me. "Can you see if our Uber is here yet? I want to talk to Sabrina alone for a second."

I wanted to stay and listen to the rest of their conversation, but I wouldn't push Jordyn like that. "Sure," I said, and I started to back away. Instinctively, I went for my phone and came up with an idea. I unlocked it and pulled up my voice recorder app.

I started a new recording and slipped my phone into Jordyn's jacket pocket and turned back around to her. "I almost forgot. Here's your jacket."

"You can hold on to it."

"I shouldn't. I'll lose it in like an hour. Just ask Sabrina."

She bit her lip, thinking back on all the times I misplaced her lipstick or sunglasses. "It's true. You better take that jacket now before it ends up in someone's lost & found."

I held it out to Jordyn, and she took it. She folded it over her arm. "Thanks."

I walked away, hoping the fabric of the jacket wasn't too thick that it would muffle my chance at hearing the rest of their conversation. About ten minutes later, our Uber arrived and Jordyn finished talking to Sabrina. In the car, I pretended to have forgotten my phone in her jacket and took it out. It had been still recording.

After I said goodnight to Jordyn, I went into my dorm, changed into my pajamas, and got into bed. I sat up as I hit the play button on my phone. As it loaded, I silently prayed I could actually make out what they were saying. It was a relief to hear their voices come out as clear as day.

I listened as Jordyn tried to talk Sabrina out of leaving with Luke. Though Jordyn admitted there was a chance Luke was right about someone posing as him online, she told Sabrina she shouldn't be so quick to take him back on the off chance he cheated on her.

Sabrina wasn't convinced. She said Luke knew about the trust issues she had and he wouldn't add to it by cheating on her because he had the same issues. I thought for a split second she might tell Jordyn about how my relationship with Luke ended. To her credit, she didn't go there.

Jordyn countered this by saying even if Luke had done nothing wrong, it didn't guarantee their relationship would work. She pointed out stable relationships aren't built off the backs of other relationships' demise. An obvious reference to Sabrina and Luke seeking each other out after he broke up with me.

This was where things got interesting.

Sabrina: Whit and Luke ended because of her actions. It had nothing to do with me.

Jordyn: That may be the case, but if you continue this relationship with Luke, you can't be upset at the karma you may receive.

Sabrina bristled at this.

Sabrina: Karma? You sound like Taylor Swift. Karma isn't some cosmic force that looks down on us and ruins our lives.

Jordyn: No, but it does come into play in relationships. People make choices and there are consequences to those choices. You made a choice to date your best friend's ex boyfriend. Luke possibly stepping out on you might be your karma. Or maybe it'll be something else. Either way, there will be consequences for your choice in partner.

Sabrina: Have you ever consider me dating Luke is Whit's karma?

Jordyn: What do you mean?

Sabrina: Whit's the one who screwed their relationship up. Now her karma is her best friend dating the guy she at one point considered the love of her life.

Jordyn was quiet for a good 15 seconds. I could visualize the disdain on her face as she absorbed what Sabrina was saying.

Jordyn: Why does it sound like you're dating Luke as some sort of payback against Whit for whatever she did to ruin your guys' friendship?

Sabrina: Maybe because I am.

Holy shit! I couldn't believe my ears. I stopped the recording and replayed the last 30 seconds. But no matter how many times I replayed the sound bite, it stayed exactly the same. Sabrina had admitted to dating Luke to get back at me for "sleeping" with Mike.

Jordyn: I'm not the biggest fan of Luke, but don't you see how wrong that is? That's not fair to him and his feelings for you.

Sabrina: I know that. Look, I do like Luke. A lot. I just like getting back at Whit more.

Jordyn: You can be fucking evil sometimes, you know that?

Sabrina: Just be grateful, all this evilness got passed down to me and not to you.

The sound of a car pulling into the parking lot came through on the microphone.

Sabrina: There's your Uber. It goes without saying, but I'm invoking sister confidentiality on this convo. No repeating this to Luke or your new best friend, okay?

Jordyn: Whatever.

Sabrina: I love you.

Jordyn: I know.

I paused the recording there, but I still couldn't believe my ears. I thought tonight might've been a waste since the damage I inflicted on Luke and Sabrina's relationship was minimal, but this? This was the smoking gun. Better than any fake scheme I could've come up with. This was actual proof of Sabrina being the conniving bitch she'd always been and how Luke was nothing more than a pawn to her. In four days' time, not only would Luke know the truth about Sabrina's true nature, so would everyone else.

17

All About Sabrina

"I'm here. Where are you?"

I was just beginning to stroll towards the campus center when Jordyn's text message illuminated my phone. Under normal circumstances, I would have sent her a quick response, letting her know I was on my way, but this wasn't any typical day. It was Wednesday night; the night the university's election results would be revealed. Positions such as president, treasurer, and social chair were all up for grabs, but it was the latter that Sabrina had her sights set on. In less than an hour, she would know if she had won or not - in less than an hour, she would be exposed as a fraud.

I never wanted it to get to this point. This should've been Sabrina's crowning moment. Her ascent to the upper echelon of the university. Except I couldn't let that happen. Sabrina wasn't the person she presented herself as. Not to her to classmates, not to friends, not even her own boyfriend knew the things she was capable. When she predictably wins, Sabrina would no longer be a mystery. She would be seen for who she truly was.

I took a deep breath and tapped out a reply to Jordyn. "On my way. See you soon." She didn't need to know I was already there. The less she knew, the less she had to deny having a role in this. There was only so much I could do to cover up my involvement in the recording bound to set the campus ablaze, but I would do everything I could to protect Jordyn from being implicated in its release.

From a distance, I saw a group of people filing into the entrance of the campus center. I would not be one of them. There was a back entrance primarily only used by the maintenance staff, but I was familiar with the layout of the campus and knew it was my best chance to get inside unnoticed.

I slipped through a side door and maneuvered my way through the dark hallways, only lit by the occasional security light. I moved quickly and could feel my heart pounding in anticipation of what was to come. After wandering through multiple seemingly endless hallways, I found the side door that led to the backstage area of the auditorium where the results were going to be announced.

Resembling the backstage of a theater show, the area was lit with bright lights and filled with sound equipment, cables, and props. I knew no one would be here yet since they were still waiting in line outside, but I wanted to make sure that everything was set up properly so that my plan could move forward without a hitch.

I moved around quickly, checking the computer that would play the candidates' choice of song if they won. For all the winners, that would be the case, except for the winner of social chair. In the off chance Sabrina lost, the audio recording would still be played. Just as the victory's theme song, not hers. But if she won, her march down to the podium would not be accompanied by an empowering pop hit, but of the audio recording shedding light on the side of her, she never wanted people to know existed. The real, truly evil side of her.

The computer was warm and already logged in. Someone had just used it. Maybe they were still using it. I needed to do this fast. I searched for the files that held the candidates' songs. After some digging, I found them. I deleted her opponents' themes, then found hers. Her selection — "successful" by Ariana Grande — was successfully deleted in mere seconds. Next, I took the flash drive I brought specifically for this out of my pocket. I plugged it into the laptop and watched it start to transfer the audio recording in place of each candidate's songs.

As soon as the file finished transferring, I knew it would be too late to turn back. Not that I wanted to. I wasn't going back or going to feel bad about this. Sabrina had done things to hurt people without a second thought, me included. It was overdue for someone to turn tables.

I grabbed the flash drive once everything was in place. I didn't think they would, but just in the off chance they did, I opened the disinfected wipes I saw sitting on a nearby shelf and wiped my fingerprints off the laptop. Sabrina will know it was me who did this, but if she had no proof, it was my word against hers.

I felt a wave of relief wash over me as I left the area. My mission was accomplished. I did what I set out to do and with no one, none the wiser. No one would know Sabrina's song was missing until after she won and by then, there would be nothing she could do about it.

I went out the same way I came until I was in front of the campus center, like I hadn't just been inside the building. The line thinned after a minute and I was inside again. This time, as a mere observer to the show.

Inside the auditorium, Jordyn and I found our seats in the front row. I stole a peek at the pamphlet Jordyn picked up and saw the results of social chair would be the third one announced. I waited impatiently for the winner of treasurer and social media director to finish their speeches so the result of social chair could be announced.

"Give it up to Craig Roberts!" Dean Clayton came out to usher our new social media director off the stage. "Next, we have the hotly contested battle for social chair. We have three candidates this year, all equally qualified, but as we know, there can only be one."

Someone off stage handed her an envelope and like a presenter at the Oscars, Clayton looked at the name and nodded. "And the new social chair of the student council is... Sabrina Price!"

The crowd erupted in cheers as Sabrina rose from her seat in the back. She looked around, dazed and confused, as if she hadn't heard her name being called out. I had to suppress a laugh; it was hilarious to watch her pretend to be in shock over something she thought for sure was going to be an easy win for her.

Luke stood, giving her a standing ovation. Jordyn and I clapped, joining the choir of applause filling the room. Sabrina stood from her seat, the cheers getting louder. Then, right where the notes of her song were supposed to play, the recording kicked in.

"Have you ever consider me dating Luke is Whit's karma?"

The clapping died once Sabrina's voice came through the speakers. Nearby I heard whispers of, "What is that?" and "What is she talking about?"

I'm sure there were more I missed, but I was too busy honing in on Sabrina's face. Her skin was sickly pale and her body stood frozen as the recording kept going.

"Whit's the one who screwed their relationship up. Now her karma is her best friend dating the guy she at one point considered the love of her life."

"No. This can't be. How did this-" Jordyn said to herself, but trailed off as the version of her on the recording asked the million dollar question.

"Why does it sound like you're dating Luke as some sort of payback against Whit for whatever she did to ruin your guys' friendship?"

Sabrina's eyes went wide as the recollection of the conversation set in. As though a fire had been lit on her ass, she raced down to the stage. "Cut it off! Cut the recording off!"

For the first time I had ever seen her, Dean Clayton looked scared. She might not have known what Sabrina was caught saying on the recording, but she scrambled like a mad woman whose life, or in this case, job depended on it.

But by the time the infamous words had been uttered for all to hear, Clayton was too late.

"Maybe because I am."

"Don't you see how wrong that is? That's not fair to Luke and his feelings for you."

"Look, I do like Luke. A lot. I just like getting back at Whit more."

The silence that followed was deafening. So quiet that the only thing echoing was Sabrina's wicked confession in everyone's ears. Everyone in the crowd turned to stare at her, shocked by what she admitted. Her face went red as she realized there was no amount of damage control able to make up for what had already been said.

Luke stood slowly from his seat. Sabrina made her way to him, but he held his hand out to her, signaling for her not to come any closer to him. "Let me get this straight. You've been dating me for months not because you wanted to, but because you knew it would hurt Whit, and that's what you really wanted?"

"It wasn't like that."

"Really?" His voice raised, no one bothering to tell him to calm down. "Because it sounded an awful lot like you've been using me to get back at her. Like this has all been some game for you, but guess what? My feelings for you are real and I thought yours were too."

Sabrina opened her mouth to speak, but nothing came out. There was nothing she could say that would justify her actions or to defend herself. Luke shook his head at her. "I can't believe I fell for this. I should've known better than to trust someone like you."

With the weight of everyone's gaze, Luke walked past her and out of the auditorium. Despite his protests, she followed him out, leaving the crowd to grapple with what they'd just seen on their own.

"Alright, fun is over. This ceremony will be rescheduled for a future date that will be announced at a different time. Please, exit the auditorium in an orderly and timely fashion," Clayton pleaded, finally breaking the silence before leaving the stage.

Though the crowd started to empty out, their whispers combined to be as loud as the original applause, gossiping about Sabrina, Luke, and me. I stayed where I was and didn't make a move to get up from my seat. Neither did the woman beside me. I didn't look in her direction. I didn't need to, to know. Just like she didn't need to look at me to know.

With a loud sigh, Jordyn finally spoke. "Do you have any idea what you've done?"

After a few moments of silence, I looked at her and said with certainty, "Yes. I do."

18

Beyond The Anger

"For a student I only saw once last semester, I sure am seeing a lot of you this semester, Ms. Robinson."

"Some would say we're making up for lost time, Dean Clayton."

The hard glare Clayton was giving me didn't budge, not that I was expecting it to. The circumstances that brought me back to her office were the furthest thing from a joke, as Clayton would point out to me. Repeatedly.

"She's not even taking this seriously," Sabrina, who sat in the chair to the left of me, seethed. "Isn't this proof enough? She's the one who illegally recorded me."

"Illegally?" I bristled. "Since when did you become a lawyer? And no, sleeping with a wanna-be one doesn't count."

She twisted her body around to face me. "Recording someone's private conversation without their consent is illegal. It's basic legal knowledge 101. I should press charges against you for what you did to me."

"You can't because you have no proof."

Clayton leaned onto her desk, rubbing her forehead. Sabrina and I had been going at it like this for close to 20 minutes, and she was still no closer to a resolution. "Whitney is right, Sabrina. You have not been able to provide me with concrete evidence to support your claims that Whitney secretly recorded your conversation with Jordyn."

"She was there when it happened and she has a motive. If not her, then who else?"

"Your sister, perhaps?"

"No!" Sabrina and I both bellowed. "My sister would never do this to me. The only way she would, would be if Whit had forced her into doing it."

"Unlike you, I would never put Jordyn in that kind of position."

"What is that supposed to mean?"

"Enough!" Clayton interjected. "This is going nowhere, and I have better things to do with my time. Sabrina, you have nothing but a theory. Get back to me when you have something substantial to prove your case."

She rolled her eyes and picked up her backpack off the floor. "Fine, I'll be back with proof soon enough. I know she slipped up somewhere, but I guess I'll have to find it on my own since you don't seem to care," she vented as she stormed out of the office.

Sabrina was hellbent on proving I had been the one to set her up. In the past, the mere thought of facing her wrath would've put the fear of God into me. However, the last 24 hours showed it was now the other way around. Sabrina was the one who needed to be scared of me and what I could do to her.

Clayton sighed heavily before looking up at me. "You know I could've given security permission to search your dorm for evidence of Sabrina's claims?"

"You should've. I have nothing to hide."

"Why don't I believe you?"

I hung my head back against my chair. I was ready to be dismissed. Hell, homework sounded pretty good at the moment. Alas, Clayton only paused for a moment and started up again. "Even if you're not the one behind the recording and it being leaked, this proves what I told you weeks ago. No matter how much you deny it, the anger you're holding onto is an issue. It's causing you nothing but trouble."

"I wasn't angry that night." I brought my head back up and faced Clayton. "The night I was raped, I wasn't angry. In fact, I was on a high. The long and brutal semester was over. I was about to go home to the grandmother I adored. And it was sad I was going to be without my friends, but at least I had friends to be sad over saying goodbye to. It was a good night. Nothing for me to be angry about. Not until he gave me a reason. I don't want to hear my anger is what is causing me trouble. The reason for my trouble has a name, and it's not anger. It's Mike. "

She glanced away from me, and I knew she understood my point. "I'm sorry. I didn't mean to offend you, but I need you to acknowledge this anger is an issue. You need to work through it."

"You see my anger as an issue. I see it as healing. It's what lets me know I'm still alive. It's what keeps me from feeling numb or broken. Do I wish it was happiness I felt 24/7? Sure, but that's not the reality I'm living. I carry this anger with me every day and I'm not going to pretend I don't or apologize for it. Stop expecting me to."

"Are you telling me you're going to continue down this path? Even though you almost reeked the consequences of it today?" Clayton asked, her eyes still on mine.

"And if I say yes?"

"I would have to warn you if you're hellbent on being angry and channeling it into your actions, the only person you're hurting is yourself. Because if I find out you did what Sabrina is saying, I'll have no choice but to expel you."

Clayton's words, combined with the look on her face, sent a chill down my spine. She meant what she said, and I couldn't afford for that to become my new reality. Being expelled would've been the cherry on top of my wretched year. "It won't come to that."

"I would like to think it won't, but you've been unpredictable as of late. This whole recording situation may lead to nothing, but you'll still find another way to land yourself in my office for another issue."

"I'll try to keep my nose clean."

"You'll do more than try. To keep an eye on you, I'm hiring you to fill the role of my office assistant. That way, you won't have time for your... extracurricular activities."

"Thanks, but no thanks. I have classes."

"You seem to think you have a say in this. You don't. It's a part-time job with flexible hours and decent pay for someone your age. You should consider this to be a good thing. Not a punishment."

Of course, it was a punishment. She couldn't prove it, but Clayton knew I was up to no good. Hiring me as her assistant was how she could keep me in her line of sight. She saw me as a ticking time bomb, waiting to go off. She wanted to do everything in her power to prevent me from blowing the rest of the campus up alongside me.

She hoped me working for her would either make me turn a corner or she would be right in her assumption and put a stop to my charades once and for all. Neither would happen because I wasn't going to put up with her. Clayton had been one of the people who wronged me. Unlike the others, I assume I couldn't get to her. She was too big. Held too much power for me to knock her down.

Staring at her then, I knew my observation was wrong. Clayton was human. If I learned anything from my history classes, it was that any human, regardless of their power, could be brought down by the hands of another.

"Okay," I said with a sigh. "I accept your offer."

She smiled at me, unknowingly setting the events of her own downfall into motion. I was ready to use her self-confidence against her. She'd been riding high for far too long, and it was time for someone to bring her down a peg or two. If no one else was going to have the courage to do it—this task was going to fall on me. Unfortunately for her, I was more than up for the challenge.

* * *

After Clayton gave me more details about the position and my start date, I returned to my dorm. I checked my phone that I shut off during the meeting and saw my texts to Jordyn were still unanswered. After I admitted to what I did, including having her act as a participant, she was upset. I apologized, but she didn't want to listen. Like Luke, she took off and told me to give her some space.

I knew Jordyn was going to put two and two together regarding the recording, so her reaction wasn't unexpected. That didn't make it sting any less. Jordyn had never been this mad at me before, including when she didn't like me. I didn't regret getting that recording of Sabrina, but if I had a redo button, I wouldn't have leaked it.

I would've played it for Luke and just him, but my blood-thirst for revenge made me care more about embarrassing Sabrina than about helping Luke see the truth about her. Now, my relationship with Jordyn was in jeopardy. I drafted another text to her, apologizing. If I needed to, I would apologize a hundred times just to get her to talk to me. It hadn't yet been 24 hours since we last spoke, but I was already desperate to hear from her.

I waited to see if she would respond, but all I got was the read receipt. She deserved to be angry at me for putting her in the middle of this after I said I wouldn't and for ignoring her one request for space. I sent one more message and for my sanity, I turned my phone face down.

In need of a distraction, I opted for a shower. I grabbed my bathrobe and headed into the bathroom, turning the hot water all the way up. I was just finishing up toweling off when I heard a knock at the door. In a hurry, I wrapped my robe around myself before answering it.

I opened it cautiously and there she was, standing outside with tears streaming down her face. "Jordyn?"

She said something, but it was intelligible from her crying. I never saw her like this before. Jordyn prided herself on being strong and showing a brave face, even when she wasn't feeling it. To see her in this state told me was wrong.

Seeing the pain in her eyes, I did the only thing I could do and took her in my arms and hugged her tight. When she was steady, I moved her inside and sat her on the bed. "What's wrong? Did someone do something to you?"

"It's Sabrina. She accused me of knowing what you were up to with the recording, that I helped you embarrass her."

I rolled my eyes. It was just like Sabrina to be this vindictive, but it was one thing to do it to me. Another thing to do it to Jordyn. "She's misplacing her anger at me onto you. That's my fault. I'm sorry."

"It's not even that she thinks I would do something like that to her. It's how she reacted when I denied it. She accused me of being a terrible sister to her. That I had chosen my friend over her."

"That's real rich coming from her." She used to choose me over Jordyn all the time. Whether it was going to the movies with me rather than staying home with Jordyn. Or going to the mall with me than attending Jordyn's middle school graduation ceremony. She always chose other people over her sister and for her to accuse Jordyn of doing that when she had always been there for her made me sick.

"You are a great sister to her, better than what she deserves. She's the one who has been a terrible sister. Don't let her mess with your head and convince you otherwise."

"For years, she treated you like you were her sister. I know your guys' relationship wasn't all what it seemed to be. It wasn't perfect, but there was a bond between you and her. I wish she had let me in like she did with you. That's why I let her treat me how she does. I'm seeking her approval, even if it's only in small ways. It's idiotic, but I looked past her flaws pertaining to me, but lost respect for you when you did the same thing. Her treatment of us was one and the same. The only difference is you got out and I'm still the fool who wants to believe she can be the sister I've always wanted her to be."

I wanted to grab Jordyn by the shoulders and shake her. Sabrina showed Jordyn her true colors again. This was who she was, and she would never change. I wanted to tell her this, but I didn't. I understood her desire for Sabrina to be something she wasn't. She had to decide what to do with Sabrina without my two cents. "You need to stand up to Sabrina. Stop letting her push you around. I know you can do it, because it's how you act around everyone else. It's only with Sabrina where that part of you disappears. Make it clear you won't accept her behavior toward you anymore."

Jordyn looked at me. She thought long and hard about the situation with Sabrina. I could see it in the wrinkles in her forehead and the slump of her shoulders. "I don't know how to do that."

"It's easy. You tell her that her behavior is unacceptable, and that you won't stand for it any longer. If she doesn't believe you, you take it a step further until she finally does."

"I'm not like you. I can't switch from caring about someone to doing something unbelievably cruel to them."

It was my mistake to think that because Jordyn was upset with Sabrina meant she was no longer upset with me. "I'm sorry for using you like that against Sabrina. It wasn't okay."

"You knew that when you did it. It wasn't something you realized after the fact," she said, her tone softer but still harsh. "The thing that gets me the most is you don't see what you did as wrong. You're sorry you had to involve me, but you're not sorry for embarrassing Sabrina or for letting Luke's heart break with an audience watching."

"I should've played the recording to Luke and only him."

"You think?"

"But-"

"There is no but. What Sabrina did was wrong, but so was what you did. Can't you see what you did was an example straight out of her playbook? You want me to believe you've changed, but your behavior is still in line with hers and you don't have the excuse of being under her spell anymore. Face it, in some ways, you're exactly like her."

"No, I'm not. Everything I have done has been in reaction to her and her actions."

"So it's okay that you used me because Sabrina did it to Luke first?"

"No-"

"But that's your rationale."

This was not how I wanted this conversation to go. I knew I had things to atone for, but I wanted to comfort Jordyn. Not have to defend myself to her. "I did a bad thing. I'm sorry for hurting you. That's the last thing I wanted to do."

"You valued hurting my sister more than protecting our relationship." I could detect the hurt in Jordyn's voice. I stood, needing to make this better.

"You're right. Sabrina hurt me in the worst way before the summer, and I wanted to make her feel a similar pain. But nothing I could ever do to her would hurt her the same way she hurt me."

"Help me understand. You've been so secretive about what ended your friendship and even though I found it annoying, I stopped pushing it. Now that you put me in the middle of this, I think I'm entitled to an explanation."

With each gulp, I could feel the tightness of the knot in my throat traveling down, settling in my stomach. I kept what happened to myself because I didn't want to ruin how Jordyn saw her sister, but I also did it because I liked how she treated me. She wasn't Clayton or Tyler or Dr. Johnson, who knew and treated me with safety gloves. I liked that. I needed that. Everything about our relationship would change if she knew, and I liked it how it was.

"I can't tell you." My voice came out as a whisper and I looked away from her. Even if I left out details, it wouldn't be enough to keep her from figuring out what happened.

"Are you worried it would affect how I see Sabrina? Because you shouldn't be. She's done enough damage to our relationship on her own doing."

Tears stung my eyes and the lump in my throat made it hard to think, let alone speak. I wanted to tell her, but a part of me was still afraid. What if she took Mike's side like Sabrina did? If my best friend in the world didn't believe me, why would the girl who thought of me being as bad as her sister?

My silence spoke volumes. I have never been so quiet in my life. Jordyn's face went from concerned to reluctant acceptance. "Okay. I will not force you to tell me. Just like I will not let you force me into forgiving you."

I slumped backward into a sitting position on my bed. Before my last fight with Sabrina, any argument we had, I knew either she or I would come back. One of us would crawl back to the other, seeking forgiveness. It's why I was never worried when she walked out of me or when I walked out of her.

Worry bubbled in my stomach as I watched Jordyn approach my door. This wasn't like with Sabrina. If I let Jordyn walk out, she wasn't going to come back.

"It was the last night of the semester," I begun. Jordyn paused, her hand still on the knob. "It was the four of us. Me, Sabrina, Luke, Mike. Our original plan was to have dinner together, but Sabrina wanted the night to last longer. We drove to the Alpha Phi. We were there for an hour before Sabrina came down with food poisoning. Luke, who was the only one of us sober, took my car and took her home. I stayed. I shouldn't have, but I stayed."

I stopped, needing to fight the tears from falling. "I drank way more than I should have and Luke hadn't come back with my car. He said he would, but it got so late and he still wasn't back. My head was killing me. I thought laying down would help, so I went upstairs. I found an unaccompanied room, and I went inside. The lights made my head hurt worse, so I turned them off. I got into bed and for a little while I slept."

My sniffles broke up my recounting of the story. I couldn't even look at Jordyn's back, that was still facing the door. It was easier for me to look at my hands as I finished. "The lights were still off when someone came into the room. They said they were Luke. I thought he was Luke."

"It wasn't, was it?"

I shook my head. "I slept with this person thinking he was my boyfriend. It didn't occur to me that what I had been told was a lie. Who would lie about something like that? All to get into someone's pants? It didn't occur to me that kind of monstrous behavior existed. But it did, and it didn't come from a stranger. It came from a friend. It came from Mike."

I put my hands over my eyes. Telling the story again was as awful as the first time. Maybe worse because I was hoping for a different reaction from Jordyn than what I got from Clayton, Sabrina, and Luke. It felt like I was setting myself up for failure.

Looking down onto my bedspread, I continued despite myself. "He told Sabrina what happened before I could, and she thought I'd screwed her boyfriend. She didn't understand or want to understand that I didn't consent to being with him. I consented with Luke. I told her it was rape, and she said that I was lying and that I wanted it. She didn't believe me."

The weight of memories caused tears to cascade down my face. My heart felt heavy in my chest. I hated this feeling and wished I could just forget everything that happened inside that bedroom, to everything that happened after, but I couldn't. It's why I was determined not to have any of those involved to forget either.

My bed shook as Jordyn sat down next to me with almost no space between us. She took my hands from my face and said, "I believe you."

It took five months after my rape to hear it, but I finally heard the words I so desperately craved to hear and it came from the person I least expected. The person I needed it most from. I bawled, my sobs echoing through the room, releasing the pent-up emotions swirling inside me. She held me as I sobbed. "I believe you."

Then she kissed my forehead and whispered something in my ear that changed everything for me - "It wasn't your fault. The drinks, the lights, the door — none of it was your fault. I'm sorry you ever were told by anyone that it was."

I felt a sudden lightness in my chest as those words sunk deep into me, calming the storm raging within me. Jordyn helped me to lie down, then asked, "What do you need from me?"

I thought about it for a moment, considering all the possible answers. I decided what I wanted most was simply her. Taking her hand in mine, I said, "Stay. Don't give me space. I know you said you needed it—"

"I don't need it anymore."

"Good, because I've isolated myself from everyone these few months, but I don't want to do that. Not with you. Please stay, and just be here with me."

"I'm not going anywhere." She took her jacket and shoes off, then climbed into bed. "Come here," she said, gesturing for me to join her.

I put an arm around her as she wrapped her arms around me. Resting my head on her chest, I could finally relax. The sound of her heartbeat and the warmth of her embrace were enough to make me forget for the time being. Her fingers ran through my hair so lovingly, I could've fallen asleep right then and there in her arms.

"Jor?"

"Yeah?"

"I don't want to be like her. Or use what happened to me as an excuse, but..."

She didn't push for me to continue, but I knew she was patiently listening. It was the only thing that kept me going. "The pain of that day I still carry it with me. I can't be the bigger person when it comes to Sabrina. I wish that wasn't the case, but it is."

"You don't have to explain. I understand. More than you think."

My eyes drifted up, but I could only see her chin. I sat up so I could see her eyes. "Care to elaborate?"

She gazed at me, then at the ceiling. "When she said I had been a terrible sister to her, a small voice inside me wanted to show her how terrible of a sister I could be. Give her a dose of her own medicine. Act like the sister she was accusing me of being, but my conscience prevailed."

"What if it didn't? What if we finally gave her as good as we got?"

"I don't know. I don't want to be a hypocrite. I was just getting onto you for going after her."

"You know why now, and you understand. Besides, it wouldn't have to be as bad as the leaked recording. I promise."

"Why? What did you have in mind?"

I walked my fingers from the button of her jeans up to the collar of her shirt. "You know how much she hates us being friends?"

She nodded slowly.

"What if we took it a step further? What if we pretended to be more

197

than friends?"

"You want to fake-date?"

"Think about it. We can pretend to be dating, and she will be so mad that she can't do anything about it. It'll drive her mad. Plus, it wouldn't actually hurt her. It wouldn't be taking things too far, like my last plan."

"This is outrageous."

"Yet you're not outright rejecting it."

Her eyes moved as if she was calculating the risks. Then finally, she sat up too, meeting me eye to eye.

"You're such a bad influence on me." She bit her lip, stopping her from laughing.

"Is that a yes?"

"What do you think?" She touched my lower back gently and brought us both back onto the bed, my head on her chest. I couldn't help but smile.

19

How To Lose Your Job In One Day

The following Monday, I arrived at Dean Clayton's office, ready to report for duty like a good little soldier. If said soldier was secretly planning on taking their commanding officer down, all while smiling in their face.

"Thank you for showing up on time," Clayton greeted me as I walked into her opened office door. She was sitting at her desk, looking less formal than she usually did. Her navy cardigan was not as crisp as usual and the white shirt beneath had a few crumbs on it. Today Clayton seemed almost... relaxed?

"Being on time is a part of the job, is it not?"

"No. No. It is. I was just complimenting your punctuality. It shows you're serious about your new position."

I was certainly serious about something. "You're welcome. What's my first task? Make a coffee run for you?"

"Haha. No. I'm actually going to work from home today. The only reason I came in at all was to welcome you for your first day on the job."

"Must be nice to have the option to stay home and do your work there than to come into the office," I mumbled, mostly to myself. Loud enough for her to hear, though.

"Home isn't always the retreat you might think it is. Not for everybody."

Her stare intensified on me like she was trying to get a point across. A point I wasn't interested in deciphering. "So, if you're not here, do I get the day off?"

"Once again, no. I thought this would be the perfect time for you to do something I've been meaning to do, but haven't had the time or energy."

"That being...?"

"Organizing my meeting minutes."

"Your what?"

Clayton got up from her seat and walked around her desk, her back to a stack of files. "Meeting minutes are records of what was discussed and what decisions were made during meetings. I have a pile of them, and they need to be sorted and filed properly."

"Alright, I can do that. Is there a specific way you'd like them organized?"

"There's a filing cabinet right behind you." I turned around and saw it. "These on my desk are from recent meetings, but I've been shifting through them, so they're out of order. You'll have to arrange them chronologically, starting with the most recent on top. Then you can put them in the filing cabinet. Oh, and please don't read the notes. The dates are at the top of each page. You won't have to look at anything else in order to arrange them correctly."

I couldn't suppress chuckling at that last part. "Afraid I'll get exposed to confidential information?" I asked, grinning.

"More like you'll be exposed to the most mind numbing boring conversations that have ever been recorded. Save yourself the trouble and ignore the notes."

Maybe she was telling the truth and there was nothing interesting to find in between those pages. Or she was lying through her teeth because she didn't want me to see something I shouldn't have. I wouldn't know unless I looked. "I won't pay it any attention. The less I have to look at them, the quicker I can leave, right?"

"Right. Well now, that you know what you need to do. I'll be off. Call if you need anything."

"I think I can handle this with no assistance. Thanks, though."

"I almost forgot." She held her hand out, showing a key in her palm. "It's to the office. Lock up on your way out and leave it on the reception desk out there."

"Thanks for trusting me with this." I would make sure she regretted it.

Clayton left soon afterwards, and I went to work. I took the files off her desk and sorted them onto the floor. There were records from each week dating back to before the semester began. On each record, my eyes traveled from the date in the right-hand corner to the notes scribbled down in the middle.

Boring.

Turns out Clayton wasn't lying. I went through at least twenty different records and found nothing that could damage her reputation. So not only was it a bore, it was also a colossal waste of time.

Giving up that there was anything there, I arranged the files how Clayton asked and gathered them to put them in her filing cabinet. While I was halfway down the aisle of files, something grabbed my attention. It wasn't a file, but a sticky note taped inside the cabinet.

On the note, in Clayton's handwriting, was a list of six different name and word combinations. They looked like passwords Clayton used to login into different accounts. My mind sprang into action as I realized what I had in my possession. Clayton must have written her passwords in case she ever forgot them, but forgot she left it in her filing cabinet, the one she had given me permission to use.

I quickly disposed of the records into the cabinet and ripped the sticky note gently off. I headed over to the desk with a feeling of accomplishment. If one of these passwords helped log me into her computer, I'd be able to access all the files onto it. If I were lucky, these passwords would help me log in to her other accounts too—email, FTP, and others.

I sat down at the desk and woke up her desktop computer. Then I took out the sticky note and compared each of the passwords against Clayton's computer. I typed the first one, typing everything correctly. It didn't work. Tried it with the second one. Same result. Finally, I test out the third one and the screen refreshed. I was in.

I couldn't believe it worked. It felt too easy, but there it was. Her home screen was an up close photo of her and a man, presumably Mr. Clayton, smiling at the camera. It felt strange seeing her happy, knowing I was there to find something to ruin it.

I opened every folder I saw on the home screen. Some were blank, either created with no purpose or the files were deleted. Some were filled with photos and documents, all seemingly harmless. Some were filled with photos and documents, all seemingly harmless. Once I went through all of them, I clicked on a browser and saw her most visited website was the university's system website for students and staff.

I clicked it and was prompted to provide a username and password. Luckily, both were on the sticky note. The only problem was it asked for a second authentication to confirm it was Clayton. I always thought that was a ridiculous feature. Who would hack into someone's university account? Now I was the person doing the hacking. I shook my head at the realization.

They gave me three options: phone call, email, or text. I choose the only plausible option—email. I entered Clayton's official school email and nervously brought up her email in the next tab. I caught a break with her still being logged in. I saw the email waiting in her inbox and I quickly clicked on the Verify link.

The website loaded with a confirmation message: "Your account has been verified! Please wait a moment for us to log you in."

I breathed a sigh of relief, but not before I deleted the email in her inbox and prayed she didn't get a notification about it on her phone. Going back to her account, it was weird to see the website from the side of an instructor. Some features remained the same, but it looked like I had entered through a brand new portal.

So much was new, but my eyes were drawn to the message features. In it were conversations between Clayton and almost every staff member. It felt like I was entering a goldmine of potential infractions that could get Clayton fired.

I didn't know where to look first. The only thing I could think of was the night I came to her, looking for help, and found the opposite. I filtered her messages to that night to see if anything would pop up. What I found was the smoking gun.

After our meeting, Clayton started a group chain conversation with one university therapist, Dr. Perry and Mr. Cole, a name I didn't recognize, but identified later as a lawyer. In the first message, Clayton said a student had come to her after hours to lodge a complaint against another student for allegedly raping her.

She admitted she told the student that an investigation would be fruitless and offered counseling instead. Dr. Perry agreed with her decision, saying they had a precedent not to conduct investigations involving rape if it wasn't clear cut. The next message was from the lawyer reassuring Clayton she had done nothing wrong legally. She didn't force the girl not to ask for an investigation. She merely presented her with the facts of the situation that lead her to agree that an investigation would not be conducive.

Reading the messages pissed me off more than I already was. It was one thing to have Clayton think she did the right thing by not pushing for an investigation. It was another thing to have a doctor and a lawyer involved in the conversation telling her she had done nothing wrong, as if it was okay to not do something.

Before I could get too heated, I read the final two messages. It was Dr. Perry asking Clayton to keep these kinds of conversations exclusive to their group chat. Clayton ended the text chain by saying the student hadn't formally lodged a complaint so she didn't believe it belong there. I reread the messages and something I hadn't thought of before dawned on me.

No one was surprised. Clayton wasn't appalled in her messages. Dr. Perry wasn't shocked to hear a student came forward with allegations of sexual assault. It seemed like they already knew the story. Almost like they had seen this coming, as if this conversation wasn't new to them at all because it was something that happened before.

The mention of a supposed group chat dedicated to discussing these issues confirmed my suspicions. The group chat wasn't hard to find. It was still a part of the university's system like the messages, but it was under private groups. What I saw told me exactly why they had made it private.

Every message was wordless, opting to attach files. I clicked on each one and incident reports took over the screen. Reports of inappropriate behavior, sexual harassment, and rape were filed, but they've each been stamped in big bold red ink with the words "closed".

There were no comments on the reports from Clayton about the findings from the investigation. Even though there was a section for her to provide an explanation and findings, it was blank.

I looked through each report. There were hundreds, dating back to Clayton's first semester as the Dean three years ago. My heart sank as I read each one and saw Clayton had done nothing. Just like she had done nothing for me.

I'd spent months worrying what happened to me was happening to other students on campus when, in reality, it already happened. It happened before me and it happened after me. How could someone who held so much power do so little for the people who relied on them? It was infuriating, disgusting, but oh so not surprising.

"You could have done something," I hissed to myself. The you in question? I wasn't sure. Clayton fit, but so did I. She should've done right by her students by properly investigating their claims, but I could've done something too.

I could've come forward with the story that she pushed me away from filing a report against Mike. Who knows what it would've done, but it would've been something. I let what she did to me go. I wouldn't let that happen again.

Taking my flash drive out of my pocket, I downloaded each of the reports onto it. Every one of them. Clayton had her chance to help her students. Now it was my turn to dish out my own brand of justice.

20

The Newspaper Trap

"What a welcome surprise," Amelia greeted me with a smile as I stepped inside of her and Jordyn's dorm.

Amelia's side was decorated with bright stars and sparkly lights. She had a poster of her favorite movie, Roman Holiday above her bed. Jordyn's side was more subdued, with cozy blankets and books, both her textbooks and her favorite horror novels on her desk.

"What brings you by?" Amelia asked as she went to her closet. It was Thursday after 3:00 p.m. and Jordyn was in class. I knew this and so did she, hence why she was asking.

"I couldn't stop by and visit my new friend, Amelia?" I replied with a coy smile.

She laughed and grabbed a pair of ankle boots from her closet. "Your new friend Amelia has a study group to meet with in ten minutes and can't afford to be late."

"So make it snappy?"

"Yes! Now, what can I do for you?"

My eyes canvassed each surface of the room as I made my way over to Jordyn's side of the room. "This is going to sound so middle school, but I wanted to see if there was any information you could relay to me about Jordyn."

"Information?" She sounded confused. She looked up from putting on her boots and eyed me. "You've known her longer than I have. What information could you need from me?"

"I've known her as my best friend's mean little sister, then as a friend. Now as a…"

Amelia crossed her arms, her eyebrows furrowed. "Now as what?"

"You're really going to make me say it, huh?"

"What ever could you mean?"

I let out a deep breath. "Now, as someone I'm interested in, romantically."

"Oh, my god!" she yelped. She didn't hesitate to come up and wrap me in a hug, saying over my shoulder, "I knew I saw something between you two at that club. You kept saying you were straight, but the way you were looking at Jordyn said otherwise."

She pulled back just as I hid my hand behind my back. I've never pickpocketed from someone before, never had a reason to. I thought I was caught, but Amelia seemed oblivious. I was actually going to get away with this.

"How are you feeling about this? Confused? Nervous? Both?"

I sighed, trying to play this up as best as I could without overdoing it. "Both, but I think I'm managing this as well as one could. I wasn't expecting to feel this about Jordyn, but now that I do, I want to make it work. I just don't know how."

"You have nothing to worry about. Jordyn likes you. She has as long for as I have known her. And I'm not just saying that. She would talk about you all the time to me."

"She would?" I asked, surprised by the simple revelation.

"At first she acted annoyed at you trying to make friends with her, then she ended up letting her guard down and started talking about how highly she thought of you."

I both loved and hated this news. I love hearing Jordyn felt this way about me, because I certainly felt that way about her. But I hated if she knew what I was up to right now, she wouldn't be so high on me and I wouldn't have blamed her.

"Thanks for reassuring me, Am. That's exactly what I needed to hear."

"Of course. I got to go now, but I can feel in my heart you and Jordyn have something special. Talk to her. I'm rooting for you two."

I walked her out of dorm and watched as she went outside, not yet aware that her campus badge was not in her pocket where she had left it. It was in mine. I waited a few moments to make sure she had left and calmly took off for the Mitchell Hall, the building where the campus newspaper room was located.

Only faculty and students who worked on the newspaper had access to the building. With Amelia's ID badge, I had access. Though I had never been inside before, I found the newspaper room with no fuss. I used the badge to open the door and relaxed that I had gotten this far without being caught.

I knew from conversations with Amelia that the staff completed any last-minute touches or changes about each edition Thursday morning, so they were ready to be printed and distributed Friday by student volunteers. I checked around the room, making sure it was only me. This next step of my plan couldn't move forward with another pair of eyes watching.

I sat at one of the computers and I couldn't believe my eyes when the screen came up fully open for me to edit. Since only the newspaper staff had access to the room, they must have felt comfortable leaving their accounts open and running. I got a glimpse of what Friday's edition was going to be. The headline story was about a new food truck that arrived on campus, and it was full of glowing reviews.

By all accounts, the food truck had earned the newspaper's recommendation. It was a tragedy the students would have to find out for themselves, because they would never read this article. Without no guilt or regret, I deleted every trace of it from the paper, along with any other stories that were supposed to be published.

The story that would grace the front page of tomorrow's newspaper would not be a trivial issue about tacos. It was a story that would forever alter the course of our campus, one that could have devastating implications. The Dean would have no choice but to face the music and, if justice had its way, see her last days in this place.

When I was finished, I wiped down every surface I touched, including Amelia's badge and the door handle. Using the sleeve of my shirt, I tossed the badge into a lost & found box I spotted on my way out of the building. It was possible I was being paranoid.

A university's newspaper being tampered with was no cause for fingerprinting, surely. Yet I couldn't take any chances. The release of the paper tomorrow would put many things into jeopardy, my future potentially being one of them. I couldn't know for certain, but what I did know was that after this night, nothing would be the same again.

21

They Shoot Robinsons, Don't They?

For the first time in two years, I woke up at 7:00 a.m. on a Friday morning. After years of begrudgingly doing it while I was in school, I vowed to never sign up for a class on Fridays once I reached college. It was the only way I could be sure to never put my body through that kind of torment ever again. I never imagined I would ever make an exception to that rule, but today was a special occasion.

It was the day of judgment for Dean Clayton and the abusers on campus roaming around without a care in the world. The newspaper volunteers would distribute the papers to stands and dorms across campus at 7:45 a.m.. After they did, nothing would be the same. So many on campus, including myself, turned an eye away from the abuse happening for a long time. But this? No one could turn away from this.

I sat in the quad, waiting for the papers to arrive. I wanted to be the first person to hold the truth in my hands. It'll be hours before most people on campus saw it, but I would take in every reaction of every student who passed by me on their way to class or across campus.

I would hear their anger, their disgust, and their sadness. For once, everyone would be forced to acknowledge the truth of what was happening and no one could deny it. It was like a dam breaking and I welcomed it with open arms.

As I waited, a few people begun appearing as they headed to class. The campus was beginning not to look so much like a ghost town, and I knew things were about to get interesting. Finally, at around 7:50 a.m. I heard a rumbling from down the street. Volunteers on electric scooters were wheeling in newspapers from all sorts of places.

I jumped up and sprinted towards one of them before they could get to me. I read the headline before I could grab a copy. On the front page read "University Corruption Uncovered: Sexual Abuse Rampant on Campus". I flipped through the pages like I was reading them for the first time and, in a way, I was.

When I wrote them, my mind was the one in control. I had four days from finding the reports to breaking into the newsroom to gather my thoughts and put them down onto paper for everyone to hear. Of course, no one would know it was my thoughts they were reading, but the feeling of nervousness about doing this story justice weighed on me.

It also wasn't lost on me that writing had never been my strong suit. I was much more comfortable telling stories with my voice rather than with a pen. But then it hit me. I didn't have to be the one who told this story. I could let the stories tell themselves.

―――――――――――――――――――――――――

Lakeview College Chronicle

October 25, 2024

University Corruption Uncovered: Sexual Abuse Rampant on Campus

by Anonymous

It's no secret that sexual abuse is an issue on college campuses throughout the world. However, evidence leaked by an anonymous source has uncovered a widespread problem here at home.

According to documents obtained by the Chronicle suggests, the university has been systematically mishandling allegations of sexual assault on campus. The documents indicate there have been numerous reports of sexual abuse on campus dating back to at least 2021. Through an examination of internal documents, it became apparent that a significant number of sexual assault reports were prematurely marked as "closed" with no signs of a proper investigation being done.

Victims' cases were routinely dismissed, and their reports disregarded without adequate inquiry. Officials including Dean Clayton, who handles student disciplinary proceedings, were aware of the reports and ignored or downplayed the seriousness of the allegations in favor of protecting the reputation of the institution.

The university's policies, procedures, and failure to properly investigate and respond to allegations of sexual misconduct have created an unsafe environment for its students. To truly understand the nature of the problem, the university is facilitating with their lack of action, read on to hear survivors' stories in their own words.

The following accounts are excerpts from the sexual assault reports filed at Lakeview College:

"We were at the Monster Mash Halloween Party at Alpha Delta Gamma, and he acted like a friend. Until he didn't. Sometime during the night, he must have slipped something into my drink because everything went blurry. He took me back to his dorm after I told him I wanted to go to mine. I couldn't reject his offer to help me because I couldn't even walk on my own. I was helpless." - Melissa Wright

"We'd been friends since we met during our freshman year of high school. But after attending a mixer together, everything changed. He wanted more than just friendship, and I didn't know how to say no without hurting him. I didn't want to hurt him, so I let him hurt me instead." - Leah Bell

213

"It was supposed to be a fun night of hanging out with our mutual friends, but she ruined it for me. I said 'no,' every time she groped me, but she would start doing it again after a while. It was like that the entire night. Maybe it was her way of flirting or maybe me laughing it off encouraged her to start it up again. I don't know, but I know I didn't like it." - Dominic Cruz

"I didn't want to come forward at first with this because he was my boyfriend. I was staying with him at his apartment off campus when he came home drunk after a night out with his teammates. I was asleep when I woke up to him having sex with me. He thought it was okay because we were together. It wasn't." - Kelsey Jones

"When I found he was gay, it felt like a dream had come true. The whole date, he was a perfect gentleman, but when we went back to his place, he started trying to kiss me. I thought it was too soon and pulled away, but he just laughed and tried again. I didn't want to be a prude, so I gave into it. I don't know if what happened between us warrants this report, but I can't get that night out of my head, for all the wrong reasons." - Malcolm Smith

————————————————————————

Stories like theirs continued. I dedicated more pages' worth of stories from other students recounting their own experiences. Even then, it wasn't enough to include every story from the reports I'd downloaded. And for every report filed by a student, there were hundreds of more waiting to be heard that weren't being told.

While I was immersed reading the paper, time slipped away from me without me even noticing. I looked up, suddenly aware the quad had become filled with students. I looked at my watch and saw it was approaching 10 a.m.. People were filing out of their classes, meaning more than just I would soon read the paper.

As I watched others pass by, two girls with trays from the cafeteria sat down at the table in front of me. One of their phones was on the table, and I noticed it was open to the paper. "This is horrible", she sighed as her eyes scanned over the stories.

"What is it?" the other asked in between bites of her waffles.

"This week's newspaper."

"You actually read that bore of a paper? Until last year, I didn't even know we had one," she replied, not looking up from her plate.

"Someone linked it in our sorority's group chat. It's different from the usual. Someone anonymously wrote a story exposing the university."

"Exposing us? What does it say?"

I tuned them out when they started reading the article, my mind drifting, heartbeat rising. The story was out there for everyone to see. Before, I could have put a stop to what was about to come if I felt like it. But now, the words were right there in black and white and there was no stopping what was about to happen.

I got up from the table, my paper clutched in my hand. Everywhere around me were people on their phones, something that was not an uncommon sight, but this time carried an entirely different atmosphere. It felt tense, almost as if the air had been disturbed with a sense of foreboding. Through every overheard small talk and exchange of disbelieving expressions, I knew the news of the university having been exposed had reached most people's ears.

If I'd needed confirmation, the crowd that gathered in front of the campus center cemented it for me. Everywhere I looked, students were glued to their phones or tablets, onto the articles that had been reposted about the university and its wrongdoing. I heard the murmurs of shock, disbelief, and rage as I joined the crowd.

The crowd was facing a group of students on the steps of the campus center, yelling about the sexual misconduct running rampant at the school and the inaction of the administration. There were so many voices yelling it was hard to tell where one began and the other ended.

The crowd was growing larger by the second, driven by an angry energy that permeated the surrounding air. Everyone wanted answers. They wanted someone to explain why the university tried to sweep reports of sexual abuse under the rug. I didn't see who brought it, but someone passed along a megaphone.

The megaphone was handed off to one of the loudest voices in the crowd, a sophomore girl who stepped up to address everyone. "I've been hearing rumors for months about nothing ever coming from the university's investigations," she yelled, her voice shaking with anger. "This article was just the confirmation we needed. I've only been here for two years, but I'm sick of us ignoring what we all know is happening. Even if you haven't been harassed or assaulted, I'm sure you know someone who has. As long as we keep ignoring what's happening to us or to our friends, the longer the administration gets to ignore it, too!"

"She's right," a second, even louder voice shouted from the steps. "If we want this to change, we have to demand it instead of suffering in silence. A brave voice risked something by leaking this story. We can't let it go unnoticed."

The voices on the steps and in the crowd swelled, a chorus of angry chants, united by the same want. Just as I was taken aback by the surge of emotion, my phone rang, breaking me out of the moment. I quickly snatched it from my pocket to answer Jordyn's call. "Have you seen the news?" she asked without preamble.

I could barely hear her over the crowd. "I can't hear you. Wait, a second." I pushed my way out of the crowd until I was standing by the theater building, the noise coming from them a distant hum. "Yes. I've seen the news. It's great, isn't it?"

"Great? Are you kidding me? It's awful."

I mentally kicked myself for my poor wording. "Yes. Of course, it's awful. I meant it's great that what's happening isn't being covered up anymore."

"Yeah. That part is good, but this whole thing is a mess. Amelia is in a frenzy. She doesn't know who wrote that article. She's on the phone confronting everyone who works on the paper and no one is owning up to it."

"Oh." I pretended to be surprised. "I thought whoever wrote it got permission to do so from the newspaper."

"No! Whoever did this did it without approval. It's why they credited themselves as anonymous. They know they can't come forward without risking their spot at the school or employment here if they're a staff member."

"That's... unfortunate. I suppose that's the price you pay for being a whistleblower."

"It won't be them who pay for it if they can't find out who is behind the article. Amelia and the rest of the staff will be the ones who are going to be held accountable."

I wasn't sure what to say. I didn't go through all the trouble I did to publish this article just to fess up to it now to Jordyn. There's no way I could, even if it meant someone else had to take the fall for it. I hoped it wouldn't be Amelia, but I had to focus on protecting myself. I couldn't afford to worry about how the consequences of my actions would affect someone else other than me.

"I wouldn't worry about it right now. The university has a lot to answer to. They should focus on that instead of whom to place the blame on."

There was no sound on the other line for a moment. Jordyn was processing what I told her and trying to make sense of the whole thing. "You're right. All we can do now is wait and see what the consequences of this article will be."

She hung up, and I was left alone with my thoughts and the hum of the crowd. I put my phone back into my pocket and looked up toward the building across from me. I didn't have to look down at the sign to know what building it was. The face looking down at me from the window was enough to confirm I was standing in front of the administrative building and that I'd just been spotted by the Dean.

I'll never forget the look on her face as she peered down at me. It wasn't the cartoony Scooby Doo villain being outed angry expression. It was a cool, calculated one. The face of someone who knew exactly what they were doing, of someone who was in control even when she was on the verge of losing it.

* * *

When you're requested by the Dean when they're in the midst of their biggest scandal, the scandal you caused, you're supposed to feel scared. I wasn't. Not in the slightest. After all, she was the one on trial. Not me.

I took a deep breath before knocking on Clayton's door. I could hear loud voices on the other end. As soon as the door opened, I saw Dean Clayton and two other officials. Their faces were red from arguing.

"Come in," Clayton motioned me to enter.

"You're seriously taking a meeting with a student right now?" one official asked her.

"Yeah. I am. We'll wrap up this conversation later." Then she looked at me and said, "Please, Ms. Robinson, stay."

I stood waiting. I only moved slightly when her two officials relented and left. Then Clayton cleared her throat and addressed me. "You can sit, you know."

"I rather stand."

She didn't fight me on it. "Okay, fine. I just wanted to talk to you briefly. I'll cut right to the chase. I know you're behind the article that was printed in the school's paper."

"If you're looking for some kind of confession by me, you're not going to get it."

"I'm not looking for anything from you. I know you're the one behind the article, but I won't pass that information along to any other officials. Your secret stays in this room between us, as far as I'm concerned."

I didn't buy what she was selling. She must've been after something.

"Why am I here then?"

"I requested you come up here so I could to tell you congratulations."

I was taken aback. "Congratulations?"

"Yes, congratulations. You got what you wanted. I've been dismissed. They're giving me until the end of the day to clear out my office."

"If you're telling me so, I'll feel guilty—"

"I'm not. I'm telling you because I want to leave you with some parting words."

"Okay..."

"You're not going to change anything."

I was taken aback again. "What?"

"You somehow got it into your mind that by getting rid of me, you'll fix the system we have here. You won't. The system will remain the same. No amount of articles, chants, or protests will change how the system operates. Do you seriously think I wanted to mark 'closed' on all those reports? I didn't."

"Then why did you?"

"It was my job."

"No!" I yelled. "Your job was to protect your students. Not to sweep the abuse they were facing under the rug."

"Stop thinking of the world as in black and white. I thought after what you've been through, you would understand you can't view the world like that."

"Are you going to tell me you not investigating students' claims of being sexually abused is a shade of gray? Because I see nothing gray about that. It's black. It's evil and corrupted, just like you."

She sighed and ran her fingers through her hair. "I see so much of how I used to be in you. I was angry at the world too, that I became desperate to change it. That's how I became a part of the system I wanted to fix because I learned a valuable lesson. One that I'm trying to teach you."

"Which is?" I asked impatiently.

"No one person can change a system. You want to change one? Change it from the inside because the people on the outside only have the power to observe."

"You say that, but you haven't changed a corrupted system. It has corrupted you and your morals."

"Do you think things here were better before me? They weren't. My job was to protect the university even at the cost of students. I knew that and I did it even when it pained me. But I did what I could, not that you've noticed. I hired multiple therapists and counselors for students to talk to. There's a scholarship fund I started for survivors. For serious crimes reported, I talked to the accused and convinced them to switch schools, so the victims wouldn't have to face them anymore. You know that one firsthand."

"Am I supposed to be thankful? Oh yay, Mike is free to assault other girls at his new school. Along with the other rapists you let leave without punishment."

"I could only do so much with what is given to me. With the limits placed on me, other people would've said fuck it and just gone along with it. I did more than most. The next person may not. Our job requires us to look out for the school first and foremost. My firing won't change that. Someone else is going to pick up where I left off. So you can enjoy this moment of being the campus hero, but know in the end, nothing will change."

I tried to process what she was saying as my jaw set in a stubborn line. "You're just saying this to me, so I'll back off. You want me to scare me into thinking if I push too hard, the system still won't change? That's not how this works. I know we can make a difference. Those chants outside are proof."

She smiled sadly, her eyes crinkling at the corners as she looked me in the eye. "Those chants will get you a lot of press and publicity, but after a while, they fade. The chants and the publicity. It'll all be gone in a few days. If you're lucky, a few weeks. Manage your expectations and prepare yourself for disappointment because in the end, there are some things we can't control."

Despite my growing frustration, I chose to control my anger instead of lashing out at her. "I'm choosing to be optimistic because this can't be the best that it gets. Therapy and a slap on the back? No, there has to be more that you guys can do than just that."

"I hope the next person who sits in this seat can do more for you than I did, but I'm afraid what we're doing now may be all you get. Now, if you'll excuse me, I need to clean out my desk."

I left her office, feeling the opposite of how I felt this morning. All that hope I had for the future evaporated, being replaced by a sense of doom and demoralization. My terrible mood distracted from where I was going when I stepped out of the building. I walked right into someone on their phone.

"Oops, I'm sorry. Leah?" I asked, as she looked up from their phone. I only saw her in passing since rush week. She was with her fellow sorority girls at their booth near the campus center, asking people to join with a heart-fluttering smile. That smile wasn't there then.

"Willow?"

I didn't know what she meant until I remembered I told her my name was Willow when we met. "Actually, it's Whit. Not Willow."

"I could've sworn you told me your name was Willow."

"I did. It was a joke. I'm sorry about that."

"Oh, funny joke," she said with no emotion. It was only then when I noticed her eyes were wet.

"Hey, are you okay?"

She tried to put a smile on her face, but the tears were still in her eyes. "Did you see the school paper from today?"

"Yeah. It's all everyone is talking about. Is it taking a toll on you?"

She looked down, trying to stop the tears from flowing again. "I'm in it. Whoever wrote it included the report I filed into their story with my name and everything. I didn't give them my permission to do that. I didn't want that stuff to be public."

My heart sunk. While I was putting this story together, I never stopped to think that someone would want their story or their name to remain private. "I'm so sorry."

"The worst part is I never told my family or my friends about what happened to me and whoever this person is got to tell them before I did. They took that from me. I just feel so exposed. I don't know what to do."

The guilt I felt was unbearable. I wanted to take back ever including their names, but I couldn't. All I could do was stand there and listen as she poured her heart out to me.

"I've been listening to this crowd for the last hour and they keep saying whoever wrote this story is brave for leaking what the university has been up to, but I don't get what's brave about them? They aren't showing their face or even telling us their name. They're using other people's stories to get attention."

"Maybe they thought they were doing the right thing?"

"Did it have to happen like though? They could've easily marked out our names and kept us anonymous like they kept themselves, but they didn't. Now I have to go home and face my friends and family knowing they know something about me I never was ready for them to find out. It's not brave to have other people do your bidding for you."

"Is there anything I can do to help? Seriously, I'll help in any way I can."

She looked up and wiped the tears from her eyes before shaking her head gently, giving me a small smile of appreciation. "There's nothing you can do. I'm not even sure there's anything I can do about it.

Thanks for asking, though." She waved goodbye to me before walking away, her head held high despite the pain she was going through.

I remained stood in place for ages, overtaken by the remorse I was feeling. I thought by getting the stories of other victims out there, I was doing something brave and courageous for all of us. After listening to Leah, I knew what she said was true. What I did wasn't brave at all; it was irresponsible and reckless. I had unintentionally hurt the people I was standing up for. There was nothing brave or courageous about that.

It was naïve of me to believe I could single-handedly bring down a corrupt system. All I did was open up more wounds for people whose trauma I could relate to all too well. In the end, no matter how well-intentioned my actions were, I had only made things worse.

22

Join Me in St. Louis

I didn't know how much time had passed since I'd returned to my dorm. I laid in my bed motionless for several hours and I didn't plan on moving. Not even when I heard the knocks raining down upon my door. It could've been the police or campus security guards here to kick off out, and I still wasn't getting up to get it.

"Whit, are you alive?" Jordyn's voice called out to me on the other side of the door and I still didn't move. "Whit?"

The next thing I heard was my doorknob turned and the presence of a body inside the room with me. "Oh yeah. I must have left the door unlocked."

"That would've been useful information for me before I knocked on the door for two minutes straight. Like seriously, I was about to call a locksmith or security to help."

My body was faced away from Jordyn, but I could still feel her worried eyes on me. "Why are you here? Aren't you visiting your family this weekend?"

"I am, and I'll be going in a few hours. I wanted to check on you before I left. Not only has Clayton been fired, but the frats and sororities are suspended until further notice since many of the reports named their assaults happening at or because of their parties."

That's what I wanted. I wanted the frats and sororities to be held accountable, but I couldn't bring myself to care. "Great. That's really great." My tone didn't match the words I was saying and Jordyn noticed.

She sat down on the edge of my bed near my feet. "You sounded fine the last time we talked. What changed?"

"The day continued is what happened. The reality of today's events hit me like a bus. Then, when it decided it wasn't finished fucking with me, it backed over my lifeless body repeatedly to make sure I was dead."

"That's an image I didn't need to see. Nor one I want you ever to imagine again." Through the covers, I felt her hand on the back of my right calf. I told myself it was her trying to get my attention, but I wondered if she knew how it would soothe me too. "Whit, tell me what's going on. That article talked about sexual abuse on campus. Did anything from it trigger you? You can tell me if it did."

"It doesn't matter."

"What doesn't matter?"

"This!" I sat up, frustrated, and I gestured to everything around us. "What happened today? What happened to me and the victims in that article? None of it matters. That story was supposed to ensure the trauma we suffered didn't happen in vain. Well, guess what? It did. None of it mattered because nothing is going to change."

I felt a wave of emotions engulf me, and tears trickled from my eyes. I wiped them away angrily. "What was the point in that article if no one is going to do anything about it? This will keep happening and more of us will continue to suffer in silence because the people in power care more about saving their own skin than they do about saving us."

I clenched my blanket until I made a fist with it. I tried to breathe, but I was struggling to keep my sobs at bay. Jordyn reached out to touch my arm. "I don't know the right words to say. For that, I'm sorry. I should've been better prepared to help you through this."

"It's not your fault. No one can do anything about it. That's the problem."

"You have the weight of the world on your shoulders, but it's not just your fight. It's all of ours. Meaningful change has to come from all of us for it to last and it will not happen overnight. For all its flaws, that story is forcing people to confront the problem instead of shying away from it. That's a start, and sometimes that's all we need."

I saw the sincerity in her eyes. She believed what she was saying. I wished I did too. "So it's okay for people on campus to continue to be sexually assaulted because one day, if we're lucky enough, things might change?"

"In no world will it ever be okay. Just like in no world should this ever be the sacrifices we have to make for change to be done, but these are the cards we've been dealt and we have to play by them."

My head hurt from the crying and the unfairness of everything. Why did people have to get hurt for a system to be better? Why did it take people suffering for a system to start to serve the ones it was put in place for? "How do you manage to not be discouraged?"

"I'm never not discouraged, but then I remember even if we can't see progress happening in real time, it is still being done. It may be small and slow, but the work being done now will make for a better future for everyone. I have to believe that."

Smiling gently at her, my arms instinctively drew her into a hug. "I thought you said you didn't know what to say?"

"That was all I could manage." She pulled away from me, yet her gaze locked on me as if she were seeing me for the first time. Every inch of my face seemed to captivate her. "But it must've been enough if I managed to make this pretty girl stop crying."

"Oh, please. Yeah, I'm pretty with my red-rimmed eyes and snotty nose."

"You are," she insisted. "Snotty nose and all. Inside and out, you're always beautiful."

I felt my cheeks burn and could see hers blushing, too. We looked at each other for a few moments, not saying a word. I couldn't speak for her, but I wanted to so badly take her in my arms and drown out the rest of the world by drowning in her. I wanted to kiss her. Finish what we started in that alley, to feel her body pressed against mine and forget about everything that wasn't her.

There was nothing I wanted more, yet I stood there frozen until she broke the silence with a whisper. "I have something to ask you."

"What is it?"

"How do you feel about St. Louis?"

I eyed her curiously, not sure where she was going with this. "I haven't been since I was a kid, but I remembered liking it."

"Would you like to go now as an adult?"

"What? Where is this coming from?"

"You know how I'm attending my cousin's wedding this weekend?"

"Yeah." I nodded, remembering Jordyn having mentioned she would be away this weekend to go attend it.

"I want you to join me. I think it'll be good for you, distract you from what's happening here. You deserve a break."

I wasn't sure exactly what to make of her request. Did she really want me to come? Or was she only asking because she felt sorry for me? It wasn't outlandish to think that when she had weeks to ask me, but didn't until now.

"I hope you aren't asking as a favor for me. I don't need to be coddled."

"You would be doing me a favor. I love my family, but I could use a friend there."

"I don't know. The last thing I want to do is to intrude or impose at someone else's wedding. They'll have to make a place for me—"

"Actually, no. Luke was supposed to go as Sabrina's date, but since they split, there's a free seat at the table. It's yours if you want it."

"I thought we establish dinners involving me and Sabrina don't end well."

Jordyn laughed, not jumping at the chance to deny it. "Think of it this way, it'll be the perfect place for us to debut as the obnoxiously happy couple we're going to pretend to be. Sabrina will have a front-row seat for it. It's exactly what you wanted."

She was right. This would be the perfect way to not only launch our fake relationship but to rub it in Sabrina's face, too. It was petty, but after the week I had, it was exactly what I needed to get back to myself. "I would love to be your date for the wedding," I finally agreed.

The look on Jordyn's face told me I made her so happy. It was happiest I'd seen her since that night back in the alley. It'd been the happiest I had been since then, too.

"Thank god because I already bought your ticket and arranged the details with the hotel. The only thing you need to worry about is packing everything you need in a timely manner because our train leaves tonight at nine."

I stood and turned away, scanning the room for my suitcase, but something in her voice made me stop and look back. "Will Sabrina be joining us on the train?"

A smirk so deliciously sinful appeared on her face. "She asked if I wanted to drive down with her, but I blew her off."

"Really?" I asked, impressed.

"What was it you said about not letting her push me around anymore? It wasn't easy, but I think I'm getting the hang of it. Besides, I figured it would be much more fun if it was just us two on the trip, don't you think?"

I returned the smirk she was giving me, feeling a warmth I hadn't felt in a long time spread throughout my body. "Definitely more fun."

23

Price vs. Price

Here I thought taking a late train ride would ensure we wouldn't have to deal with many other passengers. I was wrong. Our Chicago to St. Louis train was moderately full of people who, just like me and Jordyn, were traveling for the weekend. Walking down into the last car, I finally came across a corner where Jordyn and I could call our own.

As two passengers made their way past me, Jordyn emerged into view. I waved her over to where I was. Ever the lady, she had carried my suitcase along with hers. It took me a solid two hours rummaging through my wardrobe for anything that could remotely qualify as wedding attire. I hadn't been to a wedding since... ever. This would be my first, and I could only take a guess at what to expect.

Jordyn put our suitcases in the overhead and sat across from me. "Have you heard as couples get older, they lose their ability to hear each other?"

"What?"

"Apparently men lose the ability to hear higher-pitched sounds and women lose hearing on the lower end."

"What are you talking about? Also, you need to stop reading so many books. People think you're nerd enough as it is."

"I'm surprised you don't get it. I thought for sure you would."

I stared blankly at her, having no earthly clue what she was talking about. Then I thought about it so more and it came to me. "You're quoting Before Sunrise?"

"It seemed appropriate with us on a train and all."

"I get it, but don't you remember how you used to rag on me and Sabrina for liking that movie?"

"You didn't like that movie. You were obsessed with it. For three years, you guys whined about the boys in your class, complaining about how none of them were Jesse. Oh, why can't I find my own Jesse?"

I cringed at the memory she was recalling. Sabrina and I went around the house, moaning and groaning about not having our Jesse. It was funny in hindsight, but so embarrassing. "Did you only watched that to fun of me?"

"That was my intent, but I was pleasantly surprised by it. Your twelve-year-old's taste in movies wasn't so bad after all. I will say, though, while Jesse was nice, Céline should've been the one you were carrying a torch for. She's amazing."

"Who knows? If I watch it now, maybe I would or I'll carry a torch for them both."

"Are you trying to tell me something?"

I smiled and shrugged. "Maybe I am."

I avoided giving much thought to what me kissing Jordyn meant about my sexuality. There was no reason to. We chalked the kiss up to Jordyn wanting to fulfill an old crush and me curious what kissing a girl was like. I didn't want to think about what it meant for me in the grand scheme of things.

From when I discovered dating, I never questioned that I liked boys. Just like I never questioned that I liked the kiss with Jordyn. I didn't want my feelings for her to define me, but I couldn't deny they existed. They were there and despite our decision not to read into the kiss; they weren't going away.

"I'm not ready to whip out a specific colored flag. I'm just saying it's possible I was limiting myself before." Her reaction was as if I had shared the funniest joke, but then I forbade her from laughing. "You look like you're dying to laugh, so tell me what's so funny?"

"Well, I told you this a month ago. You know, with you and Sabrina."

"We were friends. That's it."

"Sure. Keep telling yourself that."

"I'm serious."

"So am I," Jordyn countered. "Can you really tell me there weren't times in your guys' relationship where you thought something could actually happen between you two? Think hard before you answer."

And so I did. I thought about our last day together. Me holding my breath while she rested her on my shoulder as we watched a movie. My heart racing as we sped through the mall, our arms fitting together like a puzzle. How instinctively, without saying a word, I went into her bedroom to change. How I sat on her bed and watched her put on her makeup, admiring every stroke she made.

Every memory was like a fracture in the mask I built around my feelings for Sabrina. Somewhere along the way in our relationship, I started looking at her as one looked at someone they loved. Someone they wanted to spend forever in whatever capacity they could. Because she didn't look at me in the same way, I stored away how I felt. From her and myself.

"No," I answered. "There were never times where I thought something would happen between me and her. The question you should be asking is if there were times where I wanted something to happen."

She looked at me skeptically. "Were there times you wanted

something to happen?"

The words were there, but my vocal chords refused to cooperate, leaving me no choice but to nod.

"You had a thing for her all this time?!"

"It wasn't like that," I insisted, hoping for her to lower her tone. "I wasn't harboring feelings for Sabrina for years. Every once in a while, though, when I was with her, I would think I have never felt this close to anybody else in my life. I have never spent this much time with one person and loved almost every minute. No romantic relationship I have had has ever been this fulfilling. And in even the bad moments, I wouldn't trade them for being with anyone else."

"I would think this stuff and ask myself, wouldn't it be so much easier for us if we were the ones together? Ditch the boys and see how far we could make it if we gave what we had a chance at being something more. Then I remembered I was the only one who was thinking this, and I forgot about it until I thought about it again months later."

The heavy silence that followed was suffocating, leaving me feeling uneasy. It felt like I said too much and now everything was uncomfortable. What did I expect Jordyn to say? That it was too bad I never told Sabrina how I felt when Jordyn felt the same way about me?

"If you want to throw me onto the train tracks, I would understand."

"Everything you said I already knew. Most people did. The only person who didn't was Sabrina. It's wild to think how many things might've been different if you told her. You could've been going to this wedding with her instead of me."

"Please don't think for a second what happened between us was me transferring what I once felt for your sister over to you," I pleaded. "We have our own special bond."

"Is that what we're calling it now? I hope you don't put your tongue down everyone's throat you've bonded with."

"Jor, I'm being serious."

"So am I," she sighed, her eyes darting away from me before returning. "Do I think you somehow replaced my sister with me? No, but having you confirm you felt something for her makes me question things. We kissed, Whit."

I bowed my head. "I know we did."

"It might've been a drunken, silly kiss, but I didn't regret it."

"Don't tell me you do now."

"No, I don't. It feels tainted, though. Like, did you only kiss me because you couldn't kiss her? Did you feel any kind of passion for me, or was it just a reminder of what you felt for my sister? Everything's jumbled now."

"I kissed you because I wanted you. Your sister couldn't have been the furthest thing from my mind. It was all about you and how much I wanted to show you how I felt."

"You don't have to explain." Her head shook stubbornly, a steadfast expression on her face. "We're not together. I couldn't fault you for any past feelings you had for anyone, even if we were."

"You deserve to know I wasn't using you as a stand-in for your sister. You're not her understudy or replacement, you're Jordyn and that's why I wanted to kiss you." I took her hand that was resting on the table and squeezed it. "Those questions I had are gone, along with what I felt toward her. I'm glad I never told her those thoughts I had because she wasn't deserving of being the person I thought them about. I'm here, with you, and I wouldn't want it any other way."

A sly smile formed on her lips. "These speeches are usually reserved for people who are in romantic relationships."

"In five hours, we'll be pretending to be in one. Might as well get a head-start."

She leaned over the table, her hands resting next to mine. "A head-start, huh?"

She was thinking the same thing I was, but was going to let me make the first move. I gladly obliged, leaning in and pressing my lips to hers. It felt like the most natural thing in the world. They were soft and gentle, just the way I remembered them. Her lips against mine felt like they were meant to be locked together. It was a natural, effortless connection. One I got so lost in that I forgot we were on a train with an audience.

When we broke apart to breathe, I moved ever so slightly so I wouldn't giggle in her face. "By the looks of it, we're going to pull this off nicely."

I nodded at the two fifty-somethings across the aisle who were staring at us with wide eyes. A pleased expression crossed her face, and she nodded back. "We're definitely going to pull this off."

* * *

Sleeping soundly in the most comfortable hotel bed I'd ever laid in, my eyes fluttered open to some loud banging on our door. Jordyn appeared from her room. Not wanting to be presumptuous, she booked us adjoining rooms. Now she came out of hers, groggy, and wearing a tank top and flannel PJ shorts.

"You didn't illegally record someone again, did you?"

I tilted my head and gave her a long, hard stare, hoping my laser beam glare was enough of an answer.

"Okay. Okay. Just checking."

The banging only got louder as Jordyn went to open it. "Glad to see you made it here in one piece, since you weren't responding to my texts," the voice said.

"What are you doing here?"

"Hello, I'm staying two floors down. It's not a big deal. I thought you might want a ride over to Dottie's house for the rehearsal dinner, and it's a good thing I did. You're not even dressed."

"We got in after 2 a.m.. Excuse us for sleeping in."

"We?" Sabrina walked fully into the room and turned around to look at Jordyn, but got a face full of me sitting up in bed instead. Her eyes were covered with tinted sunglasses, but I could see them widening.

"What the hell are you doing here?"

"Isn't it obvious? Just got done screwing your sister."

Jordyn covered her mouth to mask her amusement. "She's joking."

Sabrina shook like she had the heebie-jeebies. "Please refrain from joking about my sister's sex life in my presence. I rather you answer me, what are you doing here?"

"I invited her to the wedding tomorrow as my date," Jordyn answered for me.

"You're joking again, and if you aren't, this is the most inappropriate time to be telling me about it."

"I didn't know I needed to consult you on who I brought as my plus one. The last time I checked, you aren't the one getting married."

"I have made my feelings about Whit explicitly clear. Why can't you respect I don't want her anywhere near me?"

"Gotta love being talked about like you're not even in the same room," I mumbled under my breath.

"I don't care if you think I'm being rude. You have done terrible things to me, but I'm supposed to look past that because you're all buddy buddy with my sister now? No. Not happening."

"What you're not about to do is come into my room, insult my date, and force me to take sides. I told you before I wasn't going to having this and that hasn't changed. Now, unless you want me to give you another black eye, I suggest you keep Whit's name out of your mouth moving forward."

The sisters stood toe to toe. You would've never guessed Jordyn was ever considered the weaker of the two. She stood strong and defiant while Sabrina faltered under her gaze. Sensing that she had been bested, Sabrina took a step back and half-heartedly muttered an apology.

"Apology accepted. Can you offer one to Whit?"

"My apology quota was just filled," she said, making excuses for herself not to be a decent person. "Be ready in ten or I'll leave without you," she warned as walked out of the room.

Jordyn leaned against the wall, sighing. "Sometimes I don't know how to handle her. She's so hard to deal with. She drains all the energy out of me every time we talk."

"Is that why you punched her?"

"I punched her after you confided in me why you guys' friendship ended. I confronted her about her not believing you about Mike. She accused you of lying and I... lost it."

"You didn't have to do that for me, but I'm glad that you did."

"I would do a lot of things for you, Whit. You only have to name it." Those were her parting words to me before she went back to her room and closed the door. I laid there on my bed when I should've been getting ready. As her promise resonated in my ears, I silently made the same pledge to her.

With a minute to spare, we were ready and down in the lobby. Sabrina pulled her car around and was waiting for us. When we got inside, her hand was tapping on the steering wheel impatiently.

"We're here on time," Jordyn pointed out.

"If you moved with some urgency, you would've been here earlier," she shot back.

I ignored her comment and looked out of the window as we sped down the highway. When we arrived at Dottie's street, we had to park near the end of the block because of how many cars were on the street. Almost all of the Price family managed to make it to cousin Sean's wedding.

We hopped out of the car and Sabrina walked ahead of us. When she was out of earshot, I whispered to Jordyn, "Anything I should know so I don't embarrass myself with your family?"

"You've met some of them before. Dottie came to the high school graduation party we threw for Sabrina and you."

"I know, but I'm not as well versed on Bryan's side of your family." They didn't come around a lot. The most I knew about them came secondhand from Sabrina. From what I heard, Dottie did not approve of Eliza because of how she and Bryan got together.

The story goes Eliza was married to Henry, Sabrina's father, when she met Bryan. Henry traveled for work, leaving Eliza alone with a newborn. It wasn't much of a surprise to hear she found comfort in someone. The surprise came from her becoming pregnant with Jordyn less than a year after having Sabrina.

Henry and Eliza's marriage ended not that long later with no legal battles or drama. The only one who was outraged by the affair was Dottie. She was a Christian woman who resented Eliza for being a divorced adulterer and for making her son one too. It didn't help the couple moved to Wayland to aid Eliza's sick mother prior to her passing and ended up staying, taking Bryan and her new granddaughters further away from her.

Still, no matter how much Dottie disliked Eliza, by all accounts, she was the best grandmother. She visited the kids for holidays and sent presents all the time. She was even accepting when Jordyn came out, caring more about her granddaughters' happiness than her beliefs.

"You don't have to be nervous about my family. If anyone should be nervous, it should be me. You seemed to have a thing for all the women in my family. I'm afraid if I introduce you to any more of them, you'll have crushes on them, too."

"Asshole!" I yelled, playfully slugging her in the arm.

Sabrina made it to the door first, and before we knew it, it opened to reveal Dottie. "Didn't I tell you to be here at the top of the hour?"

"Please don't get onto me about that. It's Jordyn's fault. She was the holdup," Sabrina said before going inside.

Dottie's eyes fell on Jordyn and warmed instantly. "Jordyn! You made it. I'm so happy to see you."

She roped her into her arms and gave her a tight hug. It was obvious how much Dottie missed her. They hadn't seen each other in person since the aforementioned graduation party. That was two years ago, but Dottie looked how I remembered her. Late 60s, glowing golden skin, brunette hair wrapped in a scarf. She was in sweats, which was appropriate since she was indeed sweating. The preparing for the rehearsal dinner looked to have her a bit off kilter.

She stepped back to take a better look at Jordyn, taking in her blonde buzz-cut, her piercings, and new tattoo. "I was getting used to the buzzcut and piercings. Now you've gone and got a tattoo on me?"

"You don't hate it, do you?"

"I've seen worse. Do you and your friend want to come inside?"

We nodded and followed her inside. Although not huge, the place felt spacious because of the number of people in it. The wedding party crowded into the living room and connecting hallway. The house must have been filled with nearly 25 people, yet the atmosphere remained upbeat.

Laughter echoed through the room, accompanied by the lively melodies of music. I was busy absorbing the mood I didn't see who was at my feet until I felt a tug on my sleeve. I looked down and noticed the little girl who was trying to get my attention. She held out her hands and showed me her coloring book.

"You look like her," she said, smiling up at me with big brown eyes. I looked at the page and saw it was Princess Tiana.

"You look like her too."

"No, I don't. I'm too little."

I crouched down, so we were eye to eye. "It doesn't matter how small or big you are, you can be a princess. All girls are."

She touched the sides of her face as if to make sure it was really true
— that she looked like a princess, too. "I'm a real princess?"

"Yes, you're a real princess." She hugged my hip, thanking me for
making her dreams come true. She ran off, happy and confident with
herself.

I glanced at Jordyn, who was staring at me with the same admiration.
"You didn't even know that girl was Sean's daughter, and you still
helped her out."

"I knew she was your family. That's all I needed to know." I shrugged,
not wanting her to think too much of it.

"Come on, I want to introduce Dottie to you properly. I want her
to know who you are to me. She'll spread the word."

The smell of toasted ravioli took over my senses as Jordyn led me
into the kitchen. On the stove, food in tin foil was being warmed by
Dottie while a middle-aged Black man was drying the wet dishes. He
spotted us and grinned. "Jordyn! I love that tattoo. You were inspired
by me, weren't you?"

"Uncle Morris, your tattoos were not my inspiration, and they
actually hurt my case for getting one. Dad pointed to yours as a
reason I shouldn't get one."

"Your old man doesn't know what he's talking about. He never does
unless it's about the law."

Jordyn chuckled at her uncle's remark, but Dottie didn't find it
funny. "Don't talk about your brother like that. He's in the backyard.
He could overhear you."

"You gotta admit that sometimes he misses the little things in life…
like tattoos. That lawyer's brain of his is just too big."

Dottie simply shook her head. Her eyes landed in my direction and
she realized she hadn't addressed me yet. "Where are your manners,
Jordyn? You haven't introduced me to your friend yet."

"Grandma, this is Whit. You've met her at her and Sabrina's graduation party."

"That's right. You both looked so beautiful in your gowns." Dottie beamed as she reached out to give me a hug. It felt like one of Bryan's hugs, a warm bear hug that surrounded me with love.

"Nice to see you again, Dottie. I trust you have been doing well since then?"

"I am. How are you girls liking college?"

"It's going," I answered bluntly. "It's a lot of work, but we're managing."

"Get your education and you can both be as successful as Bryan."

"And mom," Jordyn interjected.

"Yeah, her too." Jordyn and I exchanged knowing looks. "Are coming to the wedding tomorrow, Whit?"

"Yeah. I'm Jordyn's date."

"Date?" Uncle Morris's ears perked up. "You two are an item?"

Before we got a chance to confirm, Sabrina walked in with a glass in her hand. "They're just friends."

"No, we're not. We're more than that now," Jordyn replied, putting my arm around her shoulders.

Dottie rushed to congratulate us. "Love really is in the air! Good for you two."

"Way to steal the spotlight off of Sean and Naomi," Uncle Morris joked.

Caught between doubt and anger, Sabrina stared at us with a blank expression. She scoffed before sitting down at the table in the room's corner.

"Something you want to say, Sab?"

"Nothing you want to hear, Jordo."

The sound of shoes approaching made us turn to the entryway. Bryan and Eliza came in from the backyard, their eyes flew to Sabrina.

Not yet seeing us. "I thought you were going to refill my drink for me," Bryan directed to her.

"I got distracted."

They followed her line of sight and finally noticed us. They walked over to us, the biggest smiles on their faces. Eliza hugged me first while Bryan hugged Jordyn, then they traded us for the other. "It's so good to see you girls. Especially you, Whit. Nobody told us you were coming," Eliza explained.

"Why wouldn't she come? She's dating Jordyn. Of course she was coming," Dottie said as she and Morris picked up the food and carried it to the backyard.

"Dating?" Eliza looked at Bryan, then at us. "Jordyn, did you forget to tell us something?"

"Maybe," she said slyly. "Don't be mad. It was supposed to be a surprise."

"It certainly is one," Bryan laughed off. "I see why now Sabrina was distracted. That caught us all off guard."

"You know, Whit, when I asked you to watch out for Jordyn, I never could've predicted this would happen. You realize you're responsible for her now, right?"

"Mom!"

"I'm sorry. I'm a little taken aback. I never saw this happening with you two. Maybe you and Sabrina, but not you and Jordyn."

"I think what Eliza is trying to say is we're happy for you girls. This is surprising, but sometimes the unpredictable things are the most beautiful," Bryan noted.

"If I hear any more of this garbage, I'm going to barf," Sabrina interrupted before standing and walking into the bathroom.

Eliza blocked out Sabrina's comment and focused on me and Jordyn. "I'm thrilled for you both, really. In due time, Sabrina will be too. Give her some time to get used to this. It can be weird when your best friend starts dating your sister. I wouldn't personally know, but it was like that on Friends."

"I never watched that," Jordyn admitted.

"Right. Well, Sabrina is Ross."

"Sounds appropriate given what I've heard of about him."

Eliza looked like she wanted to laugh, but knew that wouldn't be right. "Anyway. It was for him for like a minute, but then he realized Chandler and Monica were in love and he saw the beauty in it. Sabrina will too, if it gets that serious with you two. Who knows if it works out, we'll be attending your wedding in a few years."

My stomach dropped. This fake dating thing was for the purpose of messing with Sabrina, not for Eliza to get wild ideas about me becoming her daughter-in-law. Bryan attempted to reel her in. "Hon, they hated each other's guts two months ago. Let's cool it on the wedding talk. Let's let them figure it out and see where it goes."

"Thanks, dad."

"No problem. Now we need to freshen up. Dinner is starting soon."

Finally alone in the kitchen, Jordyn and I exhaled. "Guess the hard part is over?" I asked, hopeful.

She tugged me closer by the waist and pecked me on the lips. "Now the fun begins."

24

Her Cousin's Wedding

The rehearsal dinner went off without a hitch. For as much as I was looking forward to tormenting Sabrina with my new fake relationship, I was more than relieved the night passed without incident.

Sabrina went out of her way to sit as far from me and Jordyn as possible during dinner, never once meeting our gaze. It made our plans to get under skin a bust, but we preferred it to her ruining the rehearsal dinner. Plus, not having to play up the charade of being a lovey-dovey couple was a win. It let me and Jordyn off the hook to be normal and enjoy ourselves rather than perform for Sabrina's grimace.

After dinner, we said our goodbyes and caught a ride with Sean and his four groomsmen. They were staying at the same hotel as us, the one Sean would be wed in, and were quick to offer us a ride. Exhausted from the past 24 hours, we stumbled to our hotel room, barely making it to our beds before collapsing.

I awoke the next morning to find the room empty except for me. "Jordyn?" I called out, but there was no answer.

After I got dressed, I ventured out into the hallway to see if anyone else was up. There was no sign of Jordyn or the groomsmen. I got on the elevator and went down to the lobby. There, I saw her by the entrance chatting with a girl. At first, I only saw the back of her head, but she turned and revealed her side profile and my breath caught in my throat.

It was Jenny Liao, as in Jordyn's ex-girlfriend. Her first love, and to my knowledge, her only love. What the hell was she doing in St. Louis? She left Wayland for an out-of-state college, but surely it wasn't in St. Louis. Was it?

As I stood there watching them talk, a sick, twisted knot formed in my stomach. What was she doing here? Was this some kind of cosmic joke? I needed to get closer and hear what they were saying. To disguise myself, I hastily grabbed a baseball cap and sunglasses from the gift shop counter rack and put them on. Inch by inch, I crept closer to them, barely breathing as I strained to listen to their conversation.

For the first minute, they talked about nothing worth mentioning. I was almost ready to berate myself for thinking I would be brought up. When my name was dropped, so did my heart.

"I didn't want to bring this up during breakfast because we had so much to catch up on, but I can't let you go without asking. Is it true you're friends with Whitney now?"

"What? Are you a journalist now?"

"No, but I took a class," Jenny laughed. "Sorry. I'm not trying to interrogate you. I was just curious where that rumor came from."

"It probably comes from it being true. Whit and I became friends this year. Even crazier is that we're dating."

"I'm not surprised she's sapphic, but you as her girlfriend? I don't buy it."

"It's true. I wouldn't make that up."

"That's... wow. Didn't we break up so we could date new people, not people we already knew?"

"A journalist and a comedian now. Got any more skills? You could be a triple threat." Jordyn sounded like she was trying to keep things easygoing, but I could feel she wasn't liking Jenny's reaction to the news.

"I'm sorry again. Truly. I think I'm in shock. How did this happen?"

"She wanted to be friends. We gave it a go, and it turns out I really like her. Beyond her looks, she's funny, kind. She makes me want to be more selfish."

"That's a good thing?"

"Yeah. If it weren't for her, I would still be a doormat for Sabrina to walk over. I'm standing up for myself and asserting myself more now than I ever have before. That's because of her and her confidence in me."

"That's great and I'm glad you like her, but are you sure she likes you? As more than a friend, I mean."

"Jenny, don't do that."

"Don't do what?"

"Try to ruin something I'm happy about."

"That's not what I'm trying to do, but it's hard for me to believe Whitney would ever be interested in you romantically. That's not an insult, I promise. I just wonder if she's using you for something."

I considered grabbing the vase on the display table I was hiding behind and throwing it at Jenny's head. Did I really like Jordyn? What kind of question was that? I didn't like how she planted seeds of doubts in Jordyn's mind about me.

"Will you stop referring to her as Whitney?" Jordyn asked, annoyed on my behalf. "She goes by Whit and she isn't playing me. She likes me as much as I like her. I don't know why that's inconceivable for you to believe, but it's the truth."

"I didn't mean to offend you. Jor, I was your friend for years before we ever dated. You told me about your crush on her, and how often does it happen where the "straight girl" turns out to be not so straight and likes the girl crushing on her back? It's one in a million. I wanted to make sure that wasn't clouding your judgment."

"It's not, but thanks for your concern."

They spoke for another minute, but my ears tuned them out. Jordyn defended me to her ex, defended our relationship like it was real. Defending our friendship was one thing, but our pretend romantic relationship too? What was I to make of that? The only thing I knew was I had to make sure Jordyn never regretted defending me. She could never know Jenny was right, that what we had started off with me using her for my selfish need for revenge.

Before they noticed me, I placed the cap and glasses back where they belonged and sprinted toward the elevator. By the time Jordyn came back to our room, I was sitting on my made up bed, scrolling on my phone.

"You were up early," I commented when she stopped in her tracks, seeing me.

"I got us some breakfast from downstairs. We might have to wait a while before eating at the wedding. I didn't want you to get hungry and start complaining."

"I'm not a child you have to feed to stop from misbehaving."

"Do you want the food or not?"

I motioned for her to give it to me, and she smiled as she handed it over. I took out the sausage biscuit and took a bite. It was delicious and I couldn't help but thank her.

"No problem, just be sure to save some room for the reception dinner, alright?"

If she was close enough, I would've shoved her. Since she wasn't, I opted to ask the million dollar question. "Did you run into anyone down stairs?"

"No one from the wedding party."

Not a lie, but not the answer I was looking for. "I'm going to be straight with you. I went looking for you after I woke up and I saw you talking to Jenny. I thought you invited her to the wedding or something."

"Me with two dates? Who do you think I am? Casanova? I'm lucky to have the one."

"I couldn't think of another reason she might be here."

"Jenny has family here and when I told her I'll be in the city, she decided to visit for the weekend to see them and me. We had breakfast together downstairs."

"I didn't realize you kept in touch."

A peculiar smirk came over her face as she set down on the bed across from me. "Is that jealousy I hear in your voice?"

"No. I was merely stating a fact. I didn't know you kept in touch with your ex-girlfriend. Now I do."

That smirk didn't go away. It got bigger. "I usually hate how jealously looks on people, but it looks good on you."

"I'm not jealous. We're not together. I have no reason to be jealous."

She came over to my side of the bed and sat. She took my sandwich from me and put it in the bag. Her finger traced down my leg as she positioned herself between them. "Too bad I liked the idea of you being jealous."

"If you want me to be jealous, how about you give me something to be jealous about?"

"Something like this?" She grabbed my chin and pulled me in for a too quick of a kiss. When she moved away, I could still feel the heat of her on my lips.

I craved more as my heart raced. With a smile, I pulled her closer by grabbing her waist until our foreheads touched. "I'll need more than that before I'm jealous," I exhaled against her lips before pressing another kiss on them.

It was like the time seemed to freeze around us, held captive by this one moment of bliss. We were lost in each other, exploring every inch of our faces, while playing with the soft curve of our lips and caressing cheeks as if discovering them for the first time. Our bodies were pressed together like glue and it was enough to make me forget my own name.

The kiss deepened, passion and desire were evident in our movements as neither of us wanted to pull away. I used my tongue to explore her partly open lips, savoring every hint of sweetness that made up her. Heat surged through my entire body, replacing the air in my lungs.

I never wanted the kiss to end, and when it did, I found myself wanting so much more.

"Jealous now?"

She was joking, but I was over the jokes and the flirting that went nowhere. "No, because I can't be jealous of something that isn't real."

Her face softened, my words hitting their mark. Before she could get out a word, a knock interrupted her. "You two better be getting dressed and not undressed. Dottie wants us downstairs in 10 minutes. I won't be blamed for you being late again, so hurry the hell up!" Sabrina on the other side yelled.

"You heard her," I said, getting up and heading into the bathroom, leaving Jordyn and our conversation behind me.

My dress, the first I would wear in months, hung over the shower's rod. When I started packing for the trip, I didn't think I had a dress that would fit me with the extra pounds I'd gained, but I stumbled upon a dress my mom ordered and sent for my birthday last year that had been a size too big. I was pleased to find that it now fit me perfectly.

It was a beautiful mid-length ruby spaghetti strap a-line dress; the soft fabric floated around my body in an almost ethereal way. I checked myself out in the mirror after putting it on and I felt beautiful. Jordyn was already waiting for me downstairs and her smile told me she thought so, too.

She was wearing a tan cropped vest and trousers set. She had paired them with some black Doc Martens. Dapper didn't quite do her justice. "It's surreal to see you in a dress again, but it looks like you were made for it."

"You either really think that or you're kissing my ass to make up for earlier."

"How about both?" She laughed before extending her arm. "Shall we?"

I interlocked my arm with hers and we headed out to the banquet hall where the wedding was being held. From one end to the other, chairs were positioned on both sides of the aisle, creating an unbroken stretch. On the backs of them were white roses and white tulips, all tied up with a cyan ribbon. Down the aisle was a sky blue carpet and at the end was an arch of roses and tulips. It looked like something right out of a fairytale.

A few guests were already been seated. One of which was Dottie, who was getting up to head toward us. "You both look so beautiful today!"

"Thank you," we replied in unison. "So do you," I added.

She was wearing an aubergine sheath dress and pearls. Much like the rest of her look, her hair was up in an elegant bun. "Don't let me hold you up. Find your seats. The wedding will start soon."

Obeying her, we found our seats in the third row. In minutes, guests began to settle in, filling the empty chairs. Trying to sneak a glimpse at all who entered, I caught Sabrina's eye. She was sitting directly behind us, no more pleased about the seating arrangement than I was.

For comfort and maybe a bit of spite, I reached for Jordyn's hand. She obliged, and I could tell by the way her eyes lit up that it was no trouble for her. As we waited for the ceremony to start, a wave of calmness hit me. No matter what Sabrina did, Jordyn was the best distraction. She could relieve my worries with a single squeeze of the hand.

That was the thing with Jordyn. I never had to worry if I said or did the wrong thing with her. Not that long ago with a certain blonde, I felt like I was walking on eggshells. I worried if I touched her too much, I might scare her away. If I said the wrong thing, I might push her away.

I jumped through hoops and stayed in a constant state of anxiety to please her, but with Jordyn, it was different. There was no fear — just a feeling of complete ease and comfort. It took me far too long to realize this kind of feeling existed and now that I had it, I never wanted to let it go.

The strings quartet broke me out of my realization as it played. Everyone's eyes turned to see Sean making his way down. He settled at the end of the aisle, sporting the biggest smile I had ever seen.

The bridesmaids were out next, wearing teal dresses. They were accompanied by the groomsmen in black suits and blue ties. Then Sean and Naomi's daughter, whose name I learned was Josie, walked down, throwing rose petals everywhere.

When the opening notes of Pachelbel's Canon sounded, everyone rose. Naomi walked arm and arm with her father, beaming as she saw Sean. She looked gorgeous in her white gown with a tulle skirt and beaded bodice adorned with crystal beads. Her hair was pinned above her shoulders, a transparent veil dotted with white spots trailed behind her. Her hands were in silk gloves, her shoes a pair of shining silver pumps that matched her earrings and necklace.

As they approached the altar, Sean wiped away tears forming in his eyes. Naomi's father handed her off to him with a nod, then sat down next to his wife, Sean's mom, and Uncle Morris in the front row. Everyone followed his lead and sat. The officiant welcomed all the guests, then asked if Sean had his own vows. He did.

Sean took Naomi's hands into his and squeezed them, taking a moment to smile at her before he spoke. He declared his undying love for her, promising that no matter what difficult times they might face in the future, he would always be devoted to her and their family. Finally, he punctuated the end of the vows with "I love you, now and always."

The smile on Naomi's face couldn't be wiped off even as she begun to speak. She said she never thought she could love someone as much as she loved Sean and Josie. She thanked him for never giving up on them and promised to be just as committed and devoted to him as he would be to her.

The pastor finished by declaring them husband and wife. All that was left was to seal the vows with a kiss, and the two did just that. They embraced, creating a shining beacon of happiness in the middle of the room. We could feel the love they shared for each other, including Josie. She smiled, watching her parents cling to each other.

Morris pulled her close to him and whispered in her ear. Seconds later, she skipped towards her mother and father. The family of three embraced in a tight embrace, both parents kissing Josie on either cheek. They all held hands as they walked down the aisle. Everyone erupted in applause, showering them with congratulatory wishes.

After everyone left the banquet hall, we went to the reception being held in the hotel's garden. Candles lined our path from the entrance to the fountain. Above us, the sun still shined but temperatures had cooled off and there was a pleasant breeze. Shade from tall trees and the lanterns hanging on branches cast romantic shadows on the white tablecloths and chairs.

The band they hired sat on the small raised stage playing a sweet, jazzy tune, setting up the relaxed ambience. Compared to the banquet hall, the garden felt like a chill family reunion rather than an expensive event. Guests split off, some sitting at their assigned table and others standing by the fountain, taking in the sights and sounds while mingling with each other.

Jordyn and I sat at our table. No surprise we were seated with Sabrina, who was on her phone, pretending we weren't there. Jordyn coughed to get her attention, but Sabrina's eyes were still glued to the device.

"Nice dress," I commented, looking at her chiffon sage green attire.

"You don't have to be nice to me. God knows I'm not looking to return it."

"Sab, it's Sean's wedding. Can't we all try to get along for his and Naomi's sake?"

"I'm trying. I'm on my phone because if I have to see you two making googly eyes at each other, I'll have no choice but to stab myself in the eye with a fork."

"What is it about us being together that hurts you so much? Jealous?"

"What do I have to be jealous of? This so-called relationship will crash and burn before long because Whit won't be able to stop herself from destroying it. She'll screw you over, then find a way to make herself look like a victim. Jordo, she's an opportunist who couldn't care less about you, just what you can do for her. She is going to break your heart when she's done with you. I just hope it's before you fall in love with her," she added with a parting glare at me before leaving to get some food.

Her words hung heavy at our table. Neither of us said anything for a long moment, our eyes still on the spot she had been standing. Finally, I looked at Jordyn and saw the sadness in her eyes. "I'm sorry," I whispered. Shaking her head, she sadly smiled and went to get us drinks.

She returned moments later and handed me a water bottle. I

watched as she lifted her glass up in a toast. "To proving her wrong, but more importantly to doing what we want and not worrying about what others think."

I clinked my drink with hers, savoring the moment until Eliza and Bryan came up to us. They were glowing like it was their own wedding. "Hello girls. You look amazing. Sorry for not having time to say that before the ceremony," Bryan said while Eliza gave us each a hug.

"We have had no time alone with either of you and now you're about to leave in the morning," she complained.

"Look on the bright side. Thanksgiving is coming up. I'll be home for that."

"What about you, Whit? What are your plans for Thanksgiving?"

"I'll be spending it with Winnie. Maybe my parents, if they can take themselves away from their jobs for long enough."

"Why don't you guys come to our dinner? We would love to have you, and it gives you and Jordyn more time to be together."

I looked at Jordyn and could tell she loved the idea. "I'll have to ask Winnie, but I think she'll like the break from cooking. "

"We'll make room for you both in the hopes the answer is yes," Bryan added.

An influx of cheers from guests made us turn to the entrance. Naomi, Sean, and Josie walked out hand in hand together. Naomi had changed into a new dress, one more suited for dancing. Josie watched from the side as her parents went to the dancefloor. The sun set, sending an orange hue over the couple swaying in each other's arms. The only person who matched how happy they were was Josie.

Naomi's mom and dad were the first couple to join them, then Morris and his wife Jackie followed them. Bryan offered his hand to Eliza. She smiled and accepted. Soon more couples were out on the dancefloor.

Jordyn turned to me, a glint in her eye. "Shall we?"

"I thought you didn't dance?"

"I'll make an exception for you. Tonight only, though, so I wouldn't pass this up if I were you."

Not wasting an opportunity to see Jordyn dance, I stepped forward onto the floor with her. To my surprise, she took the lead. Even more impressive was she was good at it. She swayed me to the music's beat, only to then dip me low and twirl me in all sorts of directions.

For someone who hated to dance, she was quite good at it. I wonder how that came to be. As if she was reading my mind, Jordyn smiled before whispering, "I'm a quick learner." She pulled me in close and I rested my head against her chest.

Couples like her mom and dad passed by us, but our feet were planted in that one spot. The song ended and played into another, but we still didn't make a move to return to our seats. We swayed in each other's arms and didn't plan on stopping. We were quiet for a long time until Jordyn broke it.

"You know I'm not doing this for Sabrina, right? I'm doing this for me."

I paused, unsure of how to respond. I wasn't doing it for her either, but if we were both doing this for ourselves, that made things more complicated. "I know," I whispered back, "that's why it feels—"

"Real. It feels real," she finished.

"It felt real in the beginning too. That first kiss? Nothing felt fake or confused about it. Not to me, but apparently it did to you."

She tensed up before inhaling. "It wasn't fake for me either. I played it off like it was meaningless to save face. I didn't know if what happened meant as much to you as it did to me, so I gave us both a way out."

"I didn't want a way out. I only took it because I thought you did."

"What I wanted was not to scare you. Our friendship was just getting good, and I didn't want to ruin it by admitting I felt something deeper toward you than just friendship."

"You wouldn't have scared me. What you're saying isn't scary. It's the one thing I've wanted to hear. I like you, Jordyn. Not for show, not for any other reason other than I really, truly do."

We were so close together. I felt her heart pounding against mine as she finally spoke the words she had been holding in. "I like you too. It's why I agreed to pretend to be your girlfriend. I thought it might be my one and only chance to hold that title."

"It doesn't have to be." I pulled my head off her chest so she could see my smile. I hoped it told her how much she was making me feel right then. "You're the thought that pushes me out of bed when I struggle to see a reason to wake up. I think of talking to you and trying to get you to smile. Or get you to laugh. Oh, your beautiful laugh. I think of hearing it and it's enough to carry me out of bed. You don't just make my day better. You make it, period. We were fooling ourselves when we said this was pretend because nothing I have ever felt for you has been pretend."

"I feel the same way about you."

"Then why don't we stop pretending and do this for real? Would you like to have the title of being my girlfriend? The real one."

Jordyn chuckled like she couldn't believe this was actually happening. She leaned in close and smiled shyly. "Yes," she whispered on my lips before making them her own.

"No take-backs," I teased, drawing back.

"The only take back I want is to take you back upstairs. If that's what you want too?"

I stroked her cheek, feeling her blush beneath my fingertips. "There's nothing I want more."

25

Happy Guilt Day

A weekend away didn't ease the chaos I'd left behind on campus. The news about Dean Clayton's firing and of the expose on campus' sexual assaults had spread like wildfire. I returned to protesters camped outside of the administration building with signs demanding justice and demanding students be protected from further harm.

The protests grew louder as the week went on and with each passing day, more students joined in. Some even started boycotting classes to show their solidarity with those protesting. That is, if you believed that was their reasoning and not because they wanted to ditch. Regardless of their motivation, the protests hadn't gone away. Yet the administration had been silent about what they were planning to do about the situation, and that made matters worse.

The only acknowledgment that they were listening to us at all was the announcement that the fraternities and sororities were suspended indefinitely. However, if they thought that would calm things down, they were wrong. Students were more upset, knowing this was a result of pressure from us and yet, there was still no resolution in sight.

Campus felt like a powder keg waiting to explode. Until it did, I took refuge in my dorm. Jordyn had been around a few times to keep me company, but with mid-terms coming up, we spent more time studying and less doing the whole dating thing. That's why I was a bit surprised to see on one afternoon.

"Come in. It's open," I shouted without looking up from my textbooks or getting up from my desk.

"No warm welcome for your girlfriend?"

A warmth spread through me as I felt her wrap one of her arms around me. "Sorry. Midterms have me a little preoccupied."

"I get it, but you need to take a break. Especially considering what day it is."

My ears perked up at the sudden cheeriness of her tone. "You know, don't you?"

"Of course, I do. I would make for a pretty lousy girlfriend if I didn't know today was your birthday." As I leaned back and relaxed, she held a cupcake in front of me. "I figured since you didn't tell me it was your birthday, you didn't want to make a big deal of it."

"You would be right. It's just another day for me."

"Fair enough, but it's still worth celebrating. So happy birthday. I'm very happy you were born."

I smiled as I took the cupcake from her and ate a bite. "Thanks Jor. This is really nice," I said, meaning more than just the cupcake.

She nodded before closing my textbook for me. "Get dressed. We're going out."

"I told you I don't want to make a big deal out of today. Winnie called, my parents and I video chatted, and I got a cupcake from you. That's more than enough."

"You don't want to make a big deal out of your birthday. I respect that, so let's make a big deal out of something else. Say like our first official date as a couple?"

I should've figured Jordyn would make the day special for me even with my resistance. A smile crept onto my face. "You're insistent, aren't you?"

"Yes, but only because we're both entitled to a break. So go get dressed! We don't have all night."

I rolled my eyes but got up to do what she demanded of me. After I got dressed, we went out into the city, exploring quaint streets and unique shops before stopping for dinner at an intimate bistro with outdoor seating along the river walk. The view was stunning, but the company was better.

"Thank you for this. I needed this more than I would've cared to admit. Between the tension on campus and the pressure of midterms, I was feeling overwhelmed."

"I noticed, which is why I wanted to do this for you. I thought it would be an excellent distraction and a nice breather." Jordyn reached for my hand across the table. "We can talk about anything or nothing at all."

"I want to talk about my favorite subject: you. Anything interesting happen since the last time we talked?"

"Things have been quiet on my front. Though that hasn't been the case for Amelia."

"Why? What happened?"

With a sigh, Jordyn's face grew darker. "They found out that Amelia's ID badge was used to get into Mitchell Hall and the newspaper room the night before the story was printed. That has led them to believe she was the one behind the story coming out."

My stomach dropped. Some students made it known they suspected Amelia was the one behind the story coming out, but I didn't think their theory would go anywhere. I was the one behind it, not her. Even with her badge being used, it shouldn't have been enough to implicate her.

"This has to be a mistake. No way Amelia was behind this. She values her journalist career too much to risk it like this. Could her ID have been used by someone else?"

"She did lose it for like two days. Eventually she found it in a lost & found box. The administration didn't care when she told them that. They won't listen to reason. They believe all the signs point to her. So they suspended her from the school and the paper."

"No. This can't be happening. Where was she that night? If she was with someone, they can give her an alibi for the time when her badge was used."

Jordyn shook her head. "She was supposed to be with a study group, but it was canceled at the last minute. She went back to our dorm and studied alone. I was in a class and when it finished I went to library and stayed for two hours. I couldn't lie to help her even if I wanted to because Mrs. Campbell can attest to me being there."

"There has to be something we can do to help her. She can't go down for something she didn't even do."

"Unless you have a lead on who really is behind this, I'm not sure there's anything we can do."

The choices I had were to let my new friend take the fall for my actions or to face the consequences of what I'd done. Guilt bubbled up inside me because I knew I couldn't come forward. Not after everything I'd done to protect myself from being found out. At the same time, I couldn't just let her take the blame for me either.

"I shouldn't have brought this up," Jordyn apologized. "It's your birthday and our first date. I shouldn't have ruined it by bringing up that downer of a story."

"No, it's okay. Amelia is your friend, which makes her mine, too. We'll figure something out to help her."

Jordyn's mood lifted at that and we moved on to lighter topics, but my mind was still preoccupied with how my actions unintentionally screwed Amelia over. The burden of guilt and remorse weighed heavily on my chest, making it feel heavier. I knew myself well enough to know this feeling would not go away until I made this right. Which meant I had to find a way to prove Amelia's innocence without compromising myself. It seemed impossible, but I was determined to fix the mess I made. I just had to figure out how.

26

Stuck in Regrets

"Thanks for meeting with me. I know this is mid-terms week, so I appreciate you taking the time," Dr. Johnson welcomed me into her office with a wide grin.

It was a week before Thanksgiving, also known as mid-terms week. I'd already completed three exams and had two to go before I was free to enjoy the holiday break. Despite my jam-packed schedule, I made time to meet with Dr. Johnson. Clayton did many things wrong in her tenure as the Dean, but making my therapy sessions mandatory was not one of them.

"It was no problem. I've grown not to hate our sessions," I replied with a laugh.

"I'm happy to hear that. Sit. Let's make good use of our time and get started."

Obediently, I sat on the familiar beige couch while Dr. Johnson sat in her usual chair. "So, how have things been going with you since our last session? We haven't gotten the chance to talk since the expose was released. I imagine it had an effect on you."

"Yeah. How couldn't it? Knowing it wasn't just my case the university didn't follow through on made me angry all over again. I wanted my case to be an isolated incident, but the proof that it wasn't has brought all the pain I was feeling back."

"That's completely understandable. The university promised to protect you. To find out they hadn't delivered on their promise must have been hard."

"It was, but what's worse is their response to this. Aside from the generic PR statement, they've been silent. It's like they thought tossing all the blame on Dean Clayton and firing her would solve the problem, when in reality it did nothing to address what happened."

My chest tightened as I spoke. I wrote the expose, thinking it would force the Lakeview to take this seriously, but they still have done nothing. I'm aware I can't make them change their ways overnight, but all I want is some kind of acknowledgment that what happened was wrong and for them to actually commit to doing something about it.

"I feel your frustration. As an employee, I take these kinds of things seriously. I wish there was more I could do to help, but unfortunately, some of the responsibility rests with those in higher positions than me. All we can do is keep pushing and hope that eventually they will listen," Dr. Johnson said to reassure me.

"How do you manage knowing people are going to keep getting hurt and there's only so much you can do to help? I've been struggling with this for a while now."

"I'll say this: it's hard. There are days where I have to be okay with knowing my hands are tied and that there will be casualties in the meantime. What helps me cope is reminding myself that while I can't enforce change at the top, I can change the lives of those I can reach. I can pick up the pieces, provide them with support, and remember that even in the darkest moments, I'm doing everything I can to help others. It won't fix all our problems, but it will give those who need it hope to keep going."

"After my rape, I thought if I did everything I could to prevent someone else from going through the same pain I did, it would heal me. Now I've done all I could do and I'm not anymore healed than before. In fact, I feel worse off now because I'm carrying this burden of guilt."

Dr. Johnson looked at me with a kind understanding in her eyes before saying, "You can't expect to heal in an instant or to find a shortcut to achieve it. It doesn't work like that. Wanting to stop this from happening to someone else is noble, but it won't lessen your pain."

"I learned that firsthand," I said, exhaling slowly. "If I tell you something in confidence, will it stay between us?"

"Depends on what it is."

"It's not criminal. It'll get me expelled, though."

"It was you, wasn't it?" Dr. Johnson asked, pronouncing each syllable slowly. "The one behind the expose?" She didn't sound upset or angry. A hint of understanding laced her tone.

"I thought I was helping, but I made everything worse. I included the names of the victims in the piece, thinking it would make a bigger impact. I didn't think about what they wanted and a lot of them didn't want their names out there."

"To make things even worse, one of my friends is being blamed for the piece, even though she had nothing to do with it. I can't come forward without jeopardizing my future, but I'm sick at the thought of her taking the blame. Everything I've done to help has only hurt people more."

"Whit—"

"No, I'm not done. Can you believe that? I have more shit to atone for." I stood and paced in the small space between the coffee table and couch, growing more frantic by the second. "The one good thing I have going in my life I started it off with a lie."

My therapist blinked, her confusion obvious. "What are you talking about?"

"I sought Jordyn out, not because I wanted to be her friend, but because I wanted to use her to get back at Sabrina. I didn't expect for her to really become my friend. And never in my wildest dreams did I think I would gain feelings for her. I care about her so much. I don't want to lose her, but I'm afraid that is what's going to happen."

I plopped back down on the couch in time to see Dr. Johnson inhaling. "Was that all, or are you hiding any more tortured secrets?"

"That was all of it."

"In that case, let's break this down. One by one. Would you like me to take the Hallmark approach, or I can speak as plainly as I want?"

"The latter."

"While listening to you owe up to each of your secrets one by one, I couldn't help but notice the common denominator in each."

"Which is?"

"Your selfishness. You believed you had the right to do whatever was best for you without considering how it would affect other people. Whether it be you including confidential information in your expose to make it more interesting, you allowing your friend to take the blame for you, or you using Jordyn for your poorly plotted revenge, you were always putting yourself first."

The words stung me like a sharp needle puncturing my skin. "I was blinded by anger. I wanted to get back at the school for not protecting me and Sabrina for not believing me. I'm not excusing my actions, but this was my way of trying to get justice."

For the first time all semester, Dr. Johnson got up and sat down beside me on the couch. She looked me straight in the eye and asked, "Did you get it? Justice, I mean."

"You already know the answer."

"But I want to hear you say it."

"In small doses? Yeah. Revealing the university's wrongdoing, having some fun messing with my ex-best friend and my ex-boyfriend. Getting the frats and sororities suspended until they start doing better. In those moments, it felt like justice."

"But," I gulped down the lump forming in my throat. "Justice isn't like that. It's not about moments of satisfaction, it's about making things right. All I've done is mess everything up."

"You have a chance to make it right."

"By throwing myself to the wolves and losing my spot here, my friendship with Amelia and losing Jordyn?"

"I'm your therapist, not your life coach. My job is to give you advice, but I can't tell you what to do or what decisions to make. I will say to relieve the guilt you're feeling, you need to take real action. It's not enough to feel guilty, you have do something. It'll be difficult, but it's the only way it won't permeate through your whole life."

Dr. Johnson was right. If I really felt as guilty as I said I was, I needed to right my wrongs. I wasn't ready to implode my relationship with Jordyn or lose my spot at the university, but I was ready to face the music. As long as no one else knew.

27

Guess Who's Not Coming To Dinner

After one plane ride and a bus later, Jordyn and I returned home to Wayland. Thanksgiving was the next day, but I couldn't bring myself to feel the joy of the holiday. My mind was consumed with the want to make things right for Amelia. And after my last session with Dr. Johnson, a plan finally formed. I knew how I could help her without sacrificing myself.

In the days between my final midterm and the trip to Wayland, I composed a letter that, if it worked out as I hoped, would let Amelia off the hook without placing me on it. Not a word was spared as I penned an anonymous confession, taking full responsibility for the expose. I exonerated Amelia of any involvement and admitted to using her badge to gain access to Mitchel Hall to tamper with the school's newspaper.

My plan was to print the confession out and leave it in an envelope at the Lakeview's post office after I returned. That way, I reasoned, the truth would be revealed without my future being put at risk and Amelia would be reinstated. Sure, that meant the university would still look into who was behind the letter, but as long as it wasn't traced back to me and no other suspect was identified, I figured I was in the clear.

The plan was far from perfect, and the risks of it blowing up in my face were painfully high, but it was the best thing I could think of to protect Amelia and myself. It wouldn't take effect until I returned to campus after Thanksgiving, so until then I was prepared for the heaviness of the situation to hang over me like a storm cloud.

Jordyn noticed I wasn't in the best of moods on the way over. She chalked it up to me not wanting to return to our hometown. It wasn't a total lie, so I let her believe it.

"When are your parents getting in?" she asked as our Uber turned onto my street.

"Between tonight and never," I answered while watching the houses of my old neighborhood pass by out of the car window.

"What do you mean?"

"They have a habit of saying they're going to show up for something and not following through on it. It doesn't matter if it's a holiday or a birthday, it's what they do."

"This year could be different. Maybe they'll surprise you." Her tone was so earnestly hopeful I almost believed her.

"They won't. They never do."

I could feel her hand intertwining with mine, even without facing her. It was the only source of solace I had, and it proved enough.

After our Uber pulled into my driveway, we unloaded our suitcases from the car before we approached the front door. I told Winnie the bare minimum about my relationship with Jordyn. She knew we were together. Specific details weren't necessary. She was more surprised to hear I was dating the youngest of the Price sisters than she was that I was dating a woman.

Before I could ring the doorbell, Jordyn squeezed my arm. "Will she like me?"

"What are you talking about? You've met her before."

"Yeah, in passing, and never as your girlfriend before. What if she doesn't approve? You said she went to church. What are the odds both of our God-loving elders accept our relationship?"

I laughed and rang the doorbell. "Winnie will love you, but if for some reason she doesn't, that will not stop me from being with you."

"Really?"

"While I rather not take part in the Black and sapphic version of Romeo & Juliet with you, I will if I have to."

Jordyn's face brightened just before she leaned in and kissed me. "I love you," she whispered, her lips still pressed to mine.

The door opened, and Winnie stood before us with a warm smile on her face. She took one look at us and immediately knew what was happening; she'd seen this kind of thing before when my mom was a teenager. The sneaking kisses before the adults turned on the porch light, or worse, the sprinklers.

"Jordyn, it's so good to see you, baby. Though I would prefer to see your entire face and not your lips pressed to my granddaughter's."

She pulled back away from me. My cheeks turned a similar shade of red that mine did. "Hi Mrs. Robinson! It's nice to see you too."

She laughed and shook her head. "I'm not mad, Jordyn. Just disappointed Whit is not introducing me to her girlfriend properly."

"My bad. Grandma, this is Jordyn. Jordyn, this is my Grandma Winnie. You've two have met before, but not in this capacity."

While Jordyn and Winnie exchanged pleasantries, I took in her appearance. It'd been four months since I had seen my grandmother, and she hadn't aged a day. She was still the same short, energetic woman she'd always been with her bright smile and infectious laugh.

After a few moments of talking, Winnie welcomed us inside. "Is this your first time being here, Jordyn?"

"It is. Kinda unbelievable, considering how much time Whit spent time at our place growing up."

"It was her favorite place to be."

"It still is, just for a whole new reason," I responded, looking directly at Jordyn. She was blushing again and if my grandma hadn't been watching us, I would've kissed her right then and there.

Winnie smiled knowingly then said, "Why don't you two take your suitcases to your room and settle in? Dinner is almost ready."

"Wasn't the point of us going to the Prices this year so that you wouldn't have to cook?"

"Yes, but I wanted to make a home cooked meal for you two as a special welcome home. Trust me, I'll leaving Thanksgiving solely to Eliza and Bryan. So go on. I'll call you down when the food is ready."

I turned to go upstairs, but paused and looked back at Winnie. "You didn't turn my room into a gym or something and made this dinner as an apology, did you?"

"What use am I going to get out of a gym at my age? Then you know I love you too much to do something like that. Now go on, take your time and get ready for dinner!"

I lead Jordyn upstairs to my room. As soon as I opened the door, the scent of vanilla filled my nose. Winnie had put a candle on my desk along with a card that read "Welcome Home! Love, Winnie."

As I opened it, something green flew out of the card and landed on my beige carpet. Jordyn picked it up and handed it to me. "$100, huh? Winnie's last bingo game must've gone well."

A smile tugged at my lips as I put the money in my back pocket and let Jordyn explore my room. No matter how much time passed, Winnie would always be the same. And for that, I was grateful.

Jordyn canvassed my room, admiring my Before Sunset and Love, Jones posters. I've hanged them up when I was thirteen and never took them down. The smirk on her face made me grateful I kept them up all these years.

She kept inspecting the room, only stopping at my bookshelf, running her finger along the spines of the novels I collected. "All these books and not one single horror novel. What's with that?"

"I don't know how to tell you this, but I'm too much of a chicken to handle horror books. I can't look away from them like I can from movies. It's scarier in that media."

"What about when I would call or text you at night to talk about the horror books I was reading? You said you didn't mind."

"What can I say? I was there for the girl. Not so much the books."

She glanced down, looking at her shoes instead of me. She was uncharacteristically nervous. "What I said earlier-"

"Oh, you mean those three little words?"

"Yeah... that. I don't know where they came from. I mean, I know where they come from, but..."

"Jor, it's okay. Both you saying it and you possibly not meaning it."

She let out a hard sigh, then faced me. "I hate you because you say shit like that and I start to think I'm really in love with you. Can you do me a favor and stop being so sweet? I don't think my heart can take it."

"I can't help it. It must be love."

She gestured with her lips for me to zip it. "No more love talk. It was a mistake for me to let that slip. It's too soon for us to discussing that, let alone feeling it."

"Alright. No more love talk. I can still be sweet, right? That doesn't have to end?"

She reluctantly smiled and pulled me by my waist to her. "In moderation."

She wrapped her arms around me and all I could think was, how in the hell am I going to resist falling in love with this woman?

* * *

Dinner went perfectly. Jordyn fit into Winnie and I's dynamic seamlessly. I could tell that she enjoyed it as much as we did. To top it all, the food was delicious. Winnie cooked her famous lasagna with garlic bread. And though neither of us were of legal drinking age, Winnie surprised us with a bottle of wine.

After dinner, we retired to our rooms. I woke in the morning to Jordyn in the kitchen with Winnie helping her take a peach cobbler out of the oven.

"I thought we agreed on no cooking today. You just had hip surgery in the summer, remember that?"

"You don't have to remind me. I'm the one who still deals with the pain from it."

"Hence why you shouldn't be cooking two days in a row."

"Oh, it's just a little baking. You know I don't like going to somebody else's house empty-handed."

"Couldn't you have asked dad to pick up something from the store?" Winnie and Jordyn shared a look right then. A look I'd became all too familiar with. "Oh. I see. Let me guess, he and mom didn't get in last night like they said they would."

"They said something popped up. They apologized for not being able to come."

If I still had any faith they would show up today, I would've been disappointed. I didn't even bother asking if they would try to make it for Christmas. There was no point.

Changing subjects, I said, "Jordyn and I should start getting ready. We don't want to keep her parents waiting."

Upstairs, I took a shower and got dressed. When I finished, I saw Jordyn laying on my bed, on her phone, dressed in a long sleeve Janelle Monáe Dirty Computer concert tee and jeans. "And I thought I was dressed too casual."

She looked up at me. The happiness in her eyes from yesterday wasn't there. "You know you're allowed to be upset about your parents aren't coming, right? You don't have to put on a brave face or make jokes, pretending everything is fine."

"Except that it is. Everything is fine. I'm not pretending to be okay. I genuinely am."

Jordyn looked at me skeptically. If I wanted to convince her, I had to make her believe me. "Growing up with my parents always away taught me that if I was ever disappointed by them, the only thing I could do was accept it and move on. There will always be a chance for them to make it up for me."

"Or a chance to disappoint you again."

"Maybe, but that's not for me to worry about today. Today I get to spend time with you and I couldn't ask for anything better."

"You say that now, but two hours at dinner with Sabrina and her unpleasantness may change your mind."

"As long as I get to spend those two hours with you, I'll survive."

The sadness that had been on Jordyn's face a minute ago faded away. She jumped off the bed and grabbed my hand. "We better get going before Sabrina hogs the best food."

I drove the three of us in Winnie's car to the Price's. The door was unlocked, so we walked right in. The aroma of a Thanksgiving feast greeted us as we entered. A football game was on the living room's big screen TV. Eliza was on the couch in front of it, looking bored.

"Hello, Mrs. Price. Thank you for inviting Whit and I to join you today," Winnie said as we walked over to her.

She stood up, a big smile on her face. "First, you know you can call me Eliza. Second, it was our pleasure. Your family is always welcome here."

"We brought you this." I held Winnie's peach cobbler out to her.

Eliza waved her hand. "I've been specially instructed not to touch the food. Bryan is in charge of the kitchen and God forbid, if I were to touch any of it."

"That's probably for the best," Jordyn echoed.

"Jordyn! Not you too."

"Sorry mom, but you know it's true."

Eliza shook her head and chuckled. "You can take that into the kitchen and say hi to Bryan. I'll text Sabrina to pick up some vanilla ice cream to pair with it."

"You sent her out to the store with that crowd?" I asked, trying to suppress my laughter.

"She'll make it out of there unscathed. It's everyone else we should be worried about," Eliza said before sending the text. "Now, I need to get rid of this. Bryan wants one dinner where we all aren't tempted to pull out our phones. He asking, no, demanding everyone leaves their phone upstairs until we're finished eating."

"I love that idea. It'll make it so where we can be present with each other and enjoy the lovely meal he made for us," Winnie added with a smile.

"Leave your phones in your coats and I'll take them upstairs. You can find them in the guest room when the dinner is over." Jordyn and I gave her mom ours, then we took the peach cobbler into the kitchen, ready to say hello to Bryan. We found him mashing potatoes and humming a song we didn't recognize while he worked.

"Dad, do you need any help with that?"

He turned around, his eyes lit up when he saw us. He put down the masher and gave us a hug. "I don't need any help. Dinner is almost done, but I'm so happy to see you two."

"This is for you from Winnie." I handed him the dish, and he took it, sniffing the sweet aroma coming from it.

"I can always count on Winnie to make a mean peach cobbler," he said warmly. "How long do we have you girls in town for?"

"We have plane tickets for tomorrow night."

"That soon?"

"Unfortunately."

"Well, that just means we'll have to make the best of it before you go."

"What can we do? Put us to work," I said, eager to be productive.

"Get the table ready, then you can get yourselves ready for the best Thanksgiving dinner of your life."

"Those are big words," Jordyn teased, already grabbing the plates and silverware from their drawers.

"I'm sure he'll deliver." I grabbed the tablecloth and followed Jordyn into the dining room. The warm lightning of the room matched the warmth of the home. Thanksgiving hadn't started, but it felt like it had the makings of something special already.

We finished setting the table and went to get ready for dinner together, excited to find out if Bryan's food lived up to the hype. When we returned, my senses were overloaded with what all was on the table I had to take in. Golden roasted turkey with all the fixings, steaming mashed potatoes and gravy, casseroles that never appealed to me but suddenly looked appetizing, and a table full of desserts.

"Don't tell me you started eating without me," a voice coming from the front door called out. Sabrina revealed herself by appearing in the doorway with a tub of ice cream, rolls, and wine under her arms.

"You're right on time. Go wash up," Bryan told her, taking the stuff from her.

Sabrina glared at us before she went to the bathroom. She was still no closer to accepting our relationship, but it was alright because we didn't need her approval. Jordyn and I shared a knowing smile before Jordyn excused herself to help Bryan get everything ready.

I followed Sabrina to the bathroom, determined to try to not let our feud impede Thanksgiving. She was already washing her hands by the time I got there.

"Hey," I breathed as I leaned on the door frame of the bathroom, "I know we've been at odds for most of the year."

"That's an understatement if I've ever heard one."

"All I'm asking is that we don't let our shit ruin the holiday. Your parents, Jordyn, and Winnie deserve to enjoy their holiday in peace without us coming to blows, don't you think?"

"You worry too much. I was never going to make a scene. My parents still don't know what happened with us, except for the obvious tension they've noticed, and I would prefer to keep it that way. I assume you feel the same way since Winnie doesn't know either, right?"

"Right, so let's just agree to make it through Thanksgiving with no drama."

"My passive aggressiveness will be in check. I promise."

"Good. Glad to hear it." I turned to leave, but Sabrina's voice stopped me.

"Do you really care about her? Jordyn. I need to know if you're playing with her. She's had a crush on you since forever and I would hate it if you were doing all of this just to get back at me."

"You're the last person who should ask me that. Your treatment of Jordyn has been abysmal, and it has been for a while."

"You're not telling me anything I don't already know. I know I haven't been the greatest sister."

"And why is that?"

Sabrina hesitated before speaking. "I don't know," she finally said. "You know the relationship I have with my mom. Growing up, it felt like she put everyone else before me. Jordyn, especially. And I resented her for it, even though it wasn't her fault."

"You're right. It's not her fault that you have mommy issues and you don't get to take out your frustration with your mom out on her."

"I'm trying to be better, okay? Along with the black eye she gave me, she also gave me a wake-up call. She's my little sister and I should be more protective of her. Which is why I'm asking if you really care about her, because if you don't, end things now before she gets hurt."

I took a deep breath before replying, "I care about her more than I ever thought possible. I have no intention of hurting her, so can we stop this? Please? For everyone else's sake. Let them have their Thanksgiving without us making it uncomfortable."

Sabrina nodded, then followed me downstairs where everyone else was waiting for us. "Everything okay?" Eliza asked.

"Couldn't be better," Sabrina answered, wrapping her arm around my shoulder. I wanted to shrug it off, but I forced a smile and returned the gesture.

"Well, if you two are done being all buddy buddy again, can we finally get to eating?" Bryan asked. Everyone laughed, and Sabrina gave me one last squeeze before letting go.

We pulled up our chairs at the dining table and sat down. Me side by side with Winnie and Jordyn across from me. Sabrina was beside her while Bryan and Eliza were on the opposite ends of the table. We held hands while Bryan said grace before passing around plates for everyone to take one.

"I may have doubted you, Dad, when you said this was going to be the best Thanksgiving meal I've ever had, but you certainly outdid yourself this time," Jordyn complimented after taking a bite of the turkey.

"One day you'll learn not to doubt me."

"I'll know you're truly a primary chef the day you get mom to make a dish that doesn't taste like dishwater."

"Hey! What are these strays I'm catching today?"

"Oh, mom. Don't use slang," Sabrina implored her.

"Why? Did I use it wrong?"

"No, but it sounds funny coming out of your mouth."

"It really does," Jordyn agreed.

"Whit is the same way with me. I can't say anything without her going on a roundabout way of saying I'm old."

"Winnie, I would never call you old. I'm not trying to lose out on a place in your will," I joked. The entire table erupted in laughter.

A lot of laughing had been done by the time Eliza placed a generous helping of Winnie's peach cobbler with a scoop of ice cream on each of our plates.

"This smells heavenly, Mrs. Robinson."

"Girl, you know I don't like being referred to as that. Makes me like I'm Anne Bancroft, and the person speaking to me is Dustin Hoffman."

Sabrina blushed at her mistake. "My apologies, Winnie. I hope I can make up for it by saying you always make the best deserts."

"Made up, you have." Winnie smiled and everyone happily dug into the dessert.

Bryan leaned back in his chair after he finished his plate, taking it all in. "This is why I love Thanksgiving." Contentment was written all over his face.

"I do too. I'm hoping we can recreate this feeling in a month again for Christmas. Cynthia and Laurence are planning on making it back for the holiday. Maybe we could return the favor and have dinner at our place, then?" Winnie suggested.

"That sounds wonderful. We would love to spend another holiday with you and Whit. And I'm sure the girls would love to have as much time together as possible," Eliza said, looking at me and Jordyn.

"You make sound like we're attached to the hip. You know we can spend a minute apart from each other."

"We know you two can, but the thing is that neither of you wants to," Bryan chimed in, knowing far more about our relationship than we thought he did.

"So, it's settled Christmas at our place."

"Unfortunately, I'll have to miss it." Sabrina frowned. "I'm spending Christmas with my dad and grandparents. Speaking of which, I need to call him. Am I allowed to get my phone now? We are done eating, after all."

"Yes, go ahead."

Jordyn motioned for her to sit. "I'll get it. I need to get Whit's and my phones, too."

"I would thank you, but I know you're just offering so you don't have to do the dishes."

"And you can only blame yourself since you were the one who taught me how to get out of them," she whispered over her shoulder on her way to the upstairs.

"Might as well get started on them then." Sabrina took our plates and took them to the kitchen, but not before Eliza thanked her. It was a small token of appreciation, but I recognized how much Sabrina cherished hearing her mom say it.

As soon as she left the room, Eliza looked around, beaming. "It was so nice having you all here this evening, even if it is just for a little while. I don't know how to explain it, but I needed this."

I knew what she was talking about because I'd needed this too. Since May, my life had been a chaotic storm of depression, anger, and guilt. It'd been so long since I had a moment to just sit and be content. A moment where I wasn't angry, hurt, or sorry. This was it. This was the moment, and I didn't want it to end. Deep down, I knew it would. I just wasn't prepared for how soon.

When Jordyn still hadn't come down after we settled down in the living room, I went up and see what the holdup was. I found her in the guest room, sitting on the bed, her back turned to me.

"Hey. We were wondering what was taking you so long to come back downstairs." I said, cautiously approaching the bed.

When I got in front of her, I saw she was staring at the carpeted floor under our feet, her hands clutching her phone close to her chest. Correction. Not her phone. Mine.

My stomach dropped. A sickening feeling of dread and confusion pulsed through my veins. "What do you have that?"

"I was getting our coats and when I picked yours up, your phone fell out of the pocket."

"Jor, what's wrong? What happened? A few minutes ago, you were laughing and having a good time. Now you look like you're on the verge of crying? What happened and why won't you look at me?"

"When I picked your phone up, it turned on by itself, I swear. I wasn't snooping. The notification was on your lock screen, so it was hard to miss, hard to ignore."

I didn't know what she was talking about until I took my phone from her. I unlocked it and was sent to my email. There was a message from Dr. Johnson sent to me an hour ago, apologizing for emailing me over the break, but insisting she had good news. In a few short lines, she explained how she thought of a way to prove Amelia wasn't the person behind the expose without admitting I was the one responsible.

She didn't go into further details, preferring to discuss them in person when we came back from break. She hoped to meet with me at my earliest convenience. Finally, she wished me a happy Thanksgiving.

When I met Jordyn's eye, betrayal didn't do justice to the look she gave me. And with five words, she left me broken.

"I should've listened to Sabrina."

28

Whit Robinson's Day of Reckoning

"I should've listened to Sabrina."

The words echoed through my ears, cutting through me with ice cold precision. Of all the things Jordyn could've said to me, that hurt me the most. What's worse is she knew it too.

"Don't say that," I pleaded, my defense failing me when I needed it the most.

"Why not? She told me at the wedding that you don't care who you screw over as long as it finds a way of benefiting you. I didn't believe it, but look at us now."

Jordyn got up from the bed in a hurry to rush out of the room, but I grabbed her wrist. I held her in place, despite her struggling to break free, and pleaded again for her to stay and listen. "Let me explain."

"Explain what? That you were willing to let my friend take the fall for something she didn't do? I could look past you screwing with Sabrina and Luke's relationship by playing that recording for everyone to hear because they had it coming. But Amelia? She didn't deserve this."

"I know."

"You saw how upset I was at her being suspended and blamed for something she couldn't have done, but you still didn't want to come forward and tell the truth."

"That's not true."

"Whit, please."

"No, I'm serious. Why do you think Dr. Johnson was getting into contact with me about this? I was looking for ways to absolve Amelia and went to her for help."

"Just admit you were looking to fix things without doing the one thing that would've resolved all of this — telling the truth. It would've been so easy for you to go to the administration and tell them you stole Amelia's ID badge to get into Mitchell Hall and the newspaper room. That you wrote the expose and put it in the issue before anything could've been done to remove it. All you had to do was have the guts to tell the truth, but you couldn't do that. You wanted to help Amelia, but only if you were absolved as well."

I hung my head in shame. It was true; I wanted to help Amelia, but I was more concerned with saving my own skin. In the end, all of this could've been avoided had I just mustered up the courage to come forward with the truth. But here we were—Amelia suspended and I finally facing the consequences of my actions.

"You're right. I didn't want to tell the whole truth because I didn't want to lose my spot at the university."

"But you were fine with Amelia losing hers? You realize how selfish you sound, right? It can't just be me hearing this."

"I wasn't fine with Amelia being scapegoated. You saw how I reacted after you told me she was suspended. I felt sick to my stomach with guilt. I wanted to undo the damage I've done. That's why I told Dr. Johnson. I was hoping she would point me in the right direction where I could save Amelia from being blamed and save myself from being found out."

"You shouldn't have been looking for a way to save yourself. If you were really sorry, you would've owned up to it and taken responsibility for what you did."

"I was sorry!" I protested, my voice rising. "It took me some time, but I finally found a way to help Amelia and I was going to do when I got back to campus."

"What solution was that? What was your brilliant plan to stop Amelia from being expelled for something you did?"

I hesitated for a moment. "I was going to write an anonymous letter owning up to what I did and saying Amelia was innocent. I was hoping the confession would make the university reconsider and let her stay."

"A confession would involve you admitting something you did wrong. You! Not an anonymous source! Your plan would never work! For all they knew, they could've said Amelia wrote it to get herself out of trouble!"

The room became deathly quiet as Jordyn's words sunk in. I sighed, realizing she was right. My plan was under-baked, to say the least. I convinced myself if I came forward anonymously, it would be enough to exonerate Amelia, but the chances of that happening were low.

Jordyn's eyes were closed as she tried to calm down. "Why did you even write the expose if you weren't prepared to face the consequences of it?"

"The article needed to be written—" She cut me off before I could finish my sentence.

"I understand that. I do. What I don't understand is why you wrote the piece if you were afraid of what may happen to you because of it?"

"Because I didn't care! Not when I first thought about doing it. Or when I was actually writing it. I was so angry about the cover-ups that I cared more about the Lakeview being forced to deal with the mess they created than what could happen to me."

"But you must have known that there would be consequences."

"Of course, but I thought I covered my tracks up well enough that they could never connect the piece back to me."

"Guess what? You were right. They didn't connect it to you. They connected it to Amelia, the wrong person!" Her voice rose to another level. She turned away to the wall, her hands covering her eyes as she tried to contain her emotions. "Were you ever going to tell me what you did if I hadn't seen that glimpse of Dr. Johnson email to you?"

Though the conversation up to this point had been hard, I hadn't felt a lump in my throat until that question. Lies had gotten me here. I hoped the truth would get me out. "No. I was hoping I wouldn't have to."

"Because you were ashamed?"

"Yes, but mostly because I was afraid. I didn't want you to think of me differently because of what I had done."

"The thing is, Whit, I'm not thinking of you any differently because of what you've done. I'm seeing you in a different light because of what you haven't done."

"Tell me what I can do to make things right. I care about you, Jordyn. I don't want to hurt you more than I already have."

Jordyn turned back around to face me and said, "I already told you. You need to admit you were the one behind the expose and apologize to Amelia for waiting weeks to do it."

"Done," I said without hesitation. "I'll do it when we get back to campus."

"Just like that? What about your spot at the university? The one you were so afraid you may get expelled for?"

"You made me see the only way I can prove Amelia is innocent is by telling the truth and not hiding my name or face. I have to be the one who faces the punishment for it."

"Why couldn't you realize that before? Why did it take now for you to realize that there is no other way?"

"Because I've exhausted all my other options. Plus, I didn't have you to lose. Before, it was just my place at the school. Now, I know if I don't do this, I stand to lose you too, and I'm not willing to risk that. So, here I am telling you, I'm ready to accept whatever punishment that comes my way."

I thought I saw Jordyn's eyes softened before they became hardened again. "It shouldn't have gotten to this point. You shouldn't need me to make this decision. I am your girlfriend. I'm not supposed to be your moral compass."

"Again, you're right. I know who I am right now is not the best version of who I could be, but I'm trying to get better. I'm determined to become the person who is deserving of your love and trust."

"My trust in you has been shaken. I can't lie to you and say I'm not having some doubts about you."

I nodded sadly, understanding her feelings completely. I damaged her trust in me. I couldn't expect her to just get over it that quickly. "How do we move past this? What will it take for us to have a future together?"

She looked me in the eye and said, "I need to trust you again. Meaning, if you have lied to me about anything else, I need you to tell me right now. I don't want to find out about it later when I gave you a chance to be honest. It's now or never, Whit. Come clean about everything or this is it for us."

I took a deep breath, preparing to come clean about the one thing that's been hanging over our relationship since the beginning. "There's one more thing I haven't been truthful to you about."

"Is it what I think it is?"

"The thing you've been questioning me about since the start of our friendship? Yes, it's that..."

She sighed, not totally surprised. "Will you finally give me the genuine answer why you sought out a friendship with me?"

"Yes," I answered. "The truth is, I wanted to start a friendship with you to get back at Sabrina. It wasn't actually about wanting to be your friend, not at first. Sabrina hurt me so bad by believing Mike over me and the only way I knew how to hurt her back was by getting close to you. And even though it morphed into being something real, something I actually wanted, I'm sorry for how it started."

She took a moment to process what I said before responding. "I wish I could say I'm shocked by this, but I always had a feeling your motivates for wanting a friendship with me wasn't pure. Still doesn't make it any less hurtful, though."

"I never wanted to hurt you. It was all about hurting her. I never expected it going this far or for my feelings for you to become real."

"Where do you get off thinking you can manipulate people's feelings like that? I'm a human being, not a pawn to be used in your feud with my sister. For you to even think that was alright to do for a second says so much about the person you are."

"The choices I made were my own. I have no one to blame for them but me. But I can say with a 100% certainty that I wouldn't have done this if I hadn't been hurt the way I was. It's not an excuse, but you try having the worst thing imaginable happen to you, then not have your best friend believe you. It'll make you do things you're not proud of."

Jordyn looked down to the ground, trying to come to terms with what I said. I didn't want to push her into feeling a certain way. What I did was wrong, but I needed her to know where I was coming from.

"I'm entitled to be upset about this, you know?" She said finally. "You did something for most people would be unforgivable. Even if I understand the hurt and the pain you were going through to do something like that, it doesn't make what you did okay."

"I'm sorry. Despite what motivated our friendship starting, everything was real. Us connecting as friends, us falling for each other. It was all real, and I'm sorry that I put you in a position to doubt that."

She gave me a small nod of understanding before she spoke up again.

"Hurt people hurt people, that's the saying, right?"

"The last person I wanted to hurt was you."

"I know. We've spent enough time together for me to know your heart, Whit. You've bared it to me more times than I can count. I'm just trying to remember that in the face of all this."

"You need time, and I want you to have it. I don't want to lose you, but if there's any way out of this for us, you need to take it." I couldn't believe what I was suggesting. Time away from Jordyn was the last thing I wanted, but it wasn't about me. It was about what was right for her, and I knew space was it.

By the look on her face, I was right to think that. "Yes, I think that's what I need. Time to process this and decide if I can get past this. I know I want to, but I need to know if I really can."

"I understand. I'll tell Winnie I'm not feeling well and we'll go."

"I'll send Sabrina to get my bags before we leave. Don't worry, I won't tell her what happened."

I looked around the room, overwhelmed by what was happening. The jump between this moment and just an hour ago was so drastic it was hard to wrap my head around. "I'm guessing you'll go back with her, too."

"Yeah. Maybe you can see if you can get a refund for my ticket."

"It's not about—" I stopped myself. I wasn't sure what it was about. All I could think of was how much I wanted her to leave with me. How much I wanted for us to be okay, but what I wanted wasn't relevant. Not after what I did. "I'll see if they can do something about the ticket."

"Thanks." She picked up my coat from the bed and handed it to me. We stood there in silence for a few seconds, neither of us sure what to say or do next.

Finally, I reached out my hand as if we were shaking hands after a business meeting, not agreeing to take time apart. Instead of taking my hand, she stepped forward and hugged me tightly before stepping back and wiping her eyes with the sleeve of her shirt. "I have lie of my own to admit to."

I looked at her questioningly and waited for her to explain. She took a deep breath before continuing, "Yesterday I said I didn't mean it when I said I loved it. That was a lie. Whit, I am in love with you. Me needing time apart from you doesn't change that."

"I'm in love with you, too."

In a moment where Jordyn should've looked her happiest, her face was still marred in sadness. "Hearing those words yesterday would've meant everything to me."

"And now?"

"Now," she paused, her voice almost a whisper. "I'm not sure it's enough."

29

The "Best" Friend

I returned to Chicago two days after Thanksgiving, my heart still as heavy as the day I'd left. What in the beginning was a wonderful holiday with family had become a complete disaster. And I had no one to blame but myself.

I walked through the near empty campus, my poor mood intensifying by the sound of my footsteps echoing in the stillness. Chicago was undeniably beautiful with snow blanketing everything with a soft layer of white, and the buildings rising into an endless expanse of grey sky. Yet not even this picture book-like scene could turn my spirits around.

Jordyn and I hadn't spoken since Thanksgiving. Not that I was expecting her to reach out to me. She needed space to decide if we were going to move forward together. She couldn't do that if I was around to influence her decision.

Still, it hurt to not being able to talk to her. It'd only been two days and already I missed her. More than my girlfriend, she was my best friend. Probably my only friend once Amelia and the rest of the group finds out I was the person behind the expose. The administration office wasn't open until Monday, so I could only wait until then to find out my fate.

The chilly late November air whipped at my face as I made it closer to my dorm. I wrapped my coat tighter around me and quickened my pace. The last thing I needed was to run into Amelia, one of her friends, Sabrina, or someone else I pissed off.

When I made it to my dorm, I warmed up by making hot chocolate from a packet I brought from home. Unpacking my luggage could wait. It's not like I had anywhere to go or anything else to do until Monday. For now, I needed a moment of silence and a chance to let my thoughts settle in peace.

But before I could get too comfortable, a knock on the door interrupted me. It was a loud sort of knock, one I would give if I was angry, so I knew it wasn't Jordyn. I cautiously opened the door and, to my dismay, there was a scowling face staring back at me.

"What the hell did you to do to my sister?" Sabrina spat as she barged into the room.

"Yes, come in, Sabrina. Make yourself at home."

Her face was red, maybe from the cold, but more likely from the anger stewing inside of her. "What did you do to Jordyn?" She repeated, this time more forcefully.

"What did she tell you?"

"Nothing! I had to dig to get crumbs from her over our car ride back to campus. All she admitted to me was you two got into a fight, but I know there's more to it."

I crossed my arms, a little impressed by Sabrina showing concern over her sister's wellbeing, but that didn't change the fact I wasn't about to tell her what happened between me and Jordyn. "It's none of your business. The last time I checked, you aren't a part of this relationship."

"It feels like it, though."

"What is that supposed to mean?"

"Let's see, you became friends with Jordyn because I cut you out of my life. You started dating her when you realized you won't ever have me. Now, you and Jordyn get into this mysterious fight where neither you are speaking to each other. It's kinda like I'm in the middle of all this."

"You are delusional."

"I was hoping you were going to prove me wrong. I wanted to believe you truly liked Jordyn, that you wouldn't hurt her. But I guess not."

"You know nothing about what happened between me and Jordyn."

"Will you stop painting yourself out to be a victim? You're not. I didn't hurt you. You hurt me by sabotaging my relationship with Luke!"

"No, you did that! I just recorded it and played it for him."

"Not just him. The entire auditorium. If you really did that out of the goodness of your heart, you would have privately talked to him. Face it, you wanted revenge."

"You're absolutely fucking right I did. After all, what's wrong with petty revenge? You were my best friend, and you hurt me like I was one of your enemies. The worst thing about it is you're still convinced you did nothing wrong. The way I see it, you deserved everything I did and more."

"You're a psycho. Shifting the blame onto me for your actions doesn't make what you've done less deranged. I don't know what you did, but I'm glad my sister is away from you. You destroy everything in your life. It's why your parents want nothing to do with you."

I passed up the chance to slap Sabrina months ago. I sure as hell wasn't passing it up now. I backhanded her with an open palm, my gaze venomous. "You abandoned me when I needed you most, and now you act as if you're some martyr? You call me a psycho and deranged, you ableist piece of shit? Hello! I am what you made me."

The force of the slap sent Sabrina to the ground, but she didn't wait another second to take me on. She charged at me and speared me to the floor. I thrashed beneath her until I force my momentum and reversed our positions. Our angry eyes were locked as we struggled to get the upper hand over the other.

We rolled around, throwing punches and blocking the other's hits with our arms. If this was a normal day on campus, someone would've heard us. This was not a normal day on campus. Almost no one was there. We could've killed each other with no one finding us until the next day at the earliest.

Still, I was glad no one was there to stop this. This fight was a long time coming and as it progressed, I became angrier and angrier. The days of Sabrina's lies, betrayal, manipulation, and cognitive dissonance all seemed to crash down on me like a ton of bricks.

I screamed out in anger as I grabbed her by her sweater and shook her repeatedly. "I hate you!" sobbing uncontrollably, tears streaming down my face. "I really hate you." My grip on her sweater loosened until I was just on top of her, crying.

She lay there motionless, not saying a word. This only infuriated me more. I could see the surprise in her eyes, but still she refused to speak or explain herself. I rolled off of her and onto the floor, burying my face in my hands.

While I was busy sobbing into my hands, I felt her stay beside me. She didn't make a move to leave. She lay there unflinchingly, just listening to me cry.

"Did you ever imagine this would be where we ended up when we met on the playground?" she asked as casually as if I hadn't just pinned her to the floor.

I shook my head, my face still buried in my hands. "No. I thought our friendship would be forever because every kid thinks that way about their best friend."

"I can't remember a time where my friendships weren't transactional. You were the closest person I got to having something like that."

"Then why did you give me up so easily? I told you Mike raped me and you took his side. I was your best friend, and you just left me. I needed you and you left."

The anger in my voice was undeniable, but so was the pain in my heart. I wanted an answer why she left me so easily and why she still thought Mike did nothing wrong. I would never be satisfied by her answer, but I needed to hear it.

We were shoulder to shoulder, but her eyes never met mine. She was silent for a long time and when she finally spoke, her voice cracked as though she were about to break. "I loved him. For over a decade, my heart belonged to him. Was he the best boyfriend? No. But he was the one I wanted. I couldn't bring myself to think I was in love with a monster. No one wants to think they could fall for someone capable of something like that. I took the easy way out because I didn't want to see the truth. What does it say about me that I was with him for most of my life and never noticed the signs?"

I turned on my side to face her, even if she wouldn't look at me. "It says nothing about you. He hid who he was from everyone."

"But I knew him the best. There must have been something I missed. I should have seen it."

"So you could save me from being assaulted by him? That wasn't your job, Sabrina. No one could've stopped what happened from happening except him. You couldn't control his choices, and you can't take the blame for something he did. The only thing you could've controlled was your own reaction, and you failed that."

"I'm sorry," she whispered as tears started rolled down her cheeks. "I handled everything wrong. I should've believed you and been there for you. I was just too proud to admit I was wrong."

Sorry didn't fix anything, but I would be lying if I said it didn't feel good to hear. After months of my former friend calling me a liar, it was good to hear the truth finally come from her lips, and for once, not my own.

"And since I'm on an apology tour, I might've as well get this one out too. I didn't mean what I said about you destroying everything in your life. Your parents being away has nothing to do with you. I only said that try to hurt you like you hurt my sister."

"You always knew how to hit a nerve of mine," I replied with a hint of bitterness. "It's why I'm not going to apologize to you for anything I've done. Making you think Luke was cheating on you, the infamous recording, slapping you, I regret none of it. You had it coming."

"Do I want to know what you mean by the making me think Luke was cheating on me?"

"Nope."

Catching me off guard, she smiled. "Fair enough. You're right. I deserved all of what happened, but I already received my biggest punishment."

"A one-way ticket to hell?"

"No, losing you. We should've been best friends for life, and I'm sorry for ruining that."

"I know you are because you lost the best friend that you ever had and never deserved." I wasn't trying to make her feel worse. I was just speaking the truth.

She turned her head to me, finally gaining the courage to look me in the eye. "Sorry for failing you. For failing our friendship. Now, it's all tainted. Just one colossal failure of a relationship."

"Our friendship wasn't a failure. For almost two decades, you were exactly what I needed in my life and I was yours. Neither one of us would've become the people we are today without the other one being around. We've grown for having known and once loved each other."

"Yeah, so much growth," she said sarcastically, a tear falling from her eye to the carpet.

"Will you let finish my speech? It's the only time I'm going to be sentimental with you again."

She quieted, ready to hear the rest.

"For better or for worse, I'm not the same person I was before knowing you. I know you can say the same. The growth we had and the love we shared weren't a waste. We know the wrongs and the rights of friendship. We were each other's trial run for the real, healthier, happier relationship that awaits us. We may have used up all the love we had for each other, but we're still capable of giving it. Even if it's not for each other anymore."

She looked at me with sadness in her eyes, a sadness I didn't realize she could still feel. Her silence was broken by a single sniffle, followed by others. Reality was setting in for her, the reality I've already been living in. This was the end for us.

When her tears dried up, Sabrina chuckled. Somewhere in that, her chuckle became a roar of laughter. I'd never heard her laugh like that before. "We're having a memorial for our friendship and you're laughing?"

"I was just thinking. It's a sick joke that surely the universe wouldn't pull. But imagine if you patch things up with Jordyn and end up getting married to her. We would be sisters! Imagine that!"

I hate the universe.

30

I, Whit

The room was filled with a palpable sense of anticipation as I anxiously sat across from the disciplinary committee. An entire week had gone by since I confessed to being the mastermind behind the expose. Now I was staring at the people who held my future in their hands. The committee was composed of five members of the school faculty. Professors I never had. Professors who knew nothing about me except for what brought us all here today.

I'd expected this day to come once I decided to come clean. It still didn't make the thought of having to answer their questions an easier pill to swallow. I tried to steady my shaking hands by taking a deep breath. No matter what happened here today, I knew one thing: the truth needed to be told. Whether or not I liked what it said about me.

Question came one at a time from each of the committee members. "Did you attempt to address your concerns through proper university channels before resorting to leaking confidential documents? If not, why?" Dr. Ablack asked.

"I did. After I was raped, I reported it to Dean Clayton. She warned me off from making an official report or going to the police because she believed it was a he-said-she-said situation and it would only lead to me being hurt further. Months later, I again went to Dean Clayton, as well as the Chapter President of the Greek, Tyler Morris, about the lack of safety concerns regarding underage age drinking happening during frat parties and not having many options for them to get their dorms or homes. Neither Dean Clayton and Tyler Morris took my concerns seriously."

Another question thrown at me from Professor Stone was, "Can you provide evidence or witnesses to support the claims you made in your expose? We need to assess the credibility and accuracy of the information you shared."

"Attached to the expose are the leaked documents I discovered proving the university was not properly investigating the reported sexual assault cases. These reports were filed by students, but never addressed. As far as witnesses, no. I couldn't convince any of the students mentioned in the expose to act as a witness on my behalf. In all honesty, it had nothing to do with them not wanting to come forward about how the school mistreated their cases. It had everything to do with them not wanting to help me after I published their stories without their permission and disclosed their identities."

Admitting that would not help my case, but it was the truth and the only way I could begin to make peace with those students. The question, "How do you justify the harm your actions caused to the university and individuals mentioned in the expose?" came not long later.

"The harm done to the students? I can't justify that. It was a clear oversight on my part. I didn't think of the consequences of telling their stories when their stories weren't mine to tell. I'll have to live with that mistake for the rest of my life. However, the harm done to the school? That was the whole point. To hurt the university enough to invoke changes to be made. It may not have been the right way to do it, but after months of trying to get the university's attention without success, I felt this was my only chance to make things better."

"Did you consider the potential consequences of your actions before you did what you did?"

"Yes. I knew I would likely end up here if the truth came to light. I knew I was putting my future on the line. I just couldn't find it in my heart to care more about it than about the future of the students here at Lakeview."

Finally, after what felt like an eternity of interrogation, the last question was asked. "Do you understand the gravity of your actions? Meaning, if you were placed in a similar position again, would you make the same decision?"

Though it couldn't have helped me, I answered truthfully. "Yes. I would make the same decision again. The future of these students, the future of the students that come after us, and the ones after them matter more than mine. If my future has to be sacrificed for theirs, so be it."

Following my statement, a silence fell upon the room that was so complete and profound, it was as if all sound had been sucked out of the air. They didn't know what to make of my resolve. It surprised me too, but it felt right.

Behind closed doors, the committee engaged in a long discussion and deliberation regarding what was to come of me. After 30 minutes, they returned with a verdict. The chairperson summoned me to rise.

I stood, my heart pounding and my hands shaking. I thought I was prepared to accept whatever the committee's decision would be, but now that the moment was here, I was terrified. Because deep down, below the tough exterior, was a woman who was once a young girl who dreamed of being handed a diploma with her family watching on, cheering. A dream that comforted her in times of doubt and intensified her longing for a present pair of parents. A dream that might never be a reality because of her own costly actions.

The chairperson cleared her throat before delivering the verdict. "We have decided that though your intentions were noble, and your actions were admirable, the rules are the rules. Leaking confidential documents, not reporting Dean Clayton for her lack of action, not coming forward sooner and letting a fellow student take the fall for you, and your admission that you would do the same thing over again if a similar situation were to arise. These factors lead us to believe we must take disciplinary action."

The word "expelled" left a visceral impact, as if someone struck me in the gut. It was difficult to catch their last remarks because of the ringing in my ears. The last words I latched onto were I had a week to pack up my dorm and be off of campus.

I sat in my seat even after the committee left, still trying to grasp what happened. I was in a fog, one of my own making. Imagining the worst-case scenario happening to you doesn't do justice to living it out.

Even with a week to think about it, I still didn't know what I was supposed to do. The thought of explaining to Winnie and my parents what happened was excruciating. Returning home for Christmas without a place to come back to in the spring felt like a cruel joke. The worst year of my life was now guaranteed to end on the worst possible note.

Once I pulled myself together, I got up and walked to the dorms. I knocked on the door because it wasn't my dorm I was visiting, but Jordyn's and Amelia's. There were many things I needed to get in order before I was kicked out. None more pressing than making things right with the woman who opened the door.

"Please, don't slam the door in my face. Though I totally deserve it."

Amelia leaned against the frame of the door and folded her arms. "Jordyn isn't here and even if she was, she doesn't want to see you."

Her voice wasn't unkind, but guarded. Which, considering what

I let happen to her, was more than what I deserved. "I'm here to apologize to you. Sincerely, I'm sorry. I was hoping we could talk if you will hear me out."

"We have anything to talk about."

"Come on, Amelia. You should want to yell at me or something. I hurt you."

"I didn't expect loyalty from you, Whit. We weren't friends. You didn't owe me anything, but you knew how much my future as a journalist meant to me and you used it for your own self-interests. You risked my dreams for your story when you could've just come to me with it. I would've helped you published it."

"Really? But you would've been in the same boat as me."

"Yeah, but that story needed to be told. Just not how you did it. You were trying to help, but the trouble you caused me, the victims whose stories you used, and even yourself — it's not right. You're lucky if the school doesn't expel you."

"I'm not that lucky. I just came from a disciplinary meeting."

"That explains the skirt suit you're wearing."

I looked down at my outfit self-consciously. "I wanted to look more serious. I thought it might help me plead my case."

"Did it?"

"No." I sucked in a deep breath. "I got expelled."

Amelia, for her part, didn't smile if she was secretly pleased. "That's awful. I'm sorry, genuinely."

"You don't think it's my karma?"

"No, because despite you going about this in the wrong way, your intentions were good."

"I keep telling myself the same thing, but I did more harm than good. I got Dean Clayton fired, but who knows the next Dean could be worse for all we know. I don't know how much good I've really done."

"Are you regretting what you did?"

"No," I sighed. "I do wish something more came out of this. I feel like everything is going to go back to how it was before the story was released."

"That's always the fear when starting a conversation. You worry if the fire you sparked is going to stay lit or if it's going to be doused," she said like she was reflecting on her own experiences. "I'll say this though, your fire is still burning. People are still talking about the expose. People are still protesting. It's less than before, but it's still going. Things aren't going to revert back to before because there's more than just you fighting to keep it going."

I was taken aback by the empathy Amelia was showing me. I wouldn't have predicted it, but I welcomed it all the same. "Thank you. I needed to hear that. I can see why Jordyn likes you."

She smiled, but didn't show her teeth. "I like her too. I have a feeling you're going to be sticking around in her life and if I want to continue being her friend, I need to make peace with you. Not exonerating me sooner was wrong, but nothing that happened to me is going to affect my future. My suspension will be erased from my record, and the university will be kissing my ass for the next few months, trying to make up for their screw-up. That's why I'm not going to hold a grudge against you."

Relieved to hear her say those words, I let out a heavy sigh. "I don't deserve it, but thank you."

While I didn't know if Amelia was truly ready to forgive me, I was thankful for the gesture and was prepared to offer her one of my own. I leaned forward to hug her, but she waved a hand, signaling for me to stop. "We're not there yet. Do some more work to get into my good graces again and maybe I'll hug you."

"Fair enough," I replied. I turned on my heel, preparing to leave the conversation at that. Alas, I couldn't leave well enough alone. There was one last thing I had to ask.

"Why are you so sure Jordyn is going to keep me around? You know our relationship is on pause, right? She may decide this is too much work and show me the door."

"Jordyn loves you," she said simply, her voice firm. "If she didn't, she wouldn't have asked for a break. She would've kicked your ass to the curb, but she didn't. She cares, and she's not one to give up easily. That means something."

Her words meant something to me too. I spent the weeks apart from Jordyn considering the worst: that she wanted nothing more to do with me, that I brought more trouble than I was worth. Amelia's words reminded there was still a chance our relationship wasn't over for good — and if I kept trying and working on myself, then Jordyn might forgive me for everything and we'd be able to move forward together.

I had to keep that hope or else I had nothing to keep me going.

31

Confront the Robinsons

"Knock, knock," I announced, lightly tapping my knuckles on the wooden door frame of Dr. Johnson's office. She was at her desk with her reading glasses on, reading something on her desktop computer. My voice took her out of her concentration.

She tried to smile, but the frown on her face did not want to be replaced. "Hi Whit. I'm glad to see you. I was sorry to hear about your expulsion. If there was something I could've done beyond putting in a good word, I would've."

"Thanks for saying that, but the committee's minds were made up. There was nothing else you could've done."

She gave her an understanding nod and then signaled for me to come all the way in. "Is this a quick visit?"

"That depends on you and if you'll willing to fit me in for one last session? I'm leaving campus tomorrow, so this will be the last therapy session paid by the college."

A genuine smile appeared on Dr. Johnson's face then. "Of course I can fit you in. I want to help any way I can. Come in." She gestured for me to take a seat on the couch.

I sat opposite to her on the couch and sighed, feeling sad that this was the end. Yet relieved that I felt sad. At the beginning of the semester, I wanted nothing to do with these sessions, and now I was actually going to miss them. If that didn't point to me experiencing some type of growth, I didn't know what did.

"How are you, really? Getting kicked out of school is a tough thing to come to terms with."

"I'm getting through it. I had my time to cry and complain. Now I'm trying to look toward the future and how I can not repeat the same mistakes as before."

"What have you come up with so far?"

"Every poor decision I've made can be traced back to the night in May. I held onto my anger toward the situation and brought it into every aspect of my life. I'm realizing if I want any resemblance of a life, I can't let it or him have that kind of power over me. I don't want the story of my life to be what Mike did to me, but what I did for myself. It's just so hard to move on when it feels like he's the one in control."

"Why do you feel like he's the one in the control?"

"Because no matter what I do or how hard I try, he's always there. I wake up, and he's the first thing I think about. Is he waking up alone or is he with someone else? Was the encounter consensual or was it taken from them? Are they happy, content, or hurt and broken? Does he ever think about me because all I ever think about is him? I'm worried this is how it's going to be for the rest of my life. I'll be eighty and I'll still be thinking about him."

"The effects of rape are long-lasting, but his hold over you doesn't have to be. You'll be haunted of that night forever, but you don't have to be haunted by him. Contrary to what you think, he doesn't have control over you. Any power he has is because you are giving it to him. The moment you stop, he'll be gone. Not for good. He'll always be there, but his hold over you won't be. It's up to you to decide if you want him gone for good."

"I do want him gone," I sighed, feeling the frustration build inside of me. "You don't know how badly I do, but it's been months, and he's still in my head."

Right then, I looked Dr. Johnson in her eyes and saw her speak with the most conviction I ever heard from her. "Whit, you speak as if you are being held captive by this man. You're not. You are not his prisoner. He is yours. You get to decide when to take that key and let him out of your head, once and for all. It's difficult, but if you mean it when you say you want a life without him, then you are more than capable of making it happen. You were strong to survive this. Now it's time to be strong enough to move on from him and start living the life you want, not the one you've been confined to."

I could feel my heart thumping in response to what she said. What she was telling me needed to be done, but the doubt if I could really do it loitered in the back of my head. She told me I was strong, but I couldn't say for certain I was strong enough to move on from him. But I knew I wanted to, and that was the first step.

After our meeting concluded, I returned to my dorm. My stuff still needed to be packed because come this weekend they would remove it for me. I left my door unlocked before I left. I didn't put it past them to have changed the locks while I was gone. That was the surprise I was expecting to find when I came back. It wasn't the one I got.

There, standing in the middle of my room, were my parents. The ones I hadn't seen in person since last year's Thanksgiving. They were wearing exhausted looks on their faces.

"So… I'm guessing you heard about my expulsion," I said, closing the door behind me and walking into the room.

"Winnie told us. The question is, why didn't you?" My dad asked, his eyebrows knitted together.

"I was going to."

"When? Christmas?"

"Yeah. If you bothered to show up for it." Normally I restrained myself not to say such a thing, but I was tired. Tired of putting on a mask to protect other people's feelings instead of my own. I would not do it today and not with them.

"Is that why you didn't tell us? You were upset we missed out on coming to Thanksgiving?"

"No, I wasn't upset because I'm used to you disappointing me. I'm used to you not making time for me, not making an effort. I got so used to it I started not making time for you or sharing things with you."

They had never heard me talk like this before. They looked everywhere but at me to hide their discomfort. My mother broke the silence first. "Honey, we never meant to make you feel like that. We love you and would love to spend more time with you if we could."

"But your career is more important. Gotcha."

My father was quick to reply, "That's not true. We love our careers and we have worked hard for them, but nothing is more important to us than you. That's why we caught the first flight we could to be here for you."

"I appreciate that, but it's hard to believe what you're telling me when we don't see each other in person in a year. I recognize how important your jobs are, I really do, but your jobs as parents are supposed to be just as important. Yet you never treat it that way."

My mom walked up to me and hugged me and held my shoulders as she looked me in the eye. "You come first to us. You always have, and if we have ever made you feel otherwise, you should've told us."

"What was I supposed to say? Hey mom and dad, can you take some time off from being world-traveling doctors to spend more time with me? I would've sounded like a spoiled, selfish brat."

"No, you would've sounded like a daughter who wanted her parents around more. That's not a selfish thing to want."

"Neither are you guys loving your jobs. You choose to save people's lives, even if it means sacrificing time with your family. You're good people. You're just not good parents."

I thought what I was saying would send them into a tailspin, but they only nodded and smiled sadly at me. My dad sat down on my bed before speaking up again. "That was our biggest worry when we found out we were pregnant. Two workaholics who didn't have a parental instinct bone in their body raising a child. We were scared of messing you up because our work meant so much to us we could never walk completely away from it."

"Is that why you basically left me to be raised by Winnie?"

"We didn't leave you to be raised by Winnie." My mom sounded offended at the accusation. "We weren't going about to have a kid traveling in hazardous places so we could work. It was better for us to leave you with your grandmother, who knew how to be a parent while we worked. But make no mistake, we didn't abandon you. We kept in touch, sent packages, and came home as much as we could."

"It wasn't enough. I wanted a mom and dad who showed up on career day and made me look better than my stuck-up white classmates and came to support me on my graduation days. Parents who gave my birthday presents in person and didn't send them in the mail. I wanted parents I could tell everything to, not ones I only feel I can share the good news with."

"We didn't think you wanted that hands-on approach. You were so much like us, even as a kid, with your independence. We thought you didn't mind us not being around."

"Because I pretended to be okay with it," I fumed, like I was pointing out the obvious and they still didn't get it. "I didn't want you to feel guilty or stay home for me. I loved the independence you allowed me to have. Winnie acting as my third parent worked out for me, but none couldn't replace the love I needed from you."

My parents were quiet, absorbing every word and finally realizing what I had been feeling all these years. "How can we make this better? Do you even still want that kind of relationship with us?" My dad asked.

I waited a moment and really thought about it. The answer was more complicated than a simple yes or no. "I'd love to have the kind of relationship I have with Winnie with you both, but I don't know if it's possible. The things that have caused our relationship to be where it is now are still there. Our lack of communication, unresolved issues, and distance are all factors that have contributed to where we are."

"You're right," my mom agreed. "But underneath all our problems is the love we have for each other. Your father and I want to do better and be there for you during this difficult time in your life. Is that possible?"

I almost chuckled. They truly knew nothing about my life if they thought what I was going through constituted as a difficult time compared to the hell I'd been through in the past few months. "I feel you've missed so much of my life. It's like you don't even know me. We're strangers. I know you care about me, but if we didn't have blood connecting us, I wonder if we would have a relationship at all."

They nodded, silently recognizing the truth of my words. My mom took my hand and sat us next to my dad on the bed. My hand was still in my mom's hand when she spoke. "Honey, you're right. We haven't been there for you as much as we should've. It was never because we didn't want to be there for you. We felt like we had a duty to be there for our patients who didn't have anyone else to turn to."

"You don't have to explain. I understand."

My dad put his hand over our linked ones. "It doesn't absolve us from our responsibility to be there for you, though. You were right to call us not good parents. It wasn't easy to hear, but it's also the most truthful you've ever been with us and we want you to always feel you can tell us the truth, no matter how hurtful it may be to hear. We love you more than anything else, and we want to make this right for you."

My dad's face was regretful, yet still determined to make things better. I knew he meant what he said and he would do whatever it took to keep his promise. "Despite of all the good we've done with our jobs, you are the best thing we have ever done, and it's up to us to prove that to you by showing up for you more," he continued.

"How are you going to do that?" My words were cautious, uncertain of how this could work.

"We'll have to work this out with our bosses, but we worked enough to request time off. We already scheduled time off for Christmas, but we can ask for that to be extended into New Year's."

"I don't want you guys to miss out on your work," I said hesitantly.

"This is where we need to be," my mom countered. "Whitney, you need us and we need to be better for you. If we aren't showing up for you now, then when will we ever? It's now or never for us to prove we can be the long awaited parents you have been wanting."

There was a time where I would've doubted her, but I knew in that moment I needed to trust her. I hooked my arms around both of their necks and squeezed them into a hug. Our faces were scrunched together in an embrace before I freed them.

"Thank you. This has been a hard year for me and I struggled most of it alone because I didn't want to admit I needed help. It's why I'm where I am right now."

"Don't worry about the expulsion or your future. You're a bright girl. So this school wasn't it, there are others."

"And if you don't want to finish school right now, we can help you get a job doing whatever you want," my mom added, though she didn't know what I wanted to do. To be fair, I didn't know what I wanted either. Other than Jordyn.

"I don't know what I want to do, but I'm glad I have you both to help me figure it out."

My parents smiled at me, and I felt a tinge of confidence that things were going to be okay. My mom laid her head on my shoulder and said, "No matter what you decide to do, we will always be here to support you."

"I'm glad to hear you say that because I have something I have to tell you."

"If this is about your girlfriend. Winnie filled us in on that. We're happy for you. It's not a problem with us."

"Thanks for the reassurance, dad. I was actually talking about my name."

"What about your name?"

I chuckled at the worried lines appearing on his forehead. "I see Winnie didn't fill you in on that. I changed my name to be Whit. Not Whitney, just Whit."

They exchanged a look of confusion before returning their gaze back to me with encouraging eyes. "What led to that change?"

"It's not a happy story."

"We want to hear it, anyway."

So I told them. Told them about that night and how Mike's usage of my name made my skin crawl. How I couldn't handle being reminded of him every time I heard my own name. How I needed a clean slate and that meant being Whit. I told them maybe there will be a time in the future where being called Whitney won't bring me back to that night, but until then, Whit was my name.

There were tears, hugs, and "I love you"s all around. The conversation continued long after we finished packing up my dorm into boxes and loaded them into our rental. It continued as we drove home to Wayland. When it ended, it'd been hard, sad, necessary... and the lightest I'd felt in my entire life.

32

Christmas in Wayland

Eleven days at home didn't bring me any closer to having my future figured out. I spent my time researching schools that might overlook the fact I was kicked out of my former university for whistleblowing. Turns out, there weren't many that would. Surprising, I know.

When my efforts there couldn't possibly look more like a bust, I switched to the equally dire venture of looking for a job. Applying for jobs was as depressing and hopeless as the search for a school. There were local places hiring, including at our town center and at Natick, the town next door to us. The problem was working at a department store or a mall wasn't what I wanted to be doing with my life at twenty.

There's nothing wrong with these jobs, but I never wanted to spend my twenties stuck behind a counter. By the time I graduated, I wanted to have a job that would morph into a career, one I would be happy with and see myself in forever. Except I never figured out what kind of job I wanted.

I was a communications major, for God's sake. Perhaps the most vague, open-ended degree there is. Aside from English, of course. Choosing to be a communications major was supposed to leave me with options of what I wanted to do with my life, but I found myself as directionless as ever.

This was what I was mulling over when my mom appeared in my doorway. She and my dad kept their word and were staying in Wayland for Christmas and into the New Year to be with me. After our talk back at my dorm, my mom had been hovering over me like a hawk, but I didn't mind.

"Hey sweetheart," she said with a kind smile. She walked over and gave me a hug before sitting on the edge of my bed. "Still struggling with the job search?"

I closed my laptop and looked at her. "Yes. All the jobs I've looked at scream temporary to me. I want what I do next to be something meaningful and long-term."

"You really are our daughter, through and through." While she laughed, my heart felt warm from the sweetest compliment she ever gave me. "With our jobs, we wanted to help others as well as be fulfilled ourselves. Our path just so happened to be medicine. You'll find your path too, eventually."

"I don't know if I have a path like you and dad did. Or maybe I did, and I fucked it up by getting myself kicked out of school. Who is going to want anything to do with a communications major with no degree?"

"You're not the only person who has ever been kicked out of school. Plenty of successful people have. You don't need a degree to have a successful career. You need to find something that works for you and dedicate yourself to it."

"What if I don't find a job that speaks to me? No offense, but I don't want to be forty and still living at Winnie's," I replied.

My mom smiled at me with the same warmth as she did when I was a child. "That won't happen," she assured me. "If you can't find a job that fits your wants, then you'll create it."

I laughed. "You think I could be a business owner or something? I know you're my mom and you're supposed to fill my head up with dreams and possibilities of what I can do, but there's no way I could ever be an entrepreneur."

"You got the tools. It's not a degree, but you got the public speaking skills. You know how to network, and you got the drive. You can do whatever you put your mind to."

My mom's confidence in me was undeniable, and it felt nice to be reminded of what I'm capable of. "What do I have to offer anyone?" I inquired, my mind trying to find any objection to the idea of me starting something of my own.

"Are you kidding me? Do I have to remind you that you wrote a scathing expose on your own university for not investigating sexual assault allegations? The story you told was so powerful the university was forced into making changes."

A little birdie named Amelia told me about the policies the school announced they'll be implementing in the new year. A new anonymous system for reporting sexual assault, training programs for faculty and staff, a updated driving service for students to call and get to their dorms safely, and the creation of a student-run sexual assault support group were a few of the changes launched. It remained to be seen if these policies actually made a difference, but I was happy something was outwardly being done.

"You used your voice, and you helped an entire campus. What's stopping you from helping another?"

"You think I should enroll in other colleges and blow up their operations too?"

My mom laughed, then squeezed my knee. "Not exactly, but you can help in other ways. Telling your story is one."

My mom didn't know it then, but with that suggestion, she planted an idea that would blossom into something much bigger and great.

"I'll think about it," I told her, already considering it. "Did you come in here to give me a prep talk, or did you want something?"

"I wanted to see if you wouldn't mind going to store and picking up a few things for Christmas dinner."

"Mom, that's two days away. Do you need to get started now?"

She nodded. "It's going to be busy the closer it gets to Christmas, and I'd like to have everything on hand when I get started tomorrow. Do you mind going?"

It was hard to say no to her, so I grabbed my coat and left with a list of about seven ingredients she needed.

The store wasn't crowded, making my trip painless to get through. That was until I went into the baking aisle to get sugar. I wasn't the only one who had the same idea. Right by the sugar was Mrs. Dunne, mother to Mike.

The sight of her rendered me immobile. I hadn't seen Mrs. Dunne since my high school graduation back when Mike was known as my friend. Not what he is to me now. The urge to flee consumed me, but my feet seemed rooted to the ground. I stood there watching her like a deer in headlights as she grabbed some sugar and went on further down the aisle.

"Excuse me," a woman shoved past me with her cart.

"I'm sorry," I whispered, not wanting to Mrs. Dunne to look in my direction. But it was too late. She had already seen me. "Whitney!" She said my name with such love and kindness, as if nothing had ever happened between Mike and I. To her, nothing did. She was as clueless as I was spooked.

I smiled weakly at Mrs. Dunne when she walked to where I was because I still couldn't move. "How are you, dear? It's been too long."

I nodded, not sure what to say. Finally, I croaked out, "I'm okay. How are you?"

"I'm doing well. Life has been hectic lately, but it's a good hectic!

My family is all back in town, spread out between my house and at Ruby's. It's a full house, but family always makes this time of year better."

I swallowed the lump in my throat and asked the question I didn't know if I wanted the answer to. "Is Mike home?"

"Yes, of course. He's been back since last week. Your paths not crossing yet is surprising. I know him and Sabrina broke up, but you two were friends in your own right. I understand if you don't want to see him if you think it'll affect your friendship with her, but I'm sure he'd love to see you."

My heart thudded in my chest, synchronising to the beat of the snowflakes falling against the windows. The suggestion of seeing Mike again sent a wave of nausea coursing through my stomach. I thought if the time ever came where we would see each other again, I would be ready, but I wasn't so sure now that it was a real possibility.

Because I had to say something, I murmured, "Maybe."

"Consider it. He's made new friends at his new school. From what I've gathered, none of them are as good of friends to him as you were to him. He doesn't talk about you or Sabrina anymore, but I can tell he misses how things used to be between you guys."

He wasn't the only one. I missed thinking of him as the brother I never had, instead of the monster he revealed himself to be. The thought of him missing me, even though he caused our downfall, turned my stomach. I couldn't bring myself to respond, but I could tell my expression had changed, and that was enough for Mrs. Dunne to get the hint.

"Alright," she said with a nod. "I'll see you around, I hope." With a quick wave of her hand, she turned away with her cart and walked to the check-out line.

In the baked goods section, my nightmare came true. It may not have been Mike I'd run into, but his ominous presence was felt. What did it mean for us to both be home at the same time and our paths nearly merged? Was it a sign I should confront him, or was it the universe's way of warning me to stay away?

I grabbed the bag of sugar, paid for everything, and went home. The incident was not put behind me though. The feeling of dread remained as I wondered what seeing Mrs. Dunne meant. Dr. Johnson told me I had the power to free myself from Mike. Was this how? Did I have to face my fear and confront him?

I went to sleep that night burdened with thoughts of what could happen if I made the wrong decision. I could be worse off than before. Seeing him again could ruin the progress I'd made, but if I stayed away, I'd always wonder what could have been.

When I awoke on Christmas Eve, my decision had been made. I prayed it was the right one.

33

The Last Goodbye

Confronting your rapist at his house was never a sound idea, but something told me doing it while his house was filled to the brim with family members gathered for the holidays was probably the best way of going about it. Christmas was tomorrow and I should've been at home with my family like he was with his. Instead, I was in front of his house, mentally preparing myself for what may come. On the ride over, I kept reminding myself this was something I wanted to do. Not needed, but wanted. I hoped I had the strength to go through with it.

I stood on the Dunne's front porch for what felt like forever, but was probably closer to five minutes when I got the courage to ring the doorbell. There was silence for a few moments, but I didn't walk away. I rang it again and heard rapid footsteps nearing the door.

The moment the door swung open, I took a deep breath, feeling the icy air rush into my lungs. I don't know what I wanted to see when I saw him. Did I want him to look as miserable as he made me? Did I want him to look remorseful? On second thought, no. I definitely didn't want that. That would've pissed me off worse than seeing him happy.

In any event, he didn't look either. He looked confused, as if he had all but forgotten about my existence until I was right in front of him. He looked at me with wide eyes and an open mouth. In the past, this would have been amusing, now it was just uncomfortable.

"What... what are you doing here?" He asked after a long, torturous silence.

"You might want to shut the door. You don't want your family to overhear us, do you?" I didn't wait for him to answer. I stepped off his porch, only stopping when I was standing in the middle of his front lawn.

He nodded stiffly and followed my lead, closing the door as he walked out. In the crisp afternoon air, we stood as my heart pounded fiercely, threatening to escape my chest. To calm down, I looked everywhere but at him. Specifically, at the street I rode my first bike on and the yard that was the backdrop of my prom photos. Being here was so familiar, contrasting with this unfamiliar moment.

Turning my gaze back to the man in front of me, I cleared my throat. "I imagined this moment for so long, but now that it's here, I'm not sure what to say. Then again, it's not me who has to say anything. It's you. You're the one who owes me an explanation, an apology. Something that will help me move on from you and this hold you have over me and my life."

He took a step forward, almost closing the space between us. He was too close, so close I could smell his aftershave — the same one he always used to wear — the one he wore that night. "Go back to where you were. I can't take you being any closer to me," I warned. My stomach could only stand so much. The bile rising in my throat would be all over him if he didn't listen to what I needed. Which wasn't a bad idea...

He listened and moved back, though his hands balled into fists. I could tell he wanted to reach out and touch me, but knew better than to try. "I don't understand how an explanation or an apology is going to fix anything. Wouldn't me trying to rationalize what I did just make it worse? Nothing I say is going to make you feel better."

"I don't need you, the person who caused my hurt to make me feel better. I want an explanation. That is what I want from you."

He nodded, finally getting I wasn't leaving until I got what all I needed to hear from him. He sighed before running a hand through his hair. "I thought you knew it was me."

"Bullshit," I spat out. "I called you Luke."

"In the state I was in that night, Luke sounded a lot like Mike."

"No, you're not going to do this. You will not rid yourself of the guilt of raping me by saying you were so drunk you confused your own name with Luke's. You knew what you were doing, Mike. Admit it!"

"Okay, okay, I'm sorry," he said quickly, before I could fully explode. "You're right. Though, I had some drinks. I knew what I was doing when I watched you go upstairs. I knew what I was doing when I checked the time to see how long you've been gone for. I knew what I was doing when I went upstairs and found you laying in that bed."

He looked away from me before continuing. "I knew I wanted to spend the night with you before we spent months apart. I knew it so bad I convinced myself you were saying my name and not Luke's. That you were saying you wanted me and not him. I wanted to believe it so bad that I couldn't see what was really going on."

"You were with Sabrina, Mike. My best friend." Unlike the pain in my heart, I pushed down the growing pain in my throat.

"I know. I loved her, but I wanted you. It'd been that way for a long time and I tried to deny it because I was with Sabrina and she loved you. More than she ever loved me and if I admitted how I felt, she would lose us both. I didn't want that."

"But that's exactly what happened, and it's your fault. You took what you wanted from me that night, then you took my best friend from me by making me out as a liar. How can you say that wasn't what you wanted?"

"Sober me cared about my relationship with Sabrina and yours with her, but me who had a couple of beers didn't. I completely disregarded what you wanted, hoping I could get what I wanted."

"A free fuck, you mean. Let's not mince words here. We both know what it was."

"Yes," he admitted in a low voice. His head was hung down, still not making eye contact with me. "That's what it was."

"Didn't it bother you I was only with you that night because I thought you were Luke?"

He looked up then, his gaze penetrating mine. "Of course it did. But I was so desperate to have something that wasn't mine that I was willing to take a shortcut to get it."

I stood there for a few moments, just looking at him. How did I ever consider this selfish, entitled man a friend? He wasn't always like this, was he? If he was, how did I miss it? At that moment, I understood what Sabrina felt in reaction to the news of who Mike really was. She felt like she missed the signs of his true nature. I felt the same.

Then I realized something, and the truth was scarier. Mike wasn't a monster hiding in plain sight. He was a person who I'd turned a blind eye to. I actively chose not to acknowledge his selfishness and entitlement because it made me feel better about myself. It was easier than admitting someone like him could exist in my life. It was no different from me excusing Sabrina's bad behavior in the name of friendship.

No one could've predicted or seen that Mike would do what he did, but reflecting on our interactions now, I can see how it was headed that way all along. He always had a sense of entitlement, a belief he could have anything he wanted without consequences. I'd always thought he was flawed, but harmless, and that was my mistake.

I hadn't been willing to have an honest conversation about Mike and his flaws, just as Sabrina and I avoided having one about her behavior. I couldn't have changed either of them if they didn't want to change themselves and it wasn't my responsibility to. However, I should've challenged them more instead of enabling them. That was the mistake I'll have to live with, but I knew I would never make it again.

I asked him finally, "Are you sorry? Or are you glad you got what you wanted, even if it was under false pretenses and meant losing a friend? Was getting your fill up worth it?"

"You want the truth, right?" I nodded, giving him the go ahead. "I wasn't sorry when it was happening because it felt like a dream came true. Honestly? I was over the moon. You, the girl who was off limits for me because of my relationship status, were suddenly mine. Even if it was just for the night, I wasn't thinking of the consequences. Then I said your name, and the dream was shattered. The disgust in your voice when you realized I wasn't Luke is something I won't ever forget."

"Then your face when you saw who I was," he continued. "It was the look of betrayal—and it killed me. More than the girl I liked, you were my friend and I hurt you. I saw you run out of the room, tears in your eyes, and I knew apologizing to you could never fix the damage I did."

"I could've believed what you're telling me if you hadn't gone to Sabrina and told her what happened between us was consensual. That was a lie, and it destroyed our friendship."

"I didn't tell her the truth because I didn't want her to look at me the way you did. I thought if she believed what I told her, then at least I wouldn't hurt her as much as I did to you."

"You thought telling Sabrina her boyfriend and her best friend slept together was going to hurt her less?"

"At the time, it made sense. She would be mad at us, but she would

322

forgive us eventually. If I told her I took advantage of you, she'd never forgive me."

"Better to throw me with you under the bus than take responsibility for your actions?" I snickered in disbelief. He had no idea how much pain he'd caused with his lie. "Along with hurting me, you ruined my 15-year friendship. All because you wanted to protect yourself."

"I thought you and Sabrina could get through it. Your relationship was too strong to be broken over something like this."

"Well, it wasn't. She believed you and took your side over mine when I told her what really happened. She's come around now, but it's too late. Our friendship is broken beyond repair because of you. Was it not enough to hurt me? Was there really a need to destroy my relationship with Sabrina, too?"

He recovered his balls long enough to look at me. "I fucked up. I know I did. I'm sorry. I'll never forgive myself for what I did."

"We're on the same page then. I want to be the person who forgives and forgets, but I'm not. I won't ever forgive you for the pain you've caused me or forget it."

"Understood."

I closed my eyes for a second and took a deep breath. We're were nearing our end, but I couldn't go without letting everything off my chest. "I hate you."

"Most days, I hate myself, too."

"It'll pass for you. For me, it'll keep building and building until it finally explodes. Except it won't be your life it wrecks, it'll be mine. I know because it already has."

I could feel my voice breaking and the sting of tears welling up in my eyes. He watched me, probably wanting to say something but not knowing what. Despite how much he may try to understand the depth of my pain, he never would, even though he caused it. I wiped away at the tears and kept going. "I will always hate you, but I can't let my hatred of you run my life anymore. Because then that's on me. Not you. I accept I will never get back what you stole from me, but I'm going to aim to be happy. It is after all, the one thing you can't take away."

Mike kept his head down and nodded. Thinking there were no more words left to be said, he turned around to go inside. I called out to him so he would stop. He did, but didn't turn to look at me. He didn't have to.

"One day, you'll get asked by someone to describe yourself. You'll say you're someone's son, somebody's friend. Maybe at that point you'll be able to say you're someone's husband or even someone's father. No matter who you become in other people's eyes, you'll always be the guy who raped me. No amount of other labels you obtain will ever remove that one. It'll stick with you forever even if no one but us knows. You're the one who has to live with that, not me."

Mike's face remained hidden from me as he hung his head and walked away. I released a breath when he was gone, the tension of the moment released with it. Christmas music wafted through the open door before he closed it. It reminded me that though Christmas was tomorrow; I got my gift today.

It wasn't a Christmas miracle, but it was enough. He owned no residence in my head and he never would again. I was free, and it felt good. With a sense of peace that only came after a tumultuous storm, I turned the corner and started the long walk home.

34

Free to Exhale

By the time I finished walking home, the sky had grown darker, casting long shadows across the streets. I didn't mind it so much during this time of year. The Christmas lights on each house and streetlights adorned the neighborhood with a dazzling display of colors, adding to the beauty of the scene. Against the night sky, the bright red, green, and white lights sparkled, saturating the air with a festive glow.

Our house didn't have any lights, but I didn't mind. It was only when I stopped in our driveway that I wished we had put some up. It would've given me a heads up on who was there waiting for me.

"Jordyn?" I asked, squinting through the darkness.

"Yeah, it's me," she answered shyly as she emerged from the shadows of my porch. "I'm sorry if I scared you. I should've texted I was coming by."

"No, I'm glad you're here. I'm happy to see you. I missed you."

She looked as good as I'd last seen her in her light blue flannel shirt, blue jeans, and gray trench coat. More importantly, she looked happy. I didn't know if it was because of the holiday or because of me. I know what hoped it was.

"Why were you standing out here in the cold? Did my parents not let you in?"

"It wasn't like that. I rang the doorbell and asked if you were here. You weren't, but they still invited me in. I didn't want to be a nuisance, so I told them I would come back later. For some reason, I didn't want to go home yet and so I sat on your porch bench and waited for you."

"You came to see me?" I asked, my heart racing at the thought of her saying yes.

She nodded, her teeth biting her lower lip to keep from smiling. "I wanted to check on you. I know I said I needed space, but then I considered the year you've had and realized I was being selfish."

"No, you weren't. I did something horrible to you, the only person who've been my friend this year. You were well in your rights to want some space. Still, I'm glad you're here."

The air between us was thick with tension, and I shuffled my feet nervously. She noticed and smiled. "I never thought I would see the day Whit Robinson got flustered because of me."

"I never thought I would see the day Jordyn Price would wait an hour in the cold for me."

"Touché," she responded, chuckling. When the laughter faded, she asked me, "Where did you go?"

"What?"

"You were gone for an hour, obviously not to the store. So where did you go?"

I looked down at my shoes and sighed. "I promise I would be honest with you, so... I went to go see him."

"Him?" Jordyn's face scrunched up in confusion and concern.

"Mike. I saw Mike."

She closed her eyes, visibly not happy at my decision to do that. "What? You went and saw Mike? What were you thinking?"

"Not just saw. I talked to him."

"Are you mad? Do you know how dangerous it was to confront

him?"

"I know it was dangerous, but it felt like something I had to do. Besides, it was at his house that was full of people. I knew he wouldn't try anything, and he didn't. We talked and the conversation helped me."

Jordyn eyed me suspiciously, but I could tell she was relieved. "Well, if you're okay, then I'm glad it helped, but never do something like that again without telling someone like me first."

"Don't worry. I'm never seeing him again. I needed to get some things off my chest. Now that I have, I have nothing else to say to him. I'm letting him go."

"Really? Just like that?"

"I will always carry the trauma of what he did to me, but I'm not going to let my anger at the situation control my life anymore. I don't want to be angry. I want to be happy."

"What makes you happy?" she asked, genuinely curious about what I had to say.

"You," I said with no hesitation. Maybe it was too forward or not the right time for me to admit it, but it was true. "You make me happy," I repeated.

"You make me happy too."

More than anything, I wanted to accept what she was saying, but I couldn't. Not without seeing where she stood with me beyond this nice moment we were having. "What about the space you needed? I understand if you need more time."

She sighed, clearly not wanting to put a damper on the moment neither, but knowing we had to. "Whit, I don't like what you did. I hate to think you're the kind of person who can do something that vicious to people you claim to like, but..."

"But?" I said, hopeful.

"When you've been hurt in the way you were, it affects the way you react and handle situations. Should you have done what you did to Amelia? No, definitely not. Should you have set out to use me in your scheme? No, of course not. But can I forgive you for your worst mistakes? Yes, I can, because you're not defined by them."

She closed in on me, her fingers confidently grasping one button on my coat. "You were at your lowest this year, Whit. But even at your lowest point, you reached out to a lonely, but would never admit it, college freshman and made her feel cared for and seen. And it wasn't for your scheme. It was because you knew what it felt like to feel lonely. You have a battered heart, Whit, but what you've done with it tells me more about who you are than any of your missteps."

Surrounded by twinkling Christmas lights, I felt a sense of pressure fill my chest. In a good way. I tried to think of something to say, but all that came out was a soft "thank you."

Stepping closer, she enveloped me in an embrace. She stepped closer and put her arms around me. "It's okay, Whit," she murmured in my ear, hugging me tightly against her. She held me and whispered soft words of comfort in my ear. I closed my eyes, savoring the hug and fighting back tears.

Eventually, she let go, and we stepped apart. Her eyes didn't leave mine, watching me with a fondness that only romantic poets could do justice in describing. "You know," I said, my voice barely above a whisper, "Christmas is tomorrow."

"Huh, I hadn't noticed."

"Yeah, and since I didn't know if we would see each other, I didn't get you a gift."

"I didn't get you one either."

"It's a shame because the gift I really wanted only you can give me."

Her icy hand left her side and landed on my burning cheek. She cooled it as she caressed it gently. "I feel the same way."

With no doubt in her mind about me, she leaned in and pressed her lips to mine. My hands instinctively found her hips, and I gently pulled her closer, feeling the warmth of her body against mine. Her lips tasted of a delightful blend of cranberries and nutmeg, making me never want to let go. Something told me if it was possible, she would let me. I only had to ask.

"That was the best gift someone has ever given me," I breathed against her lips.

"I'm happy to hear that because I plan on giving it to you many more times for many more years to come."

My lips curled into a smile, my heart swelling at the thought of her future also being mine. "Merry Christmas, Jordyn."

She smiled back, her eyes twinkling. "Merry Christmas, Whit. I love you."

"I love you too."

Epilogue: One Year Later

"Are you almost done, Dr. Crane?" Jordyn joked, peeping her head into the attic I had turned into a recording space. "We have dinner to eat and presents to open at my parents'. It would be rude of us if we were late."

"I know, I know. I'm almost done, but I want to make sure it's perfect before we go."

"That episode is not coming out until after New Year's. You have time to get it where you want it to be on a day that isn't Christmas."

I sighed, knowing she was right. I saved what I had and shut down my laptop before getting up. "Alright. I'm done."

"Atta girl. As great as your episodes are, they're not worth it if you're burning out from recording and editing them."

I took my mom's advice and decided to do something with my voice, literally. I started the podcast six months ago, but I prepared for the launch of it an additional six months before that. The podcast is called Imperfect, and it focuses on stories of survivors and their responses to their trauma, always in flawed and imperfect ways.

Season one was dedicated to my story and the hell I unleashed in the aftermath of my rape. Season two just started before the holidays and it's focusing on other victims and their journeys to healing through methods not always understood or widely accepted. Slowly, but surely, it has found an audience.

The reception has been generally positive, though of course there is criticism from people who don't agree with my approach or disagree with how the survivors are going about their healing. It was expected given the premise of the show, but season two is doing exactly what I set out for it to do.

It's giving a voice to those who were not heard before, and it's showing people you don't have to be a perfect victim to be worthy of support and understanding. The podcast is still in its early stages, but I'm happy with the progress it's made. I never expected this to be the direction I took when I was looking for a job, but I loved what I was doing. I love it so much that Jordyn has to remind me when to take a break. Even when it was Christmas.

"Now that I'm getting emails from potential sponsors, I could be in the position to hire someone to edit the episodes soon."

"More time for you to focus on what you do best while someone else takes care of the technical aspects."

"It also gives me more time to spend with a certain someone," I said with a sly grin.

Jordyn rolled her eyes playfully. "Fine with me, but you're going to have to start paying rent if you keep staying over at Amelia's and mine's place."

The great thing about having a job that's so flexible means I can be anywhere to do it. I split my time between Wayland and Chicago so I can be with Jordyn as much as I can. During the spring semester, she snuck me in and out of her dorm, since I wasn't allowed to be on campus. Though I went by undetected, I was relieved when Jordyn and Amelia rented an apartment. It made our visits much easier to relax and enjoy.

"If I have to pay rent just to spend more time with you, I will do it," I told Jordyn while she grabbing our coats out of the closet. We were going to her parents' for dinner. Winnie left ahead of us to help with Bryan with a dessert. My parents weren't able to make it, but they were here for Thanksgiving and even played hosts for the Prices. It made me happy to see they were keeping their word and making an effort to spend more time with me.

After putting hers on, Jordyn held out the sleeves of my coat so I could slip my arms through it. She leaned her head over my shoulder and pressed her cheek against mine when it was on. "It won't be long before we have a place to call our own. No roommates, no parents, just us."

"I look forward to it." And I did. Once Jordyn was done with school, we were going to plant our roots somewhere and make a life together. It was a few years off from happening, but it was always at the front of our minds.

When we arrived at the Prices', we were shaking little flutters of snow off our coats. Eliza welcomed us in with a hug, ushering us straight in to the warmth of their home. Bryan was in the kitchen with Winnie, finishing up the desserts they were making.

"Finally, you're here," Sabrina said, spotting us on her way down the stairs. "Dottie would not let me get even a piece of the ham until you arrived."

"Where is Dottie?" Jordyn asked, looking around for her. "Please tell me Mom hasn't strangled her yet and hid her body."

"No, though I'm guessing she's thought about it a few times already today. Dottie is upstairs in her room. She's making some phone calls before we sit down. Speaking of which, you two need to wash up. Give me your coats." She outstretched her arms and Jordyn and I handed our coats over with our phones in them.

"No snooping," I warned when she turned away from us.

"Like I would risk seeing a nude of my sister on your phone," she retorted without turning her head. I laughed while Jordyn shivered at the thought.

I watched Sabrina head back upstairs, appreciating how far our relationship had come since last year. We weren't friends and never would be again. However, we could coexist for Jordyn's sake without coming to blows verbally or physically, and that deserved a round of applause after how last year went for us.

After Jordyn and I washed up, we went to the dining room. Sabrina was there, straightening the silverware. Winnie and Bryan were putting the food on the table. Eliza sat patiently, waiting for us to join.

"Mom! It's time!" Bryan yelled for Dottie to come down from her room.

"Boy, do you always yell in the house like that? I never taught you that. The things that woman lets you get away with are beyond me," she said, shaking my head as she entered.

Jordyn and I held in our laughter and Eliza rolled her eyes as if she'd heard this a hundred times. Dottie sat down at the head of the table, Eliza and Sabrina to her left. Bryan was on the other end. Winnie, Jordyn, and I filled in the rest of the seats. Dottie took the lead, crossing her hands in front of her as she began a prayer.

We all followed suit as we knelt, closing our eyes and bowing our heads. As Dottie finished saying grace, I opened my eyes to find everyone looking around at each other with expectant smiles.

"Well, dig in!" Dottie exclaimed.

As we ate our dinner, conversation turned from stories of the present to childhood memories to the future. Sabrina planned on doing the van life thing again over the summer. Dottie was looking forward to doing some volunteer work at her local church. Winnie was excited for her bingo games to get underway again in the new year. And Eliza and Bryan had their hands full with cases at their firm.

When the question was turned to Jordyn and me, we exchanged a knowing glance and shared a smile. It was nothing they didn't already know. College for her and the podcast for me. What made it special was we were going to be doing it together. Everything, moving forward, we were in it together. The long haul never sounded so good than right then with my best friend alongside me for the ride.

About the Author

No matter the genre or time, Dominique Davis writes affectionately about unapologetic out-of-the-box women and the people who love them. From a mother-daughter con artist duo to a revenge-driven college student, there's always something special about her characters, as she believes that all great stories should feature remarkable yet flawed female leads. Writing has been her passion since she could hold a pencil, and nowadays she divides her time between devouring books, fine-tuning manuscripts, and embracing her love for all things pop culture. You can learn more about her by checking out her website and following her on social media.

You can connect with me on:
- https://www.dominique-davis.com
- https://twitter.com/ddaviswrites
- https://www.instagram.com/ddaviswrites
- https://reamstories.com/ddavis
- https://www.threads.net/@ddaviswrites

Subscribe to my newsletter:

✉ http://eepurl.com/h6Gg0r

Also by Dominique Davis

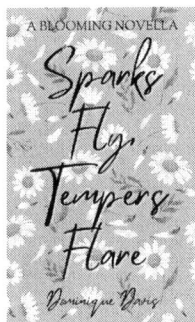

Sparks Fly, Tempers Flare (Blooming #1)
After her mother's death, 16-year-old Sloane Crawford reluctantly returns to her childhood home and the drama-filled small town she left behind. Moving in with her estranged father only reopens old wounds from his affair that destroyed her family.

Back at school, tensions flare as Sloane reconnects with old friends who resent her for abandoning them. Especially heated is her rocky relationship with her former best friend, Emory, the daughter of the woman her father betrayed them with.

As Sloane struggles to adapt to her new normal, long-held grudges threaten to boil over. To move forward, she'll have to confront the fractured bonds left in the ashes of her family's traumatic history. But finding forgiveness won't be easy in a place where the past refuses to stay buried.

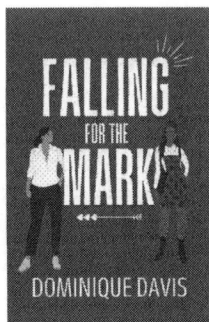

Falling For the Mark (Swindled In Love #1)
Maya is the daughter of Nicole, a cunning grifter who has been deceiving people since she was a teenager. Together, they have perfected the art of scamming people out of their money without guilt.

Their most successful con sees Nicole duping affluent men into wedding her. But when the time is right, Maya lures the mark into her bed, getting them to break their prenuptial agreement. The duo then disappear with an impressive divorce settlement. Never to be heard from again. What should be another routine con soon turns out to be anything but.

Kennedy, the daughter of their new mark, is skeptical of the pair upon their arrival. She suspects they are after her father's money and she's determined to find proof of it. Matters are further complicated when Maya and Kennedy begin to develop feelings for each other. Though both have their reasons for why they shouldn't cross the line, their growing attraction is too strong to be denied.

But when the truth is revealed, both stand to lose more than they ever could have imagined.

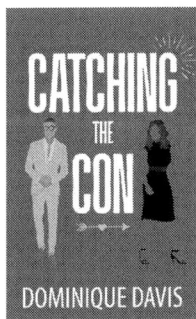

Catching the Con (Swindled in Love #2)

Reformed con artist Nicole Taylor is confronted with her past in this sequel to Falling For the Mark. Nicole's former mark is out for revenge against her and her daughter Maya. He will stop at nothing to bring them to justice, including hiring private investigator Spencer Shaw.

Spencer is struggling to balance keeping his business afloat while also becoming the guardian of his niece. When the opportunity of a lifetime arises to work with a client willing to pay any price to get a job done, Spencer jumps at the chance to save his business and secure his future as a single father. All he has to do is go undercover and collect proof of a con artist's crimes. Sounds simple enough.

But as Spencer delves into Nicole's past and gets closer to her, he begins to realize the con woman isn't who he thought she was. Despite his strong moral compass, Spencer finds himself drawn to the mysterious woman. Caught between his loyalty to his job and his growing feelings for Nicole, Spencer must decide whether to follow his heart or his head.

Between wanting to escape her criminal past and vowing to protect her daughter from the danger that threatens them, Nicole isn't expecting to fall in love. But fate has different plans in store for her. Will Nicole and Spencer find love in their game of cat and mouse, or will their respective pasts destroy their chance at a future together?

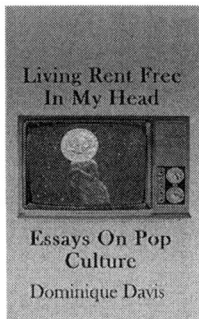

Living Rent Free In My Head: Essays on Pop Culture

For as long as she can remember, Dominique Davis has had an endless stream of pop culture obsessions playing on repeat in her head. What started as casual blog posts sharing her thoughts on favorite shows like Buffy the Vampire Slayer and Gossip Girl has grown into a full-fledged passion.

In her essay collection Living Rent Free In My Head, Dominique delves deeper than ever before into the topics, characters, and franchises that have captivated her. With insightful commentary and humor, she examines topics like our cultural fascination with celebrity relationships and asks whether it's possible to separate the art from the artist.

Whether you're a die-hard fan or a casual observer of the zeitgeist, Living Rent Free In My Head offers a fresh and engaging perspective. Dominique's voice is as compelling as the topics she covers, making this essay collection a must-read for anyone who's ever fallen down a pop culture rabbit hole.

Printed in Great Britain
by Amazon